Staying Dead

Lillith Sterling

ISBN: 979-8-9944275-4-5 (paperback)

ISBN: 979-8-9944275-5-2 (hardcover)

ASIN: B0DCGKP7N9 (e-book)

Edited by Catharine Bijak

Formatting, Editing, and Proofreading by English Proper Editing Services

Cover art by Alexandra Wolly @artbywolly

First Edition 2026

TRIGGER WARNINGS

Death/suicide

Explicit language

Explicit, on page sexual content

Drugging, poisoning

Graphic violence, stabbings, mentions of blood

Decapitation

Depictions of amnesia

Depictions of a grooming relationship (not between FMC and MMC)

PLAYLIST

Afterlife — Hailee Steinfeld

Taste of the Divine — Shaker, Azee & Cobra

Flawless — The Neighbourhood

Bad Dreams — Teddy Swims

The Sun — Brittany Broski

Back to Life — ZAYN

7 Minutes in Hell — Chrissy Constanza

Can't Keep Myself — Jeremiah Miller

Skin and Bones — David Kushner

Tell It to My Heart — MEDUZA ft. Hozier

Ten Lifetimes — Ethan Hodges

Daylight — David Kushner

No Plan — Hozier

Hurt Me — Suriel Hess

Gethsemane — Sleep Token

Shadow — Derik Fein

Trouble — Samuel Jack

Monster — colby! & Shaya Zamora

Secrets — Omido, Ordell & Rick Jansen

Die First — Nessa Barrett

Haunted — Ben Goldsmith
Past Self — Sleep Token

PART ONE

—Voltus Bulletin, posted anonymously in town square

CHAPTER ONE

Dying was the best thing that ever happened to me.

At least, it used to be.

I've always known that this afterlife of mine was on borrowed time, but Second is supposed to be a haven. A place where our souls live again before we pass on—finding Peace or a one-way ticket to the Seven Hells.

If that were true, I must've taken a wrong turn at death.

The literal knife in my back, two inches from my spinal cord, isn't exactly endorsing the serene purgatory Perry promised me.

Sitting in the puddle of warm, black blood from my assailant, I force myself to steady my breathing. But the asshole one foot away nearly punctured my lung, and all I can manage are short, sharp pants.

Edene won't ever let me hear the end of it if I try to remove this damn knife myself. If I can even make it to her.

My pulsating heart speeds to a gallop with each passing breath, the rhythm punctuating every second closer to my next death.

Hunched over the dirt in the poorly groomed alley, I slowly grip the sapphire hilt of my dagger, still lodged in the man's throat. Gods, I can't even call him a man. *Shade scum.* His black blood pooling around us is a known indicator that he long since sold his soul—feeding on those of us with any magic left.

He came out of nowhere. One moment, I'm walking home to Edene. The next, this psycho stabs me in the back.

I wipe the excess cursed blood on his shirt as best I can, then return it to the holster on my hip. My hands shake with the motion as pain and adrenaline dance through my veins.

Don't panic, Arden. Control your emotions. Perry's voice rings in my head, grounding me. Sweat beads on my forehead as I try to compartmentalize the searing wound, willing the tears building not to fall.

My thighs burn in protest as I stand, biting my hand to muffle my groan. I can't tell if I'm grimacing from the pain or the horrid smell of the Shade's blood, reeking of rotten garbage.

I should probably dispose of the body. Considering the sweltering heat of the sun will be unforgiving today, once it fully rises, it'll no longer be just my problem, but *everyone's* problem.

I don't have time. More than likely, I'll bleed out first.

None of the usual patrol guards were out this morning. They normally lurk this alley, but even if they find me, it was self-defense.

Not that trials exist. They're for those who remain in Living.

The only trial they offer us is decapitation without explanation. Orders from a kingdom long since turned to rubble.

I press against the wall and slip deeper into the alley's shadows. If nothing else, that tar they try to pass off as a life source helps conceal my silhouette. Silently, I thank whatever God hasn't abandoned me yet that the knife hasn't paralyzed me. Keeping my back as still as possible, I push forward.

Eventually, I end up at the back door of Burtons, the shop of healing fixtures that Edene runs. Reeling from the blood loss, my sweat-slicked hand slips on the door knob and I stumble into her workshop. Landing facedown onto the table she was working on, I send various herbs and half-finished potions careening to the floor.

"What in the Seven Hells, Arden!" she shrieks, her gray eyes wide as she tugs at her tight, brown curls.

"Knife...Back...Alley...Shaded," I tell her, only able to huff out words between shaky breaths. Edene says nothing as she helps lift my legs onto the table with the rest of my body, ignoring my grunts and wheezing.

"Aren't you a woman of few words? But seriously! This is clearly getting too dangerous."

I clench my fists, opening and closing, trying to ease the pain throbbing from the walk home and the brutality of slamming into the table. Edene shushes me, brushing strands of my long, dark hair off my back where they've fallen loose. The small touch eases my shoulders, comforting me. Only a year older than myself, Edene has filled in as both mother and older sister since Perry first brought me to see her.

Continuing to stroke my hair, she holds a piece of leather in front of my mouth. I clamp my teeth down on it, placing my palms flat against the old wooden table, bracing myself.

Suddenly, with efficient grace, she rips the knife out, and I release a stream of colorful curses muffled by the leather. I turn my head to look at her, panting and sweating.

Edene holds up the knife as my scarlet blood continues to drip down the curved tip of the blade. "What a nasty one, too," she says to herself. Then she points it at my face, frowning. "You better hope there's no poison on this—if there is, I'm chaining you to this workbench. Promise or no promise." I spit out the leather with poor manners and little, if any, grace.

"I'm sorry, I—fucking Gods, OW—"

Edene pours a scorching liquid onto my back, showing me exactly how much mercy I deserve. "You shouldn't swear like that," she clicks her tongue at me, "it's not ladylike."

I roll my eyes, ignoring the same lecture she's given me time and time again.

Men want someone docile to take care of, Arden.

Men don't like vulgarity, Arden.

Perhaps if the men I've known, excluding Perry, weren't so wholly and completely underwhelming, I might feel differently. The few sexual encounters

I've had in this life make me wish I couldn't remember them, the way I don't recall any from Living.

"I was *trying* to say, before you poured *acid* on my back—"

"It's antipurzon."

"*Antipurzon,*" I correct through gritted teeth. "I'm sorry for crashing in here. That Shade—he came out of nowhere. As soon as I felt the blade in my back, I swung back with my dagger and slit his throat."

The memory of slicing blindly and watching him fall face-first onto the dirt gives me a certain satisfaction. His eyes went wide and when he hit the dirt, I crouched to drive my dagger through his neck.

Just to be sure.

"Stop smirking like that, you're such a freak."

I hadn't realized my face gave my thoughts away, and as Edene curls her lip in disgust at me, I laugh, regretting it immediately.

I groan as my body protests while the antipurzon stitches my skin back together—each pull tight, sharp, and relieving as it heals.

"Every time," I breathe, "I'm floored by your skill to make something so useful. I wish we could sell it."

Edene doesn't answer as she silently cleans the blood off my back. She's made it clear why we can't.

The rigorous process the illegal potion demands makes it damn near impossible. Extracting the stolen magic from the cursed blood of the Shaded is no meager task for Edene. And while there's no shortage of Shaded, she's all that's left of the Healers that used to roam all over Second.

Magic started fading from people years ago. Some still carry bursts of it. Not all of it good-natured, as the rumors of the witches from the old kingdoms would say.

Whenever I press Edene more about magic, she simply states that *the Gods deemed us unworthy*, and she's perfectly content to leave it at that.

I sit up slowly as she drops the knife in a washbasin. Upon her return, she wordlessly holds out her hand, palm side up, waiting patiently.

Gingerly, I reach for what she wants. "I wiped most of it off onto his shirt. And the dagger, well—"

"It means a lot to you, *I know*," she interrupts, snatching it from me and bringing it to another workbench that a grown woman hasn't tackled today. She works meticulously on scraping the blood into a jar, careful not to get it on her.

I remain hunched over as I wait for the inevitable soreness to take root from the elixir, swallowing the terror of recent events. I avoid Edene's gaze as I try not to spiral.

I almost died again. I have to be more cautious. This tracking is getting too reckless, but I can't shake the feeling that the Shaded are the answer.

"Where can I burn these?" The demonic blood stains relentlessly, so there's no saving them. Edene calls it *impure.*

It's especially necessary to burn the clothes since they're evidence of a murder. No one will mourn the Shade, but killing is frowned upon by the patrol—even if we're killing people who are already dead. Or barely human.

She huffs, annoyed I'll be raiding her closet once again. Not that I'm thrilled about borrowing her floral dresses, considering they're all she owns.

Would it kill this woman to own a pair of pants?

Turning on a sigh, she says, "Take them off here. I'll burn them tomorrow after service. I'll need to wrap them up in something, but it won't help the stench." She waves a delicate hand in front of her nose, as though she can smell me from across the room. I shrug as I slip off the table, stripping off my tunic, shoes, and my last pair of pants.

A true tragedy.

In nothing but my underclothes, I head to the cluttered shop's front, making for the steep stairwell behind the counter. I keep an eye on the door, just in case someone decides to drop in before the store opens. The last thing I need this morning is someone waltzing in and seeing me practically naked.

I bathe quickly in the tiny washroom, scrubbing every surface of my body raw. I climb out, and as I dry myself, I ruffle through Edene's closet, hoping to find her least frilly dress. I wouldn't mind a plain skirted one, truly, yet every single one has to be floral.

Groaning to myself, I settle on an emerald green sundress covered in white flowers.

I prefer to sniff them, visit Violet Gardens. Not wear them.

I make my way back downstairs, careful in the slippers I swiped from under her bed. Halfway down the steps, I pause to take in the shop this morning.

She has got to organize this place.

Dark wood shelves, worn from years of use, stretch from floor to ceiling with a shaky rolling ladder providing access to higher shelves. Potions overcrowd each other, some labels looking worse for wear, constantly handled but never purchased.

Edene and her generous heart keep us at a certain poverty level just above starving. We mostly eat the same watered-down soup and stale bread, but it's enough. Whenever she does make a sale, the money typically has to go to necessities. Such as new pants. Now and then, we feast at Valerie's—our favorite café—as a treat.

When I can, I pilfer food from especially rude vendors on service days to help me stay in shape for running and fighting. I only know a few techniques that Perry had shown me before he disappeared. Deep down, I know it's not enough. While I could defend myself well enough today, tomorrow's luck holds no such promise.

Just as my foot hits the last step, the front door swings open. As though the first rays of sun are the only indication needed for a shop to be declared open.

An older woman walks in with yellowed, leather-like skin and graying hair. I plaster a fake smile on my face as she approaches the counter.

"How can I help you?" I ask, trying not to grit my teeth.

She keeps looking around as though I didn't speak at all. I don't know how Edene does this all day every day, because I'm already daydreaming about reaching over this counter to teach this hag some manners. Clearing my throat, I try again.

"Can I help you?" I ask louder this time, and she finally turns to me. Her beady, blue eyes are sharp, and every instinct I have tells me to bolt as a chill runs down my spine. Forcing myself to remain still as I hold her gaze, I refuse to let my smile falter.

"I hope so. Edene, I presume?" Her voice is clear and chilling. I'd let this woman near Edene over my undead body. I give a slight nod of my head, raising my eyebrows.

"What can I do for you?"

"I'm looking for an...*elixir*, let's call it. I heard you can make one, and sometimes, they're for sale."

"And you believe it's something I sell?"

The antipurzon. There must be too many rumors, but Edene would never offer to sell it—the woman's request has alarm bells ringing in my head.

The woman hisses at me, lowering her voice. "I'm aware of the cost, *girl*, if that is your concern. I am more than willing to pay."

Taking out a pouch from inside her cloak, she dumps it on the counter. Gold coins clatter like rainfall. My heart tramples itself at the sight.

Gods, smite me. I've never seen so much wealth in one place. A couple pieces could sustain us for months.

I try holding my face neutral as I ask, "And what is the name of the potion?"

She looks me up and down, analyzing every inch. Possibly calculating if she determines me a threat.

To her? She absolutely should.

"You know," she drawls. "Pretty, silver eyes like yours...the beauty you hold, you're wasting your afterlife as a healer. Shame the royal family of Marintha found Peace long ago. You would have made a fine bride for the crown prince."

Crown prince? Of Marintha?

"Hm, sounds like a child's dream. Marintha fell in the war—everyone knows that."

Perry had told me about it once. The legendary castle, the dangerous family who lived and ruled from it. Powerful beings, born in Second, never were a resident of Living—or so the myth states.

They wielded magic like it was nothing; no limit, no price. They had no piece of their soul to sell here, not when they were the oldest ones among us. It's rumored they consumed pieces of sacrificed souls to keep themselves tethered to this world.

I narrow my eyes at her insistence, wondering if this lady would bleed black or red. Then again, she looks like she might bleed dust.

"Let me see what I have in the back." I fake another smile as I back away and head down the hall.

Edene is cleaning the mess I made earlier, oblivious to the insane woman waiting up front.

When she sees me, she gasps. "You look beautiful, Arden!" My cheeks grow hot at her compliment. "I'm almost done here, and then we can go look at the vendors." She winks unsubtly, making me roll my eyes despite the smile creeping past my defenses.

Her continuous sunshine is always growing flowers in the cracks of my splintering foundation.

"Before I forget, there's a customer up front already."

I throw up a hand to stop her before she bolts. "We have a slight problem, Ede."

"What's that?" She tilts her head to the side, scrunching her brow.

"She asked about..." I jab a finger at the vial in her hands—the damning evidence of antipurzon. Her eyes widen with realization. She tucks the vial into her white apron, which hasn't actually been white for many years.

Suddenly, we hear a crash from the front and the door slamming shut. There's no hesitation as we run, tripping over each other to get to the front. By the time we reach the display room, two shelves of potions are empty and litter the floor. I stare in utter shock, Edene's mouth gaping at the empty shelves.

I'm more interested in the pile of gold the crone left on the counter, but it feels out of place, like a warning.

That's when I see it. My stomach free falls, dread slinking up my spine. I tap Edene's shoulder, pointing to where I'm looking.

"Well, at least she paid?"

Past the counter, only the woman's head remains—perched on the filing rod, blood dripping onto the scattered papers.

Still smiling that same, chilling smile. Eyes wide and staring right at me.

Edene turns and gasps. It's the only warning I get before she faints.

CHAPTER TWO

At least the blood is red.

My arms fling out to catch Edene before she hits the floor.

And she says, I often overreact. *Yeah, I'm the dramatic one.*

I heft her up in my arms so I can drag her with me. I reach over the counter for the smelling salts and shove the vial under her nose. Edene jolts awake, flailing her arms.

"Gods, that always smells *horrible*." She pinches her nose, as though it can erase the smell.

"I could always pinch your neck, you know. Consider this a mercy." I lunge for her, causing her to jump back, and I laugh at her skittishness.

"You're *not* funny."

"What is funny to me, though," I chuckle again, "is a healer that passes out every time she sees a murder scene."

Whenever we've stumbled upon a body on the street, dead for whatever reason, Edene faints at the sight. Being dead for as long as she has, you'd think she'd be used to it by now. Yet, if there's brutality, she's out like a light.

Edene groans, throwing her head back so hard her curls bounce as she presses her palms into her eyes.

"Arden," she whines. "The...*mess!*"

The blood has dripped all over her paperwork. It's pooling on the counter now, inching toward the precious money. I scoop the coins in my hands, dumping them into an empty jar.

"I'll clean it up. Don't stress out." I shove the jar at her. "Take this upstairs and hide it somewhere safe."

Wordlessly, she grabs the jar from me and nods her head. Once she heads up the stairs, I grab a spare cloth, wrap it around the head, and lug it to the back of the shop, placing it on a spare workbench. Reaching the front once more, I ferociously scrub the counter, sweep the glass up, and throw the bloodied papers into the fireplace.

A fire in the middle of a heat wave. *Good thinking, Arden. No one will ever suspect a thing.*

It might not be much, but it's the only plan I have. As I wring out the last of the bloodied rag, the shop door creaks open. I turn to greet the customer, but as my gaze turns, my mouth instantly goes dry.

Standing in the doorframe is a man so entrancing, every instinct tells my body to run.

He looks exquisitely deadly. Terrifying.

I'm certain that I'm no longer breathing.

Every inch of him is sculpted. His loose, black clothing does nothing to hide his tall and tanned muscular stature.

Powerful.

I stare at him, open-mouthed like a fish out of water.

He stares back, perusing his gaze up and down my body. No one's ever studied me this closely before. So openly, unabashedly.

He's silent as the door closes behind him, making my heart pound anxiously.

The sunlight looks ethereal behind him; a halo caressing the black tendrils of hair that hang over his forehead. The natural light mutes itself the closer he comes into the shop, as though it bends to his very presence. He quirks an eyebrow as he looks from me, to the fire that's now blazing, and back.

An unspoken question.

"It was...cold. This morning," I explain, my eyes trained on him.

He nods, still analyzing me with those unnerving eyes. They're the darkest brown; the golden clasp holding his cloak together reflects in their depths.

I wipe the sweat off my face with the back of my hand, all too aware of the blazing heat inside the shop now. "Yes, well, it's unnecessary now. I can put it out."

I move, but in a flash, he's right in front of me. Standing closer than most deem appropriate for strangers. I take a step back at his brashness.

"It's not bothering me," he drawls. "Don't trouble your little raven head just for me."

I straighten at his words, his tone hitting me like knives wrapped in silk. "Can I help you with something?" I clasp my hands together to resist the urge to throttle him for calling me little *anything*. But I'm not sure this is a fight I could win.

He shoves his hands into his pockets, lax and at ease. "Your hair. It's the color of ravens." He states it plainly, as though it explains why he's here.

I try to muster my fake smile, but I can only manage a slight grimace. "Can I help you with anything?" I repeat. My voice is surprisingly steady, despite the blood roaring in my ears.

Run.

"Maybe. I'm looking for something." His gaze lingers, heavy with suggestion. With a face like that, Midnight herself would be speechless in this man's presence.

He takes another encroaching step toward me, but I match it by taking a step back, hitting my lower back into the countertop. His shoes crunching over the broken glass I have yet to sweep is the only sound in the shop.

The lights seem to dim as he takes an irrevocable step again. This time I have nowhere to retreat. He braces both hands on either side of me on the counter, trapping me in.

Gods, smite me.

He smells of balsam and fresh linen. Expensive. Pure luxury. Dangerous.

"Um—what are you—could you back up?" I lift my hand to shove him back, but he only closes the space more. His chest presses into my hand, the heat of him searing my skin. His tunic feels incredulously soft, failing to hide the solidity underneath it.

He pouts, almost frowning, tilting his head. Sizing me up like his prey.

"Now, where's the fun in that, darling?"

Darling?

"What do you want?"

Lifting a hand to my cheek, he brushes something off. It's surprisingly gentle, but it burns.

I recoil from his hand, trying but failing to put that space back in between us. Realizing I still have my hand on his chest, I quickly remove it, crossing my arms.

He stares at his hand and I follow his line of sight, to the drop of blood now there. Most recently residing on my face. I try to keep my expression neutral as I meet his eyes once more.

My legs lock, my body wilting under his stare. He must hear my heart thrashing.

"What's your name, little raven?" His lips curve in a cold smirk, sounding off a thousand alarms blaring red in my skull. "You're not moving until you tell me, so out with it."

I don't move. I can't—held captive like the breath caught in my lungs.

He hums, clicking his tongue in amusement. "Raven it is, then." His voice is smooth, caressing me with each syllable.

But that's not my name, and I tell him as much. He doesn't even blink.

"I gather you must have terrible hearing."

He says nothing, continuing to let his eyes wander, when suddenly, he releases the counter, chuckling darkly. With each inch of space I'm granted, my breath returns.

Edene descends the stairs, coming to my rescue. "My apologies, sir." She gives me a pointed look. "What can I do for you?"

Giving her a dazzling smile, he says, "I just need to place a special order. If I can?" He swivels back and forth between us. The bastard seems to know I'd tell him no if she weren't present.

Edene claps her hands excitedly. "Of course! Are you searching for something in particular? I have many kinds of medicinal—"

He cuts her off with a raise of his hand. "Oh, that's unnecessary. I simply need your finest sleeping mixture."

She studies him quizzically, forever the business professional. "Tea or potion?"

The stranger seems to contemplate her question for too many heartbeats before stating, "Potions, I think, darling."

Edene, *the betrayer*, covers her mouth as she giggles at him.

Tucking a stray curl behind her ear, she looks at him with the biggest eyes I've ever seen the woman make in her life. Edene is undeniably stunning—her long, dark hair makes her even more so. While she never talks about how she died three years ago, I've always wondered what it was. She holds the kind of natural beauty many want and will kill for.

I narrow my eyes at the pair of them.

She twirls her hair around her finger as she lists the different potions for sleep aid, the pricing for each of them, and of course, the side effects.

The white-hot anger in my chest is the only side effect I feel in this moment. For her safety, of course.

That's why I should interfere.

To protect her.

"Strange, isn't it? Requesting a special order for a sleeping potion." My voice drips with suspicion. "We keep them in stock, so there's no reason for you to go out of the way and come back. I could wrap them today, personally." I beam at him, withholding all the warmth from it.

Edene pouts, disappointed that I cut in. I can already hear her voice in my head, scolding me for interrupting. I try to communicate the unease I feel with a look that doesn't land. The man squares his body at me, an amused glint in his eyes.

"My apologies, miss...?"

"Arden!" Edene *helpfully* chimes in. I glare at her, but she's oblivious to my venomous stare.

"Well," he continues. "I meant no offense. Truly." His wicked smile says otherwise. "I'm not...from here. I wasn't aware of your customs. Back home, most apothecaries I knew only made potions to order. And gathering from the state of the shop," he waves his hand over the empty shelves and broken glass. "I assumed the process was similar."

I don't believe his bullshit story for a second.

Edene pats him on the arm. "No worries! I do apologize for the mess. We had an unfortunate accident this morning. I can grab it for you now. Though, if it's more convenient, you can stop in later today." She bats her eyelashes as she looks up at him.

I know her well enough to know that she's overdoing it, even for her. When she turns toward me again, I can't decipher the look on her face.

"Let's grab them now. I can always come back if I need more." He winks at her, causing her entire face to blush.

"Perfect! I'll be right back. Don't go anywhere!" She gives him a flirty wave as she leaves, and that ridiculous look stays on his face until she's out of sight.

I keep my arms crossed, never taking my eyes off him. His smile widens, devious and pointed, making my blood boil.

"So," he mimics my stance, "interesting name." When I don't deign to respond, he keeps talking. "I wonder if it tastes as sweet as I imagine you do."

"Too bad you'll never know. I don't waste my afterlife on men as insufferable as you," I clip as I give him a onceover.

"Too bad, indeed. I wonder, however...what extent would you go for, say, the likes of her?" He points to the workroom Edene went into. He prowls around me, leaning close enough to my back that I can feel his body heat.

Please don't touch me.

Fear strangles me at the prospect, stealing my oxygen.

His breath tickles my ear as he whispers, "I wonder...what were you cleaning a moment ago?" My shoulders lock up. He notices it immediately. "Hmm. It's all a choice. I could *choose* to turn you in to the patrol. Or I could *choose* to forget what I saw."

"It's not what you think—"

"Got it!"

He pulls back as Edene thankfully interrupts again.

"If you'll be in Voltus for much longer, I insist that you attend service day tomorrow. It's quite a marvel," she says.

I'm definitely plotting Edene's demise. Soon.

"I'm sure the Gods will bless me with the presence of the two of you again here soon." He gives me a wink as he drops the money for the potion in my hand. As he's making his way to the front door, I realize—he never said his name.

"Wait," I call out.

He ignores me, opening the door.

"Arrogant *bastard,* give me your name!"

Edene gasps as he turns, my fists clenching—itching to wipe that smug smirk off his face.

"You'll see me again, little raven." With that, he slips out the door, like he was never here.

I might strangle Edene tonight.

CHAPTER THREE

Edene gapes at me, appalled by my vulgarity, I'm sure. I don't give her the time of day before declaring we have a severed head to take care of.

I abruptly turn on my heel, but she follows me to the back of the shop, anyway.

"I don't want to hear a single word, Ede," I throw over my shoulder. I focus on the workbench in front of me so I don't have to look at her. "Something felt *wrong* when he came in. His presence felt..." I snap my fingers as I trail off to find the right word.

"Sinister?" Edene offers.

"Exactly!" I turn around to face her. "Wait, what? If you knew that, then why were you flirting with him?"

"I tried to tell you, but you couldn't read my eyes!" She pauses before her face splits into a smug grin. "Ohhh. I see now. You were *jealous!*" She digs her finger into my stomach playfully before I swat it away.

"Jealous? Please. I think he's dangerous. He could be a demon for all we know."

"Oh," her voice drops an octave, "you. So. Were." She crosses her arms as we stand off.

"If you want him, you can have him, honestly. I only entertained him for the sake of a potential ally. Don't think we couldn't use a man like that to help us—to help you." She brushes her hands down the skirt of her dress. "If you insist on following that *promise* through dangerous alleys, it would help you to have a backup guy. It definitely doesn't hurt to look at him, either." She nudges me with her elbow.

I roll my eyes at her as I turn back to the head, face burning once more.

Edene comes up behind me to peer over my shoulder. "At least the blood is red," she whispers. I side-eye her. A nod is all I give in response.

"Get the bucket." She doesn't move. "Please," I add.

"There, that wasn't so hard, was it?" She pats my shoulder as she walks over to grab the big metal bucket sitting across the room. There's no sense in arguing with Edene. Ever. She will always believe exactly what she wants, anyway. If persuasion is a hurricane, she's the sole building left standing.

She drops the bucket at my feet, and using the cloth, I drag the severed head off the table. It lands in the bucket with a wet *thud.* Edene's gray eyes are lined with worry as they meet mine. "What do you think killed her? Do we—are we supposed to...bury it?"

I'm usually the one between the two of us who gets dirty. Edene has never had to hide a body—that I'm aware of—and I plan on keeping it that way.

I chuckle at her. "Don't worry, I'll dispose of it." She practically sighs in relief. I purposely omit the part where that man saw me cleaning blood off the counter. Thank the Gods it was red. I'm certain I can talk my way out of it if we're confronted. I could pass it off as a cut of my own. The glass on the floor could've cut me before he walked in. I have plenty of tiny scars on my hands to pick from before I met Edene.

Back when it was just Perry and I.

I exhale hard, letting my head tip back, the weight of the morning pressing into my bones.

The utter agony in my chest feels worse than being stabbed. He was all I had, besides Edene. Every day that he's missing is another day he could be suffering.

Edene rubs my back in soothing circles, like she can hear my train of thought. "You'll find him, Arden. I know you will. If anyone can, it's you." Her voice is soft and reassuring. She's the only one besides me that doesn't believe that Perry found Peace.

A promise is a promise.

"Why don't you dispose of...*that* first. Then we'll go see the vendors. Would you like that?"

I grimace, thinking about walking through the meat market that the citizens of Voltus have deemed *the Laine*. Edene only refers to it as *seeing the vendors* because she knows how I feel about the black market. It's no place for her to be, but it's not as worrisome if I go with her when she needs more ingredients for her potions. At least then I know she has protection.

I sigh again as I nod. She stops rubbing my back to clap excitedly. I point a warning finger at her as I say, "Only because I need new pants. I can't dress like this regularly."

Her smile only grows as she nods her head, curls bouncing. I grab my freshly washed dagger from the washbasin, inspecting the sapphire for imperfections. Satisfied that I've found none, I slip it into a spare holster and loop it around my thigh under my skirt. I pat it through the skirt once it's hidden to ensure it will not move. Edene watches my movements and gives me a sad smile.

"What's that look for?" I ask her.

"Oh, nothing really," she says. "You just look beautiful, is all. Beautiful, but deadly. It just...really suits you, I think. A rose riddled with thorns. Ready for battle. Or a picnic." She laughs, a sweet, lilting sound.

I smile back at her, lovingly rolling my eyes as I grab her leather satchel and our cloaks, necessary for our destination. We lock the door behind us, leaving the mess inside for another time.

The Laine always reeks. It smells of weeks-old ale and piss, but if it bothers Edene, she doesn't let it show. The sun boils my skin through my dark green cloak. I adjust the hood, shielding my eyes from the light. This is why I never venture during the day. Burnus and I are not on good terms. Not that I've ever met the celestial being, but my pale skin does not agree with his unforgiving rays. Edene, however, is radiant as usual, sunlight catching in her curls, making them shine with the appearance of purple waves.

The market is busier than usual for midday; people of all classes keep their heads low while they shop, hoping to go unnoticed. Edene doesn't follow suit. She walks with her head high, greeting other passersby with a smile if they meet her eye. I'm uncertain if she's the bravest person I know, or if she wishes to find Peace early.

We push through the crowd, the stench of unwashed bodies burning my nose as it mixes with the heat.

As we approach the first table, we find a rotund balding man covered in soot and grease behind it. Edene smiles her greeting as she peruses his table. He smiles back at her, but his yellowed and missing teeth give way to the hungry look in his eyes as he takes her in. His smile holds nothing of the sweetness hers has. His gaze travels up and down her figure, stopping at her cleavage.

I hold back an eye roll.

Men are so easily distracted.

He looks at me in the same manner, except I don't give off the same *feminine flower aura* as Edene. With my arms crossed and a deep scowl, I radiate more of a *try anything and I'll cut off your cursed balls and feed them to you* kind of attitude that most men don't seem to appreciate. Why settle for a strong woman when you could have one who won't fight back?

The greasy man is selling various crystals, covering his entire table in an unorganized heap. Edene hums while she browses through them, carefully examining each one. Gods only know what she's looking for. I think the woman just likes to collect the shiny rocks and pretend they "help" her.

Unsatisfied with his collection, she moves to the next table. I sign that we're not interested as we leave, but he scowls at us like we promised to buy something just by walking up. To the Seven Hells with him.

We drift from table to table, not buying a single thing. There's one selling spices, another shoes. Some faces I remember from last time, but other vendors are new. There're all brands of people—each bringing their own thing. Most, if not all, stolen from Gods only know where to sell it here for a cheaper price.

The ones more appealing to look at, Edene tends to lean in more. Bats her eyes at them, flirting as she signs what she's looking for.

I suspect she only dragged me here today to make me sweat in the heat as punishment for swearing earlier. Just as I lift my hands to accuse her as such, she hits my arm hard to redirect my attention. She takes off for a booth on the other side of the square that's selling what appears to be the finest fabric I've seen in Voltus. I quickly follow her, holding the crest of my hood to make sure it stays put.

When I approach the table, I'm hit with the sweet smell of vanilla and spices I cannot decipher. The vendor is an older woman—slender, aged, yet still beautiful. She must've been stunning in Living. Pure jealousy courses through me. She got to live long enough to age. Souls like Edene and I weren't as lucky.

She wears a long, dark purple silk shawl. Her gold jewelry glints in the sunlight, peeking through the tent overhead. Many rings and layered necklaces scream her wealth. If oracles were still around post-war, I'd expect her to be one. Only a person who could predict prophecies would be brave enough to flash money like this in the Laine.

Or a fool.

Her violet eyes match her shawl—sharp, too vibrant, like bruised twilight.

"Hello," she greets, smiling, her voice a sultry, knowing purr.

I stop dead at her voice.

She broke the first cardinal rule of Laine—speaking. We *never* speak to each other here; not even Edene and I will converse in the square. Talking leads to noise. Noise leads to being caught by the patrol guards.

A fool indeed.

Something about her sticks in my ribs like a sewing needle. I can't pin it, but I don't trust it. Glaring at her, I bite my tongue. Edene shoots me a look, but I shake my head, reminding her not to speak. If this woman wants to invite the demon guards into her home, so be it.

"If your concern is the patrol guards, they cannot hear us," she assures, speaking my thoughts aloud. "There is a veil over my booth, which blocks from sight and sound. Your fellow merchants cannot hear us, either, should you worry about being barred from Laine altogether."

The next cardinal rule: If someone is dumb enough to talk, they'll *talk*. If, by the grace of Midnight herself, the patrol doesn't come for them, they'll henceforth be banned from the market for the rest of their afterlife. Forever labeled as someone who spills Laine's secrets throughout Voltus. A risk none of us are willing to take.

Edene and I both remain quiet, not trusting the woman for her word. Although, as I look around, it appears no one can hear her. I sift through the fine linen on her table, feeling the soft materials. Edene sorts through the jewelry on a display rack, not paying attention to me or the vendor.

Her fabrics are splayed out, but neat at the same time. I go through them, feeling the woman's violet gaze burn a hole through me.

Finding a quality pair of pants, and a couple shirts worth my time and money, I sign, *"How much?"* She smiles, holding up five fingers. I hand the woman the five coppers, but she shakes her head.

"Five gold pieces?" I sign. She's out of her godsdamned mind.

I shake my head, ready to throw a punch when she speaks again. "No, love, I meant you can *have* five articles. I do not need nor want your money." She presses the coins into my palm. I stare, confused.

"No, I need to pay," I sign.

Being labeled a thief is as damning as breaking a rule. I need to be able to come back here, and I can't stand the thought of having hundreds of eyes on my every move. I pick up more pants and another shirt, dropping a gold piece into a jar she put on the table.

No one gives away things here.

"I insist," she purrs.

Edene signs her thanks, dragging me out of the booth by the elbow, and back into the open.

This woman is clearly new to the Laine, if not Voltus overall. Incompetence and the inability to adapt will get her killed. I'll be damned to invite that into my home, too.

I've never been so grateful for the shine of the sun. I hadn't realized how shadowed the booth was now that my eyes adjust to the bright light.

Why did that feel like a test from the Gods?

Edene looks at me inquisitively. Giving her a nod, I tuck my purchases into the worn satchel she brought with.

Without looking anywhere else, we head back home to discuss what we saw, and what we've stolen.

CHAPTER FOUR

My stomach lurches at the mess.

I somehow forgot in the few hours we were gone that I never finished cleaning. Edene takes her satchel upstairs, hopping around the broken glass. Stupidly, I let all the spilled potions dry, and I kick myself for not being more disciplined. Edene will freak out if the wooden floor warps. I find the broom and quickly sweep up the remaining pieces of glass into the wastebin.

Upstairs, I enter Edene's bedroom to find her sitting with her legs crossed primly underneath her. She's taken off her cloak and dumped everything out.

"What did we find?" I ask, joining her on the bed. She's got a couple crystals, a pair of slippers, and several vials of herbs and potions. Most of them small, but a few decent-sized ones as well.

"I've got everything I need to make the next batch of antipurzon," she says, her eyes taking inventory of the spread. They'd never expect a woman as proper as Edene to have such sticky fingers. The day I found out about her kleptomania, I could've wept for joy at her feet. I've never met a thief as surreptitious as her. I've never been able to master the subtle art, and she constantly impresses me. She'll have things tucked away that I never even saw her near. A true talent.

"How long?"

She doesn't meet my gaze. "Maybe a week or so. I wish they sold more of this dragon's root," she says, holding up a bottle half full with purple flakes. "It's so rare to find outside the Laine. I can only afford to borrow one at a time. And that cheapskate only keeps them half full!" She lets out a huff, personally offended.

I laugh to myself because only Edene would refer to stealing as *borrowing*. Gods bless her moral compass. It must point in eight different directions, all of them telling her, *it's okay if I do it*.

"So a week, and we'll have enough antipurzon to last us until when?"

Edene's eyes meet mine, her face splitting as she grins.

"We'll have enough to last us until next summer." The hope in my heart flutters.

A year's supply.

One year supply for potential injuries on the journey to find Perry and bring him back home. Best case scenario, we only need to reserve a bottle or two for his recovery. I try to shrug off the anxiety at the unknown as it burrows through the hope.

What if he's missing limbs? So mutilated I don't recognize him? What if he doesn't want to see me? What if he's beyond saving? *What if he's found Peace? What if everyone's been right all along?*

I refuse to accept anything as truth. I have to cling to hope; to the belief that Perry is alive. That he's waiting for me to save him.

Edene starts sorting her *borrowed* goods into different piles, while I scoop up the one with the vials and follow her instructions to put them in her workroom. By the time I return, she's already tucked away everything except the clothing I bought, folded neatly on her bedspread. As I collect my stuff, I feel something rigid in the cloth. I dig it out to find the gold coin I had paid the woman with earlier.

Godsdamned wretch.

I hesitate when my fingers brush another lump in the pocket of a pair of pants, reaching in to fish out a teal crystal. Shooting a glance at Edene, I hold it up.

"For luck," she says, shrugging. "I figured if you wouldn't ask for help, at least I could give you that."

"Why would I—" I start, but I cut myself off. "Oh." The only thing that was holding me back from searching the other providences in Second just fell into our laps.

The gold. Extra clothes. The antipurzon.

It's all falling into place. I feel excitement at the prospect of venturing out, seeing Second in all its brilliant glory, but the feeling is immediately replaced by sorrow—I'll be leaving Edene here.

I haven't been apart from Edene for more than an evening since...well, since the day Perry went missing, six months ago. My eyes and nose burn as it hits me that we have a week. One week, and then I'll be saying goodbye to one of the only people I've known as family. Looking into her eyes, I see tears lined in them to match my own.

"Oh," she gasps, covering her mouth with her hand. "Don't you cry now! Or I'll definitely cry!" Tears race down her face regardless of her protest. She wipes them away angrily as I make my way over to her, folding me into a hug.

"Ede, you're crushing my windpipe." My voice strains. "If you kill me, you'll only upset yourself more."

She laughs through her tears and releases me as I pull back. I know my face is splotchy and puffy, matching hers.

"We still have a week! No need to start with the waterworks yet."

Edene smiles sadly as she nods, wiping her tears again. She sniffles and stands, clapping once. "Let's not dwell on it. We've plenty of time before you leave, and plenty to prep for as well. Speaking of prep, what are we eating for dinner?"

Food hadn't even crossed my mind today. My brow furrows as I try to think of suggestions. "We could treat ourselves to Valerie's?"

Edene shakes her head. "No, I'd rather go tomorrow, since we'll already be nearby for service day." I want to remind her it's not that far of a walk. Considering I made the trek here while bleeding out, I'd say she'll survive in heels. I decide to keep my mouth shut instead.

Despite the hot weather outside, we settle on potato soup for dinner, which turns out to be more delicious than I anticipated. As we part to our bedrooms, Edene pulls me into another choking hug.

"I know I don't tell you enough, Arden, but I do love you very much. Like my own sister. And I'm going to miss you like hell every day. Just promise me you'll come back?" Her voice comes out small, yet the exhaustion lays thick.

I chuckle at her ridiculousness. "Of course. I love you, too." I can't help but pause. "Why does it feel like you're saying goodbye instead of goodnight?"

She releases me as fast as she grabbed me, scoffing. "I'm sorry for trying to have a nice moment," she huffs. "Gods, some people." She waves her hand dismissively and I laugh as I turn to my own bedroom.

As I open the door and collapse on my thin, springy mattress, a groan escapes me. The wariness of the eventful day has finally caught up to me, and it takes only a minute or two before the world turns black, pulling me into a dream.

The lights are so bright. Second is always brighter like this. That's what Perry says. It's going to take a while to get used to this. Perry sits across from me in the booth at Valerie's, his head thrown back, laughing that beautiful laugh. Gods, he is a wonder to watch. He's been so kind to me since he found me a few days ago, and I can't seem to keep it together.

Being dead is so strange. I figured when I died, I would've been in a lot more physical pain, but Perry tells me it's not uncommon for some of us to not feel anything.

"I don't remember much about my life," I confess to him. Perry's laughter ceases and he studies me over with sharp, green eyes. I could get lost in that forest forever and not care about another living thing again.

"Don't stress yourself out, Arden. Also, we call it an 'alive-life' here. Welcome to your dead one." He smiles broadly, then brings his drink to his lips.

Arden. That's my name. It sits on my mind like it's been borrowed. Like a shirt that doesn't quite fit.

This place has strange customs.

A different world, indeed.

"Do you know how I died? Did you, um, witness anything that day you found me lying there?" I reach inwards, trying to grasp at anything, something, to just simply remember. There's nothing.

His eyes drop, glossing over slightly, drifting to the memory. His hands fidget as he gathers his words.

"Uh, no. Typically when someone crosses over into Second, it seems to vary person to person. So, when I found you lying there on the ground, I didn't know who you were or how you got there. I only know as much as you do when it comes to your past." My face falls with the disappointment I feel from his acknowledgment. He raises a finger in the air and leans forward slightly. "But! I've heard that it comes back for almost everyone. So, maybe with time, we'll start to see pieces of your alive-life come back to you."

An ounce of hope blossoms inside my chest. "Oh, okay. We'll see then. With time, surely," I agree. My thoughts drift to those who aren't a part of the almost everyone group. I pity those Arrivals who never get their memories back. I hope mine comes back soon, because I'm not thrilled with the haze floating around in my mind. It's unnerving and disorienting.

"Memories are fickle, especially here. But don't worry about that. You have me." His hand lands on my wrist, grounding me back to the present. Emerald eyes and a warm smile entrance me in our bubble. "You're thinking about it too hard. It's like stepping into the sun after a long night. You're adjusting. You'll see soon enough." He pulls back his hand and I instantly miss it.

"So, tell me more about Second, about you. How long have you been here? Do you have all of your memories or are you like me? Do we age here? Is this a friendship now?" I ask, directing my finger between us. "How old are you? Where—"

"Holy Gods, woman! One question at a time!" He laughs at me, smiling and revealing perfect, white teeth. It's so unfair really, that someone should look like

that and be this kindhearted. While I know I'm not unattractive, I am certainly no heart-stopper, either. My long, dark brown hair contrasts my pale skin, and while I don't hate it, I wish I was tan like Perry. I resent that the paleness makes me look as dead as I feel. Whereas Perry here, in this light, looks more alive than ever. Like Second feeds his very soul and the brightness in this world is actually emanating from him and not the magic surrounding us.

"You'll age...of sorts. It's not the same, but similar all at once. When you reach a certain year, you'll notice that your features look the same after so many turns." *He runs his fingers along his jaw, thinking.* "I do have my memories. All eight years dead and thirty alive. As for friends, we can be friends."

Eight years dead. Gods, how lonely.

"What's your next question?" *he asks.*

"Can you do magic like the others?" *Better safe than sorry. If I'm going to befriend this man, I need to know what I'm getting into.*

"Yes, I used to. Before everything started slipping away. People say some providences still have magic—and before you cut me off, no. I don't know if you can or will be able to, as well." *My mouth parts slightly, and now I'm curious if part of his magic is mind reading because I didn't even get a chance to voice a second question.* "You should know, you get a tiny sparkle in your eyes when you get curious. You'll need to learn how to hold a straight face better, if you want to survive here."

"Can you read minds?" *I blurt out. Gods, smite me now. My neck and face flush with heat as Perry gapes at me. Well, now I've thrown it out in the open.*

"Um, no..." *He chuckles nervously, running a hand on the back of his neck.* "That's not an ability I've seen before."

"But you knew what I was going to ask..." *I trail off, hoping he can fill in the blanks without me having to voice anything even more embarrassing.*

"Like I said, you need to keep your emotion off your face, Arden." *He offers me a shy smile. My name coming from his mouth makes me feel a warmth all the way to my toes. I like the way he says it. Maybe he's paying more attention to me than I am giving him credit for.*

"How closely are you watching my face, Per?" *I give him a wry smile.*

"Is that the question you really want to ask right now?" he parries. "Or are you going to continue your original list?" I straighten my spine and fold my hands like he had done a minute ago.

"I have a new one, but in respect for the game, I'm declaring that and not asking." I stare him straight in the eyes, not blinking. He doesn't balk, either.

"Proceed." He nods.

I sigh, shaking my head. "You're enjoying this, aren't you?"

Perry smirks, swirling his drink. "Does it ruin the magic if I say I am?"

He winks at me, and I think I die for a second time. Unable to speak actual words, I blink at him.

"Maybe." Studying him, I wait for his response, but it never comes. "You're really gonna make me work for this, huh? Fine. No riddles. No games. Just the real story."

Perry sighs at me, like I've asked him for his weight in gold and told him to count it twice. He drums his fingers on the table, contemplating. "You want a story, huh?" I nod.

"Alive-life? Or undead one?" he questions, swirling his drink again.

"Both, if you feel so inclined. I'm here to listen. You seem like a good soul to put my faith in, so let's see if I'm right." I hold his gaze still, willing myself to not be the first to look away.

"Well, I hope I pass your strict judgement, then. I'll tell you my story, but I can't promise it's anything interesting, though." I beam at him as I settle into my seat, satisfied. Perry shakes his head at me and scoffs, smiling slightly.

He doesn't let me answer before he starts to tell me about his lives.

Back when Perry was alive, he lived with his mother, Elodie, and younger sister, Lauren. All three of them looked just alike, according to him. Same green eyes, all three with the same shade of sandy brown hair as well. His eyes look sad as he tells me about them, as though he somehow grieves them and not the other way around. I wonder if they are in Living or if they've found Peace. I don't ask. Perry continues to tell me about where he was educated, but he didn't get to graduate. I must have that same look on my face from earlier, because he stops mid-sentence.

"I didn't finish because I was murdered in my room one night. Stabbed to death," he draws his hand around to his back to show me. *"Right in the back."*

I gasp, my hand slapping over my mouth to keep it from hanging open.

"You were murdered?"

"Yep." He takes another sip of his drink as he stares at me over the rim, almost bored. As though he didn't just drop a huge bombshell on me. I don't let him off that easily.

"You say it so casually, Perry. I'm so sorry that happened to you." My heart cracks for this poor man. Perry, who shows every person he meets kindness, was brutally murdered in his alive-life.

I reach out to place my hand over his, but he pulls back slightly, halting my motion. I want to believe him—that this doesn't bother him. But how could it not?

Maybe eight years is enough to forgive and forget. Maybe he coped by helping Arrivals—maybe it dulls the pain with time.

"Don't cry for me," he teases. *"I went down with a fight, and it was a while ago, so I'm not as upset as I was when I first arrived. I mean, it's not as though I can change what happened, so there's no sense in losing focus on my life in Second."* His eyes aren't shining anymore. I'm annoying him.

Right.

"Sorry, I didn't mean to interrupt your story. Please, continue." I gesture locking my mouth so he knows the floor is his, without interruptions.

Keep your stupid emotions to yourself, Arden.

Perry continues after a beat, telling me about when he woke up here, confused, bloody, and royally pissed. I'd be, too, if I just lost a battle for my life. How he struggled at first, unable to control his rage, destroying everything he could. He tells me that he's figured out a few things along the way, finding good places to sleep, people to talk to, and where to go. He cracks his knuckles as he talks, and the sound feels too loud.

He fills most of his time helping people like me. Arrivals, he calls us. Or he spends his days tending the Gardens.

My ears perk up at that.

A garden? The thought of breathing in beautiful flowers makes my heart swell, but I'm not certain why. I barely know myself right now. I feel like this body is not my own. But my subconscious tells me this is right. I am Arden.

Perry, once again, notices my change in demeanor.

"Would you like to see the Garden?"

Should I go? Do I want to go? I might like flowers.

It's just a walk, Arden, I tell myself. I push down any doubt that it could be more.

I nod enthusiastically. I feel like a little kid being promised a present. Any hesitations I had dissipate as I slide out of the booth as fast as I can, grabbing his hand that he has outstretched to me. My heart stutters a beat as he laces his fingers with mine, and we take off running like little kids.

CHAPTER FIVE

I f it weren't for Edene, I swear on the Gods I would never attend another service day in my afterlife. The same phony vendors, mingling and chatting amongst themselves.

They sell similar things to the Laine, except everything here is legal. In fact, these are probably the vendors that were robbed. Unlike Edene, these people are greedy, charging almost *four times* more than the Laine. I might be dead, but I'm not a fool.

We set up our booth in the throng of the market square. Surrounded by several other vendors, I keep my focus on our table. I can't bear another round of small talk.

My heart still feels the ache from my dream last night. I dream of Perry almost every night since he went missing last year, but it doesn't get easier with each passing day.

Edene, however, is giddy this morning, her tears last night forgotten.

We brought most of the basic potions with us today, lining half the table. The other half holds various creams. Most are for sleep, burns, fevers, and coughs. The rest of them I couldn't even label. Edene truly has a medicinal gift, and while she is often horrible with charging her worth, that's where I step in. The dead are more manipulative than the ones in Living.

I try to shrug off the pang of worry for her business while I'm gone.

She's been doing this way before I came along and weaseled the spare room from her in exchange for my help.

I turn to speak to Edene, only to find she's deep in conversation with Chandler. The most insufferable soul I've ever met. Her short, blonde hair shifts with every bob of her head—no doubt, over-animatedly telling Edene about whatever story she heard in Saffron, the tavern she owns, last night.

Her tavern isn't exactly a high class establishment. It's rumored that the leaders of the Shaded meet there occasionally, for Gods only know what. Chandler denies it, but knowing her, she's loving the attention. It draws people in every night, as though any of them could point out the leaders. Fools.

We don't know what they look like. The only way to find a Shade is to bleed them out. Something tells me she wouldn't appreciate blood staining Saffron's floors for the rest of her afterlife.

Chandler keeps waving her hands as she talks, her blue eyes wide. Suddenly, I'm lifted off my feet, a startled squeak falling from my lips. I'm spun around as a familiar scent of cedar and clove hits me. *Kaisen.*

"Sorry, Arden! I didn't mean to spook you."

My shock morphs into elation as I melt into him. His hug is as it always is, a simple comfort. A fast grin splits across my face as he releases me from his arms.

"Oh my Gods! When did you make it back?"

His brown eyes sparkle as he smiles back at me. "Last night. I tried to stop by your place, but you weren't there."

"Oh, I moved into Burtons, with Edene." Kaisen looks past my shoulder, but she's still engrossed in her conversation. "You look good," I tell him. He does; all tanned from the sand dunes of Scarlentta. More toned, too, if his hug is any indication. His brown hair is cropped short, along with his beard.

Kaisen certainly is appealing to look at, but he's more like a brother now. We slept together one drunken night, almost a year ago when we first met. I was trying to bury my feelings for Perry in a stranger, but we didn't mesh well and decided to remain friends.

"You look good yourself, Arden." He smiles appreciatively at me, and the attention makes my face burn. He leans in closer to my ear, whispering, "Your biggest fan is here."

"I think it's your fault. She's *always* trying to get you to stay after close. Plus, I don't think she appreciated us making out at her bar that night. She's kept me on her shit list ever since."

He laughs, shaking his head. "Listen, it takes two, you know. She's not my type, anyway. And let's not pretend we only kissed in that bar. I seem to remember you wrapping your legs around me and grinding on my—"

I smack his arm before he can finish. Alcohol Arden needs constant surveillance. He laughs harder, enjoying my distress. He knows I hate talking about my sex life, especially in public.

"Oh, Kaisen! I didn't know you'd be returning to Voltus today. I would've saved you a special table!" Chandler's high-pitched voice grates on me, but Kaisen smiles.

He throws his arm around my shoulders. "Sorry, I just got into town. Had to see my best girl first. Maybe we can stop in tonight." He looks to me for confirmation that I won't give.

"Fallon, how lovely to see you here." She gives me a sour smile, staring too hard at Kaisen's arm.

"Bianchi," I say flatly. She's refused to use my first name ever since I met her. I think it might humanize me and, well, *she wouldn't want that.*

"What do you say, Arden? Just like old times." Kaisen smiles, but I look at Edene, who just shrugs.

"We'll think about it," I say. It's not that I don't want to spend time with Kaisen before I leave, but I was also looking forward to going to Valerie's instead. And a night with Chandler hovering around doesn't sound appealing.

I zone out the rest of their chatter.

"Please let me know if you see her, Edene. She's not the kind to run off and well, she's all I have. I trust that you'll keep this between us." Chandler gives me a sideways glance. "Last thing I need is for everyone to think I'm on the same crazy train as your friend there."

Edene gives her a small frown as she says, "Arden isn't crazy, Chandler. But yes, of course, just between us. If I spot Cynthia, I'll be sure to let you know."

Kaisen opens his mouth to speak when the bell tower chimes, letting us know its midday already. As soon as it stops, a deep voice breaks the silence.

"Do you have any potions left?"

My heart jolts at the voice, instantly recognizing it.

It's him.

We all turn to find the beautiful stranger from yesterday, standing next to our table. He eyes me up and down, smirking when he sees Kaisen's arm move from around my shoulders to slip around my waist. I can feel Kaisen tense, although I'm not sure why. He just met him.

Edene lights up like a fucking firework. "Oh! It's you again! You came!" They exchange smiles with each other that make my blood feel volcanic.

"Can I ask your assistance again? I'm in need of some more—"

"Chandler Bianchi," Chandler sticks her hand out to the man, cutting him off. By the glare in his dark eyes, I can see he didn't appreciate it. He doesn't acknowledge her beyond that. It makes my mouth tilt up, feeling smug.

"As I was saying, I need a few more bottles of the sleeping potions I bought yesterday."

"Did they not work?" Edene inquires. "If there was an issue with the quality, I assure you I can give you more for no charge."

He shakes his head. "No, that's not necessary. I just need to stock up on a few extra." Edene helps him with the transaction, gathering every last sleeping potion she brought with us. He keeps his eyes locked to mine during the whole ordeal.

"Lovely to see you again, little raven."

"Can't say the same." Kaisen's hold tightens onto my waist, pressing into my ribs. He doesn't move beyond that, waiting for the stranger to acknowledge him. The man notices, his smirk growing as he blatantly ignores him. Like he isn't even there.

"Oh, I hate to disappoint. Perhaps you'll let me make it up to you." His smirk sharpens, his voice too smooth. Like he can *taste* my frustration and it's the most delicious thing he's ever had. "I was so delighted by your presence last time. I'm certain we could find something...*mutually beneficial.*" His smile is devious now as I shrug out of Kaisen's hold. I grab the stranger by the arm, dragging him a few feet away with my back to my friends. Edene continues to package his order, unfazed to what's unfolding.

"What do you want?" I hiss at him. That ridiculous smile of his never falters. He knows he's won; getting me to snap first in this unspoken limbo.

I'm not sure if it's being alone with him, or if we've truly been at service so long today, but the light dims in his presence. He steps in too close, that scent of balsam and linen making me lightheaded. I have to tilt my chin up at him, and I hate it. I know the bastard is reveling in it.

"Can't a man simply want to be in the presence of a beautiful woman?"

"Listen, prick," I shove my finger into his chest, my gaze unwavering, "I don't even *know* you. Are you stalking me? Who the fuck are you?"

"Bayne." He dips into a smug bow.

I laugh coldly. How fitting. "I'm already well-the-fuck-aware you're the bane of my existence."

"You're clever, little raven. I'll give you that."

"Okay, *Bayne.* What. Do. You. Want?"

His eyes trail my frame suggestively as he straightens, and my skin heats in response. "We can discuss it tonight. If you want me to keep your secret...I suggest you make yourself free." He makes it sound filthy, like this is actually a tryst and not incessant blackmail. His eyes dart behind us to Kaisen and Chandler, who are watching us very intently. "You'll need to ditch your little boyfriend there. He can't come, darling."

My spine straightens. I scoff at him, but I can feel my ears burning hotter. "He's *not* my boyfriend. He's just a friend."

"Maybe you should tell him that."

"This is not what we're discussing! What time?" I put my hands on my hips. I can't *believe* I'm truly agreeing to meet with this psycho. Blackmailing me into dinner? Not the best of second impressions.

"Hmmm." He taps a finger to his chin, pondering. "Let's meet after seven," he says.

"Where?" I hiss at him. *Gods,* this is worse than pulling teeth.

He leans in close to my ear. "Wherever you want me."

Damn it. My traitorous body shivers before I can stop it. I yank myself away.

"Saffron. At ten. Do not, I repeat, *do not* drag my friends into this. This is only between you and me."

"Oh, I sure hope that's a promise, darling," he drawls, his dark eyes glowing with mischief. "I'm not one who likes to share." He winks as he saunters away, collecting his finished order from Edene. He gives her the money and a nod of thanks before turning to me. "Until next time, little raven." Before I can snatch my hand back, he catches it, brushing his lips against my knuckles in a slow, deliberate kiss. His dark eyes glitter as he drinks in my fury. My hand burns from his mouth.

As he leaves, Edene catches my eye, giving me a look that says, *we will most definitely be discussing that later.*

Can't wait.

Kaisen is the first to break the silence. "Who was that guy, Arden? Are you seeing him?" He sounds pissed as he watches Bayne's retreating back. I give him an incredulous look, trying but failing to get his attention.

"Are you serious right now? Please, give me more credit than that."

"Please let me know if you see Cynthia," Chandler says to Edene, who nods, shooting me another look.

"Your sister is missing?" Kaisen asks. "What happened, if you don't mind me prying?"

Chandler clears her throat, darting her eyes between all of us. "I don't know. We said goodnight. I went to work at Saffron, only for her not to be in her bed when I got home. I don't know," she whispers, her voice shaky.

It's weird to see her like this. Almost human. I almost can't see the snake I know is underneath.

"I opened her bedroom door only for her to not be there. She wouldn't just run away. As ironic as it sounds," her blue eyes settle on me, "I know she didn't find Peace. She was just an Arrival only three months ago. She loved it here, loved being dead with me."

It's so familiar, I almost feel sorry for Chandler. The thought makes me want to rip my ears off so I can't hear it anymore. *Stupid morality.* I remain impassive as Kaisen chimes in.

"Yeah, my grandmother was missing when I got back, too." My head whips to him. "I just assumed...I mean I thought..."

People are going missing. Why aren't people staying dead?

First Perry, then Chandler's sister, and now Kaisen's grandmother? It has to be connected.

The bell tower chimes again, indicating another hour has passed.

Kaisen speaks first. "Well, ladies, I should probably get some shopping done myself. I've missed this place," he bows to us, making me roll my eyes, "and it's residents." When his face meets mine again, he winks. Chandler gives him a flirty wave as they both leave us.

Turning to me, Edene gives me a look to rival even the most devious. "Soooo," she drawls.

"Uh-uh. No. Do *not* even start."

"I didn't even say anything yet! He was the one hanging all over you. *Both of them.*" She wiggles her eyebrows in suggestion.

I sigh heavily. "Ede, please. Kaisen is just a good friend. And don't even get me started on Bayne." I feel nothing but irritation at the sheer thought of him. "He's the most arrogant prick I've met in *either* life. I wish he would leave me alone."

Edene looks at me curiously but doesn't comment. Not even on the fact that I don't remember *anything* from my past life. Perhaps she really thinks it's desire pulling us together. Better for her to believe the lie, I suppose. I'll do whatever it takes to keep her safe and out of this psycho's line of sight. I take another deep breath.

"I suppose...he's not hideous. He asked me to meet him tonight." Edene lets out a massive squeal, causing other vendors to shoot us dirty looks. She bounds over to me, grabbing my arm excitedly.

"I knew it! He looks like he wants to eat you up." Her grin widens. "Which, it's been a minute for you. You should grab this opportunity by the metaphorical balls. Or literal." I blush crimson at her brazenness.

I groan, throwing my head back. Maybe I should've just told her about him being a witness to a crime. One I didn't even commit. The prospect of death by execution sounds more appealing than telling Edene about my sexual exploits.

"I'm not saying there is something there," I lie. "But even *if* there was, you already know how this works. I am not telling you details. Bare minimum only."

"Sordid details leading up to the act," she counters. "Names of one to two positions performed."

"Edene! This isn't a negotiation!" I laugh at her audacity. "You will take the breadcrumbs I feed you and let that be enough."

She pouts in response. "That's not fair. I tell you everything!"

"Against my will," I add.

"You're no fun. Maybe I'll dig it out of Bayne the next time I see him. See if he's willing to share the details you'll hide."

"Gods, smite me. *Fine.* Deal." She grins wickedly as she shakes my hand.

Midnight, if you can hear me, please smite me so I don't have to see him again.

The goddess of Night doesn't answer me. Typical.

We pack up and head home, but as soon as we get there, Edene insists on dolling me up. To my surprise; I don't hate it.

"I feel...pretty."

She's put cosmetics on my eyes and lips, and I tell myself to remember not to touch my face. I put on a fitted, black shirt with pants to match. Slipping on my boots, I tuck my dagger inside, just in case.

Edene clasps my dark green cloak around my neck, giving me a onceover when she finishes.

"You look stunning. I really hope you wore some nice underwear under all this. Or rather, a pair you don't care about, because when he sees you, he's going to want to rip them off." Her smile is mischievous as ever, and I can't help but laugh.

Edene has always had two personalities. The first is the proper lady and shopkeeper who doesn't want a speck of dirt on her skirts. The second—an absolute fiend that should be retrained with a chastity belt.

"Where are you meeting him? I can walk you there."

"Oh, no need. It's just at Saffron."

"Gods, Arden, *Saffron?* Are you trying to doom your date?" Her wide eyes almost make me lose my composure again, but I can't lose focus on what this actually is.

"It was his suggestion," I lie, smoothing the length of my cloak. "I think I'll be okay for a few hours. I'll make sure we sit in a dark corner where the she-beast can't see me." I grin.

"Just...be nice. To everyone there. Just in case. I'm definitely walking you now, just to ensure you're on your best behavior. I don't want you to get all stabby-stabby on the way there and conveniently ditch your date."

"I will do my best." I give her a mocking salute, and we head out the door.

Chapter Six

O f course the bastard is sitting front and center in the blasted tavern.

His legs are kicked out, leaning back in his chair as he watches me walk in. Part of me is really wishing I had asked Edene to stay, but if I end up having to kill him, I would hate to make her an accomplice.

I glance around the tavern, taking inventory of my surroundings as I begrudgingly walk toward the table. The place is busy, but not packed. Perfect for blending in. Bayne remains relaxed as I reach the chair opposite him. He still wears his finery of all black, looking like a Prince of Death. He grins at me, but I feel the coldness behind it. No need to pretend now that we're alone.

"Don't you look pretty. All dolled up just for me?" he coos at me. Ignoring him, I pull out my own chair and sit down without removing my cloak. "Take your coat off, little raven. Relax, why don't you?"

"You can drop the charade now, Bayne." I roll my eyes. "We both know why you really asked me here." I cross my arms and lean back. He doesn't even twitch a muscle before he speaks.

"Always down to business, hm? I think I'll need a drink first." Before I can respond, he's out of his chair and at the bar. When he turns back around, he's carrying not one, but two glasses of amber liquid. He smirks at me as he sets one down and changes his seat so that he's sitting right beside me. To anyone else, it would be a simple gesture, a first date getting more comfortable. But I see it for what it really is—a threat.

"What do you think you're doing?" I hiss through bared teeth.

"Shh, darling. It's your favorite. Drink up." He winks before taking a massive swig of his own glass, setting it down louder-than-necessary. *Your move*, his eyes seem to say, while his lips remain set in that frustrating smirk.

Stop staring at his mouth, Arden.

While I'm certain this whole "date" would be significantly easier to bear being intoxicated, I hate the idea of being even slightly vulnerable around him. I shove my glass forward as I smile sweetly at him. "No thanks, *darling.*"

Without warning, Bayne grabs the underside of my chair and jerks it right next to him, with me still seated on it. A small squeal of surprise escapes my lips, only emboldening him more as my knee hits his thigh. He leans close to my ear, brushing my hair off my shoulder and wrapping his arm around the back of my chair. "Look, you've got an audience now. Better start drinking if you want them to look away. I'd hate to make a spectacle of you."

Sure enough, as I peer around the bar, other drinkers stare unabashedly. I could stab him just for forcing my hand in such a public way. I grind my teeth as I glare at him, picking up the glass of liquor. He keeps his arm on my chair so I can't scoot away. I take a small sip of the drink, and sure enough, in my peripheral, I can see the rest of the tavern give up on getting a performance.

"I hope you're happy, asshole." I am seething as I turn back to him. Bayne's face still holds his smug expression of contentment, and it only feeds my anger. "Remove. Your. Arm. Or I'll remove it for you."

His smirk finally drops, but he listens to my command. He doesn't make any effort to widen the space between us, though, and it feels like I'm suffocating. If it were even possible, it seems like the lanterns in here dim as he leans forward to speak. "Who are you hunting?" He asks, his voice low.

That's...not where I thought this was going. "Wha-what?"

"I said, who are you hunting, little raven?" His face remains steely. If he's revealing nothing, then I sure as hell won't either.

"I'm not hunting anyone."

"Oh, I beg to differ."

"So you beg? That must be quite a sight." I can't help the self-righteous smile that crawls across my face.

"I can promise you, little raven, that most people, under different circumstances, often beg *me*." My cheeks burn hot at his words. "If you were to feel so inclined, I won't stop you. However, allow me to give you a free lesson in turns of phrases."

"How is it possible that you're so incredibly condescending and still try to flirt with me at the same time? That must be very contradictory for your soul. Good luck to you when it comes time to find Peace." I take another drink from my glass, a bigger gulp this time. I'm grateful for the burn it leaves in my chest, replacing the one Bayne put there.

He throws back his head and laughs at me, as though I've said something funny. "It's *adorable* that you think Peace is a desire of mine. So fine, you won't tell me who you're hunting? Tell me whose blood you were cleaning up the other day." I can feel the blood drain from my face and my eyes grow wide. "Hmm, hoped I didn't see? I'm not blind. Even if it never streaked across your face, surely you're not naïve enough to think the *smell* would be wiped away as easily?"

Yes, that's exactly what you thought, Arden.

"I didn't know her," I whisper, bile creeping up my throat. "I swear it. We just found her. She was just...there. A message. A warning."

Bayne narrows his eyes at me, taking in my words. "How do you track them?"

I blink at him. "How do I *what*? I'm not tracking anyone."

Bayne's face remains impassive, the poster child of boredom. "*Tracking*, raven. How are you doing it? Is it the smell?" I stiffen involuntarily at his questioning. "Does your hovering healer friend make something to draw them in before you finish the rest?"

"Do I—"

"How did you know how to kill them?"

Oh, shit. Did he find that body in the alley after I ran?

"How do you know about that?" I whisper.

He tilts his head, watching me closely. "Are you having a stroke?" Irritation mars that beautiful face of his. "I just told you, *I saw you cleaning up its blood. I could smell it.*"

Now it's my turn to be confused. "Oh, I thought...that woman wasn't a Shade." Her blood was red. I've killed enough Shaded to know the difference between something as trivial as *color.* If it were black, I would've noticed.

"Oh, I see, raven. This isn't your first time."

I shift hard in my chair, causing it to squeak loudly, but a quick glance around tells me no one is looking at us. "*Excuse me?* That's one hell of an accusation to make."

Bayne studies me, his eyes bouncing between my own. He leans into my space, bringing us nearly nose to nose. "It's interesting, you know." He lifts a hand and pushes tendrils of hair that came loose behind my ear. I freeze, but my body shivers at the touch, the traitorous bitch. "I wouldn't have pegged you as a killer."

"Well I'm not a killer, so at least we can agree you were right about that."

He rolls his eyes at me.

"Her blood was red," I tell him, and he sits up straighter.

"What did it look like?"

"Um, red?" *Is he fucking deaf?*

He shakes his head, running his palm over his face. Annoyance flashes in his dark eyes, but it's there one heartbeat, and gone the next. The cool mask of indifference sets once again.

"You said it seemed like a message? What did the scene look like for it to appear that way?" His intrigue seems genuine, but a strange feeling spreads inside me, like I *want* to tell him. As though I need to tell him.

Gods, his focus on me is...*intense.*

"She...her head." My mouth feels dry, so I down more of my drink, welcoming the burn. "I...her head was on a spike. That usually only holds papers. Well, not anymore. They're ruined now." My lips feel funny as I try to remember what it all looked like. "They were looking for something, whoever killed her."

"If you didn't kill her, why did you clean it up? Why not report it to the patrol guards? Why was Burtons a wreck if there wasn't a struggle?"

He has so many questions, my mind is reeling. He's pressing me for information, but I don't even know what he's asking. Instead of answering, I turn to stare up at the ceiling, transfixed by the chandeliers there. They shine so pretty in here...so golden.

A rough hand grabs my jaw, pulling Bayne back into my line of focus. He's holding my face with surprising gentleness, pushing my cheeks slightly inwards.

"Eyes on me, little raven. Focus. You didn't answer my question."

Shit. What did he ask me?

Oh, right. The murder.

"I don't know. The Shades, perhaps." Now it's my turn to laugh, and in doing so, he releases my face. "Why would I report it? The patrol guards would *never* believe me. I'd be damn lucky they didn't kill me instantly. I don't know where you crawled out of, but here, it's more *kill first ask questions never.* Wrong place, wrong time for her, I guess. We were robbed." I giggle at the thought. Whoever it was, thought they were probably getting something valuable. What they took was hardly more than perfume and bathing lotions.

He is silent for a long minute. "The Shaded. Are there some here?"

I shrug almost helplessly. "Not if I can help it. Are you following them?"

When he opens his mouth to respond, it snaps shut again and his gaze follows past my shoulder. I follow his line of sight to what he's looking at, and I see a table in the far corner with none other than Kaisen, Chandler, and Edene.

"Greeeaaat," I groan. The last thing I need is their judgement right now. Especially since I can't feel my face. I run a hand up and down my cheek, trying to wake up the skin there, since it seems to have fallen asleep without my permission. But I barely feel the touch of my own hand.

The three of them are staring at us unabashedly from across the room. Chandler looks smug as she tries to snuggle closer to Kaisen, who from the looks of how white his knuckles have turned, is about to shatter the glass he's holding. Edene smiles and waves when she sees us staring. Bayne has the nerve to wave back, and I am right back to furious.

I smack his hand down as I growl at him, "What do you think you're doing? I told you to leave my friends out of this."

He levels me with his dark gaze as he whispers, "I didn't invite them, darling. Must've been you. History shows you clearly love a show. What a shame." He shakes his head in faux solemnity. "I wouldn't have minded to spare them."

Fear slides down my spine at the threat, and my skin feels clammy. I look back and forth between their table and Bayne's face, so close to my own. Is he moving closer?

"Please," I whisper. "They are innocent."

He raises an eyebrow, his only response.

"They didn't...I'm the one tracking the Shades. They aren't involved." I shake my head furiously, trying to get him to understand. Bayne frowns, my vision turning blurry. *Do not cry, you stupid girl.*

He places a hand on my knee that I hadn't realized was still pressed against him. I stare down at his hand in disbelief and confusion. He gives it a gentle squeeze and I once again find his eyes. His face flickers with...anger? Irritation? But as I blink away the tears that were threatening to fall, my head starts to feel clearer again.

"Have a good night, little raven. We'll have to do this again soon. I'll be in touch." He grabs my hand as he moves to stand and kisses the back of it in one smooth motion. Slow. Unhurried. As if he already knows I won't pull away. I remain seated, dumbfounded, as Bayne turns and walks right out of the front door.

What just happened?

Before I have any time to even think about it, Edene plops down into Bayne's empty chair, oblivious to the shadows that linger in the air. "Ede, what are you even still doing here? I told you not to come." I reach for my drink, but it's no longer on the table. *That's weird.*

"I know, but I could feel the tension. The way he sat you in the middle of the tavern?" She feigns a swoon. "What I would give to be put on display like that. That man clearly wanted to send a message to this whole room."

"Yeah, he sent a message alright," I grumble.

"Ugh, *lighten up.* He's hot, you're hot. Bang it out. Fall in love, get married, blah blah blah..."

I tear my focus from the empty table. "Edene, how much have you had to drink?" I look her up and down. Her brown curls are slightly more wild than usual, and her light brown skin has a pink flush to it. I analyze her gray eyes like they'll give me the answer.

She pouts slightly, then taps a finger to her chin in contemplation. "Four, maybe five."

My jaw hangs open as I stare at her. "Drinks? Shots?" Edene never drinks this much. Not with Chandler's garbage ale, and definitely not with her tiny ass.

"I wanna *dance*. Let's dance, Arden!" she whines, but her head lobs a little as she does. I have to get her home and into bed immediately. I turn to look at the table where she was previously sitting, only to find it empty.

Edene drapes an arm heavily over my shoulders and breathes her hot breath into my ear, trying to whisper. "They snuck off. I think Kaisen could feel the tension, too. That you wanted to fuck him, that is. Bayne, I mean."

I shrug her off me, irritation flooding my veins as she tries to cling to me. "Alright, Ede, let's get you home."

She pouts at me, unimpressed with my idea. She crosses her arms, looking every bit the impotent child. "I don't want to go home. I want to *dance*."

"We can dance at home," I tell her as I try to get her to stand up. Thankfully she obeys, using me for balance as her legs wobble.

"Prom-promise?" she hiccups, her eyes wide and searching.

"Sure thing. Let's get home so we can dance." Her answering grin warms my heart, but as soon as we step out the door and the humid evening air hits us again, Edene vomits everywhere.

Gods damn me, what did I do to deserve this? Was I truly this horrible in Living that I earned such torture?

"Sorry," she mumbles. I huff a small laugh, trying to remind myself how much I love Edene, and to bask in the moment of her being less than perfect for once. No matter how repulsive it may be.

"That wasn't very ladylike," I tease her. She only groans in response, resting her head on my shoulder. "Gods, Edene, you're burning up." I can feel the heat radiating off her head through my cloak. Worry tightens in my chest, worsening when she continues to groan instead of speak.

Making the choice for the both of us, I know the fastest way back to Burtons is going to be through the back alleys. It's always a bit riskier, especially at night, *especially* when you're lugging around deadweight. But something isn't right with Edene, and the only thing I have my mind set on is the antipurzon.

I half-drag, half-carry her as we make our way home, encouraging her to keep using her legs. She isn't listening to me, and while that's nothing new, I'm feeling extra irritated. It's humid, Edene is sweating through my cloak and soaking me, and on top of that, *Bayne left* in the middle of our conversation.

Anger boils in me at the thought of that condescending, assuming, self-right-eous man. How dare he make me out to be a fool, sitting alone in the middle of Saffron? Those people know me there; I've been in Second long enough to have made enough of an impression. How *dare* he leave in the middle of our date?

Wait. It wasn't a real date, you fool.

Not that the people of Voltus would know that. So it's justified. Right.

It's going to eat me alive, at least until I find Peace. The thought seems so far away even as I think it. Is Peace what I want? Second has been all I've known. Would I find—

My thoughts are cut off at the sudden shuffle of movement behind me. I whip my head around, trying to balance both my own weight plus Edene's. Holding her up is hindering me, so I gently set her against the brick wall in the alley. I can practically hear her yelling at me for letting her sit in the dirt in her dress, but some sacrifices must be made.

I look all around me, trying to catalogue my surroundings in the moonlight, but it's hard to see anything. I take one deep breath and then another. *You're hearing things. Just ignore it.*

But awareness pricks at my scalp as I hear the telltale scrape of movement again. We're practically defenseless in an unmarked alley.

I'm full of bad decisions today, it would seem. When I peer into the shadows again, I don't see anything at first. Slowly, they appear, and I see not one, not two or three, but *four* Shades creep out of the corner they were hiding in. I suck in a sharp breath, and it will probably be my last.

Oh Gods. I'm so fucked.

CHAPTER SEVEN

"Where are you headed, sweetheart?" the first man asks, pulling out a long blade.

Double fuck.

My eyes dart to the other three: two other males and one female. Each person is strapped with at least three blades each. They all wear masks covering their faces, wrapped tightly from head to toe in the black linen fabric. All I see is four pairs of eyes, and four bodies very capable of breaking every bone in my body.

One of them would've been enough to kill me. But four? This is not a fight. It's an execution. Even if I didn't have an unconscious Edene with me, I would still be at a wild disadvantage. Panic starts to bubble in my chest as I try to keep my heart rate calm.

Without time to blink, another one of the men from the group grabs me by the throat, and slams me against the brick wall, bruising my spine in the aggression.

"Don't look so scared, princess." He gives me a saccharine smile, lowering his head and closing the space between us as he slowly cuts off my air supply. "We just want your magic. Well," he points to his companions with his sword, "maybe they just want your magic, but me? I prefer a different kind of fun. Maybe once your friend wakes up, we can all celebrate." He lets out a low whistle as his words slither over me, and disgust roils inside me. Unfortunately for both of us, I have no magic, and I never have. Though if there were a time I had needed it or wanted it more, it would be this one. I feel slightly satisfied that once they try to feed, they'll be sorely disappointed.

As he lightly drags the tip of his blade down the side of my face, his rancid breath invades senses and I gag reflexively. I'd rather die a slow, fiery death than let this man have his way with me, and like hell I would hand over Edene. I give him a weak smile, then I drive my knee up and into his balls.

He instantly drops me and we both crash to the ground. I land on my hands and knees, gasping for breath. "You fucking bitch!" He groans as he rolls on the dirt.

My reprieve is short-lived as my second attacker quickly picks me up and replaces his hand where his partner's was just a minute ago. Only, he holds me off the ground, my toes kicking for purchase. I claw at his hand, nails slicing through skin, hot blood slicking my fingers. The reek of his black blood almost makes me vomit. He's too strong for me, and coupled with the fact that they're all using their stolen magic to dull my screams, pure, unadulterated terror starts to flood my system. This is the end of the line for me, unless I can grab my own dagger and somehow fight my way out of here.

"You're gonna pay for that one, sweetheart," he snarls in my face. "You're gonna beg for Death when I'm done with you." He shoves a dagger into my ribs, and my scream barely makes it past my lips. It's swallowed by the magic, trapped in my throat. The pain is blinding, drowning out every other thought except one—*I'm going to die here.*

I try to kick my boot up high enough to grab my dagger hidden in it, but I can't reach. He's got me pinned against the wall. I glance behind the Shade. The male draws two of his blades, and the female extends her hands, fire licking the ends of her fingertips.

A part of me thinks maybe I should've let Mr. Touchy, who's still rolling on the ground, have his way instead. But it's too late for that option. I wished for a fiery death, and the Gods have always had a *sick* sense of humor. The Inferno is here to deliver the punchline.

Dread crushes my chest as the others step closer to Edene's slumped body. I open my mouth to no avail. Not a whisper. Silence. Only the sound of footsteps closing in on me.

I try to breathe in a shaky breath, but the asshole with the grip on my throat starts to twist the blade inside me ever slightly, and black spots dance at the edge of my vision. The darkness is rushing toward us and I scream silently from the pain, willing myself to be taken over by it so I won't have to witness my own death. To make it fast.

Wait.

The darkness is *moving*.

Am I hallucinating?

This must be Maveth, the goddess of Death coming to collect me. *Finally.*

No.

The shadows move incredibly fast, tripping the feet of the other two Shades. As they fall, two slivers of silver flash across their throats, splitting them open. They let out a collective gasp as they drown on their own blood. They're already dead and gone by the time my current assailant whips around and drops me, mouth agape.

Mine is stuck open right along with him. Half because, *what the actual fuck just happened,* but also, because the Shade ripped his dagger out of my stomach when he turned around and dropped me. I'm no healer, but Edene taught me that now my clock is ticking and I'm losing time, fast.

On my hands and knees, I try but fail to crawl away while holding pressure on my wound. Only, he must've known where to strike, because the blood isn't being staunched by only my hand. I glance around and see shadows moving again, right next to Mr. Touchy. He scrambles to his feet, seemingly starting to panic after watching his companion's swift deaths. Their blood begins to pool, running closer to us. The metallic scent of my own mixing with the rotting smell of theirs is overwhelming. My eyes burn and water in response; tears pouring down my face.

But before the Shade can even draw a weapon, a hand dashes out of the shadows, jabbing a sword through his neck and cutting up and out at a vicious angle, nearly decapitating him fully.

Good, I think. Fuck him, especially.

The last man standing next to me, swivels his head back and forth, clearly debating his odds on staying to fight. Suddenly, my savior steps out of the shadows, and he retreats behind me as though I make a proper defense.

Oh my fucking Gods.

Midnight, smite me where I stand, I beg of you.

One of them up there must consider me their own personal jester, because who steps out of the shadows, but *him. Bayne.* The same man who has clearly been following me home. If I wasn't currently bleeding out, I would curse everything and everyone.

Why would it be anyone else? No one is here to care about you anymore.

Bayne yawns as he stretches his arms above his head, as if he's bored of this fight already. The audacious prick. Though, I suppose he hasn't had to do much fighting. Only killing.

"It's a beautiful day for murder, don't you think?" He looks at my assailant, not the least bit bothered by the scene he's created. The Shade, however, is slightly shaking now. Coward.

"Who—who—how—" he stutters.

"Are you an owl?" he asks with the sincerest tone, as though he's genuinely waiting for an answer. Bayne twirls the point of a dagger slowly in between his thumb and forefinger. The Shade watches him bug-eyed, numbly shaking his head back and forth.

"That's what I thought. So, shut the fuck up. You're *ruining* this for me."

Bayne flicks his wrist, and a dagger flies and buries into my attacker's chest, sinking to the hilt with a sickening thud. His dark blood sprays from his mouth as he coughs—onto my face, my clothes. I retch instantaneously.

Neither of them pay my vomiting any mind as he drops to his knees beside me. Bayne walks closer, the shadows *following him.* As though...he commands them. A small gasp leaves my lips at the realization.

Oh, fuck me.

He does.

Magic. He has *magic.* It's impossible, but there's no time to process it.

The shadows lash out, coiling around the man's neck. He stiffens as Bayne leans in, whispering so only he can hear. Then—snap. His body drops, driving the hilt of the dagger through his chest with his weight.

My so-called savior steps over the dead bodies and prowls toward me. I keep my hand on my side, blood dripping furiously over my fingers as I try but fail to scoot away from him.

"Aren't you going to say *thank you*?" His lips curve up at the corners.

Gods, I want to punch him in the face.

"For following me home? For not actually learning the word *no*? You're a sick bastard, do you know that? You're a fucking—"

He infuriatingly holds up his hand to cut me off. I'd like to bite it off.

"Darling, I would let you finish, but I think we need to get you somewhere to heal. Unless, you'd rather rot in this alley, then by all means..." He gestures to the blood and gore around us with the curdling smell from the trash.

"Fuck you," I spit at him. Who does this guy think he is, my hero? He was following me home, and certainly not with pure intentions, of that I'm positive.

A wet cough sounds from the side, with a small groan. *Edene.*

"Ede? Edene!" Panic swirls in my chest again as I try to use the arm not staunching my blood flow to scoot forward.

Bayne crosses his arms, watching my futile attempts at crawling, his beautiful face deadpan and bored.

"Did you want some help with that, raven?"

I grit my teeth and ignore him, focusing only on Edene. *Pain is all in your head, Arden,* I hear Perry's words clear in my memory. *Focus on mentally walling it out, and locking it in a box, if it helps. Compartmentalize.*

Well, I'm fucking trying, Perry, and you're not even here to help like you promised you always would be.

But now is not the time to be arguing in my own head.

Edene is lying too far away, and her skin is looking lackluster compared to her normal glow. She had to have been poisoned, but we were...Saffron. Someone must've been targeting her. Why Edene...why...are my eyes so heavy?

I look up at Bayne, who has not moved in the slightest. He cocks an eyebrow at me, waiting.

"Please." My voice is barely more than a breath.

"Only because you asked so nicely, raven. Let's go." He takes a step toward me, and with what little I have left, I yell at him to stop. Surprisingly, he complies. Not without rolling his eyes, though.

"What's the issue *now*?"

"Edene," I whisper. "You have to...help her, too. She...she'll die out here." Tears threaten to fall as my throat tightens.

"What does that matter? Is she useful to you?" Bayne is unbothered, unmoving. As if I don't have a fatal wound and Edene's not turning a sickly violet color.

"Please, she's all I have. I'll—" I spit blood on the ground next to me. "I'll do anything."

His lips turn up in that devilish smile, and my stomach falls in fear of his next words.

"*Anything,*" he coos, bending over to lower his head toward mine. I turn my head to the side so I won't have to look at his stupid face. I should've known it was a futile attempt, because he grabs my jaw and jerks my face back to his.

Fury rages through me, hating how weak I feel in this moment, as my eyes water instinctively. How, even though I can't admit it, I know I probably need his help whether I want it or not because I'm not even sure I can stand, let alone walk anywhere.

He shakes his head slightly. "You should truly treat bargains more delicately, little raven. Okay, fine. You come with me and help me with *anything* I choose, and I will *try* to help your friend, too. Deal?" His voice is smooth, patient—like he's offering me a gift and not a death sentence.

My eyes go wide with realization. He cannot be serious. I'm bleeding out in a fucking alley, and he wants me to bargain with him to save me? I start to laugh, but it causes a searing pain up my side, more blood pooling out.

At my silence, he adds, "Or you could beg me. It's been a while, but I thoroughly enjoy the sight of a woman on her knees *begging* for me."

I narrow my gaze at him, letting him see the hatred in my eyes as I whisper, "Fuck. You."

The corner of his mouth tilts up as he makes a slight tsk sound. "That doesn't sound like begging to me, little raven." I know I need to, but I'm not certain I can.

Reaching into my boot, I pull out my own dagger, albeit slowly with a weak grip, but I point it at him nonetheless. Something I can't register flashes in his eyes, but it's quickly gone.

"I'd rather die...than beg you for anything," I spit at his feet with as much vitriol I can muster. Faster than I can blink, he's crouched next to me, applying too much pressure to my gaping wound. He now holds my own knife at my throat, but not enough pressure to cut the skin. I bite back another scream as my whole body recoils at the intense pain.

"You have one chance. *One.* Choose wrong, and I will leave you to die slowly in this cesspool, damning your soul to reek of the Shaded for the rest of eternity."

I'm not sure how I know, maybe it's the snarl of his lips or maybe it's his thumb trying to dig its way inside me currently, but I know he's not bluffing. He will leave me to rot right here.

Tears reflexively stream down my face, and I give him the slightest of nods.

He removes his hand from my side and stands up, the instant relief almost palpable.

"You can do better than that, darling."

Gods, I am going to strangle him the minute I'm healed. But I know what he's looking for. Absolute bastard.

"Please." My voice cracks. "Please, help her. *Please.* I'll do anything." I swallow the bile in my throat, hating the taste of every syllable. "I *beg* you."

"Only because you asked so nicely." His nose scrunches on the end of his statement, making my blood heat with rage. He reaches his hand out for my free one. "You have yourself a deal, little raven."

For better or for worse, I grab his hand, and we're instantly whisked away, shadows enveloping us as I go blind. The last thing I see is a plush maroon rug under my knees as I collapse.

PART TWO

Witches, it was told, are the reason for the extinction of
dragon-kind. The two creatures clashed on the battlefield
documented by our great monarch, His Majesty King Devon I.
Such is his wise decree that only one witch per kingdom may
remain—one to Ziineth, one to Marintha.

—A Collection of Kings Past, by Amara Santigo
For the royal Ziineth library

CHAPTER EIGHT

My head is splitting into a hundred pieces.

Okay, so maybe not a *hundred*, but at least two. The pain radiates across my forehead, pulsing in time to my heartbeat. My eyes feel heavier than ever, and when I pry them open, my eyelashes have crusted over.

Disgusting.

Laying down, I stare at an ornate ceiling; white with gold trim accentuating the square pattern. I sit up groaning, feeling like I fell off the side of a cliff and was then promptly run over by a horse. I squint around the dark room, trying to determine where I've just woken up when the memory floods in.

Images flash before me in a rush.

The attack. The Shaded. What were they even doing there? Were we followed? The ambush...my hand drifts to my throat as I remember being thrown against the cement wall—twice. That explains the soreness. My throat feels swollen shut from the bruised necklace I know I must adorn.

Oh, Gods. *Edene.*

Oh, *FUCK.*

Panic surges my whole body as I frantically look around the unfamiliar bed I'm in, like she might lie right next to me like she used to when we'd stayed up too late talking until we passed out. But she's not here. Of course, she's not.

That bastard is probably keeping her tied in a dungeon. That wasn't part of our deal, but then again, I didn't exactly iron out the finer points of our agreement.

The deal. I sold my soul. How could I forget?

This must be somewhere Bayne deems safe. I'm willing to chance this is his home.

Oh, goddess, smite me...is this *his bed*?

I shiver and as a panic tries to seize me once more, I rub my hands down my body to find I'm wearing a soft, light blue sleep tank and a pair of shorts. I can only pray that *he* wasn't the one who changed me. Mortification burns my face at the possibility that he might've. I would rather die a second time than let that heathen see me naked.

The sheets against my skin are soft like silk I've never had the luxury to know. They're a deep violet, matching the massive blanket that's now pushed down by my legs.

I start to get up when I hear a gentle knock on the door. I freeze instantly, unsure if I should answer physically or verbally. Or maybe I should pretend to be asleep again.

Oh Gods, is it Bayne?

When a second knock comes a little louder, I pull the comforter back over me and squeak out something that sounds, I hope, like *come in.*

The door opens inward and a tall figure enters, leaving the door ajar. A light flickers on from the lamp by the door and I see my visitor clearly now. It's a strange man, a few years older than me I would guess, with lavender-colored hair and warm, brown eyes that match his skin. He smiles warmly at me as he puts his hands behind his back.

"Oh, good, you're awake now. My name is Franswon, or Fran, if you're more comfortable with that. I'm the one who healed you." His voice is gentle, but deep as he talks. Relief seeps into my bones, grateful that it's not Bayne. He walks over to the massive bed and stands at the bedside with his hand outstretched for me. Gingerly, I reach out and shake it.

"Arden," I tell him.

"Oh, I know." His eyes crinkle as he smiles. "You've made quite a splash here already."

I have?

"Um, where is *here*, exactly?" I question wearily. I'm not certain I'm particularly ready for the answer.

"Oh, forgive me," he braces his hand across his chest in apology, "I forget my manners. Welcome to Meadows Parlor, Miss Arden." Franswon gestures to the room behind him.

"Meadows Parlor? Where the fuck is that? What providence are we in? Is this a fucking mansion?" I ask incredulously. Surely, it's just a nickname.

"Well, I suppose, it *could* be classified as a castle with the different wings, but perhaps the alternative sounds more satisfying, hm?" Franswon raises an eyebrow at me, waiting for my response, but I can only gape at him.

A *castle*? He brought me to *a fucking castle*? Why?

I've been in Voltus long enough to know there is no *Meadows Parlor*. Without missing a beat, Fran asks me to lift my shirt. If my jaw wasn't already on the floor, it is now.

"Excuse me?" I protest, crossing my arms protectively across my chest. He rolls his eyes at me and sighs a heavy breath. It's only been two minutes, and I can tell he's already sick of me.

"Not like that, Miss Arden. I need to check your injuries, make sure the magic is working right." The exasperated tone of his voice brings me back to reality. He is a healer. This is his job. Still, I look him over to discern if he's telling the truth, but all I find is impatience.

Reluctantly, I lift my shirt to expose my left side, twisting slightly so Franswon can see it properly. He leans over the bed, hovering his hands over the injury, careful not to touch me. I watch as he works, the dark violet bruising fading into a lighter shade of purple. His casual display of magic enraptures me, and I itch to ask how he saved me.

"Now your neck." I try to relax as Fran moves his hands around my throat. As he works, relief from the pain floods my body almost instantly, and I feel like I can breathe a full breath for the first time in days.

"How long have I been out?"

"How long ago did you wake up?" he questions.

"A few moments before you came in the room."

"Then that would make it two full nights and three days since his—I mean, *Bayne*, brought you here."

My head spins, unrelated to my injuries. *Three days? I've been passed out in this bed for three fucking days?*

"Okay, that should be enough for today," Fran announces, oblivious to my spiraling. I lightly trace my fingers over my neck, as if I can feel how it's healing. He must read the burning questions in my eyes. "You don't want instant healing of such a deep injury, or you might lose feeling in your nerve endings. Gods know, those Shaded did a number on you. Healing it instantly could even leave you partially paralyzed. Oh, well, better safe than sorry." He shrugs nonchalantly, as though he didn't just say his magic has *glitches*.

"Wait, *what?*" I squeak out. "I've never heard that before. I thought Healers could repair instantly? I just, I don't know much about magic."

"Well, it truly depends on the injury, Miss Arden. If it is something as simple as resetting a bone, or, for example, your bruising. The more life-threatening," he looks me over in a scolding manner, "the longer it can take, like your hip. Sometimes, I have to lean on nature to help. But I wouldn't fret. You should be ready to fight by the end of this week." He gives me a playful wink and grins.

"I suppose I have no choice but to believe you, don't I?" I give him my fakest smile, but it comes across more as a grimace. Fran's certainly warmer than *him*, but I would be a naïve fool to trust him simply because he's healing me.

Franswon sighs. "We don't have to do things the hard way, you and I. We can simply be straightforward. You can save all your brooding for Mr. Sardon."

He bends at the waist in a quick bow, turning abruptly for the door but I stop him.

"Wait, I have questions!" I say, raspy as all hell, but it's the best I can manage with my throat. He stops, turning back to face me.

"Right. Meet downstairs in twenty minutes for dinner, you'll find out what you need to know." He points to the door on my left along the wall. "That right there is the bathing chamber." His finger swings to the door beside it. "That one is the closet. I hope you don't mind, but I had to change your clothes from your incident. They were...how do I say this nicely? Garbage?" He scrunches his nose thinking about it. "Anyway, the closet is enchanted, so everything you pull out should fit you, and if you need anything, Jesminda will be right outside this door to help you dress appropriately." As he clicks the door shut behind him, the room feels too empty again.

I stare after him as my mind races with burning questions. My head still pounds from my headache, and yet, I'm expected downstairs shortly. Only twenty minutes to recover from almost dying for the second time, and I'm expected to get dolled up? *Fantastic.*

But I suppose I'll take what I can get.

I throw off the covers and gingerly slide my body to the edge of the bed, waiting for the pain in my side to sting once more, but I'm surprised to find it's more of a dull throb. Magic never ceases to amaze me.

Stumbling to the bathing chamber, I try to wash as quickly as I can. The warm water feels heavenly on my skin, relaxing my muscles instantly, and I can't help but groan. I wish I had all evening to soak in the hot water, but I hurry to scrub off the last three days and finish, wrapping myself in a giant, fluffy towel. What I would have given to have such luxury at my disposal at Burtons.

You already gave your soul, foolish girl. What else is there to give?

Shaking my head to clear my thoughts, I pad across the hardwood floors. They're cool against my bare feet as I enter the biggest closet I've ever seen. My mouth pops open as I take it all in.

Enchanted, indeed.

It seems to go on forever, all sides covered in various articles of clothing. Forget the shower, I could spend the night in *here.* A wall of shoes holds everything from running shoes, to boots, to the most beautiful heels imaginable. Heels I can't imagine ever owning. If the impracticality of wearing them weren't enough, the price I could get for these at Laine would feed Edene and I for *months.*

Admiring the detail on the shoes before me, I reach my hand out to run it along the shelf. I go to pick up a fine pair of black heels with obsidian diamonds on the heel when I stop.

What am I supposed to wear? Franswon never specified; he just mentioned I needed *to* dress. I start to sweat when it dawns that I have someone for this exact reason. Leaving the closet, I crack the door to the bedroom ever so slightly, peering out into a hallway just as ornate as this bedroom.

The hallway is brightly lit compared to the bedroom, but the plush, maroon rug that runs down the length of the hall catches my eye. I creak the door open further to get a better look, and I drift my eyes up to find stunning pieces of artwork lining the wall.

As if she appeared from thin air, a woman with long, red hair swoops in front of my gaze. Her arms are crossed as she glides into view, and she gives me an incredulous look.

"Please tell me you're not showing up in a towel. That's quite tacky for your first dinner." I blink at her, and my eyes widen as embarrassment flushes my face. I was so distracted by this place, I hadn't realized I was about to walk out in only a towel.

"Oh." My stomach drops as a cold draft kisses my bare legs and I choke on my own mortification.

"Uh, no..." I trail off, stunned. The woman before me looks almost un-real—like something painted, perfected. No, not something. Someone. Her resemblance to the goddess of love, Grádia, is...uncanny.

Her auburn hair cascades in thick waves over her shoulders before ending just above her waist. Two small braids run on either side of her head, presumably tied at the back to keep the long strands off her tanned face and out of her eyes. Those eyes, however, are sharp and a golden hazel.

While I've always known Edene to be the prettiest woman in Voltus, the woman in front me has an almost ethereal glow to her that makes it hard to look away.

Staring at her and the strength she clearly exudes, this woman clearly brings men to their knees. An unwelcome stab of envy flares in me, but I strangle it before it can fester.

I clear my throat and try again. "Franswon said I could ask someone named Jesminda for help if I needed assistance with getting dressed." The woman smiles at me and rolls her eyes, uncrossing her arms.

"Francie is a wise man, what can I say? But if you tell him I said so, you'll regret it. I'm always available for a fashion emergency." She grabs me by the elbow as she struts through the doorway and pulls me into the closet behind her.

"So, you're...Jesminda?"

"I am," she confirms. Jesminda is already sifting through one of the racks, pausing every so often on different pieces. I fold my arms awkwardly over my chest, unsure of how I should be standing.

She wears long, black pants that flare over her slippered feet. Her top is emerald green, with long sleeves that cuff at the wrist and a deep V to accentuate her chest. A thin gold chain adorns her neck, paired with two golden hoop earrings. At least I seem to be in capable hands.

"So, let's start simple," she begins. "How old are you? What's your story?"

She states it so casually, but the questions throw me. Somehow, I find my voice. "I—my memories are still hazy from, you know, dying and all, but I know I'm twenty-three."

Jesminda spares me a glance over her shoulder. "Your memories are still a fog? How long have you been dead?"

Do I tell the truth? I have to ponder it for a moment, counting back the months and weeks.

"Almost a year, I think. My birthday is in about six months, so I'm over the year mark, roughly. What about you?" I ask. Jesminda scoffs, feigning offense.

"Don't you know it's not polite to ask a lady her age?" She smiles at me over her shoulder and resumes browsing the closet. "I've been dead for twenty-six years now, which I guess is fitting, considering I died when I was twenty-six. Got my throat slit while I was sleeping. Barely felt a thing and then I woke up here in Second. Been a wanderer ever since."

I impress myself by holding in the gasp I desperately want to release. *Twenty-six years* in Second? She has to be one of the oldest people I've met, duration wise. Even Perry hadn't been here a whole decade yet.

"Ugh, I can *feel* you calling me old through your silence. But yes, I've been in Second for a long time."

Only one question comes to mind.

"Why haven't you found Peace, Jesminda?" My voice is barely a whisper.

She turns to face me fully now, and gives me a small shrug. "I don't know if I'll ever be ready for that. Twenty-six years may seem like a long time, but time is so different here. And if it weren't for the Sun and Burnus himself, I'm not sure how we would even tally the days." I nod, and she returns to the rack, only to pull out a silver top in similar fashion to her own, except this one has short, ruffled sleeves and not long ones. She holds it up to me, and when I nod, she tosses it in my arms and strolls over to the pants. She gives me a pair of black leggings and points to a row of drawers lining one of the walls.

"Undergarments are in there, and I'll let you pick those out yourself." She gives me a wink and starts to retreat out of the closet. "I'll be out here when you're dressed so we can do something with your hair. Although, you might want to be quick, seeing as we only have a few minutes left." I nod again and rifle through the drawers to find obscene amounts of lingerie. I roll my eyes at the sight, wondering why the hell these are even here.

You're supposed to be an enchanted closet, I scold it. *You should know better.*

I slap my palm to my forehead. Now I know I've lost my mind. I'm not *seriously* arguing with a magic closet over the underwear selection it holds.

I hastily pick out a matching set, surprised once again by the quality of the silk. I get dressed and find Jesminda sitting on the bed, leaning back on her right hand as she inspects the perfect nails on her left. She hops up when she spots me.

"Oh, goody, you're done. Now, let's hurry, we have to detangle this jungle you call hair." She ushers me to sit in front of a white and gold vanity, and starts to brush out the knots in my long hair, still wet from bathing. By the time she's done, my hair is dry. Not only is it dry, but it's smooth and shiny, looking healthier than ever as it flows past my breasts. If I didn't spend so much time hunting the Shaded, looking for Perry, perhaps it could look like this all the time. My mouth parts in admiration for my own reflection and Jesminda gives me a satisfied smile in the mirror, meeting my eyes.

"It's a lesser magic. I can enchant most of the items in this room; helps make your dead life a little less boring." She fluffs my hair, pulling it forward so the dark strands spill over my shoulders, fuller, glossier than before. She leans closer to put her head level with mine, never breaking eye contact. "*Now* you're ready for dinner."

Her wicked smile tells me that I'm not sure that I am.

CHAPTER NINE

Jesminda leads me through winding hallways until we reach a grand spiral staircase.

I can't help but wonder how in the world this girl went from a wanderer to staying here. It doesn't matter, really. It's not like she can help me escape, not when I need to find where they're holding Edene.

As I follow her, Jesminda keeps stealing glances at me. I finally get the nerve to ask her if I have something on my face, when she halts at the top of the staircase.

"Can I ask a personal question?" she asks. I nod, hesitantly. "Why are your eyes *silver*?" She gestures vaguely, as if brushing something invisible off my face.

The question shouldn't throw me, but it still does. I've grown used to the odd looks the inhabitants of Voltus would give me, but none of them would ever blatantly stare at me the way the redhead is right now.

"I was born this way, as far as I could tell you." It's the truth, almost.

She narrows her eyes ever so slightly and then shrugs, satisfied with my deflection for now.

We reach the bottom of the stairs, walking the rest of the way in silence. She leads me through turns and all the way down the end of the hall until we come to a stop in front of two large black doors that run from the floor to the ceiling. Jesminda grabs both gilded handles and swings the doors open, making a spectacle of it. Two heads look up from the table, and I immediately clock Bayne as one of them, sitting next to a man slightly smaller than him. I stand awkwardly in the doorway as Jesminda strolls into the dining room with unrivaled confidence. Not that I wouldn't act the same way if I had died looking like *that*.

"Let's eat already." She collapses into one of the remaining chairs around the oval table, sighing dramatically. "I'm starving, and if I don't eat something soon, I'm going to die again!"

"Jes, please," the mystery man gives her a flat smile, "we were waiting on you. I was being a polite gentleman. We could've long since eaten and already been done in the time it took you to actually show up. It's not my fault you don't know how to tell fucking time." His voice has a deep timbre like Bayne's, but it's missing the veils of threats behind it. He crosses his sinewy arms across his chest and leans back in his seat, smirking. Jesminda sits up straight, narrowing her eyes as she points a finger across the table.

"Don't be so crass, Axl. *You* told me to help Arden! How is it somehow our fault, when I had to get to know her first? It's hard to dress someone without a feel for their personality." Jesminda relaxes back into her seat as she inspects her fingernails, which are seemingly more interesting than Axl's reply. "Besides," she continues. "It's not like Bayne would let any of us starve. Fashion is the most important thing in a woman's afterlife, you know."

Axl rolls his blue eyes at Jesminda and glances toward me for the first time, as if remembering that I'm here, too. His ruffled, brown hair flops with the movement, but I'm not looking at Axl. I've locked eyes with *him*.

My captor. The warden.

I glare at him as my hands reflexively curl into fists and my fingernails bite into my palms. He's leaning back in his chair without a care in the world, all the while smiling at me with that dangerous look. He holds his hand out in front of the table as he says, "Sit, little raven. Unless you plan to eat standing up like a horse."

I stay rooted in place.

I ignore his blatant foregoing of using my name. "How do I know what you're serving is actually edible?" It's a fair question, really. He might've brought me here to drug me for other purposes. As much as the idea of that makes my skin crawl, I can't rule it out if no one is giving me any information.

"Rest assured, I didn't prepare the meal. Where would I have found the time between saving your ass and my *personal* life?" His eyes glint as that smile spreads, although it feels anything but friendly. My blood feels volcanic at the slight implication of his *personal life,* and for the death of me, I can't reason why I even care.

Jesminda whines, resting her head in her hands. "Oh, just *sit down,* Arden. I'm starving, and Bayne being an ass isn't going to get me fed any faster. So I need you two to kiss and make up!" She rolls her head to the side, her eyes meeting my own. "There is a perfectly fine seat right next to me, if you're not ready to make up, though. Wherever you sit, please decide quickly."

Gods, this got uncomfortable quickly.

I make my way into the seat next to Jes, and I sit down. Jes and Axl fall into conversation as servants set food on the table, but as I wait patiently in the large chair, I take in the dining room fully for the first time since walking in.

There are three large paned windows that overlook a cliffside, and beyond that, I see water all the way to the horizon. The table itself is a beautiful onyx wood, polished to perfection with ornate dragons carved into the wood, directly atop my legs. Six chairs match the table, each one accompanied with a maroon cushion. The cushions, however, match the massive, plush rug covering the expansive room. The obsidian walls bloom with monochrome floral engravings, so faint they almost disappear. While the ceiling matches the one in my bedroom, in the center of the room over the table, a chandelier hangs golden and grand, dangling with red stones.

Rubies, I think to myself. I don't think I've ever seen such clear-cut ones before and my lips part in complete awe. But I'll never tell Bayne that.

Reading my thoughts, Bayne speaks to me. "Impressed, darling? This room is special, you know." His mouth tilts upwards. "*Eating...*is one of my favorite pastimes," he whispers.

My eyes flare as my cheeks burn hot before I can stop it. I glance at Axl and Jesminda, who are too busy arguing about the roasted chicken on the table to hear him. His eyes shine mischievously at me, so I refuse to meet his gaze any longer. He's only doing this to get a rise out of me, and I won't give him the satisfaction.

"They can't hear you, angel. Lesser magic...provides us a certain privacy." His voice sounds as though it's right in my ear. Whispering, as though *he* is right next to me, and I can't help but be awestruck by his magic. A lesser magic, sure, but not a common one at all from what Perry told me.

How do they even have *magic at all?*

"No, you're not getting this through your thick skull," Jesminda groans, rubbing her temples. "It's not the same as murder; this was for the good of the chicken ecosystem."

My ears perk at the mention of murder. Are these people even sane? Arguing over *chicken?*

"Calling it an *ecosystem* is fairly generous, hm? I've never once seen you let it thrive without trying to play Gods." Axl points his fork accusingly at her.

"I'm not *trying* anything. It's a *chicken ecosystem*, and I think having to select the one we eat is a small task to grapple with, Axl." Axl's face recoils in disgust, but as he opens his mouth to speak, I blurt out the thing that's eating me alive.

"Franswon said I could ask questions."

Silence falls in the dining room, and three heads turn to stare at me. They all share a look amongst each other, speaking a silent language I clearly am not a part of.

Bayne's face is a perfect mask of boredom, but his eyes shine with curiosity. "What kinds of questions do you have? I'm sure I can answer anything you want to know." He grins at me, causing my stomach to flip. I roll my eyes, mostly at myself. Stiffening my spine with determination to make it through this meal, I turn to look only at Axl, ignoring Bayne.

"How long do I have to stay here?" I ask him, folding my hands on the table. If this is a negotiation for my freedom, I might as well treat it as such. Axl shrugs, somewhat apologetic.

"However long, until you pay back your favor." I hear the words he's not saying.

That could potentially never happen.

"Okay," I drag. "Where is Edene?"

Axl's face crinkles with confusion. "Who's Edene?" As I go to answer him, Bayne cuts him a look. His lips are moving, but there's no sound. *Stupid magic.*

"Edene is safe. That's all you need to know." Some of the tension I've held in since I woke earlier releases with the confirmation. *But where is she?*

"Where are we?"

Axl shares a look with Bayne, then folds his hands in his lap. "This is Meadows Parlor."

I have to resist the urge to rolls my eyes again. "Yes okay, *Meadows Parlor,*" I say, irritation crawling up my spine from his vague answers. "But, where *precisely* in Second are we? To the east? West? In the dunes by Scarlentta? Or by the mountains near Voltus?" Looking to the windows I had admired earlier, the ocean reflects the sunset with its incandescent glow.

If I didn't know any better, I would think this was Marintha.

Marintha has long been forgotten about, according to Perry. Once the royal family went missing, he said it fell off the map. When I felt brave enough to ask around Voltus, I got the same answer over and over—no one in Second even knows where it is anymore; those who remember it existed in the first place. The odds of being taken to a lost city feel slim to none, but no one at this table is going to spill a secret like that to me, true or not. To my surprise, Axl doesn't balk at all my questions on top of each other. He just leans back in his chair again.

"Oh," he smiles at me, "that's above my pay grade, princess."

I prickle at the thought of needing to ask Bayne himself for anything. I'd rather die for a second time, this time of curiosity. I turn to Jes, who's been doing a great job of inspecting her perfect manicure.

Gods, she needs a new hobby.

She shrugs slightly, pursing her lips as she shakes her head at me slowly, confirming who I really need to ask. Clearly, they both answer to him. It's the last thing I want to hear.

Slowly, I turn to glare at Bayne, devilish smile spread wide across his face as he wiggles his fingers at me in a little wave. He sketches a brow, baiting me to ask.

I cannot fucking stand his arrogance.

I look away from him before I think too long about embedding my dinner knife in his jugular. "Alright then, what's within your pay grade then?" I'm sick of these games already.

"Baby, I can tell you anything that doesn't compromise security," Axl says. "Anything that won't endanger the lives of those who rely on Meadows." He winks at me, and I feel more than see Jes rolling her eyes beside me.

Security? What are they protecting here?

"Okay," I say carefully. "Whose house is this? Who owns Meadows?"

"Technically speaking, it was inherited by Bayne here," he points at the devil himself, "but it belonged to a relative."

Despite myself, I spin back to Bayne, mouth hanging open. "No one has tried to ransack this place or tried to take it from you?"

Most luxury living places in Second have been destroyed or fought to the death over. The latter is usually the reason for the former.

"No one is stupid enough to try, darling," he purrs at me.

I look him over, and I'm not sure what he sees on mine, but his face becomes hard set, like stone.

"You—" I start, but he cuts me off with the wave of his hand.

"If you have any more questions, they'll have to wait. I have a meeting to attend to, and you should rest." He stands, pushing his chair back from the table. "Jesminda will lead you back to your room. Don't worry, darling—I'll see you in the morning." Anger at being interrupted surges in waves, but before I can retort, he excuses himself from the table. Axl follows him in suit and Jes stares at me, momentarily lost.

"I've fought in several battles, you know. I may look beautiful and harmless, but I have thorns. And while I like you and all, I'm no babysitter. No offense." She looks me up and down as though she's choosing her next words carefully.

She's a warrior. I wonder what battles she's talking about, but I don't interrupt.

"Even if you don't like me yet—or the boys, for that matter—you'll warm to me." She smiles broadly. "Everyone does eventually. Those other two? I'll make an offering to Midnight on their behalf." Her smile turns feline, and a thought crosses my mind.

That maybe she's more terrifying than Bayne.

CHAPTER TEN

This white and gold ceiling is already starting to haunt me. Morning light creeps in from the oversized window of my room, casting a glow on the gold edges. My mind is reeling from the last twenty-four hours. I hate myself for allowing myself to get into this situation.

Edene. It's all for Edene. It's worth it as long as she's safe.

The anxious feeling in my chest keeps expanding as I try to take deep breaths.

What kind of sick bastard even offers sanctuary in exchange for...for what? What does Bayne want with me? Why did he drag me here, to Gods only know where, only to keep me prisoner? What kind of *favor* requires me to live with him?

Darker, more dangerous thoughts start to bubble their way up in my mind and I shake them off. My bones ache from the frigid air, as if the castle itself is listening. I narrow my eyes on the gold squares, lying flat on my back, my arms spread to either side of me.

I don't want to think about dying at this moment, which is new for me.

I'm always thinking of dying; of Living. I close my eyes, still trying to even the pain in my chest with deep breathing. Perry showed me this trick once, where if I can draw in a breath deep and hold it for a few moments, it helps to relieve the pressure slightly when I exhale. It's not doing me a lick of good now, though.

I wonder what Perry would think of my bargain. Always the calculating man, with a strong sense of discipline; for me and himself. Thinking of Perry always makes me resent my subconscious for the fuzzy memories that have yet to show themselves to me in Second. I wish I was a normal being of the world, but I'm cursed with the most horrid luck. On top of not remembering how I passed in my Alive-life, I often struggle to put a clear picture together of my family. If I have any at all.

I've prayed to the Gods that some sliver of my memory will come back. Worry and dread eat away at my skull that they'll remain a haze forever. My memories that I've made in the past year while dead however, are crystal fucking clear. No matter how brutal some of them may be and I wish they would disappear.

Perry, you bastard. You said they would come back.

Opening my eyes, I rub my hand over my chest, trying to relieve the ache there. It's futile though, because it's been six endlessly long months since Perry disappeared, and it's been there the moment I realized he wasn't.

With my stomach growling and pulling me out of my wallowing thoughts, I sit up and climb out of bed, already missing the warmth of the covers as soon as my bare feet hit the cold floor. I walk over to the window, pulling back the floor-to-ceiling, white curtains. The light shines on the walls, emphasizing the black-on-black wallpaper.

This room is a prison cell.

I sigh and stare at the scenery before me. The cliff is a steep drop, enough to make me feel dizzy, even staring through the safety of the window. The far hillside is covered in lush greenery, making me yearn for the days I took for granted in the Gardens. Is it still close by?

The sun is still rising above the horizon, which means it's still early enough that I could try to look around this place without being caught. Is it possible? It has to be—I'm determined to get out of this bargain, out of this *prison*, and intuition tells me that I'll find the answers in here.

I make my way into the magic closet, fighting the urge to be annoyed with the spell, realizing how insane I sound, even in my own head.

I quickly slip on some black leggings and a black sweater to help fend off the cold in this place. You'd think his royal-pain-in-my-ass could afford to keep the castle warm since it has yet to approach winter naturally. Yet, here I stand, frozen to my bones, having to wrap my arms around myself to get my blood flowing, and my nipples feel like they could cut ice. Ice that's clearly being pumped through the air.

I pull on black slippers to match, exit the closet, and I slowly open the bedroom door, looking both ways just in case the devil himself stationed another watch dog. While Jesminda seems friendly, I won't be here long enough to find out. That goes for Axl, too.

Franswon will probably be visiting my bedroom to process my healing. Fuck. I didn't think this through enough. He'll surely tell Bayne if I'm not in bed, so I'll need to hurry. I close the door as quickly and quietly as I can, keeping my head on a swivel. Part of me aches to analyze and admire the art on the walls, but I stay focused on my task, promising to come back to them.

I tiptoe down the maroon rug, grateful it helps to swallow the sound of my footsteps. I don't remember which way Jes took me to dinner last night, so this is going to have to be a guessing game. One I hope won't accidentally lead into someone else's bedroom. I make it to the end of the hallway, taking note of the art on this corner. It's a painting of the ocean, the moon cascading over the water and lighting up a beach. I take a mental picture to remember my way back.

I turn the corner, and there's a set of double doors at the very end, both sides of the hall holding various artifacts on tables. This place feels more like a museum with every passing minute.

Making my way to the double doors, I pull on them, but they don't budge. Swearing under my breath, I turn back around. *Surely*, I'm not naïve enough to believe it would be that simple, but can't a girl hope that for once, something is?

I walk down the opposite hall and it, thankfully, reveals stairs going to a third floor.

At least it's not another dead end.

I make my way up the stairs, praying to Midnight the wood doesn't creak. As much as it pains me to say, the architecture in this place blows me away. The elegance feels fit for royalty. While it's a beauty to behold, it's a blatant reminder that I do not belong here. Someone with no magic, no power, dispensable to these people. The starkness of the house calls me out with its very existence, like it wants to make sure I know what my true place is.

Reaching the top of the spiral staircase, I'm almost out of breath. *I really need to work on that.* I can't even climb the stairs. How can I run away, let alone actually *run*? I swear I can hear Bayne's mocking laugh in my head as I picture running away and only making it twenty yards before I'm out of steam.

Bracing my hand on my hips to try slowing my breathing, I make my way down the new hallway. This one is simple, unlike the others. The walls are different too, covered in a dark wallpaper with what I think are...are those *ravens?* Unease settles in my stomach like a foreboding. The gold trim takes my breath away as it pairs with the navy background of the wall. Well, any breath I had left, anyway.

I make my way to another set of double doors, similar to the ones downstairs. I reach out for the handle and when it opens, I lose a breath I didn't realize I was holding.

Thank the Gods.

I step into the room, instantly blown away. It's the most magnificent library I've ever witnessed. Books stretch from the floor to the ceiling. Some look timeworn, older than a century and falling apart at the binding, while others look recently printed. I greedily run my eyes over the expansive room, and that's when I notice the railing. I walk toward it and I let out a small gasp. This is the library of my *dreams*. It has two levels, with a black spiral staircase on the left side, allowing one to move between them. The far side of the library has vast windows and glass doors, which allow access to a balcony. There's a fireplace on the opposite side, and surprisingly, it's already lit. With the obsidian wood everywhere, the whole room is beautiful—too beautiful. Like everything else here, it demands to be admired. A gilded cage. Catered to me.

I've always loved books, though there isn't much time to read in Second. I only have a couple books to my name, anyway, and when I do have time to read, it's only for an hour or so. I like to think I read often in my Alive-life. I have vague memories of a young girl reading for hours, curled into a sofa and drifting into a different world, a different life. I suppose Second isn't that different. Not that I've ever thought otherwise.

I walk to the wall with the fireplace, and I run my hands over the tomes around it, a warm feeling flooding my veins. Not the fire, but my very soul, warming. My heart is drawn to the written word, so it seems I can't avoid its seduction in any life. I find one with a green cover, with gold embellishments, reminding me of Perry. I pull it off the shelf and read the worn cover.

Cooking with Dragons

A How To: Dragon Fire Meals

What the hell?

I'm so confused by the subject matter, I reshelve it immediately. *Who is cooking with dragon fire? And who is dumb enough to believe dragons still exist?*

The now-mythical creatures are talked about often enough, but I've never come across anyone who's even seen one before. They went extinct a long time ago, and most of us have long accepted that. At least, those of us from Voltus don't believe in fairytales.

I keep browsing, not sure what I'm looking for. Maybe a book that will tell me where I am, for starters. I find another one, searching solely on my intuition as my guide. Pulling it off the shelf with a careful hand, I notice it's very worn and the spine is peeling from the glue. It's black, smaller than the first one I grabbed, and it has no title written on the front. I run my hand gently on the cover, not wanting to damage it further.

If there weren't so many obscene windows in here, letting in all this sunlight, I bet you would've had a longer life, little friend.

I scoff, opening the cover. The poor books in here, abused by the presumable decades of light—

"Do you always have to wind up in places you're not welcome, angel?"

The deep voice startles me, and I slap the book shut again, hiding it behind my back and spin around to find Bayne standing dangerously close to me. His scent invades my senses, the heady mix of balsam and linen overloading my brain. The fire gives his body an effervescent glow, reflecting off the little golden clasp on his cloak. Combined with his all-black attire and shadows, it suits him. A true Prince of Death, like the day we met.

What am I saying?

He's starting to haunt me. Even when he's not there, he is.

"Who says I'm not supposed to be in here? You?"

He smirks at me, but there's no humor in his eyes. Only annoyance. "Yes, angel. Me. You *did* notice that it was locked downstairs, did you not? I know you can't possibly be that vapid, but do I really need to tell you how to read between the lines? Or in this case, what's blatantly written in front of you?"

Embarrassment floods my cheeks knowing that he was watching me the whole time. Letting me think I could sneak around. But my blood burns—hot, warring, and unrelenting. "Oh, I'm *sorry* your *royal highness*, am I to be secluded to my room for all of eternity? I didn't mean to overstep your plans, including trapping me in this *castle*." I give him a sweet smile, hoping he can feel the hatred rolling off me.

He leans in even closer, our noses almost touching, but I refuse to back down. I keep my chin lifted in defiance, slightly worried that he might get *other* ideas. He holds my gaze and gives me a wry smile.

"You could always try to run, you know." His eyes darken with each whispered word as they bounce between my own. A dare.

Arrogant dickhead.

I'm sure he would love to watch me try. He and I both know, if I make one wrong step, I'm dead. He's made that abundantly clear, through his warming hospitality.

Fuck him. Two can play at this game.

"And deny you the pleasure of my company? Even I couldn't be so cruel, your highness." I feign a pout, placing a hand over my heart.

He tilts his head to the side, and the fireplace lights his face up more until I see the dimples he has on his cheeks. They frame his perfect lips, which are still set in that condescending smirk of his. His gaze is scrutinizing, roving all over my face as though he can see the thoughts twirling through my head.

Stop looking at his mouth, you stupid girl!

"Do books interest you, raven? We hold quite the collection here at Meadows." When I don't reply, he whispers, "Or are you just curious about me? I wonder, why *do* you call me *your highness*? Is it because you feel the urge to get on your knees for me? To bow to me?" Bayne's nose brushes the end of mine, sending shockwaves across my skin at the contact.

My cheeks redden with the implication as I give in and jerk back from him. "I assure you I feel no such urge, nor am I interested in you in the slightest! All you do is piss me off and hold me prisoner to *help you* with Midnight only knows what. You're no prince. I might call you a royal, but it's the silver spoon stuck up your ass that drives the nickname. Someone so tactless and vain could never actually be royalty, for you have no sense of the burden. The only reason I'd get on my knees for you is if you were to cut the tendons behind them."

"So intriguing, little raven. You make threats and pick fights you would never win, with no concern for your own death." His gaze peruses down my body, like he's analyzing all of my weakest points. "Maybe I'm not a prince, but don't speak to me about the burden of a crown when you have not borne the weight yourself, either. You should pick a different goddess to pray to. Midnight can't help you in here, darling."

"Does that have to do with why you all seem to have magic and the rest of Second is forced to rely on healers? Why *do* all of you have magic here? *How* do you have it? Speaking of healers, I want to see Edene."

Bayne's face remains impassive and impossible to read beyond his scrutinizing dark eyes.

"Be a good angel and be downstairs in thirty minutes. We're having breakfast." Bayne slowly reaches an arm up and around my back, his fingertips gently brushing my upper back. My spine stiffens at the intimacy, just as he snatches the book out of my hands. He stands up straight, no longer invading my personal space, but the smell of him lingers.

I scowl at him, ordering me around like a puppy. "If you think for *one second—*" He cuts me off with the raise of his hand again, and I consider *cutting* it off completely. But truly, though the promise of death in his dark eyes makes me pause more than anything else, it doesn't smother the fury I want to spew at him.

"Oh," he drawls, like he can see it in my eyes, "you *will obey*, raven. You owe me, remember? *Please, anything you want,*" he mocks my words from when he saved me and Edene. My scowl deepens, which only causes him to smile broadly.

He shakes his head as he starts to back away, still smiling to himself.

"What is so godsdamned funny? This is not a joke to me! This is my undead life and I will see her." My voice cracks like a whip. "Stop playing games." *What a pretentious prick.*

"Oh, I do love playing with you, little raven." His brows knit together, then smooth back out as he contemplates his next words. "You are a vision to behold, raven. Even when your eyes wish Death upon me."

With that, I scoff at him, storming past him and out of the library, practically running back downstairs. I turn the corner, looking for the moon painting. Spotting it, I continue my tantrum all the way to my bedroom, slamming the door as hard as I can. Why should he get to see me unravel? I need as much space as I can put between us as possible.

CHAPTER ELEVEN

*"**D**o you think we would've been best friends in our Alive-lives?" I look up at Perry, who's lost in thought as we walk around the Lake. The sun has started to set, as Burnus must be tiring out for the day. I turn away from Per, waiting for him to answer my question as we head toward Violet Gardens.*

The Gardens are my favorite place that Perry has shown me. He's been so kind and patient with me, even as I impatiently wait for my memories to return. It's only been a week, and while Perry says it's normal for them to come in pieces, it's starting to feel like nothing is coming. Ever.

"I would like to think so." He smiles at me, and my heart flutters in my chest. What a heavenly sight. He has the most amazing smile. I need to keep my heart out of this, but Perry feels so safe. In a way that no one ever has. At least I think, considering I barely have any recollection of anything else. But I trust my intuition, and Perry is my safe place.

"What were your friends like, when you were in Living?" I ask. His eyes go slightly distant, but he still holds his smile for me. He sighs.

"They were...complicated. But I miss them, nonetheless. What about you? Do you remember anything about your friends?" His smile turns sad, and I want to reach up and caress his cheek; tell him to not feel pity for me.

"No, not yet," I say. I shrug, tucking my hands into the pockets of my pants so I resist the urge to touch him. "But I'm not giving up hope, you know. I'm going to try to get them back every day."

He gives me a small chuckle as he looks at the ground. "So determined, Arden." His gaze finds mine again, ensnaring me as he brushes a leaf out of my hair, sending sparks through my body. "I think they'll come back to you. I'll try to help in any way I can."

I blush, turning away from him to study the violets all around us. He's so sincere, taking care of me, physically and emotionally, and yet, I can't help but wonder when the other shoe will drop.

"Thank you," I mutter. I can't even look him in the eye most of the time. Something about those emerald eyes feels like a lure. A lure to what, I'm not certain. But it can't be all bad, right?

Not when Perry is so...good.

So right.

Breakfast is normally my favorite meal of the day. Amazingly, Bayne has managed to ruin that, too. When I reach the dining room, there is no Jesminda and no Axl. Only his royal highness pain-in-my-ass.

For only two of us, there's an obscene amount of food. A spread of various fruits, bacon, eggs, and toast. I want to glare at him, but my mouth is too busy watering at all the choices. The food was in fact not poisoned yesterday, and it seems my brain recognizes that there's no danger. Although, Bayne seems to be reading, not even bothering to glance up as I sit down at the furthest seat from him.

I reach for the fruit first, filling my plate with pineapple and watermelon, then moving on to the rest. I'm more than content to eat in silence when in my peripheral, Bayne looks up and clears his throat, as though he only just noticed I've been sitting here.

"You're late," he states flatly.

"Breakfast doesn't have a time limit. It's the first meal regardless of when you're eating." I don't even grace him with looking up, keeping my eyes on my plate.

"I don't give a fuck what you *call* your first meal, darling. I told you to be here twenty minutes ago. I'm not a patient man, and I'm not sure when you got the impression I am." I can feel his eyes bearing into me, but I refuse to look at him.

A hum is my only response.

He shuffles his papers in front of him, and I hear, rather than see, him push away from the table. I finally chance a sideways look his way, only to notice he didn't even eat. He's standing in front of his empty plate, glaring at me with a cold expression, those dark eyes devoid of kindness.

"Finish eating, then get changed into something you can sweat in. You're going to start training. Today. No ward of this house is going to be as defenseless as you were against the Shaded." He brushes invisible dirt off the front of his shirt, marking this as the end of the conversation.

"I'm not training, especially not with you. Let's be honest here, I'm not your ward. I'm your prisoner."

"Maybe, but you're by far my prettiest prisoner." He winks at me, walking around the table to where I'm seated. He leans in, bracing one hand on the table, the other on the back of my chair. My breath hitches at his nearness. His voice drops to almost a whisper as he says, "You should know how to end another man's life, angel. I'm afraid your signature move of kneeing them in the groin will only get you so far."

I try not to blush at the backhanded compliment, but there's only so much a woman can do when a gorgeous man calls you *pretty*. Even when he insults you at the same time.

"You're a dog," I grit out, shoving down the rising feelings in my chest. I refuse to back down from his jabs.

"Woof." His breath coaxes the shell of my ear, my flush deepening. "Let's test that theory then, hm? Let's see if your bark is worse than my bite." His breath caresses down my neck, and it takes all my willpower to not squirm in my seat. The shiver down my spine is solely to his proximity and not the innuendo. Right. I'm only uncomfortable.

Looking at him, he winks at me again—*he really needs to stop doing that*—before turning to walk out of the room. I mentally throw daggers into that sculpted back, imagining them sinking all the way to the hilt as they bring him to his knees. The image makes me smile.

Not him on his knees, that is. The knives.

Right...

My inner voice needs to learn when to shut up.

CHAPTER TWELVE

There's a strange man standing in the hallway.

He's tall, with rich brown skin, and built like a fucking brick wall. I have to physically look up at him, because my eyes are level with the middle of his chest.

His arms are crossed, but he has a smile and warm, hazel eyes. He's young, although he definitely looks older than me. He's stunning. Not in the way Bayne or Jesminda are, but in his own stature. I can't help but stare at the whole of him with my mouth open.

"Who are you?" I blurt out. He laughs a small chuckle, deep and resounding.

"Name's Harrison. You're the little sprite giving Mr. Sardon all that trouble?" He looks at me curiously, almost confused.

"Mr. Sardon? Do you mean that devil man who *imprisoned* me in this house? Giving *him* trouble? He hasn't even seen trouble yet." I glare at Harrison, not wanting to make an enemy of the giant in front of me, but too stubborn to let him think I bow to whims of the likes of *Bayne*.

He gives me a hearty laugh, and says, "Oh, yeah, you're the little sprite causing trouble all right. And last time I checked, you made a bargain. Far cry from imprisonment, if you ask me." Harrison taps his lips with his index finger, like he's actually thinking this over.

Harrison has an easygoing demeanor, a complete contrast to the others, and I like him almost immediately. Until he nods his head at me and says, "Let's go. Time for training."

I don't move. "And where is training, exactly?"

If Harrison is annoyed by me asking questions, he doesn't let on. "The training gym, little sprite," he deadpans. I roll my eyes. "Come on, we're already late. You may not care about your head on a spike, but I would prefer to keep mine attached to my body."

Harrison moves out of the way for me as I close the door to my room and follow him down the hall. We walk side by side quietly as I watch my feet on the maroon carpet. The silence is deafening, and I wonder if he can hear it, too.

"Would he *really* put your head on a spike? Isn't that sort of old fashioned?" I ponder out loud. Harrison rewards me with a small chuckle.

"Maybe, maybe not." He gives me a sideways glance. "Is that something you might want to test him for? Mr. Sardon isn't exactly a patient man, you know."

"You don't say," I snap, refusing to acknowledge that he told me that himself just a few hours ago. "I don't know. I don't know any of you, really. And according to *Mr. Sardon*, I am not even allowed to leave my room. So you tell me, Harrison, would your attitude be any nicer than the one I've supplied? Would you accept your imprisonment, or would you defy the warden?"

I'm not even sure why I am asking this of him, considering the logical thought is that Harrison, of course, is loyal to Bayne—whatever that means. And I'd be a fool to not recognize that.

"I see your point, little sprite. Have you tried, I don't know, maybe getting to know us? I've been in actual prisons, ones behind enemy lines, and trust when I say this is not as bad as it could be. You're not chained to the bed, are you?" There's a haughtiness to his hazel eyes that has my brows knitting together in response.

"Are you suggesting—"

I'm cut off by Harrison opening a door to an expansive gym, covered with mats and various weights around the room. The far wall is one giant mirror, and catching a glance of us in it, the reflection makes me want to laugh. The utter size and height difference between us is comical. I look like a doll he might carry around by the arm. I'd never considered myself small until this exact moment. No wonder he keeps referring to me as *little sprite*. It doesn't make me bristle like *little raven*. Maybe because it's said as a joke and not a claim. Or maybe it's because he's not a total asshole like Bayne.

He walks over to a seat of weights, and crosses his arms over his chest again, standing with his feet apart. I haven't moved more than five feet into the room.

"Well? Are you coming or not?" he asks. His gaze flickers over me like he's measuring something. Strength? Stubbornness? I can't tell.

"Debating it," I counter. I want to tell him no, but the truth is, I don't have the luxury. "What's in it for me?"

"*Everything,* raven." A breath ghosts my neck. A shiver locks my spine before I can stop it, but I barely have time to recoil before fingers tighten in my braid—right where I tied it for training. "It will have *every benefit,* but you gotta put the work in, darling." His voice sends a shiver across my skin as he gently pulls back on my braid, exposing more of my neck to him as he forces my head against his chest. I struggle against his hold, not wanting to be his captive in more ways than one, but I can feel the bands of shadows holding me still.

"Let go of me," I grit through my teeth.

To my utter shock, he listens. "For now." Bayne releases me as I practically scurry to Harrison's side. Harrison, who just gives Bayne a flat smile. I think I like him less now. "Why were you late, Harrison? Not like you to be running behind."

"I think the answer you're looking for is right in front of you, sir," he replies, gesturing to me. I run my hands over my braid self-consciously now, worried the royal pain messed it up.

"Get started," Bayne clips. "Don't waste any more time, and let me know when you're done." Harrison gives him a nod as the thick shadows swirl around Bayne, and he disappears as quickly as he arrived.

"Does he always have to do that? What a prick." I cross my arms as I turn to face Harrison, who only gives me a small curve of his lip.

"Do you see what I mean, little sprite? I told you," he puts his palms together as he enunciates his next words, "spike. Head. Let's get started with some stretches."

By the time we are finished an hour and a half later, my legs are completely useless. After stretches, Harrison made me lift weights that felt like they weighed as much as me, if not more. Seeing him lift them one-handed did not do my ego any justice. After strength training, he made me do pushups, and these horrible things he called *burpees*. If I wasn't already dead, I would've wished Death herself, Maveth, to smite me where I stood.

After the initial torture, Harrison brought me over to a mat on the ground. He held his hands out and told me to give him my best shot. I think I delivered the same amount of damage that he could equate to a feather doing to him. If he thought the same, he didn't voice it. He remained stoic the whole time, only giving instructions. He took my training seriously, despite being so carefree beforehand. And while I can't stand Bayne, I felt myself wanting to give effort for Harrison. He seemed much better company than Bayne, anyway, who was about as fuzzy as a sewer rat.

I lay flat on my back with my arms out, sweaty and panting, staring at the ceiling, begging for it to stop spinning.

"You look like you need water and a good meal," Harrison says, extending his hand to help me up. He isn't even sweating, and I look like a greased pig. I take it graciously, groaning through the pain currently racing through my body. Pain I know is only going to worsen by dawn break.

"I think I need to be reborn, because I'm officially on life number three, thanks to you." Harrison laughs, and I can't help but crack a small smile back at him.

"Go rest, little sprite. Same time tomorrow. Actually, scratch that. Ten minutes earlier tomorrow. You know, decapitation pending and all that." He gives me a friendly wink and I laugh breathlessly, since there is no oxygen left in my body anyway. I give him a half-hearted wave goodbye before making my way out of the door and back to my bedroom to bathe, and eat, and hopefully fucking *sleep*.

Of course, Bayne suddenly blocks my path.

"Good workout, angel?" He looks so cocky and smug that if I had any energy left, I would slap it off his stupid face.

"Move," I deadpan. Any other day I'd have some kind of retort. If I could lift my arms, I'd strangle him.

He grins an evil smile at me. "You can't even fight me with that mouth of yours, huh? I bet you're so tired, you're practically incapacitated. It's a good look for you, darling." He steps out of the way, finally. As I walk past him, he leans in to whisper, "If you ever feel like you'd want a *different* type of workout, you know where I live."

I glare at him with as much hatred as I can muster. "Fuck. You."

He winks at me as he walks into the gym, grinning even broader.

"Anytime, anyplace, raven. But don't keep me waiting too long—I'd hate for you to miss out."

My traitorous body shivers in response, but I shove it back into that neat little box and make my way upstairs. Slamming the door on my way out, I wish I could slam it hard enough to close him out of my mind.

CHAPTER THIRTEEN

Swirling the bubbles that surround me, I bask in the warm water, silently thanking Midnight for the quiet, albeit temporary luxury. Leaning my head back on the edge of the tub, my eyes beg to close, heavy and unrelenting. My fingers have long since started to prune, but I give myself permission to breathe in the perfumed oils a little longer. Taking a deep breath, darkness consumes me.

"Perry," I laugh, "where are we going?"

He tugs my hand as he races on, laughing with me. "We're on an adventure, Arden! There's so much to show you!" We run through the Gardens, the fields of flowers all around us. The scent of violets smells like home to me, and I take a deep breath. Perry has longer legs than me, and he's practically dragging me behind him.

I struggle to keep up with him, but he doesn't notice.

"Well, slow down! I can't run this fast!" My laughter never stops. Neither does Perry's. He's running too fast. "Perry, hang on, you're hurting my arm," I cry.

Perry doesn't answer me. He keeps tugging on my hand.

"Perry, stop, please." I try to dig my heels into the ground, but it's not slowing him down. He doesn't relent on his grip.

I pull back, trying to yank my hand out of his. It's as though Perry is made of stone, and my hand is wrapped in dried cement. I yank harder, and I feel the bones in my hand break with a sickening snap, and I scream in pain.

Perry finally stops, and he turns around. Fear courses through my blood, chilling my bones and warping my vision. This is not Perry.

It's Perry's body, with his perfect hair and his beautiful smile I miss so much.

Perry is not here, *I tell myself.*

Wake up, stupid girl.

Where Perry's green eyes should be instead are two swirling abysses of black. They make his smile look so warped, and as the thought crosses my mind, the world around us starts to melt. He leans in, and he whispers, "What's wrong, Arden? Never seen a dead body before?"

I try to scream, but my voice doesn't work. My throat feels raw.

Wake up.

The demon reaches a hand up to push hair behind my ear, and I flinch hard. He smiles at me in a way that makes my stomach curdle.

Wake up.

He leans in closer, and I recoil.

"So pretty, so delicious,*" Perry croons.*

WAKE UP—

I jolt awake from my nightmare, gasping for air, sputtering water out of my mouth. Jesminda has me by the shoulders, and helps me remain sitting upright in the tub while she pats my back as I cough up bath water.

"Are you crazy? Or just suicidal?" she asks me. I don't blame her accusations, I must look wild, having nearly drowned while taking a bath. "I get that you might not like living here, but killing yourself is *so* not the way to get back at anyone."

I glare at her as I try to stop coughing. "I wasn't trying to kill myself, I think I fell asleep and..." I shake my head, shivering from the cold and from the dream I had. "And some—something *had me* in my dream," I hiccup, looking into her hazel eyes. They reflect the worry I feel encompassing me.

"What was it?" Jes swallows.

"I don't know," I whisper. My throat feels shredded internally. Reaching up to rub it to no relief, the thought passes that I may have been screaming underwater. "I've never had a dream like that before. Or a nightmare, rather."

Jes releases me and walks over to the wall to hold up a towel for me. I stand up and graciously accept it. She holds out her hand and helps me step out of the tub. My skin is wrinkled from head to toe. Gross.

"Jes? Is something wrong?" I ask.

She sketches a brow at me. "I could ask you the same thing. I've only known one creature to haunt dreams like that, to take physical hold in dreamscapes." Her eyes look haunted. She continues to analyze at me, as though whatever demon had a grip on me might crawl out of the bath with me. "Get dressed, girl. We've got to talk to Bayne."

With that, she leads me to the closet. Jes sits on my bed, long legs crossed and leaning back on one hand, inspecting her nails. Like she saves people from drowning all the time. Guilt stabs me that her perfect outfit of white slacks and a light pink blouse are now soaked with my bathwater. If it bothers her, she doesn't bring it up. I stop in the doorframe to the closet.

"Hey, Jesminda?" She perks up at the mention of her name. "Thank you, for uh, saving me." I blush, embarrassed that she saw me naked and writhing like fish when I was underwater.

She just shrugs as she looks at me, giving me a small smile. "No big, A, you would've done the same."

We both know that's a lie, that in reality, I want nothing more than to be free of this place. No offense to Jesminda. It's not that I *want* her to drown, but I wouldn't go out of my way to save any of these people. They might not be the ones who stuck me here, but they're far from innocent in my eyes.

Yet a thought refuses to stop nagging at me.

"How did you know...that I was in danger?" I try to read her guarded expression, eager to see what lies behind.

"I—my power—um..." She puffs a defeated breath as she collapses her hands into her lap. "It's my gift. I just...know when someone's in trouble. I've never met another Siren, but I've had a lot of time to become comfortable with it. Twenty-six years, to be frank." She gives me an apologetic shrug. "But either way, I could sense something was wrong in the house, it was only a matter of *who* was in danger. It was lucky I found you when I did." Her small smile returns, and I stare blankly at her.

Part of me is in awe over her power, since I've never even *heard* of a Siren before. But another part of me is still wary; certain she isn't telling me the full story. I want to ask a million questions, but I don't want to appear too eager.

"Oh, well, that's helpful," I reply, because what the fuck else am I supposed to say when someone admits to having a weird and unique power? And said someone works with the person holding you captive?

"Yeah, but let's hurry. I want to catch Bayne while he's in a good mood."

I hurriedly put on something comfy; a navy, long sleeve tunic that hugs my curves. I pair it with black leggings that flare at the end, and slide my feet into the slippers that I'm secretly starting to love.

"Let's get this over with," I groan, and Jesminda doesn't waste a second as she leaps off the bed and ushers me out the door, toward wherever Bayne is lurking.

Holy. Burning. Hell.

When Jes said we were going straight to where Bayne was, she wasn't kidding. Because she dragged me right back to the gym. Where Bayne is still working out.

I shamelessly stare at his bare back, sweat glistening off his bronze, muscular skin. He continues to spar with Harrison, and it's nothing short of a spectacle to behold. His muscles flex as he throws punches at Harrison, and the black ink of his tattoos stretch with each jab.

Tattoos.

My heart does a little flutter, and my blood pools in my core.

Stop, Arden. He's the bad guy.

But I can't look away.

The both of them move with an elegance I envy. I must've looked like a wounded animal in comparison. Bayne doesn't acknowledge us as we walk in, which is fine by me, considering I'm too busy devouring him in my head from my position. Not that I would ever admit that out loud.

He is...gorgeous.

He looks like something I wouldn't mind drowning in.

I shake my head to clear my unwarranted thoughts from voicing themselves. Because the last thing I need is for that man to think I want him. I don't. I'm simply just admiring the beauty in front of me. Deadly things usually come in the most beautiful packages, anyway.

"You can stop drooling, darling. It's not polite to stare." Bayne calls from the mat, giving Harrison two more punching combinations before they peel away from each other, both breathing heavy. Guess they're finished.

Jesminda doesn't make an effort to move, as she stands beside me fidgeting.

"I will not even dignify that with a response," I huff at him, crossing my arms over my chest. I *was* ogling him, but there's no way for him to even know that; his back was turned. The egomaniac is swinging blindly, and I won't give him the satisfaction.

Bayne strides toward us, eating up the distance rapidly. He gives me a once over, eyeing my still-wet hair from my bath, as he crosses his arms. "You look like a drowned rat," he states arrogantly.

He looks beside me to where Jesminda stands. "Well? What did you want?"

She swallows, looking nothing like the confident woman I met the other day. He lifts an eyebrow at her, impatiently waiting. "It's back," she whispers. Bayne's eyes flare slightly, the only indication that something is wrong. I keep looking between them, trying to understand what they've cut me out of.

"Are you okay?" His voice is gruff with concern. He looks her over in a much more loving way than he did with me a second ago. Jealousy tries to rear her ugly head, but I shove it down, ignoring the irrational feeling.

"It wasn't me this time."

Those dark brown eyes find mine as he looks...surprised? "Are you sure, Jes? Tell me you are one thousand percent sure."

"I'm sure."

Why does it feel like she just signed my death warrant with those two words?

Bayne steps closer to me, never breaking eye contact. The smell of sweat on his skin is distracting, but I refuse to lose my focus. His eyes darken, his mouth only a few inches from my own.

"I think it's time we had a little talk, angel."

Standing in a strange room, Jes, Axl, and Bayne are on one side of a long, round table, me on the other. I suppose it will always be this way. Me versus them.

They stand in a small circle, speaking in hushed whispers, not bothering to hide the fact they're talking about me.

"We need to see what it's doing back—"

"What we need is to cut her open and see *exactly*—"

"If the two of you don't stop your bickering, you'll scare her off before we can ask anything," Bayne cuts them both off with a hushed command.

"She is right here, you know." I stand with my hands on my hips, and three heads whip to me, as though they forgot they dragged me in here with them.

Axl wants to *cut me open.*

Definitely filing that away for later.

Jesminda is rattled, fear painted across that beautiful face. She twirls a long, red curl around her finger mindlessly. Something is definitely wrong.

Bayne steps away from them and closer to me, slowly. Treating me like I'm a skittish animal and he doesn't want to spook me. He raises both hands in surrender as he keeps closing the space between us.

"Listen, angel. We just want to know who you are. *What* you are. Why don't we all sit down—"

"He just said he wants to *cut me open*!" I point an accusatory finger at Axl. *So much for keeping that tucked away.* "What kind of people are you? I did nothing to any of you!"

Before I can blink, Bayne is on the other side of the table, his hand under my chin, holding me with a bruising grip. Tears well in my eyes out of reflex when my head bumps the wall as he pins me.

"You don't know what you're even saying, raven. Qin can only visit three kinds of people." He points back to Jesminda. "A Siren," he points to his own chest, "a Vail, or the Shaded. Now, which are *you*?"

I claw at the hand holding me, drawing his blood. Bayne doesn't even flinch.

"I'm not asking again. Which. Are. You?"

"Fucking Hells, Bayne, if she can't move her jaw how can she fucking speak?" Axl says, surprising me. Bayne releases me, but I feel no physical relief. He glares at Axl, and they exchange a look, promising retribution.

Turning back to me, Bayne levels his glare through me. "Speak."

"Don't bark at me like I'm a fucking dog, *your highness*. I don't know what that thing was, I certainly don't have any fucking magic, and I sure as shit have no clue what the fuck a *Vail* is. *You* should know my blood is red, as you seem to forget that's how I ended up here! So perhaps in the future, you should talk to your prisoners before you attack them!"

Bayne says nothing, but he looks at Axl again like he's waiting for something. Axl only nods in response.

What the fuck was that?

"You're excused." Bayne walks away from me, holding up his hand to dismiss me.

"Fuck you," I spit at him.

"Bayne—" Axl warns, but it's too late. Bayne is quick, latching his hand around my throat this time, cutting off my air as he holds me against the wall. My feet don't even touch the ground anymore as he brings me to his eye level.

"Do that again," he whispers darkly, bringing his face dangerously close. His eyes are cold, void of any emotion except anger and visceral hatred. "Disrespect me in my own home, and I will snap your little raven neck and clip your wings for eternity. I will keep you chained to me, forced to live out your worst nightmares. Qin will be *nothing* compared to the way I'll haunt your dreams. Are we clear?"

I can't do anything except barely nod, but he sees the attempt and drops me to the floor. Like I'm the garbage he found me lying in back in Voltus. I cough, grabbing my throat, trying to ease the burning in my lungs and stop my eyes from watering.

I look up to find he's already gone. Jesminda and Axl remain, and Jes can't even meet my eye. Axl's shine with pity, and it honestly is not much better.

I continue to cough as I stand, and Axl takes a single step.

"No," I croak. "Don't."

Somehow I hold myself together long enough to make it back to my room before the tears come. Hot and unrelenting they pour, and a sob makes it past my shredded throat.

The emptiness in my chest is a chasm, trying to devour my entire soul. Frustration wars with the never-ending hopelessness inside me. How did I get myself into this? The whiplash of trying to reason with myself about my situation gives me a headache.

I lay down on the floor, rocking slightly.

Edene. It's all for Edene.

Where are they keeping her? All they can tell me is that she's safe? That's bullshit. I need answers, and I need to see Edene.

Exhaustion threatens to consume me again, and as much as I want to stay put, I know from personal experience my body will be worse for wear after a night on the ground.

Getting off the floor, there's a small knock, barely audible. *Should I even answer that?* Deciding it could be Franswon, I move toward the entryway. Dragging my feet, I crack open the door just enough to peer into the hall.

Jesminda. Her head is bowed, eyes cast downward.

"What do you want?" I ask. My voice sounds as defeated as I feel.

Her golden eyes meet mine, guilt and shame warring inside them. I wish I cared at all.

"I wanted to check on you." Her voice is small, so unlike the boisterous woman who demanded I dress in finery. "I wanted to see that you were okay."

I scoff, but it hurts and sounds more like a croak. "I'm clearly *not* okay. Go away. I don't want your pity, so long as you serve that demon."

"It's not like that, Arden. I owe Bayne my afterlife, it's not that simple. And I wanted to speak up, but I can't. I wanted to step in, especially when he held you off the floor." She pleads with me, her eyes lined with unshed tears.

"Funny. You did nothing to stop him. Yet you claim we can be friends." I feel nothing but the hole in my chest as I try to care. The emptiness wins.

"Bayne is under a lot of pressure, and he's not himself lately. I can't undermine him, not as a Siren, you don't understand—"

"Oh, I understand perfectly," I cut her off, anger simmering at her pitiful apology. "You saved me just to put me at his mercy! Which he has none of, if you hadn't noticed. And you want to be my friend? To the Seven Hells with you! You're a monster just like him. You want to *help*? Bring me to my *actual* friend, Edene. The one you're all holding against me."

Jes looks like I've slapped her as tears race down her face, mirroring my own. She runs off down the hall, crying. I can't bring myself to care as I slam the door. There's no lock, because why would there be?

Screaming in frustration, I punch the door as hard as I can. I don't feel a thing as adrenaline courses through me.

Looking down at my shaking hands, I notice that my fingers are still caked with *his* blood, from where I scratched him earlier.

It's not red.

My stomach free falls when I look closer.

It's not black either.

It's bright, cobalt blue.

Perry. His hand is warm against my own, his strong chest is a comfort to my back. His arms wrap around mine, one on my elbow, another helping me hold the bow. My arms shake slightly from holding the string taut. Or possibly having him in such close proximity. The smell of him is heady and intoxicating. Distracting.

"Focus on your prey, Arden." His breath coaxes my ear, sending shivers down my spine.

"I am focused."

He breathes a laugh at me. "Keep your elbow level. Use your pointer finger," he adjusts my fingers under the arrow, "to keep your aim straight. Shoot for the heart, or the eye, if you can. We can always get more money for an unmarked skin, but not starving is more ideal. When you're ready, let it go."

I focus on the deer over the brush, drinking from the stream. It has no idea that Death waits for it right here in the forest. I almost don't want to kill it. I know I have to. I know we need the hide.

I release the arrow.

It zips through the air, fast and whistling. I can't watch, squeezing my eyes shut. A scream rips through the air, and I open my eyes to the horror before me.

There is no deer.

I put an arrow through Edene's heart.

No, no, no.

Her beautiful face is carved with betrayal, her curls as wild as the last time I saw her.

No.

Blood tears stream down her face, marring her brown skin.

I drop the bow and Perry comes into view. His emerald eyes are shining with pride as he holds my face in his hands. "You got the deer on your first try. I'm impressed."

Tears spill over my lashes as a sob escapes my lips. Perry looks confused.

"Why are you crying, Arden? It was just a deer. It's necessary to survive. We have to keep moving. I'll grab the deer, and we can make our way back." His thumbs brush my cheeks. He leans forward and kisses the tears off my face, and I close my eyes to the sensation, my breathing stuttering.

He rests his forehead against mine, his breath mixing with my own. He lays a featherlight kiss to my lips, and the gentleness makes more tears fall.

I let them flutter back open as he pulls back. I gasp, falling back onto the unforgiving forest floor. This isn't Perry at all.

It's Bayne.

Sweat completely soaks my body as I bolt upright. I press a hand over my racing heart to slow the stampede in my chest.

What the actual fuck?

My skin crawls with the memory of my nightmare. I don't even remember falling asleep. I get out of the bed and make my way over to look out the window. There's nothing but black skies lit up by the moonlight and stars, cascading twinkling over the ocean beyond the cliff. I press my forehead against the cool glass, grateful for the reprieve on my heated skin. Taking a deep breath, I press my hands on the window. I wish I could shatter it and feel the breeze on my skin.

I wish Perry were here to hold me. To chase all these nightmares away. I don't want to analyze them too hard. Edene dying by my hands, Perry's kiss. My nightmares are morphing with my memories, and it's giving me a migraine to separate what actually happened from what is twisted.

Edene is alive. She is safe. You didn't kill her.

A tear escapes my too tired eyes. Pulling my hand away, I see the blue blood still caked under my nails. I fell asleep without washing up, but I'm glad I didn't now.

A Vail, a Siren, and the Shaded.

I shake my head free of Bayne's ridiculous accusations. He's clearly a man scared of his own shadows. *He still has my dagger and my crystal.*

The crystal isn't a weapon, but I want it because Edene told me to hang onto the dumb rock. If I can't have my own weapons, they shouldn't deny me a pretty rock to hold.

Franswon came to heal me again after Bayne's attack in the meeting room. The mender didn't blink twice at the bruising he'd left on me. The people here at Meadows must be used to it by now. He's an unhinged *demon*. Yet, they protect him.

I can't help but wonder what else they're hiding here.

And I know just who to press for answers.

Chapter Fourteen

I really hate this fucking ceiling.

It mocks me every morning, a cold reminder that I'm still stuck here. With the Devil incarnate. Midnight smite me, for I would rather change places with Edene. She would've already found us a way out.

I throw myself out of bed and dress for training, skipping breakfast. Fuck the three of them. I'm only talking to Harrison and Fran from now on.

Throwing open the gym doors, Harrison is wrapping his hands in a black cloth. He turns, surprise in his raised eyebrows.

"You're up early, sprite."

"What's that for?" I point to the wrap he's tying off.

"It's just a wrap to help with grip on a sword. Did you want to work with swords today after your workout?" I give his face a once over to see if he's jesting, but there's no mocking in his hazel eyes.

"Am I *allowed* to?" It's a genuine question, but I can't keep the sarcasm from my tone. He laughs heartily before responding.

"In here, I'm in charge. So if you want to practice swords, we'll do that."

My smile is genuine for the first time in days. Harrison is my new favorite person—second only to Edene.

Harrison makes his way to the sparring mat, gesturing me to follow. "You *have* used a sword before, right?" I nod.

"Once or twice. I did have this dagger...it was a gift. From a friend of mine." He takes a ready stance, and I follow. We circle around each other on the mat, waiting for the other to make the first move.

"You had it? As in, you lost it?" He takes a swing with his right hook, and I duck just in time to miss the blow to the face.

"It was stolen from me." I kick out for his side, and he catches my ankle before it hits his hip. Instead of taking me down, he drops my leg, nodding.

"So you're wanting to steal it back, I'm guessing." He gives me a devious grin, his white teeth contrasting his dark skin.

I throw a punch directly for them. He quickly dodges, so I use my other to punch his stomach. He grunts, but it doesn't even make him move. He grabs my wrist and spins me around, pinning my arm against my back. Not quite painful, but enough to feel a stretch in the muscle.

"You need to catalogue your surroundings, Arden. You can't come swinging at someone twice your size with nothing but your fists and your anger." I use my free arm to swing back and hit him in the balls.

He releases me as he falls to his knees. *"Fuck,"* he breathes, laughing through the pain. "Yeah, that'll work." His voice is strained, and I have to roll my lips to hold my laugh in.

He staggers back up, steadying himself, then beckons me to come back at him. I heed his warning this time and wait for him to charge first. I throw myself to the floor, rolling away from him and popping back up when I have a good distance.

"Heard you made Jesminda cry yesterday. Wanna talk about it?"

"With you? No thanks." We circle each other again.

"Well, you're running out of options here, Miss Arden. Not very many in Meadows are willing to chat with you, anyway."

"Who gives a fuck? Are you trying add to my list of people I'm ignoring? Are we sparring or gossiping?" Annoyance fills my veins, as though Harrison would even understand.

I need to remind myself that no matter how easygoing he may seem, Harrison is still here. He's still serves part of this prison.

Harrison gives me his worst, or a quarter of it. I take every punch, every edge of pain and hold on, knowing I deserve it. I deserve to feel like shit, especially after the way I treated Jesminda, and now Harrison, too.

She still could've spoken up.

Unsure how to broach the questions that burn me inside out, I blurt, "Why does Bayne have blue blood?"

Harrison stops mid-step, face slack with shock.

"I'm sorry." He blinks rapidly. "What did you just ask?"

I repeat the question, steadier this time. "Why does Bayne have blue blood?"

"Um, it's a Vail thing, I believe," he says but his voice lacks its usual conviction—and I don't think I'd trust his answer either way. But he's the only one I know I can ask.

"Oh," I reply. We leave it at that.

I'm too tired for sword practice at the end. He promises another day, and I would thank him, but I can't even think past putting oxygen back in my lungs.

When I get back to my room, I opt for a shower instead of a bath, scared to fall asleep and encounter another drowning nightmare. Falling back under the covers, I slip into another silk set that I'm secretly starting to love having at my expenditure.

I'm about to drift off for my nap when several loud raps at the door jolt me fully awake again. I get up to answer, thinking about how I'm going to apologize to Jes for yelling at her.

I fling it open to find Axl with his hand raised again and Bayne behind him, holding up the wall. We all seem surprised to see each other.

I know why I'm surprised, but they were knocking on my door...so why is Axl's mouth hanging open and Bayne looks like he's choking on a bone?

"Can I help you?" I keep one hand on the door, the other on my hip. Axl's cheeks blush, and he tilts his head back, staring at the ceiling, his brown hair falling off his forehead with the motion.

Weirdo.

"Um, we need you in the library. When you're ready for the day. You didn't come to breakfast, so we came to you." He runs his hand on the side of his neck, and I notice for the first time that he has tattoos over the back of his hand. They disappear under his pale blue shirt. I'm sure it brings out his eyes, if he could even meet mine.

"Okay." I go to step into the hallway when Bayne steps in front of me, blocking the exit with his arms. I sigh, exasperated. "What now?"

His dark brown eyes look wholly black right now, only making the gold all the more striking. "Maybe you should put some clothes on, little raven."

I furrow my brow in confusion. "What's wrong with my sleeping silk? It's not like—"

"It's fucking *see through*," he seethes. My face burns with embarrassment, and I quickly cover my chest with my arms. "So unless you have plans to be fucked in the library, I strongly suggest changing. I'm good with either decision, angel." His grin is lascivious as he looks me up and down with obvious appraisal.

"Pig," I scoff at him, disgusted. He's absolutely as deranged as I thought if he thinks I've forgiven him for attacking me. I step back, trying to kick the door closed as I turn around, but it never clicks. Looking back, he's still watching me with that unfiltered hunger.

"Maybe do another twirl for me. The back view is just as tempting as the front."

I hold one arm across my chest as I flip him off, walking into the closet to find something less revealing.

When I'm finally dressed in *several layers*, I reenter the hall and find the two of them still waiting for me. Bayne rolls his eyes at all my clothes.

"We already saw it all, raven. You're being overdramatic now."

"I, for one, did not see anything you didn't want me to see, and I respectfully will wipe the images from my memory as best as I can. Respectfully, of course." Axl's nervous chatter fills the silence as he leads the way, Bayne and I in tow. We meander down the hall toward the library. It feels closer to a military prisoner march to me.

We walk right past the moon painting again, and it catches my eye as it did the first time. Although, it feels like there's a familiarity to it now. I must be growing used to it, having passed by so often.

When we turn the corner and find ourselves in front of those massive onyx doors again, it dawns on me; one of them has to have the key. Especially since this time, we're going into the lower level that apparently needs to remain locked. Axl reaches forward first, twisting his wrist over the gilded handles, and I hear a significant *click*. He glances back toward us, his face cut in a smug grin—making him look too much like Bayne. Axl pulls on the door, and it opens with ease.

There's not enough time in this afterlife where I can picture myself getting used to the casual displays of magic.

Ostensively, Bayne shrugs as he follows Axl, reading my thoughts as he says, "It's not that unusual, angel. Locksmiths are a copper a dozen." Axl turns a playful glare on Bayne, only making him smirk. "What? It's true. Not my fault your family line wasn't gifted something unique."

My confusion must show on my face, because Axl takes one look at me and explains, "Each of the family lines holds a different magic."

"Is that why we came to the library?" I ask, glancing between them. In this light, the two men look like they could almost be brothers. I take the moment to really look at Axl.

He's handsome, sure. Built like Bayne, honed for fighting, but his presence is different, and being slightly smaller than Bayne, he's not as menacing. Be it, the ever-present playful grin on his face, or his sapphire eyes holding a glimmer of mischief, Axl certainly seems to be less on guard.

Bayne's eyes are dark and possessive, his hair is inky black, his face is always clean-shaven. They're such a contrast to Axl's brown hair and the constant stubble he adorns that it hits me.

Axl seems to exist as Bayne's lighter half.

Something feels weird about the revelation, but my thoughts are cut short by the two of them staring at me.

"What?"

"*You* asked *me* a question, kid. But you weren't even listening to a thing." Axl scratches his scruff on his chin as he looks at me, puzzled.

I can't remember what I even asked. I need to stop losing myself to my thoughts before it gets me killed.

"He said, you're here to fulfill your favor to me." Bayne takes a step closer to me, his shadows moving under him unnaturally.

"In the very library you locked me out of? What changed your mind?" Fear tries to take hold of me, but I use every ounce of defiance to stay rooted to the spot.

"Who says you weren't allowed in here? You're a ward, not a prisoner." Bayne's face remains impassive with the lies that slip off his tongue, but his eyes give away his mirth at my anger.

"Why, you little fucking—"

He holds up a hand and a band of shadow wraps around my mouth instantaneously, shutting me up. Bayne is in front of me in a blink.

"You really should watch that filthy mouth of yours, raven. I'd hate to cut out your tongue, clip such beautiful wings. I haven't gotten to see how far they can fly yet."

Like Maveth below, would I ever let him near my mouth.

I burn the vitriol through my gaze locked with his, hoping he can feel it radiating off me.

"Bayne, let her go, we need her." Axl sounds tired in his plea, and truth be told, I almost forgot he was here, too. The shadow disappears, but it leaves a strange tingling sensation across my mouth that has me wiping my lips with the back of my hand.

Bayne chuckles at me as we follow Axl, who has made his way over to one of the bookshelves, creating a stack in his arms. The lower level of the library is much more expansive than the upstairs portion. There are several sections under the balcony that never seem to end, books covering every available inch of the onyx wood shelves. There's a sitting area on this level as well, welcoming the browser to read by the fireplace. That same mantle holds books on both sides of an old gold clock that doesn't seem to be working anymore. The walls surrounding us have that same mysterious wallpaper. *Raven birds.*

The windows expand over the same wall, a continuation of the ones upstairs. The onyx wood follows the theme; every exposed piece of wood is made from the stuff. Including the four academic tables that separate the sitting area from the shelves.

Bayne pulls out a chair from one, gesturing for me to sit in it. I glare at him, deliberately walking past the chair to select one at an entirely different table. As far from him as possible.

Axl slams down six books on the table in front of me, causing me to jump a little. "These are for you. For your research."

"For my research? What am I researching?" I try but fail to keep the incredulousness out of my tone.

Bayne comes up beside Axl, placing his hands on either side of the stack of books. "You owe me a favor. Remember, angel? You probably remember little of our conversation, but we need to know how to track the Shaded. You said you don't know how? Learn. My library is now yours to use. Figure out how to track them, and then we'll move onto phase two."

"Phase two? You get *one* favor—"

"I get your help with *anything I want*, remember?" he cuts me off. "I did tell you that you should be more careful with your bargains, didn't I? The only person responsible for your poor decisions is *you*." Bayne's eyes narrow at me, dissent evident across his face. "Research." He jabs a finger on top of the books to pronounce his demand.

"So, what if it's not in these six books? How am I supposed to know what I'm looking for?" Overwhelming anxiety starts to take form inside me as I realize this daunting task most likely has no end.

He'll keep me here forever.

"If they're not in these six, you'll keep looking," Axl answers for him. "You're just looking for anything around the start of their arrival in Second. Any first or secondhand accounts, really." He gives me a sheepish smile. "And, I'll be helping you for the time being. Since, you know, Jes is..." he trails off, but he doesn't need to finish.

I know good and well that Jesminda doesn't want to see me right now. And I can't say I blame her, either. Bayne yells at me all the time, and I would find Peace happily if I never saw him again.

"So, why am I training everyday if you needed me for research?" My eyes bounce between them, beckoning an answer. Bayne straightens, smoothing the fine fabric of his tunic.

"Phase two, little raven. Better get reading. And try not to make Axl cry, too. You're too beautiful to actually lock in dungeons, but that doesn't mean I won't if provoked."

Axl looks nothing short of offended. "Hey! I'd like to think that—"

His defense dies on his tongue as Bayne disappears in a swirl of shadows. Axl slumps his shoulders with a sigh. "Well, Arden, I hope you read fast, because this is going to be a while."

Internally I groan, grabbing the first tome.

Life of the Forgotten:

A study in Death and dying

I hold it backward to show Axl, who's already flipping through the pages of his own book. "What the fuck is this going to have on the Shaded? This has nothing to do with them."

Axl's blue eyes meet mine with curiosity. He squints to read the title, as though he wasn't the one who pulled them off the shelf.

"Is it true what Bayne says?" he asks.

"That depends," I huff, cracking it open anyway. "He talks a lot. Most of it is vulgar and borderline harassment."

Axl chuckles as he shakes his head. "I meant, is it true that you were tracking them in Voltus? The Shaded." He drops his volume to a whisper, even though we're the only ones in here.

I frown at his questioning. "I didn't particularly *track* them, as he may think. It was more often they found me. Whether or not I wanted them to."

Axl's confusion matches my own. "They were tracking you? Is that why—*oh*, that makes a lot more sense."

"What makes sense?"

"So, why were *you* hunting them in the first place? Gods know that migraine they give you makes even the most docile feel vicious."

What in Midnight's name is he rambling about?

I give his legs a swift kick under the table.

"Ow! What the fuck was that for?" Axl glares at me as he bends to rub his shin.

"I *said*, what makes sense to you? Are you going to dodge all my questions or do I need to keep kicking them out of you?"

He curses under his breath, mumbling something about *just like him*, whatever that means. "It makes sense why my cousin said you weren't affected by the Shaded. Because if you had any magic, which you don't, then they can siphon it through your blood."

"I already know they can do that. What does me being powerless have to do with being hunt—wait a fucking second, did you say *cousin*? As in, Bayne is your Gods-cursed *cousin*? You're related?"

This really shouldn't be so surprising to me, considering how similar they look to the other. But at the same time, the two men couldn't be so different.

Axl throws back his head and laughs, deep and rich enough that almost makes me smile in reflex. "Ah," he settles back as his laughter subsides, "yeah, most unfortunately, Bayne is my cousin. Couldn't you tell? Didn't think you were the all looks, no brains type."

My cheeks flush with heat, embarrassment or at the compliment, I'm not sure.

"I suspected, but I know how rare it is for families to find each other after their death. So I assume nothing. For all I know, you just look alike."

He sketches a brow as he smirks at me. He truly is handsome, in that Prince Charming kind of way I used to read about. When my books weren't assigned to me.

"Arden, we're not dead."

Chapter Fifteen

"**A**rden, we're not dead."

"What?" I think my ears are ringing.

"What part are you struggling with, kid?"

"We *are* dead, you dumbass. That's precisely how we ended up here."

Axl returns my snark, his usual demeanor of flirtation gone. "I meant that *we*, as in, *Bayne and I,* are not dead. We never have been. This is the only life we have known. We were born here."

My temper is gone as soon as it flares, replaced by confusion again.

"Explain," I demand.

"We are Vails," he states plainly.

"You all keep telling me that, like it's supposed to mean anything. What the fuck is a *Vail?*" I cross my arms, my stack of books long forgotten. Axl gets up and starts skimming the shelves. He must find what he's looking for, because he snaps his fingers before pulling a thick, black book off the bottom shelf. If one could even call it that. It's closer to the size of three books.

It hits the table with a solid thud, Axl sliding it across the top and spinning it around. There's no title, only small royal blue embellishments around the edges, and I open the worn cover. Quickly skimming over the first page, I look up at Axl.

"A history of Vails?" I question. His eyes shimmer with mischief in response.

"Oh, yeah, baby. A complete history, full of facts, magic lines, and Gods know what else." He plops back down into his chair, kicking his feet onto the table top. "I never read it, but I hear it's got some good information."

"Why do you even have this? Why would you need it?"

"Uh, to *learn*? Haven't you ever had to attend an educational class before?"

"Have you?"

Axl's face is unblinking as he says, "Yes." It's without hesitation.

"I...I do not remember," I whisper. The secret falls out of me, as embarrassment flushes my face. Axl studies me, puzzlement knitting his brows together.

"What do you...you do not remember? Are you forgetting things?" His voice is a hushed whisper, but I swear I see a flash of fear in his eyes.

"What? No! I just—I woke up in Second without memories. It's not uncommon. But I'm one of the unlucky ones who never got them back. So I don't remember what Living was like. For me, at least."

Axl's face relaxes, and his easy grin returns. "Ah, that we can work on, kid. For now, read. Then we can practice some magic, see if we can't bring those memories back for you."

As much as I try to shove it down with everything else, I can't help the ball of hope that stirs to life at his promise. I close the book on Vails, promising myself to return to it. Axl brought up a good point, and I can't help but internally kick myself. How have I gotten so complacent about not remembering? Is it simply because Perry is missing? Because I promised him? My heart squeezes, but now is not the time to spiral.

Picking up the copy of *Life of the Forgotten*, I start reading.

When I finally find her, Jesminda is standing in front of the dining room windows. The sun gleams through the glass as Burnus greets her, his rays caressing her beautiful face. She twirls her hair around her finger, but her eyes are glazed with unfocused lingering as she watches the water dance.

"Jes?" I speak softly, so as to not startle her.

Her head turns toward me, and as soon as I see her sad golden eyes, guilt stabs me for being the one to put it there.

"Hi," she whispers.

"I just wanted to apologize. For yelling at you." I take a deep breath. "You could've spoken up, but I get why you didn't. Why you don't."

Her eyes go wide. "You do?"

I shrug. "I mean, it's the same for all of you, isn't it? You're scared of him?" My questions are serious, but Jesminda grins.

"Oh, I'm not scared of Bayne." She laughs. "He knows better by now." I raise an eyebrow, waiting for her to finish. "Oh, I suppose you don't know. I saved his life once."

"Wouldn't that make him in *your* debt?"

She shrugs again. "Not quite, but it's complicated."

"I've got time." I'm sick of not having answers.

She sighs, opening the balcony doors, gesturing for me to follow. When I step outside for the first time in Gods know how long, I'm hit with the sea breeze. The sun is behind the clouds now and the salt in the air makes me take a deep breath, my eyes fluttering shut for just a moment. That's all it takes for Jes to notice.

"I know," she says, her smile smothered with sadness again. "I love the sea, too." She takes a deep breath. "A few years ago, there was a war in the kingdoms."

"I know this already," I interrupt. Perry told me about the tragic war Second faced—how the five providences tried to band together, but the Shaded had already infested the lands. There were too many in each providence, and the royal families were killed, drained for their magic. That's why we answer to the patrol guards in Voltus. They're what's left over from the two kingdoms we used to live under—Ziineth and Marintha. Both decimated and all royal lines ended.

Jes frowns at me interjecting.

"You might know a version, but I was *there*. I fought and watched friends die right next to me. The war cost us a lot. Too many people, too much death in a place where the dead are supposed to live again. To stop it, Bayne was willing to die. You must know, for a Vail to die, it's like a piece of the afterlife goes missing. They're born from it, the same way you and I are born into Living, but different all at once. Their ancestors—they were powerful. More than you and I can imagine. But that magic was in their very blood, and each Vail line had a responsibility to their magic, a price to pay."

My eyes widen as shock flashes through my system. "So it's true? The royal families had to consume pieces of other people's souls to maintain their power?"

Jes knits her brow as the wind picks up, blowing auburn strands around her face. "Where did you learn that?" Her tone is genuine, but there's a snip of disbelief behind it.

"My...friend. Perry."

"And this friend, is he a Vail?"

"He wasn't, to my knowledge." Her usually sharp eyes soften.

"Ah, well, either way, your *friend* was mistaken. The royal families definitely did not consume other people's souls." She laughs, but it's not to be hurtful. "Maybe they would've survived if they had. But alas, their blood magic keeps them tethered. They live for our eternity, and then even more after that. I think time would have to cease to exist for them to pass *naturally*, as we might call it."

"And if they did, then Second would cease to exist?" Part of me doesn't even want the answer as anxiety coils in my stomach.

She ponders it for a minute before responding. "Potentially. Let's hope we find Peace before we ever need find out." I nod my agreement, turning to lean against the warm stone railing.

I briefly close my eyes again, letting the breeze flow through my own hair.

"I gave up my song," Jes whispers so softly, I almost don't catch it.

"Your song?"

She nods. "My Siren ability, it used to be more powerful. It wasn't just the warning bell you know it to be now. I could sing, persuading almost anyone I wanted. Living was...a dream. But that's why I owe him everything." She faces me now, pulling my attention back to her and away from the waves. "Bayne gave it back to me. And a gift like that, I can't ever repay it."

"But...you gave it up? Why? What for?"

"Because some things, some people are more important than power, Arden. I went twenty-two years without it. I didn't need it anymore." Her small smile is sad, but the glimmer of nostalgia rims her irises. "It wasn't worth keeping if it meant losing Bayne or Axl. But when I'm ready for Peace, it'll be like coming home."

My heart splinters another fraction as I think of Perry. Of finding Peace.

"Yeah. Home," I tell her.

I don't know what a home is anymore.

At some point, Perry is going to kick me out.

I pick up the shattered pieces of the bowl, careful to put them in the trash bin and not scrape my skin. I've got the last of it in my palm, ready to throw the evidence away, when a loud slam tells me Perry just got home. The sudden loud sound startles me, and I drop the shards ungracefully on the pile. One of them manages to cut my palm decently, red pooling in the center of the wound.

"Fuck—" Pain slices up my arm, like I cut a vein.

A small thud, then, "Arden?"

I press a small cloth onto the cut, trying to stop the bleeding. Perry comes around the corner and into the kitchen, watching me bend over the sink as I try to keep blood off the floor. His green eyes calm my racing heart, bringing me to the present.

"Hi." I blush, the compromising position making me feel all the more exposed.

"Hi." He smiles warmly, and I feel it all over. "Wanna tell me what happened?" Perry looks around the room, and I can see the moment he realizes what I did. "You cut yourself?" he placates.

I nod.

"C'mon, let me see." Perry walks closer, and the smell of him alone makes me want to wrap him in a hug. The smell of the trees and burning wood wafts with him, like every day he spends out there in the forest is curling under his skin permanently. And I don't hate it in the slightest.

Perry peels back the cloth, now soaked in blood, making me hiss through my teeth.

"Gods, Arden, this needs to be seen by a healer."

I study him while he inspects my hand, waiting for him to snap out of it and remember that we cannot afford a healer. He never does.

"Where in Second are we going to find the money for a healer, Per?"

His eyes snap to mine, questioning. "I might know someone who would do it for free." He rewraps the cut, and intertwined my good hand with his, pulling me out the door.

We stay like that, slipping between alleys, hoping not to be seen by patrol guards. Demons on leashes, Perry told me last week. He holds onto my hand, supporting the weight of my heart with each gentle squeeze. He only lets go when we come up to the back door of a workshop. The dilapidated wooden door has no windows, holds a small silver doorknob, and across the top in worn paint it reads: Burtons.

Perry knocks on the door, a discreet rhythm tapped out on the wood. Two raps come from the inside in response. When the door swings open, I'm taken back by the woman standing there. Her tight, brown curls fall carelessly around her face. She's devastatingly beautiful. Her skin is a light brown, a complement to her gray eyes. Part of my soul feels like I know her already, but I don't want to scare her—considering the only reason I think that, I know, is my eyes are silver. Not gray, but close.

Hers are wide, taking us in with a gasp, wiping her hands on her not-very-white apron—covering most of her lavender dress, strewn with daisies, I believe. She looks behind us, side to side, then ushers us in quickly.

Cradling my hand, I take in the workshop with awe. It's simple, but in disarray. Something tells me the healer would know exactly where everything is despite the mess. Concoctions sit out on the various work spaces, a large wooden workbench in the center holding the most interesting of them. They all look so...colorful. I squint, trying to see them better, but the woman slaps Perry on the arm, drawing my attention.

"Ow, Edene, that was uncalled for." He rubs his arm in mock hurt.

"I thought I told you not to bring others here! Are you trying to get me arrested?" Her voice is a shrill scream, negating the whole point of remaining quiet earlier.

"She's hurt. I didn't know where else to go, okay? I couldn't have just let it get infected." Edene narrows her eyes at Perry, like an older sister ready to start scolding.

Instead, she only huffs then turns to me, holding out her slender hand.

"Can I see your hand, love?" Wordlessly, I place my wrapped hand on her palm, wincing as she peels off the useless rag staunching the blood in poor fashion. Without looking, she tosses it at Perry, who barely dodges it, glaring at her. She pays him no mind, inspecting the laceration.

"Okay, you have two options," she says, her eyes meeting mine. They flare just a fraction with...something, but it's gone before I can decipher it. She glances at Perry again, almost nervously. "First option is stitches. Second is my own...elixir for healing."

"It's like acid, Arden. Horrible," Perry chimes in, and I find his gaze, steadying myself.

"How long would the stitches need to stay in for?" I need to be able to hunt with Perry. My archery is getting better every day.

"Three weeks, to be safe."

"Three weeks! Are you fucking kidding me?" I squeal in disbelief, but Edene is frowning at me.

"Yes, love, three weeks. Don't swear like that, it's not very ladylike." I return her frown, but she ignores me, tapping me on the nose. "Or the elixir. Your pick."

It's a no brainer. I need my hands.

"Think about thi—" Perry starts.

"The elixir," I say at the same time. I don't look his way, but in the corner of my eye I see him throw his hands up, exasperated.

"No one listens to me," Perry grumbles, crossing his arms. He's so cute when he pouts, I smile to myself.

"Okay, up on the table you go," Edene says, moving to help me step up on a stray bucket, but Perry is there faster, shooing Edene to grab her stuff.

His eyes lock onto mine, and I lose myself in that forest—my favorite forest—as his hands slide to my hips, his touch sending chills over my skin. He hoists me up on the workbench, making it look effortless. If he were to take one more step, he'd be between my thighs, and the possibility of that alone has heat shooting low in my belly.

"Thank you," I whisper. He smiles that brilliant smile at me again, and despite myself I lean closer, mirroring it on my own face.

"Please do not dry hump each other on my workbench, okay? This is a professional workspace," Edene cuts in, shattering the tension that was hanging in the air. My face burns hot as Perry steps away, clearing his throat.

Gods, how am I supposed to go home with him after this?

Edene has a small vial of dark violet liquid and a piece of leather. Holding the leather up to my mouth, she instructs me to bite down, and I almost spit it out instantly. My nose crinkles at the horrible taste, but before I can react, Edene cuts off my hand.

I scream into the leather, tears spilling hot down my face in reflex. I look down and feel no relief to my hand still being attached after all. Because, holy shit, does it burn.

I writhe in pain, trying to ease it any way I can, biting as hard as I can into the disgusting leather. Edene places a soothing hand on my wrist and my back, *shushing me as the elixir stitches my skin back together. I stop screaming as I look at her—most definitely looking wild, I'm certain—and she smiles deviously.*

The skin on my palm pulls tight, sharp. As if an invisible thread is weaving it back together, taking away the initial pain and replacing it with relief.

Magic.

CHAPTER SIXTEEN

"**W**hy do you keep calling it an undead-dead life?" Bayne's voice silences the chatter at breakfast, everyone turning to look at me.

What are you really? I want to ask. Instead I settle on, "What do you mean? That's what we call it." I can't say I'm not confounded he would even ask me such a thing.

"Who calls it that?" His face twists, like he's eating something sour. "That's the dumbest thing I've ever fucking heard. And I've had to listen to Axl judge his burps based on duration and smell." He takes a bite of his food, keeping his eyes trained on me.

Perry. Perry called it that. We called it that. Back when we was *something I could claim.*

"You woke up on the wrong side of the bed this morning, Bayne," Jesminda cuts in, tossing her long hair over her shoulder. "Maybe you should go see if Harry needs help this morning if you're going to act like a brute for no reason."

Axl cackles, slapping Bayne on the wrist. "Gods, cousin. You've even upset Jes. Maybe we should leave some thoughts *inside*, hm?" The three of them chatter on, blissfully unaware.

I've stopped listening, not hearing if he replies or what he says. I glance at my left palm, my dream from last night still prominent in my brain.

Gods, I miss Perry. I miss Edene. Why can't I see her? I know she's alive, but how many days can fly past before she's not? And my promise to Perry—forget it.

If he were still here, still in Second, he wouldn't have just vanished. We were supposed to find Peace *together*. The ache of grief pierces my heart, and simultaneously weighs down the fruit I just ate, threatening to bring it back up.

Jesminda taps her red nails on the table in front of me, garnering my attention. "Why don't we go get you ready for training? It's a busy day today." She locks eyes with Axl, who also excuses himself as we stand to leave.

Bayne studies the three of us like we're plotting something together. All I want is to be left alone. Every night, every dream brings a deeper heartache. A cavern in my organ so wide, it's starting to become irreparable.

I follow Jes aimlessly as she tugs me by the elbow back to my room, depositing me at the door. She's forgotten all about me as soon as Axl walks by, whispering something about hourglasses, which makes her laugh. They practically skip down the hall as I reenter my room, closing the door on whispered giggles. It does nothing to ease the pain of fractured pieces of my heart slipping into my lungs, making it impossible to breathe through the pain.

Nonetheless, I dress for training, opening my door to find Harrison waiting to escort me again. His dark brown skin looks glossy today, like he bathed in oil.

"Why are you so *shiny*?" I ask him.

He laughs, a genuine sound, slightly cracking my moody exterior. "It's a new treatment I'm trying out, to protect me from the sun. I'm not exactly Burnus' favorite." As I snick the door shut, I whip my face to his in shock.

"Really?" I can't help the smile that creeps up my face this time. "Because I'm pretty sure there's not a soul in this afterlife he hates more than me." I roll my sleeve back a little to expose my pale wrist, holding it up to show him as we walk. "See this? My skin has this shade, and bright red. Nothing in between."

"Oh, my apologies, little sprite! I forgot I was in the presence of a woman worthy of a God's wrath." He sketches a mock bow, a laugh slipping past my lips. He straightens immediately, shock written in his features. "Wait, wait, did I just make the moody, swearing, grumpy sprite *actually* laugh?" He chuckles, shaking his head in disbelief. Then he holds his hands palms up to the ceiling. "I'll be going to temple again, my Gods. Because apparently the Seven Hells have frozen over."

I smile at him, a real one. Allowing even the smallest light of potential friendship to sneak through the cracks. Harrison isn't so bad, anyways—except while training.

When we enter the expansive room, I see the setup has been changed. Now, where weights used to be, there's a small assortment of blades. Daggers and swords alike, ready for practice.

Excitement bubbles in my chest, but is halfway shot down when he tells me we still have to work out first.

"If you can't lift a sword when you're tired, you'd be useless on a battlefield. Dead, in fact. For the second time."

I nod, beginning my workout.

When I'm slick with sweat and out of breath, Harrison approaches me with the black wrap I saw him wear before. He hands it to me, after showing me first how he wraps his own hands. He helps me tie it off, and it feels clunky, almost.

Maybe I used too much cloth.

I walk to the rack of blades, trying to find one appropriate for my size, but also trying to swallow the disappointment I feel when I don't see my own dagger amongst them. *Of course it's not that easy, foolish girl.*

I find one I like and test the weight of it in my hands. A little heavy, but perfect nonetheless.

The wrap really does help maintain the grip on the hilt, but I make a mental note to definitely not wrap as many times as Harrison suggested.

"You ready?" he asks.

I've never been more ready in either life, it feels.

"Fuck yeah."

He grins at me, guiding me over to a test dummy. He demonstrates a few strikes first, then tells me to mimic him. I do, but the first few swings are awkward. I grimace as I try to hold it steady, unused to the heavier weight.

"It's all good. Let's take it slow. One strike to the shoulder—" He slices the dummy's straw packed shoulder. "Next strike, you block his retaliation." He bounces on the balls of his feet, ready to parry a blow that isn't there. "Last, go straight for the gut." He stabs through the test dummy's stomach, straw exploding out the back end. But once he pulls the sword out, the dummy heals itself, ready for more practice.

"Woah," I say, unable to hide my reverence at the casual magic. I don't know if I'll ever get used to it.

"Yeah, I'm pretty good." He smirks at me as I shove him with my free hand, then ready my stance.

"Let's try again."

It's been twenty grueling days of monotonous hell. Eat, train, read. Rinse and repeat. The only useful information I've discovered through reading so far is that if Shades cannot ensure the blood they steal is fresh, it risks improper magic retrieval. The magic in fresh blood can't be substituted, and if a siphon attempts an improper withdrawal, the magic can be rejected.

Most days are spent with either Jesminda, Axl, or Harrison. Bayne hardly graces us with his presence, and I can't say that I'm all that upset by it. He seems to have Axl and Jes on a rotating babysitting schedule, no doubt the two of them reporting my every move.

Even at mealtimes, Bayne will be there, except he's reading those same papers. If the others are there, sometimes he'll chime in a time or two with a comment. But he keeps his distance from me. His flirtatious taunts are gone, replaced with a brooding I want to cut off his sculpted face.

Occasionally, I'll run into Bayne in between our training sessions, and while he throws in a *little raven* here and there, the bastard can't be bothered.

It's infuriatingly rude.

He *took* me, refuses to let me see Edene, won't give me *any* information, and now, he's never around. What could be so godsdamned important? What could he *possibly* be doing that's so imperative?

Harrison doesn't have the answers, either.

In training, he brushes off my questions, my concerns.

"I just don't get it." The metal of my two daggers screeches against the blade of his sword. "What is he up to? What. Is. So. Fucking. Pressing?" I enunciate each word with a jab of my blades, gritting through my teeth.

He blocks each strike effortlessly, my anger simmering in response.

"Maybe," he swings, making me take a step back to dodge, "he's just busy with Meadows' operations. You don't have to be privy to everything, little sprite."

I huff at him. "Maybe *you* don't need to," I point one dagger at him. "But I deserve a semblance of respect. Especially when the one who refuses to do so is withholding my belongings."

Harrison still hasn't located my teal crystal. If I last long enough to see Edene again—and I fully plan on doing so—she'll kill me for losing it.

"I'll keep looking, Miss Arden. Till then, focus."

I charge for Harrison, letting my rage fuel me into a fury of steel on steel, each clash sending reverberations through my locked jaw, but I ignore the pain. Funneling down every burn, I refocus it into anger. I lose myself to it, letting the inferno swallow me whole.

That's when I flick the blade down in my hand, and kick Harrison straight in the face. The impact nearly shatters my foot as agony shoots up my leg. Kicking him is equivalent to hitting a stone wall, but even stone crumbles. He falls back on his ass, the mat beneath us barely cushioning his blow as he lets out a surprised *harrumph.*

We stare at each other in stunned silence.

I can't believe I struck him so solidly. To his face, no less.

"Are you okay?" My voice squeaks as it rises with panic.

He chuckles at me, shaking his head. "Oh, I'm good. Where did you learn that? Because that certainly wasn't anything I showed you." The relief that he's okay calms me down, grateful I didn't actually hurt him.

"Oh, good. Didn't want you going soft on me." I smile, bending down to rest my hands on his shoulders. Laughing, I smack a kiss on his cheek right where I kicked him. "All better." I pat his face. When I pull back, Harrison looks like he might be sick, and is no longer smiling.

"Maveth take me," he mutters under his breath.

My scalp prickles with awareness, and I immediately know who's here.

"Get. Up," Bayne growls, his stride angrily eating up the distance. He only looks at Harrison. "Go. You're done for the day." He obeys without a word, as if the tank of a man couldn't take Bayne. The clipped tone, the blatant dismissal, heats my blood to a boiling point.

"He didn't do anything wrong." Bayne cuts me a glare, but I already hold one for him. I fold my arms over my chest, unwilling to let Harrison take the fall for...what? What could he *possibly* have done—

"Is all this because I kissed him on the cheek?" I laugh, cold and mocking. "Gods, because you're what? A little *jealous*, your highness? Grow the fuck—"

Bayne lifts his hand, cutting me off. But it's the look of retribution in his eyes that gives me pause. "*Jealous?* Oh, no, little raven, I'm not jealous. I'm taking away your little game here. I won't sit by and have my staff be manipulated by a Voltus *rat*. These are not your friends." He invades my space, his scent overwhelming my senses, but I block it out. "They are here as resources, and since you can't seem to *behave*," he spits the word out, like the syllables taste sour as his nose almost brushes up against mine, "I'll be the one to personally handle your training from now on. Your research, too, if you can't manage to keep your hands to yourself."

"I will *not*—"

"Oh, but you will, darling." Our breaths share the same oxygen, and it feels hard to breathe, but I refuse to back down. "You'll need to stop conveniently forgetting that you belong to me. *You are mine.* Until I decide to let you go."

My breath stutters as the world seems to crumble around me. *I'm going to be stuck here forever.* I'm not sure if it's the training today, the scare that I almost hurt Harrison, or this incorrigible *ass,* but for the first time in a long time, I feel myself wanting to crawl into a ball and disappear.

You're smart, Arden. Know when a deal presents itself—recognize when you have the upper hand, even when your opponent makes you think you don't. Perry's voice in my head steadies me, reminding me that even if he's not here, he's with me.

"I'll train with you. But if and *only if* you give me my stuff back. That you stole from me."

He pulls *my dagger* out from behind his back, taunting me as he holds it between us. "Oh, you mean this?"

I lunge for it, but he's quicker, stepping back and holding it high above his head, effectively keeping it out of my reach.

"If you think I won't just climb on top of you to get it back, you're sorely mistaken, your highness."

"Ah, see? There it is again." His smile is sinister. "You, threatening me with a good time—to *climb me.* Don't make promises you can't keep, little raven." His smile drops as he watches me intently. "Speaking of highnesses, where did you get this, I wonder?" Bayne twirls the blade in his hands as he circles me on the mat.

The breath in my lungs seems to have evaporated as I remain still.

"See, this doesn't belong to you." He holds it out to me.

"It was a gift. From a friend."

"Hm, *a friend.*" He seems to contemplate it for a moment. "Unless this friend was of the Ziineth royal bloodline, this is not yours to wield." His eyes grow dark as he keeps them trained on me. "Considering this particular heirloom has been missing for over a year. Since the royal family was murdered by the Shaded, in fact. Just brings up a lot of questions."

My mind is racing with the information Bayne is telling me, yet all I can focus on is how *he* knows this. All this reading has opened up small corners of my mind to the royalty in Second. Royalty that Perry never told me much about.

As though he can see my brain processing his words, he gives me one last shove over the edge. "Go on. Ask what you're dying to know."

"Are you?"

Bayne only gives me a sardonic brow in response.

"Are you royalty? Are you the Prince of Marintha?" I impress myself with how steady my words come out.

Bayne shrugs.

"Did you just fucking *shrug* at that?" If it's one thing he has, it's always the audacity.

"Seems like you already figured it out, anyway. Didn't you always know? At least some part of you? I'd think so, angel." I shake my head, but his smile remains lethal, telling me he sees right through my lies.

CHAPTER SEVENTEEN

*H*e's *going to kill me.*

Bayne doesn't fight fair.

He uses his shadows to his advantage, vanishing from one side of the mat to the other. Every time I try to charge for him, he uses them to trip me. If I fall one more time, I might scream until my throat is raw. This is all a game to him. A fucking game.

Landing on my face for the fourth time in ten minutes really has a way of humbling a girl.

"Stop. Doing that," I grind out.

"Work a little harder, raven. Maybe you wouldn't fall if you were watching where you're going."

I glare at him over my shoulder as I peel myself off the floor again. "You tripped me! There's a big difference between the two!"

He shrugs, his face a mask of boredom.

Gods, I wanna punch that look right off him.

When I'm standing again, he's gone. It's only when I feel a sharp tug on my braid yanking my head back that I realize where he went.

His grip is strong, holding me in place when I try to pry his hands out of my hair. "My only question today," his warm breath coaxes my ear and I refuse to let my body react, "is how did you manage to manipulate Harrison so thoroughly?

Working with blades when you can't even properly defend yourself." I keep trying to wrench his fingers from my scalp, but he only tightens his hold, making me feel every painful point. He drags his finger lazily up and down the side of my neck, toying with me, and I can't hold back my shiver anymore. My traitorous body gives him exactly the reaction he's trying to elicit, as he chuckles to himself.

"Who says I manipulated him?" I breathe out. "Maybe he just betrayed you for the simple fact," I thrash in his hold, "that you're an *asshole*."

"Oh, darling." His laugh is sinister. I can practically feel the darkness crawling over me with his next words. "That'd be a Death sentence for him. He's not an imbecile. Harrison has served the crown for centuries, and he could never betray it."

His words clang in my skull, fighting for dominance with the compromising position he still holds me in.

He could never betray it.

Not, *would never*. But rather, he *cannot*. Jesminda was right. This shit is so beyond complicated. No wonder none of them stand up to him.

He releases me, shoving me forward, making me stumble as I try to keep my balance. Whipping around to face him, I scowl, only to find his retreating back.

"Same time tomorrow, raven. Don't be late."

I brace for pain that never shows its face. Wrapping my hand around the staff of the bow, I nock another arrow and line it up for my target.

"How's your hand feel?"

"It's fine," I tell him. Because strangely enough—it is.

Perry releases his shot beside me, the telltale whistling cutting through the wind as his arrowhead finds its mark easily, effortlessly.

I groan, pointing my bow at the ground. "How are you so good at that?" I want to stomp my foot like a child at him. At the unfairness.

He laughs, tossing his head back. When he meets my pouting face, his green eyes sparkle in the sunlight slipping through the trees above us. He is so captivating.

Being dead with Perry is an unreal dream—if I could remember any from Living. But I'm okay with this as my one and only reality.

"It just takes practice, Arden. You just need to focus. Here," he helps me pick the bow back up, aiming once again at the target, "pull back, and release when you're ready."

Except I'm not ready. Because I can't breathe with him right behind me. My breath stutters in my chest, refusing to cooperate with my lungs.

"Breathe, Arden."

I huff a laugh. "I can't with you tickling my neck! It's impossible to focus on anything, let alone a godsdamned target."

I feel rather than see Perry's grin as he moves his mouth against my neck in slow, languid kisses.

"Perry!" I protest, but he knows I don't mean it. Every word is a damn lie.

"Whaaaat?" He draws it out, punctuating it with a kiss. I sigh, tilting my head for him to give more access, closing my eyes to the bliss, letting it take over. "Arrrrdennnn," he whispers.

"Mhmm?" Words are long since incoherent, muddled by what he's doing to me.

"Focus, doll."

"You don't play fair, Per."

This makes him laugh again, like my lack of control is funny. I suppose it is laughable.

His hands find my hips, one slowly slipping forward, as he shows all the restraint in the world. Restraint I simply do not have.

"Hit the target, get rewarded." Another kiss, right behind my ear. I have to bite my lip to stifle a moan.

I nod, lining the arrow up again, albeit a lot shakier than the first time. Pulling it back, I let it fly, just as Perry slides a hand back now, dangerously close to my ass—ready to make me risk it all out here in the forest.

I miss.

"Too bad, doll." Perry removes his hands and mouth from my skin, and I immediately mourn their loss. "Guess we'll have to play later."

Swinging my fist only to connect it with nothing—again—I yell in frustration. Bayne evades every swing, every day I've trained with him. His fucking evaporating trick is getting so old.

Granted, this is only the fourth time, but I would've bet good silvers that I could've at least made contact.

His answering chuckle does not help my rising blood pressure, ready to erupt in fury at any moment.

"I'm over this! You want to spar with me? Fine. Then we need to level the playing field." I whip around trying to find him, when he's suddenly behind me.

"Level it how?" There are notes of genuine curiosity in his deep timbre.

Time to play.

"First rule," I hold up a finger, "no magic. I don't have any, so it's unfair to accurately determine my skill."

He lifts an unamused brow at me, his face practically written with the words, *please be so serious, raven.*

"Rule two—we play with swords." I hold up another finger.

"And the third?" he mocks me, holding up three, making me roll my eyes.

"No playing dirty."

He clicks his tongue. "Now who's not playing fair? That's my favorite way to *play*." He winks, a flush creeping up my neck that I viciously scramble internally to shove down.

Bayne walks to the display of swords, selecting one he finds acceptable. I study him, watching as he tests the weight of it, bending his wrist back and forth. I don't even realize that I've become mesmerized by the flex of muscles in his arm until he clears his throat. My eyes snap up to his, humor and cockiness swimming in his dark brown gaze.

"When you're done deciding how delectable I look, please find some time this morning to pick a weapon, hm?" That insufferable smirk is plastered on his face, and I have no one to blame except myself for putting it there.

I was staring.

I blame my subconscious, sending me the best of memories as dreams, that simultaneously hurt in the worst way.

Perry has haunted me since he disappeared, but this is a new form of torture. I feel like I'm relieving our entire relationship—as if even my brain can't comprehend why he isn't here anymore.

The heavy punch of grief to my chest saps all my strength instantaneously. I drag over to the all-too-familiar rack of weapons, selecting the daggers I'd used with Harrison.

As soon as I pick them up, I set them back down. "Wait." I grab the black wrap, interweaving it around my wrist, over my thumb, and back down. When I go to tie it, however, is when I remember that Harrison used to do this part for me.

I shoot an anxious glance over to where Bayne stands with his sword hanging by his side. Surprisingly looking relaxed, for once.

I keep trying but failing to tie the wrap. I keep my back turned so he can't see me struggling. I focus on the task at hand, my thoughts betraying me as I use my teeth to attempt a knot.

Just because he knows he looks good, doesn't mean he needs to flaunt it all the damned time. He grates on my last fucking nerve, I—

My thoughts are cut off as a warm hand covers my own, stopping it from the shaking I didn't realize was happening. I glance up to lock eyes with Bayne, as he murmurs, "Let me help you."

I nod, if only out of shock alone.

He unwraps what I've already done, and when my wrist is bare once more, his fingers expertly redo it. His gentle touch traps my breath in my lungs against my will, so I train my eyes on his hands—anywhere but his face. Every brush of his fingers on my skin sends lightning through my veins, and I hate every single moment.

What about Perry, Arden? my inner voice scolds me. *You're so selfish, forgetting him so easily. What happened to loyalty? What about your promise to each other?*

A slight squeeze to my hand rips me out of my head once more, and I look up at Bayne, who just finished the first hand.

"Are you okay in there, angel?"

"In where?" My voice sounds small as I try to quell the tears that burn my eyes, trying to build.

He taps the side of my head, *the way Perry used to.* "In there, wherever you just went."

I shrug. "Not your concern, princeling."

He smirks at the nickname, looking all the more regal for it.

Wordlessly, he rewraps my other hand, much quicker this time, tying it off securely. He only pauses to brush his thumb against my forearm, where skin meets the cloth. For the first time, I don't shove it away.

I let him be the distraction I need to get out of my own thoughts. I let him stop me from tumbling down my mind's internal staircase.

I watch him, mesmerized by the gentle touch. He's been gentle before, but never without calculation. I study him; his shadows don't appear as prominent as they usually do—his own eyes transfixed on his thumb as it sweeps back and forth.

Now who's lost in their head?

Only difference is that I have no clue what he's thinking.

What am I saying? I don't care.

I jerk my hand away, clearing my throat. Those dark eyes snap to my own, as I whisper a small *thanks.*

He nods, but as he walks away to pick up his sword again, I watch his hands by his sides—his fingers flex and curl, as if they hurt. As if they ache.

I pick up the daggers I chose, shaking my head to clear it.

Before I can speak, Bayne swings his sword down, and it's solely reflex that has me blocking it with my own blades.

"What in the Seven Hells!" I exclaim, adrenaline making my heart race. He drags his sword horizontally, the screeching steel making my ears want to bleed.

"You said no playing dirty, raven. You didn't say no surprise attacks."

I attempt to parry his attack, but he's quicker than I am, moving with elegance and a flawless balance I can only dream of. In either of my lives.

Sweat starts to drip down my back, and I'm even more grateful for the wrapping on my hands, or I definitely would've lost my grip by now.

One hard elbow to my wrist has one dagger skating across the mat. I watch as it slides away, my hopelessness rising with it. My other blade is a joke in comparison to his, and I regret my choice in weapon.

"That's enough for today, darling." Bayne moves to store his sword, but as he puts it down, I charge at his back.

I never said I agreed.

Before I can make contact, he whips around, snatching my wrist in his hand, locking it in place above us. He clicks his tongue in admonishment at me. "I thought you were smarter than that. Though surprisingly, it's not the first time I've been wrong."

He twists hard, forcing me to drop the blade. My gasp covers the sound of it clattering to the ground.

"You approach it all wrong, darling." He releases me, but something keeps me rooted to the ground as he starts to prowl around me. My heart is still racing, from the fight or his damning proximity—I'm not sure.

"What do you mean?" I breathe.

"You have to focus on where your opponent is weakest." My mouth drops open, not quite believing what I'm hearing. Bayne's hand drags across my back as he walks to my front, sending a shiver down my spine. A stupid, wry smile is on that mouth, and if I wasn't so shell shocked, I'd try to punch it off him.

"I can...I can hear your thoughts." I remain dumbfounded, and he takes advantage, wrapping his leg around mine to take me to the floor. He keeps me pinned with his hips, my arms pinned in one of his hands.

"Better stop listening then," he speaks inside my head again. *"Because they are about to become absolutely filthy."* His free hand travels slowly over my exposed throat, drawing a delicate line across the length of it. My pulse is rapid under his finger, and I watch him as he follows his hand.

"Dead." His eyes snap to meet mine, his brown eyes even darker now, foreboding. "Start over." He rolls off me, and we start again.

Chapter Eighteen

"There's no information on the royal family of Ziineth in here?"

"Why would there be? This isn't Ziineth." Jes looks at me dubiously over the top of her book. The same book that is clearly about poetry, and *not* the Shaded.

Although my own tome is on the ancestry of the royals of Marintha, so who am I to pass judgment?

I keep glancing around the library like the answer to all my prayers is around the corner, and it's only just out of reach.

"What are you even reading?" Jes' golden eyes narrow at the book in my hands, so I quickly tuck it under the table, but it's too late. "The royal family, hm?"

Blush creeps into my cheeks, giving me away if the book hasn't already.

"It's not what it looks like," I rush out.

"What does it look like?"

"Um," I pause. "Like I'm being creepy?"

Jesminda laughs, making her eyes sparkle. "I wouldn't worry about being *creepy*, Arden. I'd say it looks like you have a crush more than anything else."

"I do *not!*"

She shrugs, refocusing on her own book.

"Jes, I have no such feelings, I can assure you," I scoff, bringing my book back onto the table, a tad more aggressive than I intend.

"Then you wouldn't need to be secretive, you know. You can just ask if you have questions." She flips a page, but I'm not convinced she's even reading it.

"You say that like all of you don't dodge every question."

Another infuriating shrug as she continues to flip another page. "What do you wish to know?"

I try to think, but my mind feels blank. An empty void—like every time I try to remember Living.

The silence between us stretches as I think, pulling like a visible string. It grows impossibly taut, until finally I cut it.

"So since he's the crown prince, does Bayne—"

Jesminda chokes on nothing, her eyes growing wide. "I'm sorry, *what*? He told you?"

I smile. "He confirmed it without actually saying those exact words."

She relaxes back into her chair, folding her arms, both of our books long forgotten. "Is that why you're reading about the royal history then? To find out when he became the *crown* prince?"

"Partly," I admit. "But also to see if he was lying."

Her brows knit together. "Why would he lie to you? He hasn't thus far."

I cross my arms, mirroring her. "And how would I know that? Oh, wait—because you all won't even let me bathe without keeping a shadow over me."

Jes sighs, rolling her eyes and moving to pick her tome up again. "You're bonded, Arden. If you die, he dies. And the last thing Second needs? One of the last Vail dying because some girl was reckless with her safety."

I blink. *"Bonded?"* I squeak out. *Midnight fucking smite me where I stand.* "You're protecting me? Since when?" I stare at her, bewildered.

Another heavy sigh leaves her pretty face, flipping another—definitely un-read—page.

"If you hadn't made a bargain and then sealed it, it wouldn't have been necessary."

Now it's my turn to be confused. "What do you mean, *seal* it?"

"*Midnight*," she swears, "—girl, when you ate the food at the table with us. The first night you woke."

"When I ate with you? That doesn't make any—"

Before I can finish my thought, Axl barrels into the library. He nearly breaks the door, slamming it into the wall with a *crack*, reverberating through it.

The sound makes us both jump.

"Sorry," he breathes between heaving pants.

Jesminda speaks first, jumping to her feet. "What happened? Why are you out of breath?"

He swallows, trying to collect himself. "Bayne said we have to go. Now."

I jolt to my feet, ready. "Where is he?"

When we reach the meeting room, I can't help the wariness that crawls over my skin. *Last time—he hurt you.*

Only this time, there is no divide. Jesminda stands next to me, Axl next to Bayne.

"What are we here for?" I break the silence.

Bayne studies me, those dark eyes unreadable as they flicker between my own steely gaze. "We need to go back to Voltus."

I recoil in shock. "Voltus? Are you letting me out of the deal? What of Edene? What about—?"

He raises his hand, silencing me. "We need to collect something I left. In your old shop."

I tilt my head, still not understanding. "In Burtons? You left something in the shop, and now it's so urgent we must leave immediately?"

I don't believe him. Not for a moment. He's lying to me.

"Yes," he nods, "Axl and Jes will stay here, protecting Meadows."

"You mean Marintha," I correct him.

Axl's face slackens with shock. "Oh, fucking smite me, cousin! What *are* we telling her now? I can't keep up!" He flails his arms in exasperation, and if there weren't something secretive slinking around this room, it probably would've made me laugh.

Bayne shoots his cousin a scathing glare. "I didn't tell her," he growls. "She figured it out."

"Bullshit," Axl mumbles under his breath, crossing his arms in a pout. Although Bayne either doesn't hear him, or doesn't deign to pay him any mind.

"You and I will go, raven. They won't suspect you coming to collect your own things."

"Who's they? What are we collecting?" A thousand more questions burn in my mind, but I hold them in.

"The Shaded." He doesn't elaborate, doesn't answer my follow up question. *Prick.*

"What are we getting? I'm not helping you unless I know." I put my foot down, as if I hold any weight over the situation. It's a façade, but he seems to see right through it.

"Something of value. And maybe a few sleeping potions, too." He takes a step closer, the light in the room dimming.

I roll my eyes, resisting the urge to punch his pretty teeth in.

"What's the value?"

"Nothing to worry your little raven head about, darling."

"If we're going, and you're not telling me, I want something else."

He takes another step toward me. If he were to take one more, I'm all too aware that our chests would surely touch.

"Whatever you want, darling," he whispers.

"I want out of the bond."

Bayne rolls his eyes, annoyance radiating off him. "You can't be released from a bond without fulfilling it. Pick something else."

I chew my lip, trying to decide. It's not a difficult choice. "I want to see Edene."

Something flickers among the gold flecks in his eyes, but it's gone in an instant.

"Done," Bayne says.

Jesminda gasps so loud I almost throw my hands over my ears. Axl swears, their discernment swallowing each other in the clamor.

"Enough," he commands, turning to his cousin. "Axl, you'll keep guard here, defending—if necessary, with Jesminda." He finds her, then me. "Jesminda can help you pack, little raven."

Jes scoffs, and glancing over at her, it's a shock that she doesn't just storm out of the room. "If *necessary*," she hisses, "I'll be sure to inform you, your highness. Especially if I have to—Gods forbid—wield a fucking weapon!"

Her anger carries a physical heat on its back, warming the whole room. Internally, I plead with her not to lash out.

Only for the reason that I spar with Bayne every day, and he's way too damned fast for me to help defend her. I turn back to the prince.

"When do we leave?"

"Now."

Chapter Nineteen

"**C**an't you just enchant this bag to be the same size as my closet?"

I give Jesminda my most pleading look, but she throws her head back in laughter. I scowl at her in response, but it's missing any threat behind it. I keep stuffing more clothes into the impossibly small bag she loaned me, trying to decide what needs to come with. *Curse these sleeping silks. Now I can't live without them.*

Jes stops me mid-cramming, holding my face in her hands. "You're going to be fine, Arden. Just try not to kill the crown prince, yeah? That'd be bad for appearances." Her golden eyes glimmer with mischief, but I still force myself to pout at her.

"You're *sure* you or Axl can't come? Oh! Why don't you go in my place?" It's futile, I know, but she can't ever say yes if I don't ask. Her hands fall from my cheeks, finding her hips.

"Yeah, and spend a few days traveling with Bayne? No thanks." She scoffs. "Love the guy, truly. Like the brother I never had. But anything longer than two days, and I'll kill him."

"Oh, and I won't?" I sketch a brow at her.

Tapping the side of my temple, she grins. "You can't, remember? Looks like you're stuck with him." She places a hand over her heart, placating. "I appreciate you taking one for the team."

I shove her back playfully. "Oh, fuck you, Jes."

She cackles as she exits the closet, throwing over her shoulder. "You wish. I'm very *flexible*." Rolling my eyes at her, I snap the pack shut, hoping I'm bringing everything I need.

When I sling it over my shoulder, I enter my room to see not Jesminda, but rather Bayne occupying the space. My scalp tingles, like the bond tethers us with a physical hold as strong as our mental one.

He looks beautiful, his cloak already on as he stares out to the waves hitting the cliffside, the afternoon sun reflecting on the water. The image of him standing there, watching his kingdom from my bedroom window, is ensnaring.

Turning his head to the side, he finds me watching him like a fucking creep. *Way to go, freak. Focus on literally anything else, Arden. He's going to think you actually want him.*

"I'm ready," I tell him. I bend to pick up my dark green cloak, the soft material brushing my fingers reminding me of the last time I wore it. I was going to meet Bayne for our "date". Gods, Edene. Tears threaten to burn in my eyes, but I take a deep breath, pulling them back so Bayne doesn't see.

He spins, the train of his cloak swishing with the movement. He closes the space between us in only a few strides. That dark gaze runs all over my face, like he's looking for something. Lies? Deceit? It won't be there. Edene needs me, and if this bond keeps me from killing him, then I'll keep myself in check until I can. I'll go willingly for the time being.

As if he found the answer he wanted, he smirks. "I have something for you, raven."

"What is it?" Curiosity always has been my most damning trait.

His chuckle is dark, skittering chills across my skin. "Since we'll be returning to that garbage pile you call a hometown, our stories need to align. They'll need to believe it. I know you understand the weight of that."

Edene's life.

"Yes, I understand. What's our story?" I cross my arms, waiting. His answering grin is pure evil, and I already know I'm going to fucking hate it. And not just because it's his idea.

He reaches into his pocket, keeping his fist closed. I watch carefully, like it might be a trick. He flips his hand over, opening his fist achingly slow, dragging this out for the sole purpose that he can. It takes a lot of willpower to not break his fingers so they remain *open*.

My eyes flick to his. "Maybe sometime today, your highness, so I don't die for the second time out of boredom."

Bayne doesn't say a word, that devious grin still plastered on his face as his eyes flick to his now open palm. Sitting in it are two silver rings. One is a plain band with faint engravings of blooms on it. The other—an intricately woven band, like two vines come together to hold the most stunning amethyst. My breath catches in my throat at the raw beauty of it, enraptured by its shine. I reach my hand up when I catch myself, snatching it back before I touch it.

*A ring? Why would he...*Confusion muddles my train of thought when the realization snaps into place. I glare up at him. "Oh, *fuck* no."

Bayne's grin is gone, his face the perfect mask of boredom. Like he has the right to be exasperated with me. Fucking prick.

"I am *not* wearing a fucking ring. No, I refuse." I shake my head repeatedly, but I already know his retaliation is coming.

"Raven," he sighs, "did we not just go over this? Your little friends need to think you left of your own accord. It will draw too much attention if you try to—"

"Why, because they might try to free me? Because Gods forbid someone have free will and—"

Bayne roughly snatches my wrist, his grip bruising and unforgiving, effectively shutting me up. "*Because,* we can't afford any major displays of attention. Our mission is to slip in, slip out. That's all you need to know." I feel rather than see the cool metal against the skin of my ring finger. The gentleness of the gesture is jarring compared to the demanding grip on my wrist. His fingers brush my skin softly, almost beguiling. My breath hitches, my skin pebbling before I can stop either from happening.

"So, they'll think us married then?" I keep my eyes on the ring and where his fingers twirl it absentmindedly on my finger. He doesn't respond right away, and

I find his eyes again, only they're almost wholly black. As if I'm hallucinating, there's a flicker of something in his eyes that looks deceitfully close to *raw hunger*. But I blink twice, and it's gone as quickly as it appeared.

Bayne nods slowly. "They'll think us married, little raven. If you can actually convince them. Since history shows you're so...*snuggly*."

He releases my wrist, and I snatch it back, breaking the tension building. Tension that came out of nowhere. *Stop letting him distract you.*

I can practically hear Perry scolding me from the corners of my mind. *Eyes on the destination, Arden. Stop looking behind you.*

I clear my throat and take a step back to breathe. "When do we leave?"

The smug bastard grins. "Now. Grab your bag, *wife*."

I roll my eyes, flipping him off as I sling the bag over my shoulder again. Turning back to face him, Bayne's hand is outstretched, waiting for me. Reluctantly, I grab it, internally groaning and already regretting this.

As soon as my fingers brush his, he yanks me into his chest, causing me to rely on him for balance. That evil smile is back in place as he whispers in my ear, "Hold on tight, angel."

The shadows envelop us instantly, and despite myself—I cling to Bayne as hard as I can, my fingers digging into his soft tunic and hopefully the bastard's skin, too.

When the shadows evaporate, I swear I feel a phantom hand push my loose hair behind my ear, but when I turn, no one is there, and Bayne's hands have not moved from my waist.

"Where the fuck are we?" His deep voice is snarky, and it almost makes me laugh, as his lip curls up at the sight of flowers before us. My smile is genuine as I take a deep breath and take in the endless rows of flowers—colors exploding all over the hillside. It's been so long since I've stood among the flora and fauna that the ache splitting my chest in two threatens to bring tears.

"Welcome to Violet Gardens, your highness."

Bayne releases me as he sneezes, and for the first time ever, he looks so blessedly human, I can't hold back my laughter.

I double over as he sneezes again, and catch his glare, which feels mountains less intimidating now. "Don't tell me you have *allergies*, your highness? Surely someone as powerful and mighty as yourself wouldn't suffer from such a mortal hindrance?"

Bayne closes the distance he put between us, the sun looking less bright now. "Oh, you think that's funny, little raven? We'll see how funny it is the minute we're back home and there's no witnesses." The tip of his nose is slightly reddened, stealing all the teeth out of his bite.

It feels like a challenge. And now we're on my home turf. "We'll see, princeling. Let's go get your precious little sleeping potions. Maybe Edene has some stashed away for your little allergy problem." I laugh to myself as he groans behind me. But I've already headed to the town square, practically skipping as I swish my loose pants through the tall grass.

I'm home.

CHAPTER TWENTY

I fucking hate service day.

I should've known that the *one day* I return, it's godsdamned service day. Bayne follows close beside me, the heat of him keeping me warm, despite the chill in the air. I pull my hood tighter over my head, hoping to avoid anyone we may know.

"Arden?"

Oh, fuck me.

We turn around, both of our cloaks mingling in the breeze, like Second itself is trying to scream we showed up together. My stomach drops the minute I hear that voice. *Oh, Kaisen. Sweet Kaisen. Please,* please *walk away.*

Kaisen drops the piece of clothing he had in his hands the second his brown eyes see my face.

Fuck, fuck, fuck.

"Raven, I don't think this is the time or place. Try to keep it in your pants." Bayne's voice curls seductively around my mind, reminding me to try to shield the fucker out. I imagine building a wall around my mind, but it's not very effective, since I can still hear his laugh echoing in my head. I glare at him, only to find him watching Kaisen with a bored look as he marches toward us.

"Arden!" Kaisen opens his arms, only to immediately lower them. The relief on his face quickly morphs into confusion. As if offering an explanation to our situation, Bayne wraps a possessive hand around my waist. His thumb is dangerously close to my breast, squeezing my rib gently. The small motion freezes my breath—my heart accelerates before I have the chance to stop it.

I tell myself it's because we've been here for *three minutes* and already Kaisen's caught us red-handed.

"Hi, Kaisen," I squeak out. His hair has grown, as well as his beard, showing how much time I've been gone. I offer him a weak smile, using the heat of Bayne's hand to ground me.

"I would ask where the hell you were, but I guess it all makes sense now." His answering sneer is ice water in my veins as he folds his arms over his chest. It makes my brow furrow—he's *never* been cruel to me in the short time I've known him.

My mouth opens to retort but it's Bayne who interjects.

"We're actually in quite a hurry, if you don't mind. *My wife* and I have some...marital duties to get to." I feel rather than see Bayne's gaze caress my whole body, devouring me. My skin feels like it's on fire. Either from the embarrassment or verbal lashing my *husband* has coming his way.

"You're *married?*" Kaisen's face is slack with disbelief. "To this prick?" His voice rises in volume, pulling unwanted attention from bystanders. "Are you fucking kidding me? You're joking, right? You've only been gone four months!"

Oh, Midnight. You owe me for this one.

I slide my hand over Bayne's, displaying my ring next to his, my fingers interlocking between his own like it's familiar. Like they were always supposed to go there.

Kaisen's jaw hits the floor.

"It's not a joke, Kaisen." My voice is surprisingly steady with the lie. "We're married."

"It's probably time you left," Bayne cuts in. "She didn't want you then, and doesn't want you now. Go find something else to fantasize about, because she's with me." His hand moves achingly slow, sliding down my body to rest low on my hip, goosebumps following in its wake. I try to tamp down my body's useless reactions, reminding myself this is for show.

It's an act, Arden. Relax and play your part.

Kaisen's face is bright red; his mouth is sputtering, but nothing is coming out. Without another word, Bayne uses his grip on me to spin us back around. As we walk away, he releases my hip, only to find my hand and intertwine his fingers with mine. The sudden sensation stuns me into submission as he pulls me along.

As we weave through the booths, I keep my head down to the murmurs of vendors. Bayne pulls me into an alcove, effectively ditching Kaisen in the sea of chaos. The adrenaline pumping through my body keeps my heart racing like a galloping horse.

"Stop shaking, raven." Bayne's hushed tone is laced with annoyance.

"I didn't even realize I was," I whisper back, failing to return any venom back. He squeezes my hand, reminding me I'm still holding his. I pull my hand back as I look into his eyes, searching them for...I'm not quite sure what. Empathy? Comfort? Whatever it is, I know better than to look for it in Bayne.

With a nod of his head, I follow him through an alley, slipping into a café I've never visited. Never had the money or time, really. As Bayne holds the door open for me, I'm hit with the overwhelming aroma of coffee beans, fresh baked pastries—and I think I instantly start to drool.

Bayne's hand finds my lower back, ushering me along through the tables, but all I can focus on is the warmth of his hand seeping through my cloak. Against my better judgement, the action of possessiveness makes me squeeze my thighs together. *It's just an act. It's only your body reacting to the false display.*

Pulling our hoods off, we approach the counter to order when I hear the worst possible sound.

Chandler's laugh.

Bayne and I lock eyes, dread residing deep in his face and mine. But when I turn and see her sitting at a table, I find her wrapped under the arm of a man, looking at him like he hung the moon and the stars. His back is turned, but I would know that form anywhere.

The floor feels like it's moving out from under me, as Bayne gives me a puzzled look, following my line of sight. As if they can feel us staring, Chandler and the man turn to face us. Suddenly, I connect with a set of emerald eyes I know better than my own, and it takes everything in me not to retch immediately.

Perry.

He's here, he's—

"Arden?" Those green eyes—the ones I love so much, the ones I've grieved every day—they look at me now like a stranger, as though I'm trespassing on a private moment.

"Someone you know, little raven?" I ignore Bayne's question as it bounces around my empty skull, landing on the back burner while my world is being tilted—no, *flipped*—on its axis.

He's here, but his arm is around *Chandler.* Her blonde hair sways as she looks back and forth between Perry, me, and Bayne.

I thought he was dead.

I thought he was missing.

I've been—

Perry murmurs something to Chandler, who nods like the obedient bitch she is. As he stands, he extends his arms—*like he's done so many times before*—and smiles. "Arden, how have you been?"

I'm going to kill him. Right here.

"Wipe the murderous look off your face, raven." Bayne grips my arm, holding me back. *"We have an audience."*

I don't give a fuck about an audience, though. It's taking every piece of my mosaic heart not to shatter again at the mere sight of *Perry.*

When I don't make any move to reciprocate, Perry frowns, lowering his arms. He looks at Bayne's hand on my arm, then at the prince himself, as if noticing his presence for the first time.

Which I know is calculated and a façade. Everyone notices Bayne.

"Arden, are you okay?" Worry knits his brows, and maybe Arden from last year would've fallen for it. But he owes me some answers.

Bayne and I move as a unit as we close the space in between us and Perry, Bayne's hand moving from my arm to my hip, tugging me close to him. The action looks intimate and familiar to others, but in reality, it's to prevent me from stabbing this fucker right here, right now.

"*Ohhhh*, I'm great, Perry. How are you? Oh, wait, you're great! You found a new shiny toy to worship your feet. Only this new model doesn't have a brain, so it makes her easier to *fuck*, huh?"

Perry rears back as though I slapped him.

"What are you talking about, Arden? I've been back for months—everyone said *you died*. That you found Peace, I mean, you're not seriously upset with *me*, are you?" He gestures between me and Bayne. "You clearly moved on, too."

Tears burn my eyes and my throat, but I swallow them under the waves of rage, refusing to let them fall. "Where. Were. You." It's not a question anymore, not for him.

"I was captured," he whispers, his face looking crestfallen. A pang of guilt tries to worm its way through, but I cut it off at the head. "I was trying to find something Edene had asked me for, but I was cornered by four Shaded. I didn't even have time to think—they took me and tortured me for my magic, but it's faded since I've seen you last."

"Why would they capture you? Shades never take prisoners." I don't believe him, even though the small part of my heart that still holds love for him begs me to.

"I...I'm not sure." His hands fidget as he speaks, his nervous tic. "I slipped away before I could figure it out, but they dragged me all the way to the outskirts of Archendia, where it meets Ziineth. I came home as fast as I could, but when I got here, you were gone and so was Edene."

I look down at my hand, adorned with the amethyst ring. Perry follows my gaze.

"Oh, you got married?" He gives Bayne a onceover. "Is this your husband?"

"Yes," Bayne interjects while my thoughts spin to decipher the story Perry told us. Like it's anything but the painful truth.

Perry holds out a hand, ever the gentleman. "It's good to meet you..." He trails off for my *husband* to fill him in, assumingly blissfully unaware that's not who he is to me.

Bayne remains still, his face the impassive mask he loves so much. He doesn't speak or move, he just watches the scene all unfold. He's watching the rest of my heart shatter in real time. My heart is splintering, puncturing my lungs, making it hard to breathe.

All I can do is shake my head in disbelief. *It's not true, it's not tr—*

"I'm sure we'll see you around," Bayne interrupts my spiraling, his hand flexing where it rests on my hip. "My wife and I need to get settled. We're not staying long, just grabbing some things she left behind."

I can't even look at Perry. The feeling sitting in my gut feels a lot like *betrayal*, and for the death of me, I can't pinpoint why. Maybe that's why when Perry tries to say goodbye, I ignore him. Maybe that's why I turn to Bayne, grab his hand like it's rightfully mine to hold, and walk right out the door. Leaving Perry in the past, where I've already mourned him.

Stepping out onto the street, we look for somewhere else to eat.

I need a fucking drink.

In my head per usual, Bayne says, *"Let's get something a little stronger than coffee."* I never thought the day would come that I'm grateful for the princeling, but here we are.

"Thank you, I'd thought you'd never ask."

His brows raise in surprise. "Did you just say, *thank you*? I wasn't aware you knew the word *thank*, raven."

"Of course I know how to say *thank you*—wait, just *thank*?" He isn't making any sense.

"Well, given how many times you've told me *fuck you*," Bayne cuts me a sideways glance. "I'm well aware you know the word *you*. *Thanks* was never explicitly in your vocabulary, however."

I shoot him a scowl, but it's missing all of its usual heat.

Bayne stops our walk, smiling lasciviously as he pokes the wrinkle between my brows. "So feisty, darling. I love it when you resist me." He leans in close to whisper in my ear, my breath hitching in my lungs at the action. "Makes chasing you all that more thrilling."

"You're chasing me?" I breathe, grateful as he stops invading my space.

"Through every life, little raven." He brushes a piece of my hair behind my ear, his fingers ghosting over my cheek as he pulls back. "Did you forget that you belong to me?" He clicks his tongue. "Don't cross me if you don't know the consequences, raven. That's how you end up over my knee."

My whole body feels like it's been lit on fire. I press my thighs together, despite my stubborn will to be unaffected. My throat feels impossibly dry, making it hard to swallow.

You're not into that, Arden. You're not into him.

I do the only thing I know how—escalate.

Fluttering my lashes, I drag a nail slowly down his chest, keeping my eyes locked on his that grow a darker brown every second. "*Promise*, your highness? I'm not sure a princeling even knows how to delve out...*punishments*," I whisper for emphasis, continuing the game we always seem to play. Bayne is frozen to the spot, unmoving, unflinching.

Well, that's disappointing. I was hoping for some kind of reaction.

I pull away from him, focusing on finding a drink, somewhere—anywhere. I need it now more than ever, since I apparently keep embarrassing myself today.

When I get a few feet in front of him, I hear Bayne curse under his breath, then finally follow me. The scuff of his footfalls and his quiet murmurs make me smile to myself, feeling like I won for once.

CHAPTER TWENTY-ONE

Stepping into Saffron feels weird, and I'm trying to be comforted by the fact that Chandler will be *occupied*—nope.

Not thinking about them tonight.

Sliding into the stool furthest from the door, I'm hoping we can hide in the shadows. At the very least, keep an eye on the door. Bayne slides in next to me, not even bothering to look around the busy tavern. He waves down the bartender, ordering several glasses of liquor.

Without thinking, I grip his arm as the barkeep walks away. "Are you trying to get us killed?"

"Relax, raven." He doesn't even bother a glance toward me, his eyes following the man making the drinks. "No one's dying tonight. Well, not any more dead than they already are."

Rolling my eyes, I release him, unclasping my cloak for the first time since arriving. Relief floods my veins as I can breathe again. Maybe it's just a feeling of normalcy—after months of what's felt like being held underwater.

The man arrives with the drinks, sliding one to me. Bayne raises his in a salute to me, then drains the entire glass in one gulp. *That shouldn't be hot.*

It isn't, I mentally kick myself.

Bayne motions to my glass, still full. "Your turn, angel." I glance at the glass, then back at him.

"You didn't even let me order. What if I don't want this?"

He rolls his eyes, and in pure *royal pain* fashion, he yanks my stool even closer to his—our breath sharing the same air.

"I'll tell you what, raven." His deep timbre is smooth, seductive. To anyone else, it's a married couple having a tiff. But this is *us*. It's so much more than that, and he knows it. "For every glass you drink, you can ask one question, and I'll answer it truthfully."

I frown at him. "What's the catch? Why now?"

He laughs, genuine and carefree—catching me so off guard I almost fall off the stool. "No catch. Only if you can remain sober enough to keep asking."

"Let's play, princeling." I grin, and he reflects it back.

I throw back the first glass, the clear liquid burning like hell, making me cough and sputter as Bayne laughs at my expense.

"Oh, yes, little raven. Let's *play*."

When I stop choking, I glare at him, but it's clear I've made a grave mistake. But it's too late to back down. He won't win this time.

"First question. Why do you want to find the Shaded?"

Bayne sucks in a breath through his teeth, contemplating. "For my aunt. Next drink."

The next drink appears quicker than the first, and I throw it back, praying to Midnight I won't taste it as much. She never listens—I taste each burning drop.

"Why for your aunt?"

Bayne shakes his head. "Nope, ask a different one."

"You never said—"

"Neither did you, darling. My game, my rules. Told you to be more careful when you bargain." Rolling my eyes, I pick a different one—one that's nagged at me for a while for some reason.

"How did you meet Jesminda? Since you're related to Axl, how'd she come into the picture?"

"That's two questions."

"That's not an answer."

He sighs, then says, "She saved my life once." I tilt my head at him, desperate to know more. As if he sees it written in my eyes, he pushes the next glass toward me. I empty it before I can second guess anything.

I shake my head as my body tries to reject the liquor and the burning that follows, willing myself to power through. "What's the deal with the raven wallpaper by the upstairs library doors?"

Bayne flinches, clearly not expecting this line of questioning. "That was my mother's wing."

Oh.

I take the next glass, already ready, if just for a reason not to respond. It doesn't burn as much as the last one. "Do you ever wear a crown?"

A faint smile tilts his lips, like he's recalling a good memory. "There was a time I never took it off. Quite a, what was it again? A *pompous prick*?"

My cheeks burn as he winks at me, drinking his own glass. The liquor is stronger than I remember, keeping my whole body flushed.

Just the liquor, though.

Not Bayne, of course.

My hands find the cool glass before me, which miraculously is full *again*. I drain it like the others. "What is the extent of your magic?"

"I wouldn't know. I save it for special occasions."

"Define a special o-occasion," I hiccup.

Bayne glances sideways at me, definitely noting my impending intoxication. "I determine when it's necessary. Next."

I frown at him, pouting. *Pompous prick.*

"I heard that, little raven," he whispers in my head. It wraps around my own thoughts, seductive and entrancing. The intrusion makes me gasp, still not used to the sensation.

He chuckles, taking another sip of his drink. I focus on my own that just keeps refilling itself. I'm going to die for a second time. Only this time around will be infinitely more embarrassing. Because Bayne is absolutely drinking me under the table. In *Saffron* of all the cursed places.

Infuriating.

I throw back the glass, not even taking time to think of the next question. My throat is numb now, and the slight buzz throughout my body feels pleasant.

Well, as pleasant as I can feel in Bayne's presence.

Looking back to him, I notice he's waiting.

For what, I'm not sure.

I squint at him, just as he asks for the next question. *Riiiiight.*

"Have you ever been in love, princeling?" I search his eyes, waiting for him to shut down. He isn't freezing me out, but he's unreadable.

"I have," he states plainly.

I scoff at him, disbelief bleeding through me. "Yeah, real convincing."

He holds my gaze, unflinching, enunciating each word.

"I. Have. Been. In. Love." I nod, unsure how to respond. "Have you, raven?"

"Yes," I rasp, my throat going impossibly dry.

"Him?"

He doesn't specify. I know he means Perry. I nod, and I swear I see a flash of...something flicker over his face, but it's gone before I can decipher it.

Bayne drains the rest of his drink, and the bartender replaces it before it even hits the counter. *Damn.*

I'm the one asking questions, yet I feel like I'm the only one who's truly exposed.

CHAPTER TWENTY-TWO

"Do you think I'm prettier than her?" My words slur as the vision of Bayne before me tries to double. I'm not sure how long we've been playing the game, or if I'll even remember what he's said at all.

He laughs, taken aback. "Prettier than who?" He looks around the tavern as if my mystery girl is standing behind him.

I wish she was. I'd rip her stupid blonde hair out and gouge—

"That girl wrapped under that prick we ditched earlier?" He interrupts my thoughts with his question. I nod several times, just to make sure he sees it. He grabs my chin gently, making me stop. He leans in close, stopping my heart altogether as sparks skitter over my skin. "You're more radiant than any other soul in this damn life, Arden."

The sound of my name on his lips makes my lips part. He pulls back slightly, those beautifully dark eyes bearing into mine.

He's definitely a gift from the Gods themselves, carved out piece by rugged piece and put together to form one...perfect...man.

He laughs, his smile full and genuine. "I appreciate the sentiment, little raven." His thumb traces my bottom lip, and I forget to breathe. I forget to care that he heard my thoughts at all.

Leaning forward, I close the distance between us so our foreheads are almost touching. Our mingled breath tastes like the alcohol, permeating the air with sin.

Sins that I'd need to attend temple for the rest of my afterlife to be forgiven for.

I close my eyes as my nose brushes his, and he sighs. They snap back open when I feel him pull away. The rejection hits me like a stampede, reminding me he doesn't want me and I don't want him.

My heart tramples itself in my chest, stealing what little air I had left in my lungs.

I can't believe I almost did that.

Bayne stands, tossing some silvers on the counter for the barkeep, and holds out his hand to me. I shake my head, pouting like an adolescent. "Let's go, raven." I refuse to move, my embarrassment rooting me to the spot.

He steps into my space, breathing heavily. I wonder what it looks like when he loses control. I wonder if he would lose control with me—

What am I saying?

"Now," he commands.

My hand lands on his chest, drifting slowly down to his belt. I keep my eyes locked on his, trying to stop the world from tilting as I try to undo it. "You don't want me?" I whisper—I think. He stops my hand as I start to unravel the first strap, making me pout again. "Fine. If you don't want to pla—play with me," I hiccup. "I'll find someone else in here." I look around the poorly lit tavern, not seeing much of anything.

Something in the back of my head tells me this is Bayne's shadows, making it harder to see.

"If you even so much as *think* about leaving here with another man while your hand wears my ring, you'd be signing his death warrant," he says, promising and possessive. "I'd bring a Hell so vicious, Maveth herself would be shaken."

My breath cuts off in my chest, weighing his words. His eyes flicker into both of mine—searching? I never know. He's an enigma.

His voice drops even lower, speaking directly to my soul. "He could beg for the possibility of Peace, and he would never know the meaning of the word. Leave with another, and I promise, little raven, he'll leave this life in pieces. Understood?"

I stare at him with unadulterated wonder, mouth open, trying to process through the alcoholic haze. Yet a part of me has never felt more sober. Sighing, Bayne rolls his eyes as he dips down, wrapping his arms around my legs, throwing my body over his shoulder. Like I weigh no more than a doll.

If the world was spinning before, it spins twice as fast upside down. When I try to focus my vision, it worsens until darkness overtakes me, and all I feel is bliss.

My eyes don't peel open until I feel Bayne set me down on a bench. He holds my head as he speaks, but I don't hear it. The world is spinning, and my eyes can't focus on all the swirling colors.

"What?"

He sounds underwater.

"I said, we'll need to stay somewhere safe tonight and leave in the morning."

"What? Why?"

He doesn't answer, but I follow to where he points at the sky, indicating the sun has set already.

"Can't you just," I wave a hand over his stature, "shadow us back? You did it the first time."

Bayne sighs, like I'm a small child who never learns. "It doesn't always work like that. And given your state of being, I'm not taking any chances going back to the flower fields at this hour."

"Oh." I frown, understanding weighing down my urge to leave.

"That's why you brought a *bag*, raven. So we wouldn't rush our search." He gestures to the pack I didn't realize I was clutching in my hand.

"I know that," I bite back. His answering smirk tells me he doesn't believe me in the slightest.

"Let's go," he says. "I know somewhere we can crash."

Picking me back up, he cradles me in his arms this time, and it helps the world feel less dizzying. Stopping in front of an inn, he sets me back on my feet, asking silently if I can stand on my own. I give him an affirmative nod.

Voltus has never been known for its stellar hospitality. Being away for a few months, I can see why Bayne had such a foul taste in his mouth the first time he came to town. The only inn we could find with a vacancy is hardly an inn at all. I'm not sure if the wallpaper is supposed to be peeling off, but it's the least of our worries.

"I only have the one room," the older gentleman behind the desk tells us, stroking the back of an orange cat. His gray hair stands out to the tanned wrinkles on his face, like running this hovel has drained his afterlife of youth. I try blinking to focus, but I can't stop staring at his weird ass cat.

"One room is fine," Bayne says, and I cut him a glare hot enough to melt steel. *"We can't buy what the man isn't selling, little raven. Relax."* He speaks into my head.

"I'll relax when I die for the second time," I cut back.

Bayne smirks, keeping his eyes trained on the man in front of us.

"Okay, two silvers, lovebirds." I roil in disgust before quickly tamping it down, almost forgetting about the rings on our hands. Bayne hands over the payment for the small bronze key. We nod our thanks, making our way to our room. Bayne's hand finds my lower back, the heat of him sending a wave of awareness through me.

"That is so unnecessary, your highness."

He leans in close to my ear, as if the bastard knows it's a direct line to send shivers over my skin. "I beg to differ, *wife*. The man is still watching, and I'd hate for us to spend our first night married with the patrol guards, hm?"

He has a point. Not that I'd ever tell him that.

When we reach the room, he holds the key out to me to open the door, clearly incapable of doing it himself. I snatch the key out of his hand with a huff, ignoring the shit-eating grin spreading over his face. As it creaks open and we step inside, I stop in absolute, gut-wrenching horror—causing Bayne to collide into my back.

"Oh, *fuck no*," I murmur a curse.

This has to be a sick joke.

Why, why, WHY?

Bayne grunts as he runs into me. "What are you—" he stops, taking in the room. Then the bastard laughs, like this is the funniest thing he's ever seen. If I wasn't tired, intoxicated, and pissed off, it might be endearing.

What am I saying? He's nothing if not a nuisance.

The room is quaint, with a tiny window filtering in moonlight. The wooden panel walls are casting an orange glow by a single bedside lamp. And a *single bed*.

"Oh, darling." He huffs a breathy laugh as he takes off his cloak, letting it hit the floor with a sensual thud. "I hope you don't snore." The grin splitting his face is depraved, reveling in the uncomfortable circumstance. "Try to keep your hands to yourself, won't you?"

Bayne starts to unbutton his tunic, and every second he reveals more of that bronzed skin hypnotizing my eyes like a spell, drawing me into his deft fingers.

"I'm not sharing a bed with you." I snap my wandering eyes to his face, determined to swallow the blush that's threatening to creep up my neck. A lasting effect of the alcohol, I'm sure.

His hands stop, leaving his shirt half open and *Gods*—if it isn't a holy sight. He looks like a fallen divinity from the clouds themselves. My tired brain is too drained to filter out *who* stands before me.

"I don't think you have much of a choice, raven. There's only one bed, and I'm not sleeping on the floor. I don't think you'll want to, either, considering I already know you'll burn those boots the minute you're back in Marintha."

"I just, I've never—" He shoots me a surprised look as I fall over my words.

"Angel, I never said I was going to fuck you. Your virginity is safe—for now."

"I'm not a virgin, you insolent *dog*. I just haven't spent the entire evening with another man since..." *Since Perry.* The embarrassment is too much to hide as it burns my face. I look down, unable to meet his eyes.

"I promise to mind my hands." His voice is giving him away—that smirk I know is there, screaming *I'm lying*.

Digging through my bag, I cringe with dread as I remember what I actually packed, thinking I would sleep alone. *My fucking sleep silks.*

"I'm going...to change," I say, looking around for privacy. The only place that might work is the washroom, but it's a bit small.

"Go ahead." He grins at me, waiting for the show he's definitely not getting.

"I'm waiting for you to turn around!" I clutch the silks to my chest, and he seems to notice them for the first time.

"Raven, if you're wearing those, there's no point in me turning around."

"I'll be under the covers on the opposite end before I let you turn back."

"Before you *let me*?" he scoffs, incredulous.

"Yes."

He chuckles, but to my surprise, he turns and faces the wall. Keeping an eye on him, I quickly strip out of my clothes, pull on the silks, and slide under the covers. I shimmy all the way to the far side of the bed, against the wall, furthest from him.

"Okay, I'm covered now."

Bayne turns around, an amused glint in his eyes when he sees me huddled under the covers. Without another word, he removes his shirt and reaches for his pants before I squeak.

"Oh, I have no qualms if you want a free show, little raven. Better close your eyes if you don't want to see anything."

I squeeze my eyes shut, not trusting him to get naked just to spite me. I don't open them again until I feel the bed shift beside me and the covers pull away slightly. The room is darker now, but I can still see Bayne as he fixes his pillow, which is not much more than a couple of feathers shoved in a bag. Watching him do something so domestic is enrapturing. The crown prince, roughing it in the slums of Voltus.

He catches me staring. "What?"

"Nothing. I'm just waiting for you to stop moving the whole fucking mattress so I can sleep." He rolls his eyes at me as I toss and turn, giving him my back. When he finally settles, the space between us feels like a chasm, and I can't shake why I even care at all.

The cold air from the outside creeps in through the walls, chilling me to the bone.

"I thought I told you to stop shivering." he scolds me.

"I can't help it if I'm cold," I snap back at him.

Before I can protest, strong arms wrap around me, one over my stomach, one over my collarbone. Bayne pulls me into his chest, the heat of his body warming me from the inside out. It takes all of my willpower not to squeeze my thighs together at the ache building between them. It's been forever, it feels, since I've been held like this. Like I'm something precious, something worth holding.

"If you tell a soul that I held you, I'll kill you."

"Yeah," I yawn. "Sure."

His breath tickles my neck, ruffling my hair as he chuckles, but I'm too tired to give a damn. His chest reverberates with the laugh and for some reason, the feeling is comforting. We lay in silence for what feels like ages before I break it.

"You know, he didn't even like her," I whisper to the darkness. Tears burn in a threat to spill, but I refuse to let them fall. I refuse to cry for Perry again.

Bayne tightens his hold on me, as if he can squeeze the heartache out of my body. "Yeah?" His voice is groggier now, like he's about to fall asleep.

"Yeah." I sigh. "She was always rude to me, and he swore she was a pest. We used to make fun of her sometimes." I huff a laugh. "Now he's seeing her? It just doesn't make sense."

Bayne doesn't speak for several minutes, and I think he's fallen asleep, until he lets out a deep sigh. "Sometimes, little raven," his breath ghosts the back of my neck, "sometimes our opinions of people change. For the worse, for the better."

Like us? I want to say.

But I don't.

I let sleep take me prisoner and pretend that I'm safe in Bayne's arms, even though everything I know tells me I'm not.

Chapter Twenty-Three

Finally approaching Burtons, something in the air feels *off*. Perhaps it feels lackluster with Edene no longer here, but the air feels even colder here when it should feel like home. Right?

The unease has me stepping in closer to Bayne. Only the unease. Not because I'm drawn to him.

My head throbs with a dull ache—embarrassment of the previous night threatening to swallow me up and send me to my second death.

My bones feel the chill before I see it. The front door is cracked open, shadow spilling out onto the sidewalk. Bayne and I look at each other at the same time, a wordless conversation passing between us.

This. Is. So. Bad.

Hesitantly, we creep forward, not to startle whoever might still be inside. But as Bayne opens the door further, the sight before us suffocates my breath. My heart stops beating, as it simultaneously pounds ruthlessly in my chest.

The shop has been *eviscerated*.

Once carefully stacked potions on the shelves now decorate the warping hardwood floor in a cacophony of shattered glass, cork, and wire stoppers.

"Gods, do you think they found what they were looking for?" Bayne's comment is meant to be teasing, but the ringing in my ears is blocking out everything except the utter destruction before me.

Gone. It's all gone.

Every single thing that Edene worked so hard for, day after day. Every smile to a rude customer, just hoping they would continue to return so we could eat that week. Every single Shade I slaughtered, just for a glimpse of a better afterlife—none of it remains. The life I lived here with Edene, wiped from my past.

"Raven, I—are you crying?" Bayne's face is marred with confusion, and I brush my fingers over my cheeks to bring them back wet.

I guess I am.

The tears flow harder now, hot and messy, and for the first time, I don't care if he sees. His face blurs as my eyes continue to spill over. My knees feel weak as a sob wracks my chest, and the second they give out, Bayne catches me.

I can't even be upset with myself for letting him hold me again. He supports my weight as the scent of balsam and linen overtakes me, my head falling into the crook between his neck and shoulder. The tears are endless, and when I feel a hand lightly brushing down my hair on the back of my head, coupled with a barely audible shush, I lose all sense of composure.

"Little raven," he whispers, his breath ghosting the shell of my ear. "I hope you know that if you cut your knees on this glass, I would have no explanation, and I think Franswon might never let me live it down."

I can't help but release a choked laugh, laden with water. "He—he'd probably think you dragged me across it," I hiccup. "I'd think the same thing. You're an ass."

His laugh reverberates through his chest, and despite myself, the sound makes me relax a fraction. My lips crack into the tiniest of smiles before I force a frown.

No. You will not be charmed by him.

I pull back slightly, his hand now cupping the back of my head, like it's where it belongs. "Oh," my voice is small now, overshadowed by grief, "I got your shirt wet." Our eyes lock, and the slight humor in his is so godsdamned steadying. Even as it disappears with his next words.

"Raven," his brow furrows, "I don't give a fuck about my shirt."

My mouth parts at the growl in his tone, as my eyes flick between his own. His pupils look blown, those damning eyes looking wholly black—the resolve that was hanging by a single thread *snaps*.

I bunch his shirt with my fist and yank his mouth on top of mine.

There's a split second of surprised hesitation from Bayne the moment our lips touch, but it's all he needs before he slides his hand from my hair to the back of my neck, holding me in place. He must feel my pulse beating rapidly under his thumb—caressing me as he deepens the kiss.

My fingers slide through his hair, the strands of ink even softer than I imagined. Anything—*something*, to pull him closer, to take his breath and use it for the both of us.

The feel of him is so damned euphoric; I moan into his mouth, letting go. He uses the invitation to slide his tongue against my own, and it feels like I've been brought back to life. Our mouths rival for dominance, but for once, I willingly let him win and take the lead.

Sparks explode inside me, lighting up every nerve. My breath becomes more desperate between each kiss. Every touch messier than the last. His groan spurs me on, his other hand moving to grip my ass, squeezing as we stumble backward, my back hitting the counter.

The counter. Burtons.

Oh, fuck I—

I shove Bayne back, wrenching his lips from mine, shattering whatever the fuck this was. His eyes are fully black now, his lips swollen, no doubt reflecting my own. We're both breathing heavy, locked in a haze of hunger and arousal. I stare at him in disbelief, my fingers reflexively running over my lips, still feeling the sting of his mouth.

"I-I, why did you do that?" My voice is hushed with disbelief. *I can't believe I just kissed him. I can't believe Bayne just kissed me back. I can't believe I liked it.*

He scoffs, raising a sardonic brow. "You kissed *me*, little raven." He darts his tongue out to wet his lips, and the movement makes me squeeze my thighs together. *That tongue was just on the inside of my mouth. Why did he taste so good?*

"You pulled me in for a kiss, remember?" He takes a step closer, glass crunching under his feet. "*You* grabbed *my* shirt, kissed me first. Not saying I didn't enjoy it." He chuckles darkly, and it skitters chills over my skin, contrasting the heat surging through me. "You did taste...*so sweet*." He drags his thumb over his bottom lip, and the motion keeps me mesmerized, simultaneously catching my breath in my throat.

He takes a final step, closing the space between us once more by caging me in to the counter. His nose is nearly brushing mine again, our breaths sharing the same air.

"Tell me," he breathes. "Tell me...that didn't electrify you in a way you've never known. Tell me, and I won't do it again." He leans in closer, and my heart threatens to explode out of my chest and fall on the floor.

Before I stop myself, I slap him across the face. Hard.

His face jerks to the side, his expression back to being flat and unamused. When his eyes find mine again, they've iced over.

"I'm going to let that one go. Because I know you're mad at yourself and not me. Because you cried today. But that's it. You get *one*."

I nod imperceptibly and he pushes off the counter, giving me the space to breathe again.

"I'm going to search down here, you go upstairs," Bayne commands me.

"What if I wanted to search this floor?"

"You're right, angel. How could I give up an opportunity to go through your old underwear drawer?" His smile is nothing short of evil. The bastard is plotting my demise, I'm sure of it. He turns to walk up the stairs, and before I think better of it, I grab his arm to stop him.

He stops, looking down at my hand on him, then meeting my eyes once more.

"This is the second time in five minutes my wife has put her hands on me. Either she wants to fuck me, or she makes *very* poor decisions."

I drop his arm immediately and take a step back. "I—I'll check upstairs. I don't want you to steal any panties for your own use." I fold my arms over my chest, hoping to quell the incessant nerves racing through me.

"Darling," he whispers in my ear as he walks past. "I wouldn't need your panties." He brushes a piece of dark hair off my shoulder, and it sends sparks all the way to my toes before I can tamp it down. "I know you'll be crawling into my bed soon enough. This little fight is just that. I'll be here to kiss and make up when you're ready."

I scoff before I bound up the stairs two at a time—anything to put distance between us. My breaths come in short, quick pants, and I feel deprived of oxygen.

Definitely not thinking about the way his tongue—

No, Arden. Get a grip on yourself.

Sleeping potions. Find the sleeping potions.

Compared to my closet alone at Marintha, my old room is a broom closet. Looking over the space, it's strange how only a few short months ago, this was my everything.

I shouldn't have let the luxury seduce me the way it has, but it felt against my will at the same time. Like I was drawn to it. Not just the material things, but the people, too.

I focus on turning over the room, leaving no pillow or blanket unturned. There's nothing here, just like I suspected. Sighing, I collapse on my makeshift bed—before I knew what a real bed even was. Bayne's a horrible influence on me. He's *warping* my mind, I'm sure of it. Every day, I feel myself losing focus more and more. The Arden I was four months ago would've been itching to get back here, but the woman I am now? She isn't sure how to say goodbye to the opulence that's integrated in her daily life.

My head is spinning, throbbing with the past and present hitting me like a thousand horses. And that kiss—*that kiss.* What was I fucking thinking? Can I even call that a moment of weakness? Was it just a second of loneliness or something more? I don't want Bayne. He won't even say my name, for Gods' sake. I hate him. And I hate that he's left me in knots over something so stupidly simple as a kiss. I hate even more that a minuscule part of me wants to do it again.

I don't want to check Edene's room. The simple fact of knowing she's alive really isn't enough anymore. I don't understand this game of limbo they're keeping me in. Why can't I see Edene? If she's fine, there's no reason I should be denied to see her. He said I can, but I don't trust him to keep his promise.

She isn't okay. But she has to be. This is *all* for Edene.

I check her room as fast as humanly possible, pausing only when I find extra crystals shoved between her mattress and the frame. It's a small assortment of colors—teal, pink, purple, white, and blue. But the one I can't take my eyes off is a black crystal I've never seen before. The weight of it even feels heavier than the others, like it's denser. *Strange.* Why would Edene have these rocks between her mattress of all places? And why is it so dark?

Perhaps I've just never noticed them or looked too closely before. But the damn thing seems to radiate energy—one I'm not sure I like. I pocket it to be safe, but I should tell Bayne. Or hit him upside the head with it. The thought makes me smile to myself with devious satisfaction.

"What the hells is that evil ass smile for, raven?" Bayne's deep timbre startles me as I get off the floor, whirling around to see him. He's leaning against the doorframe, waiting for my response.

"I found something interesting," I admit, pulling the black stone out of my pack. His brows knit with concentration, taking the crystal from me and holding it in his own hand.

"Hm."

"That's it?" I look incredulously at him. "Just a *hm*?"

Bayne gives me a flat stare. "I'm just curious, darling, that's all." He tests the weight of it in his palm again. "Why would a healer and a wannabe assassin have crystals for hexing?"

I reel back at his accusation. "Excuse me?"

"You're not excused. That was a genuine question. What exactly was your little friend up to?" His tone is accusing, threatening without naming the punishment.

"She collected those rocks," I tell him. It's a half truth. Edene stole most of them. "She thought they brought us protection. They just look like rocks to me."

Bayne rolls his eyes, murmuring something about *insolence.* "Angel, these are no mere *rocks.* They are powerful ward stones, and in the wrong hands, they can do a lot of damage to a soul." He waves the black stone between us. "I don't know what hex is on this one, but I'd rather not find out since I'm quite attached to keeping all of my body parts."

"These...ward stones." I rub my temples, trying to grapple with the information he's feeding me. "They can make someone explode? Lose body parts?"

"Not all of them. The different colors mean different things, really. Do you have any others?" I pull out the other colors I found in the mattress. Bayne nods, like he's assessing each one in my palm.

"Purple," he drags a finger over it, and I quietly gasp, feeling his body heat through the fucking rock. "It's for persuasion," he purrs, dark eyes watching me closely. "If you wanted to be more convincing, you would wear this one. Blue is a power amplifier. If you have any," he whispers, sealing it with a wink. He drags his finger over the others. "Pink for strength, orange for transport, and teal for luck." I don't know why this feels like a game, but I know that I'm losing—when I don't even know the rules. "White is special." The words curl around us, and I see his shadows coil around his arms like an extra layer of armor.

"Why is white special?" I whisper, playing into it even though I know it's a setup. My stomach twists in the prolonged silence, my heart racing, waiting for his killing blow. He tilts his head at me, assessing.

"It's the most useless of all." He brushes a loose hair behind my ear, his shadow caressing my cheek. "It's for love." He almost looks lost, contemplating. "Love is the most powerful thing you can have, angel. No godsdamned rock will wield what your heart sings. It can't hold onto a feeling that lives among the stars."

I pause, soaking in his words, the look on his face as he...did he speak from the heart for once?

"Don't look at me like that." Bayne's face sours, snapping me back to the present.

"Like what?" I snap.

"Like I'm something worth saving—worth knowing. You'll only find disappointment, little raven."

I scoff at him. "Gods, you truly are the most fucking dramatic, incorrigible, arrogant—"

He chuckles, cutting me off mid-sentence. "There she is."

I swing my arm for his face without thinking, but he catches my wrist before I make contact. His eyes darken, lethal promise swimming in his irises.

"Didn't I say, you only get one?" His voice is low, laden with withheld retribution. When I don't respond, his grip tightens, then he drops my wrist, like it's nothing more than an irritating bug. "Let's go."

"Did you find what you lost?"

He nods. "I think I did."

Bayne holds out his hand this time, and reluctantly I take it, letting the shadows envelope me, wishing this was one memory I could lose.

PART THREE

Dreamscapes are never safe for those susceptible to Qin's influence. Extreme caution must be used if power remains uncultivated. Blood demands a price for balance. May the God have mercy on the Siren should they not heed warnings. Damned are the Vails who survive.

—A Tale of Folklore, Author Unknown

Chapter Twenty-Four

*"H*appy Birthday, Arden."

Perry's eyes match the forest surrounding us, glittering in the sunlight streaming through the branches. His smile—that beautiful smile—dazzles me as he stretches his body out next to mine on the worn blanket on the ground.

"Thank you," I whisper, my face growing hot under his intense concentration. I can't remember a time when I wasn't enamored with him, and I have no desire to.

Perry is all I care about.

He brushes a piece of my dark hair behind my ear, then taps my temple, making me smile. "I have something for you, doll."

"What is it?" I can't help my brows that raise in curiosity.

"It's a special gift, one that I had made for you especially." He turns, reaching into the brown leather satchel he got from Edene. When he reveals his hand, he pulls out the most stunning dagger I've ever seen.

A gasp falls from my lips as I sit up, unable to hide my shock.

The dagger is beautiful, lethal. The sapphire-jeweled hilt draws in my eyes, contrasted perfectly with the silver edge of the blade itself. The sun bounces off it as he twirls it, a single black silk ribbon tied around the cross guard.

Perry sits up with me, holding the blade out to me. "Perry, how did you afford this?"

We can barely eat, especially with winter fast approaching. An extravagant purchase is not in the cards for us.

He shrugs, the picture of nonchalance. "Don't worry about it, doll."

"But—"

"Arden, it's your twenty-third birthday. I think it calls for some celebration. Let me worry about how I got it made, okay?"

The sincerity in his tone, his face, makes me want to trust his words—to not worry. But even as I shove it down for this moment, I know that future me will.

I nod, placating him. He gives me another smile, leaning forward, places his hand on my knee. Asking.

I return his smile, closing the space between us, wrapping my arms around his neck. My lips brush his in a small, chaste kiss. Even still, my heart has never felt so full of love—of warmth and safety.

"Thank you," I say against his mouth. "It's beautiful."

He kisses me again, longer, fiercer, as his hand slides up my thigh to find my hip. "You're beautiful, Arden. You're all I've ever wanted."

My heart soars, overflowing with pure love.

"You don't think that..." I trail off, shaking my head, unable to voice the insecurity.

Perry pulls back slightly, his eyes flicking between my own, trying to piece it together. "Think what?" His other hand twirls around the end of my hair absentmindedly.

Distracting me. Emboldening me.

"You don't think you'll need more? Want to find more?" I whisper. I want to look away, but I hold his gaze.

"Arden, you are my more. There isn't anything else—anyone else."

His words quell the unease that was starting to build, squashing any doubt.

"You're my more, too, Per." I kiss him again, as he pulls me fully onto his lap, following him down on the blanket once more.

Glaring at the gold squares has become a part of my daily routine. It's not the ceiling that I'm mad at—truly.

My heart is at war with itself inside me.

That's not war, it's guilt. Guilt toward someone who isn't even committed to you anymore. Insolent girl.

I groan, pressing my hands into the backs of my eyes. What is *wrong* with me? *What is wrong with Perry?* The man that I knew—the one that I loved, he would've never just left.

Right?

I'm sick of dreaming of him, of giving him any more power over me than he already had. He doesn't deserve my grief, he didn't deserve my *searching*. My longing.

And Bayne.

Gods, Bayne.

Why did I do that? Why did I kiss him? Because I did. He was right, the smug bastard. *I* made the first move, not him. Sure, he was there, but I'll be kicking myself until I find Peace for that.

It makes me hate him all the more.

How dare he take advantage of me like that? While I'm upset, vulnerable, and above all else—like I'm his?

It felt different in Voltus, like maybe my actions didn't have the inevitable consequences they normally have.

Is that why I did it? Why I kissed him even though I hate him?

Because beneath it all, there's an attraction—no.

I can't even allow myself to think that way because he is a monster. *Isn't he?* Do monsters hold you in the dark? Do they squeeze you tighter, despite being incapable of comfort?

Perhaps it was a moment of weakness on both of our sides. But it won't happen again. It can't.

It's the instant reminder that the princeling still owes me his half of our deal. He's going to let me see Edene today. Whether he wants to or not.

"When does one typically need to collect on the reward of a deal?" I skip all pleasantries as I throw open the doors to the dining room, Jesminda trailing sleepily behind me.

She clearly did not sleep at all last night, either. However, I struggle to feel sympathy for her when she got to remain here with the better cousin.

A quick glance at the table tells me that Bayne isn't even here. I ask Axl where he is, only receiving a shrug in return.

"I would assume he's doing *prince* things," he spits out Bayne's title as he pushes food around his plate with a fork.

When he glances up from his pout, he doesn't even see me for a moment—those blue eyes cut to Jesminda first, then me. His eyes soften with his tone, as if realizing who came in.

"You both look like shit."

Jes scoffs, feigning offense she clearly doesn't have the energy to give. Her scathing look at Axl does nothing to mar her beauty. Even sleep deprived, she looks ethereal.

"Oh, shut up, Axl. Eat your Gods-cursed breakfast," she scolds him.

A smug grin is all that he gives in reply, before turning to me as we join him. "She's normally this cranky when she doesn't sleep." He gives me a conspiratorial wink. "What kept you up?"

Your cousin. Perry.

"Slept like a baby, actually."

He cocks a brow at me, humming his disbelief. "Sure, baby. Let's go with that."

Jesminda groans beside me, cutting a glare to him. "Didn't I tell you to stop calling everyone baby? It's gross."

Axl's grin grows wicked. "Oh, really? Because last I heard—"

Jes kicks him under the table, eliciting a faux protest. "That was rude."

Rolling my eyes, they catch once more on the chandelier above the table. The rubies glisten in the morning sun, refracting little rays of scarlet light.

Funny.

I stand to remove myself from the situation, needing to find Bayne all the more urgently. "I'm going to find the princeling," I announce and both their eyes snap to me. "We have some things to discuss."

Without giving them the chance to protest, I leave the room to the sound of hushed whispers and the burning sensation of their stares on my back.

He's asleep.

His legs are crossed at the ankles, atop an ottoman as he leans back in one of the oversized chairs by the fireplace. I debate starting a fire just to see if he wakes up.

A book sits precariously on his face, efficiently blocking the sun that streams in from his eyes. His hands are laced together across his stomach. The picture of relaxation.

I should stab him.

Marching over to him, I shove his legs off the rest, effectively making him sit up, the book falling off his face into his lap. The face it reveals, however, is unamused.

"I was resting."

"The rubies," I seethe.

He raises his brows, waiting for me to continue.

"The chandelier. In the dining room. They're not *rubies,* are they?"

Come on, say it.

"What do you think they are, darling?" He wears his favorite mask of boredom—unreadable, infuriating with a slight smirk added.

"*Ward stones,*" I spit out, his smile falling. "You absolute bastard. So. What do those do? Hm?" I keep my hands on my hips, tapping my foot as I wait for his inevitable lie.

"Scarlet is for sealing a bond."

The words clatter in my brain, my ears ringing in the silence that follows.

"So that's why you insisted I eat at your table? Why I had to endure all of this," I wave my arms wildly, gesturing around the library, "just because you lied and deceived me?" My anger is reaching a boiling point, asking to spill over.

Bayne crosses his arms, leaning back once more as I tower over him. "I never lied. At one point, you owed me a favor. I was simply sealing the bargain with the crystals."

"You *incredulous, abhorrent—*"

"*I so love it when you talk dirty to me.*" Bayne's voice invades my head, cutting off my insults.

"Get. Out. Of. My. Head."

"You went into mine first," he counters.

"No, I didn't—" I start, but I stop. Because I did. I slipped his insults directly to him, not even realizing I stopped speaking out loud.

"Ah, yes. The dawn of realization, little raven. You always do look so beautiful when you remember that I'm always right."

I scowl at him, pressing my hands over my ears. "Stop that, I can't stand it."

"Can't stand it?"

"I cannot stand *you!*"

He gets up, now towering over me as I fold my arms over my chest, keeping the rage inside.

If only killing him wouldn't kill me. The things I would do.

Bayne closes what little space we have between us, our noses nearly brushing as he whispers, "Then kneel, if you must."

I reel back, the sheer audacity like a slap to the face. Before I can retort, he continues.

"Why did you do it?" he whispers, his voice suddenly twinged with solemn.

"What did I do?"

Honestly, the list could be endless, Edene's voice in my head tells me, and I swallow my growing smile. She always did scold me for my *antics.*

It could be the kiss, it could be avoiding him—praying to Midnight that he would let me out of training today. *Gods, I miss Harrison.*

"Why did you work at the apothecary?"

My face scrunches with confusion.

"Oh—I—um. It was complicated."

Bayne nods, pushing a piece of hair behind my ear that fell in front of my face. The move is gentle, assuring. But he does it often. And I'm no fool to his tricks.

"Define *complicated.*"

"Why? So you can use it against me?" I breathe out the words, lacking conviction.

"Maybe, darling. Maybe I just want to get to know you, that's all."

"You don't need to know me. You only want to use me."

He tilts his head, considering. "Why do you think that?"

"Why would you want to know me?"

He smiles, almost genuine, I feel. If anything about him even could be. *That's a recipe for disaster, foolish girl. Don't go looking for signs of redemption. He even warned you not to.*

"What fool wouldn't want to know you, little raven? You've got such radiant, warming energy, it's hard not to be drawn in." Sarcasm drips from his tone like honey, sickly sweet.

Without thinking, I shove him on his chest. He doesn't even move an inch. In fact, I'm quite certain he got closer.

"You're a prick," I say.

He's silent for a heartbeat, then repeats himself. "Why did you work at the apothecary? I won't ask you again."

I roll my eyes, gnawing on my bottom lip as I try to dig for the memory. "After he left…" I trail off as Bayne's eyes grow impossibly darker, as if his shadows swim within his very irises.

He nods, urging me to continue.

"After he left, I had nowhere else to go. I didn't know anyone else, didn't trust anyone else. So I fled to Burtons. Some foolish part of me hoped maybe he would be there. That I wasn't going crazy."

The words fall out of me without restraint. "But he wasn't. Obviously." My gaze drops, but his hand tilts my chin back, forcing me to look at him once more. "So, then came Edene. She helped me while I was grieving, but she wouldn't allow a freeloader, so I pitched in."

I don't have to tell him how I helped, understanding written in his features. Hunting the Shaded, making poor deals. That's how I ended up here with him, after all.

"So that's why when I ask to see her, it's not a small thing to only know *she's okay*. Edene is my everything."

There's more I want to tell him, more I feel *safe* enough to say, but his damning thumb keeps tracing the edge of my bottom lip—pulling it free from the clutches of my teeth, not realizing I did it again.

"Thank you for telling me," he says, and I nod, though I'm not sure why.

He doesn't pull his hand back, holding the moment captive in time.

"Stop biting your lip, raven," he whispers, and his eyes find my mouth, following the path of his thumb.

I want to say *don't tell me what to do,* but I ask instead, "Why?"

"Because it drives me wild," he breathes, his lips only centimeters from my own. "Because it drives my thoughts to a place you said you didn't want to go."

I step back, shattering the rising heat in the air, coiling around us, within me.

"You can't kiss me again," I tell him.

"Didn't kiss you the first time, darling."

"Well, it was a mistake, and it won't be happening again."

His laugh is as smooth as it is cold, sending a chill down my spine. "If you say so, angel." He picks up his book, sitting back down when Axl and Jesminda come through the door.

Our heads collectively whip toward them, and I thank Midnight above for giving me the pretense of stepping back. Had they entered thirty seconds ago, it would've been a much more embarrassing moment.

One I'm not sure I could explain.

"She's awake," a familiar voice says, but it comes from behind them. The pair of them step aside, letting Franswon through, his lavender hair in disarray.

Bayne shoots a look to me, assessing.

"You wanted to see your friend?"

I give him a nod.

"Let's go visit her."

CHAPTER TWENTY-FIVE

Thank whatever God hasn't forsaken me yet, because I would've wept before even Maveth for this. When I'm transported to a bedroom I've never seen before, Edene is sitting up in the bed, unharmed and watching the sea out the window.

"Ede?" I croak out, my voice cracking with relief. She turns to where the five of us stand at the door, and gives me a weak smile.

Steel to liquid silver, we lock eyes. After everything the last few months, it's difficult to squash the swell of sadness, grief, and exhaustion. Coupled with the weight of the world falling off my shoulders, I'm no match for the burn in my eyes.

"Hi, stranger," she squeaks, her own voice groggy from misuse.

I bolt over to her and throw my arms around her body, squeezing until she makes a whimpering protest.

"Oh, sorry!" I laugh through my tears, her mess of curls are blurry in my watery vision.

"No, it's okay," she croaks out. Edene runs a hand down my back in soothing circles. Just like she used to—just so Edene.

"Arden," Franswon's soothing voice sticks out in the crowd, "we should inform you of something you were not privy to before." I turn to face him, reluctant to take my eyes off Edene, just in case she's not real.

Curiosity has always been my biggest flaw.

"You mean what you did not trust me to know," I say. Partly because it's the truth, but also because they don't deserve my sugarcoating.

Franswon nods, continuing. "Edene here has fought hard," he trails off, looking to Bayne. Surely the crown prince wouldn't forbid me from knowing *now*, right?

"Edene was poisoned," Bayne jumps in, nearly startling me. My mind reels at his words, endlessly spinning, making me nauseous.

"I already guessed that much. But who would poison her? Was this why you wouldn't let me see her?" I stand, closing the distance to him. "Was this why you kept her locked away in this room, like some sort of disease-ridden Shade?"

Bayne's handsome face twists solemnly, not wanting to confirm my fears, my worries, out loud to our audience.

Jesminda breaks the silence first.

"It wasn't just *any* poison. It's Shade poisoning that infected her, Arden. We did whatever we could, but now that she's better, you're able to visit." She gives me a hesitant smile, pity floating in her amber gaze.

My eyes dart between the pair of them. This almost feels like an intervention, and I'm most certainly on the outside.

"Shade poison?" I sound as small as I feel.

Bayne nods, but it's precious Edene who answers.

"Yes, Arden. My body is still fighting it, but I'm doing better."

I survey the room, unsure who to look at. Against my better judgment, my eyes find *him*.

I shouldn't find solace there, shouldn't feel safe. But he's become my constant over the last few months, and despite myself—despite hating him, I don't feel as much anger when I settle into those beautiful, dark eyes. The light I usually find in Edene is trapped in the gold flecks of his irises, that inky black hair like a halo of shadow, bleeding over his forehead to frame his face.

As if I let him into my mind, he sends me a reassurance across our mental bond, like the tether takes a physical hold.

Like he can feel my despondency, my spiraling.

"It's okay, angel. Take a deep breath, center yourself."

I do as he recommended, turning back to Edene as I press my hand to my stomach. As though it can subside the rising anxiousness within me.

"What did it do?" I ask, gingerly sitting next to Edene on the mattress. It's plush, so at least she hasn't been suffering there.

"Nothing too drastic," Fran assures me. "We're still working on the kinks, but Mr. Sardon was gracious enough to find what we needed."

"Franswon, there's no need, she already knows who Bayne is. She's well aware—" Axl starts, but I cut him off.

"Wait, what did you find?" I look up at him expectantly, but his face is unreadable.

"Well, that's why we needed to go to Voltus, raven. For the antidote your friend here used to make. It was the only thing to save her from becoming a Shade."

"That's not how it works," I tell him.

"Arden, what do you mean?" Jes cuts in. "Yes, it is."

"No, Perry—"

Bayne crosses the room over to the bed, effectively stealing my air. Or maybe it's the promise of contrition on his face that gives me pause. "Do not utter that pathetic excuse of a man's name ever again," he seethes, silencing the whole room.

A flush threatens to make its way to my cheeks at his display, his blatant disregard for our audience—the fact that we have one, for starters.

I nod, mouth agape.

Edene laces her fingers with mine, and her once elegant fingers feel bony and cold against my callused ones. "It was the antipurzon, Arden." She gives my hand a gentle squeeze, then before I can stop her, yanks it toward her. "What the fuck is this? Is that a wedding ring?" she shrieks, and my face flushes scarlet, burning with the mortification that I forgot to take it off.

I try to take my hand back, to no avail.

Surprisingly, Bayne comes to my rescue. "I informed her of the necessity that a disguise would bring in the outside world. Seems raven has some sticky claws." He smirks, the corner of his lip curling.

The irony of him saying that to me, in front of Edene, is not lost on me.

"It's gorgeous." The awe in Edene's voice stops me from tugging my hand again.

"Thank—" My words die on my tongue when I notice in my peripherals Axl, Jes, and even Fran staring—no—*gawking* at the ring.

"Am I missing something?" Edene asks.

"The ring," Bayne starts, "belonged to my mother."

CHAPTER TWENTY-SIX

"Why does she have that?" Axl's tone is lethal, one even I wouldn't dare take with the prince.

Bayne puts his hands in his pockets, leaning against the wall by the bed. A physical barrier between Axl and me, I note.

"Because it belongs to me. Because I don't need to explain my actions to you."

"Did she give it to you? Was that why you went—"

Whatever Axl planned to say, I'll never know. Because Bayne orders everyone out. Except me. Well, Edene, too, of course.

Axl wears a promise on his face. A promise to return to this, privately.

Edene shares a look with me, but I can already tell her strength is waning. It's in every flutter of her eyelids, every deep breath she breathes. I would know her tells in every life.

A funny thought occurs to me as the others file out, making me snort to myself. Bayne and Edene look at me perplexed, as though I'm the one on my near-death bed.

"What?" Widening my eyes, I pass them my most innocent look. Edene pinches me.

"Don't act all innocent now," she scolds, yawning behind her hand.

"She's never been innocent." Bayne grins at Edene, his knowing smile reflected by the playful glint in her eyes.

"Oh, absolutely not," she coos. "She is much too reckless to be mistaken as someone with innocence."

"Hey! I could be innocent! I'm *nice*." I give them a halfhearted smile.

Since when am I the one to be picked on here?

Exchanging another look with each other, they both burst out laughing. For a moment, I'm so entranced in watching Bayne laugh that I barely hear Edene's weak cough. Barely see the blood that splatters on her hand before she tries to hide it.

But I see it nonetheless.

"What's happening to you?" I whisper.

She blinks at me a few times, frowning. Her gray eyes look glassier now than they did a moment ago, and she yawns again. I watch Bayne expectantly, but it's not surprising that he doesn't explain.

"We should let you sleep," he tells her, gesturing for me to get up and let her rest.

"I'm fine, Arden, truly." Her smile is weak as sleep threatens to overtake her once more. She lays her head down on her pillow, whispering *I love yous* into the feathers.

Standing, I take the prince's outstretched hand, his shadows wrapping around us, depositing us into the castle gardens. Gardens that I wasn't even aware of. The sudden sunshine is bright, making me squint my eyes, blinking to clear my vision.

"What's wrong with her? I thought she was fine? Wasn't the antipurzon helping?" I wildly search his eyes for answers, but he's unreadable.

"As much as it pains me to admit," he drawls, "I'm not as talented with potions as your apothecary. So I can't say why she's so tired, but know that the poison is mostly worked out of her system. We're trying to do whatever we can, little raven." He tucks my hair behind my ear, but I see it more than feel it this time.

Everything feels numb. Because Edene is *not* okay.

I shove his chest, pushing him away from me.

"You lied to me!" I point an accusatory finger in his face. "You told me she was okay!"

"Actually darling, it was *Axl* who informed you that she was 'alive'. It's no fault of mine that you took that for what it was."

Anger boils my skin, white hot. Over a *technicality*? Why is everything a game to him? My blood feels as though it could melt brick if I wanted. I just might try.

"So not only did you purposely mislead me, but you *also* deigned to forget that we have a deal? One where, in exchange for my help with your little research, *you were to help Edene*. Sound familiar, princeling?"

I rip the ring off my finger, thrusting it back at him. He takes it, never breaking eye contact like a silent game. Except he's the only one playing.

He smiles at me, but it's cruel, wicked, and without any warmth of the last few days. *Or even just mere moments ago.*

"I said explicitly that I would *try*. And I did. I got the potion, I gave it to her, and I tried to wake her numerous times. Did you ask me that?" He steps closer, and the once shining sun dims, bending to his shadows. "No, you didn't. If you could get past your own ego, then maybe you'd stop living in denial."

"Denial?" I scoff at him.

"Yes, darling." The distance between us is gone, his forehead almost touching mine. He bends even lower, his breath coaxing over my ear, making me shiver. "You're in denial that you want me," he whispers.

I shake my head from side to side, closing my eyes. He grips my chin, firmly but gently, holding me in place.

"Yes, you do. And that's okay, little raven. I'll be here waiting when you've decided that royalty is no longer beneath you," he strokes his thumb over my jaw, "but rather, when you decide you want a royal *beneath you*."

I gasp, but when I open my eyes, heart pounding in my throat, I'm alone in the garden. Bayne is gone.

Stranger things have happened than watching Harrison try to fit at the tables in the library, too small for his towering frame, but yet, every last one of them fails to surface as I watch him struggle to get comfortable. Rolling my lips together, I try to stifle my laugh.

"Watch it, Miss Arden. I'll flip this whole table." His hazel eyes dance with mirth, even as his tone does not reflect it.

Giving him a mock salute, I get up to wander the shelves, wondering what book seems to call to me. If the princeling isn't going to hold up his bargain, then neither am I.

I'll be reading for enjoyment, thank you.

Browsing the titles, I keep going back to that same tome Axl brought out my first session. *A History of Vails.*

I pull the massive book off the shelf, ungracefully lobbing it onto the table. The noise makes even Harrison startle. I mutter an apology as I sit down, avoiding his dubious gaze. He picks up a book of colored pictures, not even trying to help.

I hope this has what I need. At least, for the time being.

Flipping through the pages, I skim the information, most of it uninteresting. Something sparks in my chest when I see *Ziineth Royal Family* scrolled across the top of the page. Greedily, my eyes devour the information, but there isn't much to read.

In the War of Souls, it is hereby this general's decree that the royal family of Ziineth has indeed perished.

All remains have been turned to ash, returned to the Gods as all Vails should for final resting.

The bodies marked are two female and two male. Two children and two adults. Devastation to the land cements what we already feared—there are no survivors from the castle.

—*General Elodie Marlowe, service to the Ziineth crown*

Who the—

"Harrison, what do you know about a *General Elodie Marlowe?*"

He looks up from reading, scrunching his brow. "Not much, why?"

"Well, what do you know? And maybe I'll tell you why."

He chuckles, deep and amused. "Okay, well, she served the Ziineth crown, from what I understood."

"So, she doesn't anymore?"

"You can't serve people whose bones are now ash, can you?"

I shrug, unsure how to answer.

"Is that all you know?" I press him, but I'm not sure why I even want to know. *Perhaps it's the not knowing in your own life that demands you learn the fate of strangers.*

"I mean," he rubs the back of his neck, contemplating, "we had a slight...*fling* as you might call it." He blushes, refusing to make eye contact with me. If he would, he'd see just how wide my eyes are.

"Wait, *what!*" I screech, only for him to shush me, mumbling something about being in a library, but I can barely hear past the thundering in my ears, desperate to know more.

"It was a small thing, Miss Arden. Small enough, the others do not know, so let's not tell them, hm?" He nervously meets my gaze, but I reassure him it's safe with me.

If only for the reason that not even the princeling knows. It feels good to have a secret of our own. I smile to myself at the thought.

"Don't do that. That looks fucking evil," Harrison feigns disgust, and it reminds me so much of Edene, I laugh. "Not sure what's funny," he huffs, "but you're secretly creepy. I liked you better when all we did was spar and *gossip.*" He pops the 'p', only making my cackle grow.

I close my book, giving up for the day. "Can we go see her?"

He looks to both sides, making sure the coast is clear. We're the only ones in the room.

"Let's go. In return for your silence," he adds. I mimic locking my lips closed, following him out of the library.

Edene is in and out of consciousness the entire time I visit, not able to converse more than a few sentences before sleep drags her away from me.

This is almost worse than not knowing. Almost.

Part of me can't believe Bayne kept her in the uppermost part of the castle, furthest away from me, but in the same breath—I do. Because it's what he does. What *they* do.

Manipulate.

I trust Harrison, but then again, what has he ever had to hide from me? Brushing the light brown curls off her forehead, I stand from the bed and turn to face him.

"Have you had any more luck searching for my crystal?" My eyes betray my thoughts, cutting back to my drowsy friend. "She'll be quite mad if I don't have it. You know, when she's not surrounded by strangers and can actually talk to me properly."

Every word was mumbled, her eyes remained glassy. It couldn't have been easy, sleeping in a poison-induced sleep for the last few months. She seems to fight it, but the question still remains: who would poison her? It had to have been someone at service day, one of the vendors.

"No, I'm sorry, sprite. I've kept my eyes peeled, but I haven't seen a teal crystal."

Ward stone, you mean.

I give him a rueful smile. Before I can reply, Harrison's eyes grow wide.

"I forgot, I'm supposed to meet his highness for his training. He decided to move the times again." He shifts on his feet, giving me a sly smile as he leans on the doorframe. "Do you see how you're going to end up getting my head on a spike? I've only got a handful of minutes until I'm due, are you okay to get to your room by yourself?"

I nod, trying to keep the surprise and giddiness off my face. He leaves me alone with Edene, and I can no longer hold my grin back.

CHAPTER TWENTY-SEVEN

Edene would tell me that flying down several flights of stairs is not proper for a lady, but I'd have to tell her that sometimes it's certainly necessary. I'm not sure how long I have before Bayne comes looking for me if I don't show up to training on time.

Axl, Axl. Where are you?

I race to the library, but the second my hand wraps around the gilded handle and I tug, disappointment smacks me. Locked.

Okay, Axl loves to eat, right? That's what Jesminda says?

Fuck, I really need to start listening to these people more.

Taking off for the dining room, I throw up an extra prayer to Midnight—or whomever is listening—that I need him to be there.

Sucking wind, my lungs feel like I've swallowed fire, burning me from the inside out. When I finally reach the familiar onyx doors, I push, only to—

Is that...moaning?

Shock riddles my system useless like a bolt of lightning, rooting me in place. Granted, it doesn't keep my ear pressed to the door, but I'll certainly blame it on that if anyone sees me.

I don't hear anything now, besides a small scuffling noise. So I knock.

Opening my mouth to holler for him, Axl slips into the hall, surprised to see me. But the most jarring thing is how *disheveled* he is. His normally crisp, light blue button up is wrinkled to each of the Seven Hells. His face is flushed, hair wild—

Oh, sweet, holy Gods, I'm not thinking about this now. Especially not about Axl. I cannot—*do not* need to know what he was doing in there.

Trying to hold in my physical revulsion, I give him a weak smile.

"Hey, Axl."

"You look like hell, Arden."

I scoff. "You're one to talk. You look like you fought a wild dog." I can't keep my lips sealed as curiosity rears her ugly head in my mind. "What *were* you doing in there, anyway?" I peer my head at the door he's already closed as if I can see through it. "Why was this door locked? It's never locked."

Axl flushes scarlet, his blue eyes looking all the more prominent for it.

"Fixing something." He curves a brow, crossing his arms disapprovingly.

I nod, more than willing to leave it at his flat expression.

"Did you need something? Or are you just snooping around again?" He squints, looking over my shoulder, but his eyes hold no coldness as he teases me.

"I was looking for you, actually."

"Oh!" He wraps an arm around my shoulders, leading me back toward the training gym. "Whatcha need?"

"Well, you promised me we could do some memory work...you know, to help bring back my memories?" I nudge his side, pulling a laugh from him.

"Right," he drawls, "well I don't have time right now, and neither do you. So, let's reconvene, maybe after training, yeah?" He's nodding before I can even confirm. Shoving me gently toward the direction of the training room doors, he winks before giving me a sly *see you later.*

He's so...bizarre.

Shaking my head, I dash back to my room to get ready for training. Wishing now more than ever I had magic to wield. By the time I'm dressed and once more in front of the doors, I'm winded. And my workout hasn't even started.

I don't need Bayne to get suspicious, even though I did nothing wrong.

He'll find something.

Sighing, I swing open the doors, only to discover the room is empty. Afternoon light streams in the far windows, giving off a soft glow. But the equipment? Looks untouched.

The sparring mat? Not a drop of sweat.

Harrison said they would be in here...didn't he?

I rack my head as I stroll further into the room, and the second I see the shadows ripple at my feet, I know I've fucked up.

They wrap around my ankle, sending me careening to the floor. A startled gasp is all I can manage and when my body hits—

Wait, I didn't hit the floor?

Whipping my head side to side, a band of shadow caresses the side of my face. I jerk away, only to realize the same shadows hold me up. Panic starts bubbling up in me, seizing the very blood flowing through me. I forget how to breathe entirely.

"Hello, little raven," his deep timbre echoes in my head, toying with me. Slowly, I'm lowered to the ground, set gently on the hard floor.

"You sure know how to make a girl feel welcome, princeling." I pause, stretching the silence between us like a taut thread. "Where are you?"

"In your head." He snickers.

I roll my eyes, already sick of his taunting games today.

"Where are you, *physically*?" I keep looking around, but the shadows are getting denser, making it appear like it's nighttime.

"Look at you, angel." His voice coils around my mind like a snake. Ever the predator. *"Looking quite delectable in those tight little pants you've put on. Just begging to be unlaced,"* he drawls.

Heat sears my face, embarrassment and desire shamefully coursing through me at his words.

"Stop," I hiss. I take a couple steps forward, but when I trip a little on something, I give up, holding my arms out for any semblance of my surroundings.

"Now, where's the fun in that? I do love watching you squirm for me."

"Nothing I do is for you. And it won't ever be."

His laugh echoes, throwing off my sense of direction. *"Everything you do is because of me, darling. You belong to me."*

I scowl, shaking my head, as if he can see it. Hells, I'm not sure what he can see at this point.

"Oh, yes, you do. And that stubborn look on your face?" He groans, and I wish the sound didn't have my thighs pressing together, but arousal claws its way between them. *"It's like you're just waiting for it to be wiped off with a kiss."*

I shiver, despite my best attempts not to.

"Well that won't happen again," I say, *"it was a mistake. I was upset and vulnerable. You took advantage of me."*

My hands, still outstretched, suddenly hit something solid. As I rub my hands down, it feels hard but there's something soft, like a fabric—

"Did you get a good feel?"

I jolt back in surprise, the shadows dissolving in an instant to bring back the light missing in the room. "What is *wrong* with you? I swear, I've never in either life seen—"

"You rubbed all over me." He feigns a gasp. "You were taking advantage of *me* this time." His lips settle in that ridiculous smirk.

I give him a hard shove, but he doesn't budge. "You're a prick."

"Prince," he corrects. "I know how easy it is for the smallminded to get confused." He winks, walking onto the mat.

"How am I smallminded?"

"Sorry, darling, I didn't realize you woke up this morning and started to care for anything outside your little bubble? Do go on, I'm all ears."

He grins at me, waiting.

"Fuck you."

"Wow, what a mouth on you," he says, something glinting in his eyes, but I can't read it. "I liked it better when you used it for more *fun* activities...like moaning for me."

I don't think, I just move. Sending my fist flying toward his face, he catches it before I make contact. He tilts his head, and that's the only warning I have before he throws me to the floor. I land face down, and within a breath he's on top of me, straddling my legs.

"What a feisty little thing you are today, raven. Are you...*frustrated*? I'm always willing to lend a hand."

I try to push off the floor, but he's always one step ahead, and he pins one hand to my lower back, the other right by my face. Forcing me to physically look at how he can overpower me.

"Don't you know that I always win, darling? I don't know who taught—"

I don't hear the rest of what he's trying to say because I jerk my head forward and bite his hand, hard.

He grunts, flipping me over in the same breath. He moves so fast, his shadows returning as they keep my wrists tied together, under his hand, pinning them above my head. But it's the hand around my throat that I worry about.

He's not applying pressure, not even closing my airway a little. But the threat of it, the possessive control he exudes, tells me he could. He has.

His eyes are blown, dark as the retribution promised within them. I hold his gaze steady, unwilling to back down.

He bends closer, keeping us nose to nose as he loves so much. That's when he whispers, "Don't you know, you shouldn't bite the hand that feeds you?"

"I'll bite it again if you keep putting it near me."

"Oh, darling, I don't mind a biter." He brushes his lips against my ear, and it takes all my willpower just to not melt into the sensation. "But there's more fun places to bite."

CHAPTER TWENTY-EIGHT

I sit at the table, waiting for Perry to finish making our dinner. I keep my dagger in its sheath on my hip, but for now, it's carving into the sad, rotting wood.

I trace a 'p' first, trying to get the curve of the letter just right, but also carefully keeping the pressure from going too deep. I carve an 'a' and a cross in between. When the carving is complete, I trace a heart over the letters, smiling to myself.

Perry hums to himself in the kitchen, and peering over my shoulder to glimpse at him, I smile.

I love him.

I love him. I love him. I love him. Dying was worth everything, as long as I have him. I may not remember my life in Living, but I have never known such true arrant happiness in my past life, of that I'm sure. My heart bursts with the joy I feel just by basking in his presence. Perry is such vivid color, in a world that could've been so black and white.

I smile, content as I get up from my chair to be with him. Be near him. Being more than five feet from him makes me feel like I might combust.

He sees me heading toward him, and his smile grows wide as he beckons me closer. His eyes—my favorite shade of green—dance, reflecting the love I feel in my heart. I take one step in the kitchen when I hear a knock on the door.

We both jerk our heads toward the sound, silencing our home from our domestic buzz.

A small prick at the back of my head says to answer, but I shake it off, smiling at Perry once more. I want to kiss him, let him know how much he means to me.

Another step, another knock. He reaches out his hand, reaching for me. My heart starts to pound.

"You're almost there, doll," Perry's soothing voice whispers. When my own hand stretches out, our fingers almost brushing, the front door shatters, sending splintering wood across the entrance.

I shriek, jerking back into myself. It feels like Perry is slipping through my fingers like sand.

"Perry!" I call out for him. The worry and concern sketching his face mirror my own.

"Arden! Are you okay?"

I call out again to let him know I'm okay, but the words are cut short by a wave of onyx shadow flooding the floor around me.

"Arden, come here, doll! It's the only way you'll be safe."

"He's lying."

I gasp, finding Bayne beside me. He tucks a strand of windblown hair behind my ear, my eyes filling with tears as my chest fills with an ache of sadness.

"What do you mean?" I search his face, only finding his usual stoicism.

"Arden! Please!" Perry's cries are desperate now. He feels so far away. Bayne is so close, so warm, so—

"Don't listen to him, little raven." His hand rests on my cheek, his thumb making very distracting swipes of comfort.

It almost burns.

"Arden, please! I need you!" Perry sounds like he's crying. I try to turn my head, but Bayne won't let me.

"Don't, raven." His voice is sterner now. I wonder if he'll force me not to if I try. I think I'd like it if he did. I always like playing with him.

When I turn, it's not Perry but rather—the demon.

Its black, sickly claws drip with poison, reeking vile liquid all over my beautiful home. I shriek again, only to find solace with Bayne, behind his arm.

He draws a sword, holding it steady between Qin and us. "Arden, get back!" Bayne pushes me back further, but I trip. I forget to scream as I fall...falling down...into pitch black.

Gasping for breath no longer in my lungs, I claw at my throat for air that is not there. I'm falling, I—no.

It was a dream.

It was him. Qin.

He's morphing what few memories I have left of Perry, what little good I remember of him. Before he started sticking his—

Bile rises in my throat. Ripping off the covers, I sprint to the washroom right as my bedroom door swings open. I don't pay it any mind. I don't have the luxury.

As soon as my knees hit the tile flooring, I retch into the toilet, the vomit burning my throat. Someone comes in behind me as I hold onto the toilet for support, tears blurring through even as they remain tightly shut.

It hurts, Gods it hurts.

A hand rubs my back, soothingly, calming me as I finish.

"I know it hurts, raven. You're okay."

Bayne. He's here.

I vomit again for the last time, sitting back on my knees, still hunched over. I feel dizzy, and the room is tilting on an axis I'm unaware of. I just need to rest my eyes. I just need to rest. Laying my head on my arm, I try to slow my breathing. My skin is slick with sweat, disgustingly so. I'm not sure how Bayne can even touch me right now.

Wait.

He's touching me.

My body stiffens, and turning my head, he shuffles into view, crouching on his knees. I hadn't realized he was on the floor with me. Since when does royalty get on the floor?

"Are you going to vomit again? Do you need help standing?" He looks genuine in his concern, and it's a new look for him.

A better look. A dangerous look.

He saved me from the demon, in my dream. Why? He wouldn't even save me from my own—

"Why are you looking at me like that?" His face twists with confusion, tilting his head. His inky hair flops across his forehead, *almost making him look boyish.*

He laughs, a small smirk of relief tugging at his lips. "I'm glad that after thirty years in this castle, a woman still considers me to look like a boy. Exactly what a man likes to hear, raven."

"Fuuuuuuck," I groan, "I didn't mean to say that out loud."

He taps the side of my temple, making me flinch. *Perry used to do that.*

"You didn't have to, remember? You're shoving thoughts my way." He gestures a hand over me as he stands. As if I'm not much more than a spilled drink on the floor waiting to be cleaned. "Well, it's probably due to the state of you, honestly. A one-time pass is all you get."

I groan again, closing my eyes, begging the room to stop spinning. As if the Gods can hear me complain, the room shifts violently, my head now bobbing. Peeking open my eyes, I'm in Bayne's arms. My limbs hang awkwardly over his, but he cradles me close to his chest. Despite my sleeping silks, my sweaty skin, he carries me back to the bed.

"You saved me," I whisper to the backs of my eyelids.

"I saved you?" Bayne questions.

"Yes," I breathe. In my dream, he saved me. Why doesn't he understand?

"What did I save you from, my little raven?"

My.

He said my.

A slip—a minor one. It changes it, changes everything too much.

"Qin. You saved me from Qin." The words fall out as darkness threatens to pull me back under, right as he tucks me into bed once more. I feel something brush my cheek, but when my lashes flutter open once more, I'm all alone.

Chapter Twenty-Nine

The words on the page in front of me are making my eyes cross. Or maybe it's the fact that Bayne is reading in front of me. Except he's not actually reading anything, he's just staring at me like I have two extra heads today.

I'm sick of it, frankly.

"Can I help you, princeling?" I set my book down to glare at him.

He breaks his stare, trying to put on that mask of nonchalance he adores, but it's too late. I already saw him.

"Can't I just stare at my favorite prisoner?"

I roll my eyes, picking my book back up. Already regretting that I even asked.

"I thought I wasn't a prisoner," I mumble.

"You always complain about it, darling, so how was I supposed to read your mind?"

"You invade my head *all the time*," I remind him.

"You push those thoughts to me. I can't help it that you're a lost cause."

Ignoring him, I hold my book up higher to block him from view, but it only makes him chuckle.

"What are you even doing in here? Isn't babysitting beneath you as a royal?" *Royal pain in the ass,* I laugh to myself.

"*Heard that, raven. Do better.*"

I scowl, unimpressed.

It's weird, almost. That I dreamed of him last night, twice, and now he's here, like a guard dog. I thought I woke to throw up, but when I actually woke, there was no evidence. I even had on a different sleep set. The only explanation is that it was a dream.

A very real dream.

So much so, I almost asked him at breakfast, but decided better of it. Why would he save me? Why would he help me? It was just a dream. A very strange, realistic feeling dream.

And Qin—it came again. I should tell him. But as I'm about to, my eyes catch on an interesting passage.

Vails create bonds as powerful as their own lines allow. Do not attempt to bond with other beings, for the risks taken will not yield desirable results for the weaker party. If both beings are not of the Vail, retaining a soulbond is a great error. The weak will be damned, a servant of Maveth the Fearful for the rest of their eternity.

Peace does not come to those who bend Her laws.

Vails...can't bond other souls? What the—

"Did you fuck me over?" I practically screech the accusation, not really wanting to hear his answer, but I need to hear it all the same.

He scrunches his face in consternation, eyes drawn to the ceiling. When they meet mine again, I know I'm about to be met with horseshit.

"Pretty sure I've never fucked you." He smirks, then whispers, "I'd remember."

"*This,* you incorrigible bastard," I seethe while I flip the book toward him.

He reads it, instantly rolling his eyes. Annoyance drips from him as he commends me on *accomplishing nothing.*

"What do you mean *nothing*? I'm researching, like you fucking told me to!"

"Pretty sure I told you to research the Shaded, no?" He glances at my book cover. "That's a book on Vails, angel. If you have questions, you only need to ask. I would've saved you the anger when I tell you we do not *have* a soulbond. It's not possible, since you're just an Arrival."

"You're such a prick, you know that?"

He clicks his tongue in admonishment. "*Prince,* darling." A sneer mars his pretty face.

And that's all he is—a pretty face. He's not the man I dreamt about last night, because the selfish bastard in front of me wouldn't think twice about saving himself first.

I slam my book shut, picking up another on the public records of Second. Less interesting, in my opinion. And I'm certain that there's no information on the Shaded in here, yet these are the books his *highness* picked out.

My eyes immediately gloss over the first few pages, and I swear I might die of boredom.

"This record says there's people who live in Ziineth," I say, cutting the silence. That's not right. Perry told me ages ago that no one lives there anymore, it's a wasteland. "Didn't they all die in the war?"

Bayne ponders it for a moment before speaking. "The royals died, sure. We all could feel it, in the very ground they were laid to rest. But the rest of the people who survived the war, sure, they're out there, living their lives."

He turns a page in his book, frustratingly resembling Jesminda and her own 'reading' tactics.

"But no one lives there anymore."

"What are you talking about?" He sighs like I'm a petulant child. "Of course they do. They think we all perished, hence the veil surrounding the castle, but they certainly still inhabit that providence." He narrows his eyes at me, confusion twisting his features. "Even if they had all been wiped out, when more Arrivals died, they may have ended up there when they crossed over. It's just naïve to think otherwise."

Naïve?!

Standing up, my chair pushes back abruptly. "I think I'm done for the day, actually." I start to collect my stuff into a pile, even though I haven't read much today. *This is precisely why I don't sit in here with him.*

"Second is much bigger than that pitiful corner you call home, darling."

I stop what I'm doing, ready to throw all of my books at him or beat him with them.

"Voltus is the largest providence, Bayne. That's a fact—one that not even you can change, your highness," I sneer at him.

"That's where you're wrong, darling. I *can* change that. But I don't have to. Because Marintha is the largest. Always has been. Always will be." His voice is steady, but a muscle feathers in his jaw, giving away his frustration. "Just because your precious little boyfriend didn't fill you in on the true history of your people wiping us off the map, doesn't mean it was the *right* information."

"Just because a man was my friend, doesn't mean he was my boyfriend."

"Oh, my sincerest apologies, raven. Tell me—did you sleep with him?" He lifts a mocking brow at me, waiting.

I blush furiously at his brash question, my mouth opening and closing like a fish out of water, trying to think of something, *anything*, to not admit it.

"That's what I thought." He smirks at me, fueling my need to rake my nails across that face of his.

"Fuck you."

Bayne doesn't flinch, his face the epitome of boredom. "Come up with something new, darling. That one's a bit tired."

Sparring is quiet today.

Whether it was our fight in the library earlier or something else, we're both distracted.

I wouldn't know between me or Midnight what stick is up his ass today, but mine has something to do with his...lack of clothing.

He showed up for training shirtless today, every glorious swirl of ink on his bronze skin on display.

I'm certainly not gawking. That would be...wrong of me. Probably.

His chest is carved with muscle, like he was born for battle, for fighting. The sweat makes it glisten, truly not helping me keep my distance.

The worst part? He's completely unaffected.

If he lost his shit on me after almost wearing my sleep set to the library that day, I wonder if he'd be as good a fighter if I wore only my restraining band over my—

Oh my Gods, what am I even saying?

I don't want him.

In fact, out of all the bad decisions I've ever made in this life, I think he would be the worst. Kissing him was certainly a mistake. A lapse in judgment that will never happen again.

But every time I feel his skin brush mine, I'm fighting an entirely different battle.

Every swing of his sword is slightly sloppier than usual, and I can barely keep up with my own sword.

I miss my dagger.

When we finally finish for the day, I'm breathing heavily as I lay on the mat, praying for the room to stop spinning. But when he's about to leave, something prickles in the back of my mind, and I sit up and stop him.

"You said," I pant, "that if I have a question, all I need to do is ask."

He nods, and before I think wiser of it, I pat the ground in front of me, beckoning him to sit down.

To my surprise, he does.

"What's that," I gesture over his form, "shadow swirl thing you do? It's interesting. Can you go wherever you want?"

He huffs a laugh, cracking a rare, genuine smile.

Fuck, not helping the ache—NO, ARDEN.

"It's referred to as phantom traveling," he says. "Pretty unique to myself, my lineage. However, no. I can't go wherever I want. Long distance travelling requires me to be at full strength. Otherwise, I'd need a ward stone."

I nod once, not wanting him to change the subject. "So, like you mentioned a few months ago, with the family lines? That magic is unique to your bloodline?"

He nods slowly, then holds out his hand.

"The shadows are simply the doorway." His shadows curl around his arm, his wrist, before spilling onto the floor like liquid. "My mind is the key to that door, keeping a hand on them, telling them where to go."

"And the tattoos, are they a part of that?"

He looks down at his chest, as if he doesn't remember that the ink is even there. His hair flops with the motion, slightly damp with sweat, and I can't help but remember how soft it felt between my fingers as—

What is *wrong* with me today?

We have certainly spent way too much time together.

"They can be for control or protection. In remembrance. For my aunt..." He trails off, letting the silence grow too loud before continuing. "She's slowly losing her memory. She's passing, affected by the same Shade poison as your apothecary, except she's been poisoned for many more years than her. The elixir I took from Burtons, it didn't make any difference." His eyes find the ground, and part of me wishes I could offer a comfort beyond *I'm sorry*, but words always fail me at the most important times.

"I should...go," he says.

I stand to leave first, but he phantom travels before I have a chance. My hand is still outstretched in the space he occupied moments prior, and I almost convince myself that a trace of shadow curls over my palm.

CHAPTER THIRTY

"**F**uck, I'm so late," I mumble to myself.

I completely slept through breakfast, blissfully unaware that everyone in this stupid prison who has been up my ass the last few months suddenly doesn't care if I eat.

But Bayne must've missed breakfast, too, because he didn't come for me, and if the sun that finally woke me through my curtains is any indication—he's waiting for me in the training room.

I can't say I'm upset with my results so far. My reflection in the mirrors show a body that's toned now, my own muscles flexing in different lights.

I feel strong. *Powerful.*

I race down the hall, giving my favorite moon painting a glimpse, like a compulsion.

I really need to ask Jesminda the next—

Rounding the corner of the hall, I almost slam straight into the back of Jes who, very suspiciously, just snuck out of—Axl's bedroom...?

She slowly clicks the door shut, careful not to make a noise, and the sight elicits a grin on my face that's nothing short of evil.

"What are you doing, Jes?"

She nearly jumps out of her skin, a small yelp escaping her. Her face is flushed nearly as deep red as her hair. Fanning herself with her hand, she scolds me, "Arden! Do not do that! Gods, you scared the shit out of me."

She reminds me so much of Edene, that a small pang in my heart tells me to visit her today, since I haven't in a few days. Guilt starts to eat at me until I refocus on Jesminda.

I open my mouth to respond, when I look at her a little closer. She smooths her top, but it looks *off.* It's much lower than normal, as if it was ripped slightly. Her chest is flushed, too, matching her face. Her normally perfectly arranged hair isn't even braided back. And is she...*sweating*?

Closing my mouth, I'm about to shake my head and turn around, wanting absolutely nothing to do with this, when *Axl* files out of the bedroom after her and tramples me.

"Fucking smite me," he mutters as he rights himself. When he sees me, his eyes flare with shock. "Oh, hello, Arden." He gives me a shy smile, trying to regain composure.

"Oh," I say, taking in the sight of him. He matches Jesminda: flushed, sweaty, and his floppy hair is sticking to his forehead.

"OH. Oh Gods, no. No, NO." I wag my finger between them. "I want no part of this! I never saw you!" I slap my hands over my eyes as I storm past them, hoping to rub the burning image of Jes and Axl having sex out of my mind for the rest of my now-damned eternity.

Fading laughter follows me as I hurry down the hall to the training room, putting as much distance between us as possible. I hear a faint slap, then Jesminda whispering, "You were supposed to wait for ten minutes, you imbecile!"

When I reach the door to the training room—my now safe haven—I slip inside as fast as I can, realizing too late the room is dark. Again.

"Harrison? Bayne?" I call out. My nerves are immediately wired, keeping my head on a swivel. I can't see a damned thing. I try to let my eyes adjust but to no avail.

"You're shaking, little raven." Bayne's smooth voice echoes in my mind, and I roll my eyes realizing this is just him and his playful little shadows, trying some sort of *training exercise* again.

"Bayne, stop being annoying and drop the shadows," I demand.

"Perhaps you'll have to find me in them first." His voice is teasing and it almost makes me smile. Playful Bayne is a much more preferable teacher to brooding princeling.

A much more distracting teacher, albeit.

A band of shadow runs across the small of my back. It's almost sensual, causing me to whip around. *"Come on, raven, you can do better than* that.*"*

"Stop speaking into my head. We're alone in here, it's not necessary." I shake my head slightly as if that can knock him out of it.

"If you practiced blocking me out in your mind," he drawls. Another shadow twirls a piece of my hair, sending prickles up my spine. *"Then we wouldn't be having this conversation. And don't ever assume there aren't prying ears. Information is power, and power is control. Do not. Lose. Your control."*

My breath stutters in my lungs as his words wrap around my mind, or what feels like my very soul. I close my eyes to the sensation, allowing myself to embrace it slightly.

"If you think you're going to beat me with your eyes closed, you're worse off than I thought." I feel the shadow drop the piece of hair it held, and I loosen a deep breath.

"Maybe," I jab back, mentally. *"Maybe I'm trying to focus, princeling."*

"Ah, look who came to play today." His tone changes, heating my skin with the promise in it.

Gods damn Axl and Jes for distracting me, dragging my mind to sex instead of focusing on training. I take a few calming breaths, trying to settle my rising heartbeat and the pulse I feel between my thighs. The most *inconvenient* timing.

"Are you even on the same world right now, Raven? You seem...distracted. Deliciously so." He's whispering now, but I'm starting to learn it's because he doesn't want me to gauge the distance between us. Unfortunately for him,

it's also his tell. *"Your thoughts seem to be running in more...pleasurable directions."*

I squeeze my legs together, ignoring his distraction. Another band of shadow brushes against the heated skin of my neck, my traitorous body shivering in response.

I tell myself it's a natural reaction, trying to reassure myself that I'm not attracted to Bayne. He is an *asshole*, a liar, and above all—dangerous.

As the shadow moves its way from the base of my neck toward the sensitive skin behind my ear, I strike.

I whip my hand out across my body, grabbing hold of the shadow, as it turns into a hand. The shadows smothering the room dissipate, and I scowl as the sunlight now streaming in through the windows reveals a grinning Bayne, standing right in front of me, his face inches from my own. I smell the intoxicating scent of balsam and linen, but I choose to ignore how good—or bad—he smells.

I'm *also* choosing to ignore how the slight sheen of sweat on his neck doesn't bother me the way it would on someone else. Despite being sweaty, I still want him pressed against me again. I miss the way we molded together that day in Burtons, and while I know it's a horrible idea, I want to do it again.

I shouldn't, so I won't.

But I want to lick the sweat right off his sculpted body.

"If you wanted to hold my hand, raven, all you had to do was ask."

I scoff as I shove his hand away from my neck, but that doesn't stop the heat from flushing up and into my cheeks.

"So, you found Axl and Jes, I see," he coos, and it's like I've been dumped with a bucket of ice water. I take a step back, putting some much-needed distance between us.

"What? How do you know that?"

He closes the space between us, but not as close this time. He reaches up and taps a finger to the side of my temple.

"Your memories," he says. "At least your recent ones, you push them my way whether you're aware of it or not." He drags his finger down the side of my face lightly, falling to my cheekbone. "You. Have. To. Shield. Raven. Not every Shade can get into your mind, but the ones that can will take advantage of it. And if you don't learn and start mastering it, you'll be finding yourself at their mercy."

His eyes look wholly black as I hold his gaze. The intensity makes my spine tingle, like he thinks I'm someone worth protecting.

Foolish girl, making foolish bargains. Lying to yourself will only break your own heart, Arden.

My voice of reason scolds me alongside Bayne. My training session only just started, but between the two of them, I already feel overwhelmed.

"So you know about them then? Axl and Jes?" I keep holding his gaze, refusing to look away first so I don't lose this game we play. A game, I'll admit, that's all in my head.

But is it though?

Sometimes I swear that he shows that he feels this pull between us the way that I do. But other times, he's still that cold bastard that I made a deal with in that alley.

I think I'm going crazy.

Bayne leans closer, and the sunlight dims once more. *Gods, he's* too *powerful.*

"Do you truly think me that obtuse, little raven? I've got way more important things to worry about than who my cousin is fucking."

The declaration shocks me, but I'm silenced by it. Because he's right. Why would he care about castle gossip anyway?

"I miss Harrison," I grumble, not giving a damn if he can hear me.

"I'm sure he misses you, too," he mocks me. "Now pick up the damn sword and start practicing before I put you on your ass."

"I'm going to marry him, I'm sure of it."

Perry is everything I've ever wanted, so when I tell Edene, I feel my chest deflate at her disapproval.

"And what makes you think that after knowing that boy for four months that he's marriage material? Surely you can meet other men around Voltus, right?" She organizes her cabinets as I swing my feet from where they hang off the workbench.

Visiting Edene while Perry goes to the Laine has become my favorite activity.

He won't let me come with him, though, and while it hurts my feelings, I know why I can't.

It's not safe for women there. Even with my new dagger, I know that it's not worth the risk.

"There are other men," I twirl the blade in my hands, unable to look Edene in the eye, "but there's no one like him."

She sighs, shuffling several small vials filled with violet sand into a basket. "Arden, there are plenty of guys with mediocre dick and pretty faces in the village. Gods bless, I mean, the sex with him cannot possibly be that good!"

My skin heats to a scorching temperature at her brashness, embarrassment and politeness warring for attention within me.

"That's incredibly personal!"

She turns to give me a disapproving once over. "Not really. Because if it was good, you wouldn't be embarrassed to say. And clearly he's not hitting something right, so how can you sit in my home and tell me you're happy to spend the rest of your eternity with..." Her words fail her a moment before she finds them. "With that boring, average man!"

She angrily wipes her hands on her apron, picking up her basket once more. As she does, a forgotten vial falls off the counter, shattering over the floor, sending the purple sand everywhere.

Edene smacks her forehead, her curls bouncing with the reverberation.

"Gods, why, why, why today?" Looking at the ceiling, she shakes her head in exasperation.

"Here, let me help you clean it," I hop off the table, starting to clean up the pieces when one of them nicks me. A small bead of scarlet blooms on my finger, making me wince.

"Oh, be careful!" She kneels beside me, out of the mess, but when she takes my hand to wrap a small bandage on my finger, she pauses.

Well, she's stunned, really.

"Um, are you alright?"

Her gray eyes snap to mine, all the previous lightness gone. "Your blood is red," she says, her voice a harsh whisper.

I look to both sides of the room, wondering why this is surprising.

"Yes...it is. That's normal, Ede," I search her eyes as she just stares at me, like she's never seen me before.

"Why is it red?"

"That's the color of blood. I'm not getting what you—what color should it be?" Panic and dread swirl and press on my chest like an anvil, waiting to crush me at any moment.

But her light comes back.

"Right, it's supposed to be red," she says, wrapping the finger, but I notice a drop dripped onto her white and yellow floral dress. It looks like a dreadful stain on the sunshine fabric, soaking into it with each passing second.

"There, all done," she smiles at me, but I'm not letting this go.

"Wait, what color is your blood?"

Without question, Edene picks up my dagger where I abandoned it on the table, slicing a small cut on her palm.

Red blood, similar to my own, pools instantly at the cut, proving both of us are safe from the poison of the Shaded flooding the alleys of Second.

"I'm not a Shade," I say, feeling the need to defend myself.

Her eyes grow wide, apology written in her beautiful face. "Oh, no! I'm so sorry, forgive me, I didn't mean to offend you, I just—"

"You just wanted to be safe, I know. Fuck," I laugh, "I understand, you don't need to explain."

She nods, giving me a relieved smile that fades almost instantly into admonishment.

"You shouldn't interrupt, you know. It's quite rude."

"Well, fuck me, I wasn't trying to be."

"Don't be so vulgar, either, men don't like that." She wags a finger in my face before grabbing the broom to sweep up the sand, grabbing my attention.

"What is that?" I point to the mess she's still cleaning with my now bandaged finger. Perry is never going to let me come here alone again if I keep hurting myself.

"This is—was—dragon's root. It comes as flakes, and I grind them into a sand, to make that healing elixir I used on you a few months prior. Hard to come by, but also when you do, it's so damned expensive."

"How do you afford it?"

She meets my eyes, mischief and something sly dancing within them.

"Do you want to help me get more?"

Chapter Thirty-One

"W hy. Must. You. Be. So—"

"Handsome? Breathtaking? *Irresistible?*" He laughs as I grit out my words between sword slashes, working out my anger.

Edene is still in and out of consciousness, and every day when she doesn't wake, when her beautiful, brown skin turns another shade paler, it fractures a piece of my already broken heart.

"I was going to say *irritating*, princeling." I swing again, the steel clanging together echoes off the walls, the reverberation shuddering all the way to my clenched teeth.

He pauses for a moment, placing a hand over his heart, feigning hurt. "You wound me, darling."

I use his pause against him, striking while he's not ready, but he deflects my blow easily, effortlessly knocking me off balance.

I stumble, and Bayne wastes no time wrapping his leg over mine, taking me to the floor. As he pins me, I lose my grip on my sword, watching it skip across the mat.

Useless thing.

Bayne's dropped his own blade to keep my hands pinned by my head, and when I turn to look, I try my best to bite him again, but it only makes him release a dark chuckle at my expense.

"Look at you, pinned down." His grin is devilish as he peruses my body, taking his time. I can't help the rush of heat that flushes under my skin, spreading fast like spilled ink. "You look good enough to eat."

I buck my hips, but it's no use. He's too heavy, too strong.

"Get *off* me," I hiss.

"Or what?" He leans in, breathing in my oxygen. "What are you going to do? Attack me with your mouth again? Darling, you'll have to be much better at restraint if we're going to have some fun." He tilts his head at me, then winks.

I wish I didn't feel aroused by him pressed against me like this, holding me down so I can't fight back.

What is wrong with you, Arden? Fight!

I buck again, but he doesn't move an inch.

"Keep doing that," he whispers, "and there will be hell to pay." His breath coaxes the shell of my ear as my breathing accelerates. I should tell him no, I should tell him—

He nips my earlobe, trailing ghosts of featherlight kisses down my racing pulse. My eyes flutter shut at the sensation and before I can stop myself, I moan.

Biting my lip, I try to take it back. But it's too late.

I can tell by the way his body goes rigid that he heard. When he pulls back to look at my face, his hands move to cup my cheeks. Using his thumb, he frees my lip out from between my teeth, and his brown eyes are once again nearly black—as if shadows slowly bleed into his irises.

"What did I tell you about biting your lip, little raven?" All the air in the room seems to dissolve as his shadows leak from him like a black sea.

I don't answer, using my now free hands to shove him off and to the side of me, rolling us over so I now sit astride him.

Pulling out a spare dagger, I hold it to his throat, but he only grins as it ghosts his skin.

"Look who's finally learning," he coos. "Guess she can be taught after all."

I roll my eyes, but halt when I feel his hands grab my hips, keeping me atop him.

Don't think about it, don't think about it, don't think about it.

This is the perfect position to—

"How would you kill me in this position?" he whispers. "I want to know."

I pretend to drag the blade over his neck, my eyes tracing the movement.

"Probably going for the throat," I say.

He rolls his eyes. "That is such a basic—"

"And then I'd stab clean through it, just to make sure all your pretty blue blood decorates the floor just the way I like."

He releases a deep breath, his hands dropping from where they sat on my hips. I climb off him, trying to ignore my racing heart.

It's too much. I need to get out of here.

I toss the dagger back to its stand, my hands shaking from the adrenaline rush.

"Did I say we're done?" he demands, but I ignore him, throwing open the doors. It's not until he appears in front of me, guiding my back to the wall, that I even realize he followed me.

"Did I say that we're done?" he repeats.

"No," I breathe, "but I'm done."

"What, no goodbye kiss?"

His eyes bear into me with intensity as he holds my chin, gently but firm. As if I could look away if I wanted to. His usual scent of balsam and linen mixes with the light sheen of sweat. It's intoxicating, and I hate myself for wanting to breathe it in deeper. Breathe *him* in.

His head lowers ever so slightly, and I mirror his movement. As I do, his hand slides from my face to around the back of my neck, sending goosebumps in its wake. His other hand finds my hip, nearly closing the space between us entirely.

I hate but crave him all at once. The bastard knows it, and there's no playfulness in his eyes tonight.

No, his eyes are full of pure hunger and lust. As much as I might regret it tomorrow in the daylight, I slide my hands up his chest and over his shoulders. He's built so strong, I can't help the heat that coils low in me just at the feel of his firm body.

I shake my head, answering his last question.

A smirk plays across his beautiful mouth, clearly pleased with himself. "Are you happy with your decision, darling?"

"Hmm?" I reply, not really retaining what he's saying. My eyes follow the curve of his lips. His deep, smooth voice holds me captive, and all I can think about is how sweet that mouth tasted on top of mine, and how desperate I am to taste it again.

"Your decision to deny yourself," he whispers, leaning even closer. My mouth parts in anticipation, his breath mingles with my own.

For a second, I don't speak. Because the moment I do? I'm lost.

"Deny myself...?" My question is breathy and full of want.

"Yes, little raven. You deny yourself the pleasure you could have. The pleasure you *crave*. I can feel your heart racing. Right...*here*." His thumb brushes up and down the side of my neck where my pulse beats uncontrollably. "I wonder," he whispers, "are you wet for me, Arden?"

I groan in response, the sound of my name on his lips heightening the rush of his filthy words. I dig my nails into his shoulders as the air thickens. His lips are centimeters away from mine as his other hand still caresses my hip along the waistband of my training pants. I've never been so disappointed that I don't have a skirt on as I am at this moment.

"Use your words, angel. I want to hear you say it. I want the sweetest mouth I've ever tasted to speak the truth for once—to hear it say how much you want me." His own truth mixed in with his command liquifies my restraint.

I shouldn't say it, but my lips part anyway. "I hate you," I whisper. "And I hate how much I want you, despite that."

His following smile is feline and full of heat. "You can tell yourself lies all day, Arden. But I know." His hand finds the laces on my pants and undoes them effortlessly in one sharp tug, pulling a small gasp from me. "Deep down, right where it matters, anyway, your body sings for *me*, like it was fucking *made for me*. Isn't that right?"

Without another word, I pull his face to mine and seal our lips together. He tastes as sinful as I remember, and I moan into his mouth. He uses my permission to move his wandering hand down into my pants and behind my underwear. I never answered his question, but I didn't need to.

"Fuck, Arden," he says against my mouth. "Is all of this for me, angel?" His fingers slide back. Forth. Then again, and again. My breath stutters—I can't answer. He grins against my mouth, knowing the truth.

What a smarting son of a bitch.

I bite his lower lip in answer, eliciting a groan from him. Laughing as I let him go, he darts out his tongue to taste the spot where I split his skin. Bayne tightens his grip on the nape of my neck right as he presses down on my clit. A moan rips out of me, sending my knees buckling, only held up by the pull on my hair.

"Always picking fights you know you won't win." He kisses me again, roughly invading my mouth and robbing me of air. I kiss him back just as fervently, pulling him closer as I wrap my arms even tighter around his shoulders. Throwing my leg over his hip, Bayne uses the advantage to slide one finger inside me, pumping it in and out slowly. He captures each moan with his own mouth, adding a second finger. "Goddess smite me, Arden," he breathes against my lips. "You just might be the thing that actually puts me in the grave once and for all."

I ignore him as I ride his hand, building that high in my core. He crushes his palm against my clit as I buck my hips against him shamelessly in the hallway. Awareness prickles my scalp.

"Oh my Gods, we're in the fucking hallway." I want to care that Jes or Axl or fuck—Harrison—might walk up on us, but I can't seem to find it in me to care about anything through the fog of lust.

"We are *in the hallway."* He smiles lasciviously at me as he speaks into my mind. *"Did you somehow forget between your biting and riding my hand like a bitch in heat that other people live here, too?"*

My stomach clenches at the thought. If I wasn't already sweating from training and my building orgasm, the thought of someone walking up on us in such a compromising position would have my skin dripping with it.

"Seven Hells, Arden. You like that, don't you? You just squeezed my fingers so fucking tight at the thought of being caught, I can barely move them." His breaths mimic my own, but it isn't to make fun of me. Bayne grinds into my

thigh, his cock so hard I can feel the ache through his leathers. The friction only sharpens the pleasure. *"Aren't you quite the surprise, little raven. Who knew an actual animal lived under that thorny exterior? Too bad for your fantasy, though. No one else gets to see this body except me from now on."*

"That's what you think—" Bayne rips his hand out of my pants as he scoops me up over his shoulder, effectively cutting me off as we phantom travel to a bedroom. He unceremoniously throws me on the bed, my body bouncing slightly. I look around to see where we are—my bedroom. I kick my shoes off quickly, so as not to stall for even a moment.

"Oh, I'm sorry, raven," he coons, pulling off his own boots, one at a time. In a blink, Bayne is quickly kneeling on top of me, grabbing the waistband of my pants, moving to rip them down my legs. "Did you want to finish that sentence?" I shake my head, my heart beating fast in my chest. The arrogant grin that follows makes me wish I did. His hands shove my legs apart as he drags them up the length of my bare skin. "So soft, so beautiful," he murmurs, so quietly I almost don't hear.

I sit up and remove my shirt, throwing it to the floor to join my pants. Bayne's gaze heats all over my body as he kneels between my thighs, greedily taking in every inch I've exposed. He grabs the hem of his own shirt, still slightly damp from our workout, and removes it. Any worrying thoughts vanish as I selfishly feel his sweat-slicked skin and rest my hands on his hips. Not having a thought or care in the world, I lean forward and lick his stomach, keeping our eyes locked in the haze. Bayne sucks in a sharp breath, and I grin.

"I've been wanting to do that," I whisper, biting my bottom lip, knowing it drives him crazy. I look back and forth between his eyes, and his beautiful face looks feral with need as he grabs my shoulders and shoves me back down. A surprised gasp falls from my lips, but he quickly covers my body with his.

With one arm braced next to my head, his other reaches down to his pants and pulls out a knife, flashing it before me. Fear tries to flood my system, and Bayne must see it on my face because he laughs at my squirming. He taps the tip of the blade to the binding over my breasts that holds them in place.

"I do hope you're not attached to this, angel." He slides the blade down my body, eliciting goosebumps along the way until he finds my underwear. His grin is nothing short of evil as he slides the knife between my skin and the fabric. "Or these."

In three quick cuts, I'm naked underneath him, and he tosses the knife to the floor with a clatter, joining the rest of our clothes.

Both of us are breathing heavily as he sits up, taking in my naked body for the first time. He palms himself through his pants, never taking his eyes off me, open for him. I swear my chest might cave in if he doesn't touch me soon.

"Do you need some motivation, your highness?"

I draw my hands up my stomach, and his eyes snap to mine. I run them over my breasts, rolling my nipples through my fingers. Sparks shoot all the way to my toes as he watches every movement. I slide one hand down, when he pins it, halting its trail.

"Ah-ah. That's not your orgasm to take. I'm more than well and selfishly motivated." Bayne tosses my hand off my body and catches my mouth in another kiss. His hands skim all over, running up my sides, down my thighs, and back up to grab my breast. He mirrors the movement I made when I touched myself, but he's rougher.

Bayne kisses down my body, leaving a trail of fire and need in his wake. I've never been so turned on. I'm as sure of it as I know the blood in my veins is red. He wastes no time in teasing my body, drawing a nipple into his mouth, flicking his tongue over it as his fingers make their way back between my thighs. My moans turn into sharp breaths as he works his talented hand in and out, deliciously slow. He curls his fingers up inside me, making me yell out.

He lifts his head and there's nothing but visceral hunger in his gaze. "Oh, *Arden,*" he whispers my name like a prayer, laying a featherlight kiss to my sternum. "You'll need to scream like that every time. I want to hear every sound of pleasure I can pull from your perfect body."

I can't speak as he pumps his fingers faster, working in tandem with his mouth now on my other breast, and I can feel the pressure building in my core. *Yes, yes, yes.*

"Come on my face and mark your scent on me for the rest of your afterlife." His voice is velvet as it wraps around my mind.

He moves his mouth down, sucking my clit, and I do as he asked of me. I *scream.* My hands tangle in his inky hair as I ride his face, bucking my hips up to grind against him. His fingers don't stop, working with his tongue to scrape every last tremor from my slackening body.

Bayne finally releases me, slowly stilling his fingers as the aftershocks wear off. His dark laugh caresses me as my breathing tries to level out, and I release his hair. Sitting up, he withdraws gently, and I catch the thick outline of his cock straining against his pants.

"You're wearing too many clothes, Bayne."

His answering grin is sly as ever. "For once, little raven, we agree."

I move to help him pull his pants down, but he's quicker than me, and they're on the floor in an instant as my focus is pulled to his cock as it beckons between us. I wrap my hand around him, pumping slowly and squeezing, watching to gauge his reaction. His breath hitches in a sharp inhale, and I grin like the devil before me. Using my thumb, I run it over the head, spreading his arousal. Leaning forward, I lick it to taste him. It's fucking *magic.* I seal my lips around his head, teasing him with my tongue like he did to me. His groan mixes with my own, but before I can move any further, he grabs my hair and pulls me off.

"Later," he pants, his chest heaving. I nod my reply. He lets go of my hair to shove me back down to the mattress, grabbing my hips to flip me over, and I squeal. He pushes my chest to the mattress, forcing my ass into the air like a present to him.

"Good fucking Gods, Arden. You should see yourself right now. You've never looked more delicious than you do right now, dripping onto your bed, ready for *me."* His hands run down my back as he grabs my ass, leaving kisses behind.

"Shut up and fuck me before I walk out that door," I scold him impatiently. "OW what the fu—"

Bayne bites down, definitely leaving a mark, then slaps my ass in scolding.

He shouldn't secretly know that I love it, but somehow, he does. I hate him as much as I want him to mark me.

"You won't. Not just because I wouldn't fucking let you, but because you need this as much as I do. Scratch that itch, Arden. I'll make damn sure it's deep enough you feel me tomorrow." He lines himself up behind me, and I can feel him barely slide the head in when he stops.

I look over my shoulder, barely breathing. "You can't actually scratch the itch if you don't—"

Bayne seats himself fully inside me, effectively shutting me up. I feel so full my mouth hangs open with the scream stuck in my throat.

Blissfully, he moves, his hands still bruising my hips as he punishes me with each sharp thrust. My cries turn into moans as he finds a rhythm that has me building right back to the edge faster than any other man I've been with. I involuntarily squeeze around him, making him swear. He spanks me again, then I'm jerked up by my hair as he continues to move inside me.

"Fuck!" I can't help but whimper at how much fuller it feels from this angle. Bayne yanks my head back so it's nearly resting on his shoulder, and I can see him in my peripheral.

"If you keep squeezing me like that, angel, you're not going to get to come at all. Understood?" He threatens me, tightening his hold on my hair while all I can manage to do is gasp for oxygen. My inner fighter wants to make it a game, get him to come first, but not at my expense.

"Ye-yes," I breathe.

His answering laugh is as malevolent as it is hot. Using his grip, Bayne tilts my head and licks the side of my face, groaning.

"Look at that. Ravens can be trained to behave after all." He doesn't wait for a reply as he moves his hand from my hair to wrap around my neck and squeezes. Simultaneously, his other hand moves its way back to my core as he finds my clit again. He drives me higher and higher, his own breath becoming more ragged as his thrusts get jerkier, both of us on the edge of oblivion. "Don't forget to scream my name as you fall apart for me, Arden."

"Fuck, *Bayne!*" His whispered words send me over that cliff, and I freefall as I come harder than I ever have in my life. We fall forward and I catch us on my elbows. Bayne removes his hand from my throat to help support his weight now covering my back. His talented fingers keep stroking me, drawing out my pleasure as he grunts, then moans my name as he follows me over the edge. He spasms inside me, his forehead resting against my back as we both breathe hard, coming down from the heavens.

It may be the state of delirium, but I think I feel Bayne lay a kiss to my spine in…reverence? Or is it thanks? I can't be certain and I quickly compartmentalize it away. That road will only lead to getting emotionally involved, and that's not anything I can afford to do. Especially since I hate him ninety percent of the time.

At least I've discovered one redeemable quality.

The man knows how to fuck.

Bayne wraps his arms around my waist, rolling to the side and pulling me with him; his front flush to my back. He's still inside me, but I can't bring myself to care as bone deep exhaustion creeps in. His hand splays across my stomach as the other drags the hair off my face, but my eyes have already started to drift close.

How can someone so dangerous feel so safe?

He tightens his hold as his lips find the shell of my ear. For once, I don't ignore the goosebumps that rise. "I think you might be a witch, little raven. That's the only explanation I can think of."

I want to ask him what he means, but the darkness pulls me under first.

CHAPTER THIRTY-TWO

Dawn lights up my room in hues of purple and pink I've begrudgingly grown accustomed to. My eyes flutter open, and when I go to move, I stop. There's an arm draped over my waist and a body at my back.

Bayne.

Did he spend the night in my bed?

The answer is obvious as he lies next to me. I turn over to face him, relieved to find he eventually pulled out of me before he fell asleep. Prince or not, he looks like Death herself crafted him.

His lips are parted slightly as he breathes deeply. His hair falls over his forehead in messy waves of ink. He looks so entirely peaceful in his slumber that all I can do is lie here and admire him. I study his face, his sharp cheekbones and fluttering eyelashes encapsulating how unfair it is for him to look so devastating.

My eyes drop back to his mouth. The mouth that was *all. Over. Me.* My thighs clench in memory. The way he coaxed the pleasure out of my body like it's an instrument that only he knows how to play. Remembering the delicious feel of his tongue all over me, I try to quell the urge building in me to wake him up and do it all over again.

As if he can feel me staring, a singular eye pops open. "Arden? It's early. *Why* are you watching me—" Bayne bolts upright, frantically searching around. His dark eyes are wild when they meet mine. "Did I sleep here all night?!"

I bite my lip to hold in my laugh at him. "Um, yes?"

"Fuck."

Bayne rips off the covers and scrambles off the bed to pick up his pants, pulling them back on with haste. I sit up to watch him, but can't help the amusement I'm barely holding back. I've never seen him so flustered. He swears under his breath as he steps on something.

"Where is—oh." He bends over again and retrieves his knife, sheathing it at his hip once more. I squeeze my legs together as I remember how he cut off my underwear with quick precision. It shouldn't be arousing, I swear, but it is. He finds his shirt, holding it in his hands—more than likely because walking around shirtless is less obvious than wearing yesterday's clothes. He pats his pants like he's still looking for something when he finds me staring again.

"Are you laughing at me, raven?" His eyes darken with the promise of retribution. If revenge is what I experienced last night, then I will gladly be collateral damage.

Unable to hold it back anymore, I grin. "I wouldn't dream of it, princeling."

His face breaks into a smile matching mine, and that's my only warning before he's over me in an instant, his mouth devouring everything my own has to offer. His kiss isn't quite as punishing as it was last night, and the softness of it has my heart lurching.

Stupid, stupid organ. Knock it off.

His hands move down my body as I melt into him again, taking on his groan as my own, running my hands in his hair to keep his lips sealed to mine. Rolling to the side, his hand finds my ass and a small squeal leaves my lips as he squeezes. It must break the haze we were falling back into, because he gives me one sharp spank as he untangles himself from me again and stands up.

"Someone hates me a little less now, hmm?" I chuck a pillow at the smug look on his face, but he catches it. "Ah, there she is. See you soon." He winks at me as he retreats from my bedroom.

As the door clicks shut, reality starts to sink back in through the silence.

What are you doing, *Arden? What about Perry? Over him that fast, huh?*

Guilt sinks into my stomach, wiping away all the bliss from the last twelve hours. I didn't have a dream about Perry.

I didn't have any nightmares, either.

I don't even bother to pray to Midnight for forgiveness as I drag myself to the shower, knowing I deserve every bit of spite to come my way for letting a beautiful prince distract me with sex.

Breakfast is silent, despite having Jes and Axl as company. If they know what transpired last night, they don't make a comment. Although, they may have indulged themselves again. Maybe that's why none of us speak more than to pass food to each other.

We don't acknowledge Bayne's absence, and I push the fact that it bothers me at all out of my mind. There's no place for it here.

I'm staring at my fruit, pushing it around my plate when Jes excuses herself from the table. Axl and I both jerk up to watch her leave, but my gaze cuts back to him. He can't hide the longing that flashes over his features quickly enough before he sees me staring. He looks like he's been up all night, but not the same way I was. He clears his throat to speak.

"I'm to help you with your research today," he says, his words clipped. "Then more memory work."

Our *memory work* has consisted of Axl telling me to sit in a circle of salt, and *making mental offerings to Midnight so that she may forgive me* or whatever nonsense he spouts for an hour every other day.

I frown at him, annoyed by the blatant fact that Bayne has clearly chosen to avoid me today. "What about Bayne?"

"He's busy." He deadpans.

My eyebrows raise in shock, considering Axl is usually the least strung out of all of us. I can't help the vitriol that spews back at him.

"Well, I'm sorry you have to babysit me today, prick. But feel free to leave me to my devices in the library. It's not like I can burn the place down with a couple of books." I shove back from the table to stand, my chair scraping against the wood floor.

"Arden, I—" His apology is clear in his eyes as he internally struggles with whatever he's trying to say.

"It's fine." I force a smile at him. It's not him I'm really mad at, just like I'm not the one he's torn up about. "I'll meet you in about ten minutes? I just need to grab something first."

Axl gives me a grateful smile and a swift nod, probably relieved that we're moving past whatever *that* was. It's alright with me, because the last thing I want to do is talk about my feelings with the cousin of the man I'm feeling them for.

And not all of them are hate anymore.

CHAPTER THIRTY-THREE

I keep the small black book tucked under my arm, grateful for the distraction of Jes this morning.

Axl told me to keep my memories documented in the book, but so far, it's only my nightmares of Perry right now. I'm not even sure why Axl cares so much. It's not like remembering my life in Living will help me in this one.

In fact, I'm certain it's only been hindering me this whole time.

We march up the stairs as she yammers on about Axl, the ocean, and something about his eyes? I've tuned her out mostly, vibrating with the need to show what I've found to Edene.

If she's awake today.

There's so much to fill her in on—the biggest one being Bayne. Or perhaps the one I know she'll be the most interested in.

I smile to myself as I hear her questions play in my head.

How was it?

How did it happen?

What positions did you try?

Are you going to do it again?

The only issue is, I certainly don't have all the answers for her. Not when I don't even have them for myself. He's complicating my entire—

"Are you even listening to me?"

Two golden eyes narrow at me in accusation, and the blush on my cheeks shows every ounce of guiltiness. I didn't even realize we reached Edene's door.

"Kinda," I lie.

Jesminda sighs, pouting her bottom lip. "You totally weren't. What *were* you thinking about, anyways?"

I want to laugh at her sudden redirection, but I'd rather not give away information for free. "What do you think I was thinking about?"

"Don't answer a question with a question, Arden." She crosses her arms, not budging.

I'm certainly not going to tell her I was thinking about Bayne—who has successfully avoided me all day—when she was confiding in me about Axl.

Okay, Arden, selective truth.

"I'm just thinking about what I'm going to talk to Edene about. She hasn't been awake much since she woke the first time."

Her expression softens, and my guilt instantly skyrockets. *I'm going to the Seven Hells. Why am I even lying?*

"Well, why don't we open the door and check?"

I nod, trying to prevent myself from being an even worse friend to Jes.

Except, we're not really friends, are we?

I grab her wrist before she turns the handle, stopping her.

"Hey, we're friends, right?"

Jes scoffs, pulling her hand back in fake outrage. "How can you even ask that? I thought we were this whole time!"

I smile at her, rolling my eyes. "Such a drama queen. You and Ede would get along for sure." She opens the door, and to both of our surprise, Edene is sitting up in the bed, totally lucid for once.

"Arden!" She smiles, reaching both of her hands out like a small child asking to be picked up. My face mirrors hers, and I rush over to her bedside with Jesminda in tow.

I throw my arms around her, and her embrace is surprisingly strong.

"Damn, Ede, let her breathe."

We pull apart to stare at Jesminda, using the nickname only I ever have. She looks at us with an unspoken question, and I tell her the answer she's looking for.

"It's not exclusively for me, but no one has ever used it. Probably thought I'd cut them or something." I look between the two of them, grinning. "I'm not sure why, though. I'm always a ray of sunshine."

The two women laugh at me in unison, but I don't care. I'm just elated to hear Edene's laugh after thinking for so long that I might not get to again.

I look to Jesminda, hoping she's forgiven our earlier squander. "Do you think we can have a moment alone? Not that I don't love you two bullying me, but I just have some..." I trail off, gesturing to Edene.

"Say no more," she says, tossing her hair over her shoulder. "I'll be out here, talking to myself."

I roll my eyes as Edene giggles at her, and the sound is such a weight off my shoulders that it makes my eyes water. The minute the door shuts, she has her hands cupping my face, her eyes roaming over me looking for harm.

"Why are you crying? Are you hurt?" Her hands smush my cheeks in, muffling my words.

"Well, I will be if you keep twisting my neck like that."

"Oh, sorry," she says, dropping her hands.

I laugh, giving her another hug. "I'm just happy you're awake. You've been in and out so much, I have so much to tell you and—"

"ARDEN FALLON, *is that a hickey*?"

My face heats, but I don't think he marked me at all. Did he?

I swear, I'll kill him.

"Uh, no? Where?" I strain, trying and failing to look at my own neck. That's when Edene taps the space behind my ear where—yes, he probably left evidence of our encounter.

I hide my face in my hands, unable to look her in the eye. Grabbing my wrists, she pries my hands away.

"Arden, I have a question." Her tone is serious, and for a moment I worry that she'll judge me for sleeping with him.

I nod, waiting.

"How was it?" Her smirk is as damning as the all-too-familiar mischief glowing in her gray eyes.

Rolling my eyes as I fight a grin, I whisper, "Really, really good."

Edene squeals, throwing herself back on the array of pillows. "I'm so happy for you! Tell me *everything*!"

I shrug. "I mean, what's there to tell? It was just sex. There's no need to blow it into something it isn't."

Her brows draw together in a frown. "You don't sleep with just anyone. How could this possibly be *just sex* for you? Do you not like him?" She gasps hard, a hand flying over her mouth. "Did he force himself—"

"Oh Gods, Edene, no!" I smack her leg lightly.

"I had to ask." She shrugs at me. "So, then what is it?"

What is it. What a hell of a question.

Because what *isn't* it?

"It's complicated." I grimace.

"I hate that answer. Actually, no. I don't accept that answer." She points at the door. "That man had his *mother's ring* on your finger, and you're going to sit here and tell me that the two of you fucking means nothing?"

My mouth opens, then shuts again.

"I liked it better when you were in a coma."

She smiles, knowing she has me backed into a corner. Because she's right. Technically, Bayne did put that ring on my finger, but it was for show, for an excuse. So why does that feel like such a stretch?

Because two days ago, you hated him.

"I'm going to hold your hand while I tell you this, because I know you'll freak out." She takes a deep breath, and I follow suit, readying myself. "He's visited me every day."

"Wait, what? Who, *Bayne*?"

She nods. "Yeah, he has. He talks about you a lot, too, you know." She squeezes my fingers. "Granted, not all of them are good things, but—"

"Hold on, did the two of you talk shit about me?"

Edene frowns again. "Arden, it's so rude to interrupt." I roll my eyes as she continues. "As I was saying, yes, he didn't always say nice things about you, but I don't think he knew that I could hear him. I was comatose, not actually asleep."

"Men."

"Men," she agrees. "But one day he did mention that you bit his hand, and I wish more than anything I could've borne witness to that, because being trapped alone in my own head was horrible. And that was a spot of light, regardless of whether or not it was meant to be."

A smile spreads across my face at the memory, but it quickly morphs into a frown.

"But why did he talk to you? Why would he vent to a comatose patient when he could talk to his own friends?"

"Maybe he wanted to talk to someone who couldn't answer. I don't know, truly. But I don't plan on asking." Her smile turns devious. "I like that I have this over him, and he won't know what I've heard versus what I didn't. Perfect blackmail."

I laugh, and it's easy. Falling back into rhythm with her, just like we used to. But I have to shatter it.

"Edene, I have my own question."

Her eyes are bright and attentive, palpable worry written in her stormy irises.

"Did you know about those crystals you hold? The ones you store in your mattress?" Her face drains of color, but she breathes out a quiet confirmation.

"Did you know they're ward stones? Bayne and I, we found them and he explained how dangerous they are. I'm not mad, I just—I just wanted to know if you knew."

I search her eyes for any indication of...secrecy? Calculation? I'm not sure anymore, but her silence says more than she ever could. *She knew.*

"I know that they used to be ward stones," she starts, "but the magic is long gone. The Shaded made sure of that during the war last year. Drained about every damn one."

My eyes widen at her profanity, but I let her continue. "I should've told you, but I thought they were powerless, I swear."

I shake my head, "No. Bayne said he could feel the power in them, like a vibration or a hum. I felt it, too, in some more than others."

"I didn't know, I'm sorry." She gives me a placating smile, and I force one in return.

I don't know when she started lying to me, or when I started to be able to tell the difference, but it feels like a sword to the heart either way.

Since when is Edene someone I struggle to trust?

Since everyone after has given you reason to doubt.

I'm not sure I know anyone in this castle.

CHAPTER THIRTY-FOUR

When we finally part her room, it's all forced smiles, and *see you laters* so she can rest again. But I fear that I won't rest well for a while. My head is spinning so hard it might just split in half.

"Are you okay?" Jesminda puts a hand on my arm, whispering so Edene can't hear through the door.

What do I even tell her? Yes? No?

Why is Edene lying to me, and for how long?

"Can I trust you to keep it quiet?" She nods, gesturing for us to head downstairs. "Edene just lied to me," I whisper.

"About what?"

"She claims she didn't know about the ward stones having magic in them. But she *did*."

"Well, how do you know?"

"She didn't pull on her curls. She always does it when she apologizes. And it just dawned on me that she doesn't do it when she's crafting a lie. It sounds crazy, I know, but I know Edene. She was lying to me."

Jes seems to contemplate this for a moment.

"So if she was, what then? Maybe she's trying to protect you or something."

I shake my head. "No, Jes. She had a black one, with hexes on it." Her sharp answering gasp is the only confirmation I get as we keep walking in silence.

It isn't until we reach the training room that she offers me an apologetic smile. "I'm not really sure how to help you. If you say she lied, then I believe you. And if you need a friend, I'll be enjoying the sea breeze. But maybe she has her reasons. Just give her time to come clean."

I tell her thank you as she walks away, but not before giving her a hug. I'm grateful for her constant support, even though guilt eats away at me, thinking of how I could've been nicer in the beginning. My stomach twists as I remember how I pushed her away when she only wanted me as a friend.

When did it all get so complicated? When did Marintha start to feel like home?

I open the training room door to find it's totally empty.

"It's not surprising anymore," I call out to the room. "There's only so many times you can pull this, you know."

No answer.

"Bayne?"

Where is he?

I try to garner my senses, to feel him nearby as I've grown familiar with. I check every corner of my mind, but there's nothing except a void. The pang in my heart at that realization is as disturbing as it is daunting.

I don't care. *Why would I care?* If he thought—

The familiar prickle dances over my skin, informing me he's here. Spinning around, I catch the last of his shadows slipping away to reveal a smug ass grin.

"Miss me?"

"Hardly," I scoff.

"That's not what you said when you were screaming my name last night, raven."

"Are we here to train, or are you here to flirt?"

He walks past me to the swords, throwing over his shoulder, "I'm always here to flirt with you. I thought that was obvious."

Picking up my favorite daggers, I point one in his direction as he takes position. "Don't act like you care about me now, princeling."

Sheathing his sword, he closes the distance between us, slowly, methodically. Reaching behind him, he pulls out my dagger—*the one Perry gave me*—holding it between us.

An offering.

I stare at him wordlessly.

"I can have it back?" My eyes widen, disbelief coursing through me.

He shrugs. "Only if it's not going to wind up in my back." He pauses, flexing his fingers over the handle before relaxing them again. "Understand, however, that it's not yours, regardless of how it came into your possession."

His eyes are cold, a muscle feathering in his jaw as he speaks. When I nod, he places it into my outstretched palm. It's gentle and charged, but something has shifted between us.

I'm not sure if it's the sex, or if having it back means I'm one step closer to...to what, exactly? Having my old life back of scrounging every penny? It's not like I need to look for Perry anymore.

"Thank you," I whisper.

Maybe I could be happy here. At least, until Edene is better.

"I can see your mind racing, little raven, what's going—"

He stops suddenly, his head whipping around.

"We need to go."

"Wait, what? Right now?"

I tug on Bayne's sleeve as he tries to storm past me, but he rips his arm out of my hold.

Prick.

Just like that, the moment we shared is shattered.

I knew I should've never slept with him, because in glimpses like these, he couldn't be further away. And I don't know where we stand most of the time.

Do we hate each other?

It used to be so clear, but it's as if I'm swimming in muddy waters now.

Do I even care if we do?

Everything is so complicated, and yet so simple.

"Because it's urgent, raven," he hisses between his teeth. He continues down the hallway, rushing...somewhere? That's the most aggravating part—he still doesn't trust me.

I stay on his heels, not letting him get out of this so easily. "Well, you can't just bark orders at that we're leaving, and then not tell me anything!"

A sudden wail from the end of the hall has us both frozen for a heartbeat. One glance at each other is all it takes before we take off running. Thank the Gods that I've been training every day, otherwise I'm not sure I could keep up.

Skirting around the corner, we come across Jesminda and Harrison standing in the hall, their heads bowed. They look up when they see us, both of them with tears in their eyes. Haunted expressions lie on their features, heavy with the shadows only grief can give.

"She's...she's gone, Bayne." She reaches out a hand hesitantly, but the moment she grazes his sleeve, he jerks out of her range, plowing into the room. Peering in after him, I see an older woman lying still in the expansive bed. Her skin is a sickly purple-gray, and her short hair is white. Axl kneels at the bedside, head in his hands. Bayne approaches his cousin, offering a single hand on his shoulder. He bows his head, too, but it's what he does next that surprises me most.

He kneels beside Axl, wrapping an arm around him, drawing him into a hug. Axl turns and silently cries into his cousin's shoulder.

It's his aunt.

I don't know the woman in the bed, don't know when or why I started to cry for her, but I am. I bow my head like the others, unsure of how to act in this kind of situation. I only raise it when I feel something rub at the small of my back.

Jesminda.

She gives me a weak, watery smile as she approaches the men silently, waiting. As if he senses her, Axl reaches for Jes. She slides her hand into his, and the moment he looks upon her face, fresh tears flow.

I need to leave. This feels too intimate, personal.

Would anyone care if I died—other than Edene?

Probably not.

But when I turn and my watery eyes meet Harrison's, I can't help but give him a hug. It's brief, but the tightness behind it lets me know what he cannot say aloud.

That he needed it.

"Where did you go? Are you...are you alright?" Bayne's voice rings in my head.

"I'm fine," I tell him. Because I am. I just need space. I can't ignore the fact that even though he's hurting, he's still making sure I'm okay. Why? Because I left?

Everything is scrambled in my mind, my heart. It feels like I'm trying to paint a picture in the dark, but all the colors look exactly the same.

"You still need to be ready. We're heading for Scarlentta." A beat, then he continues, *"We need to scatter the ashes where she was born. Out of respect."*

I whisper back an agreement in my mind, as if I know anything about letting a Vail pass on. Besides what I've read, anyways.

I want Edene, but unlike the prince, we don't have a mental link. I have so many questions for her, and I wish she would just wake up.

What does she know about the ward stones? Why is she lying to me?

Once I enter my bedroom, collapsing on the bed, I rub my temples. Everything hurts as my head pounds within my skull. When did everything I know get turned upside down?

I'm so entranced by my thoughts that I don't even see him enter the room.

"Take your time, little raven." His voice is soft now, softer than I've ever heard it.

I nod, sitting up but unable to look at him. At that face that's slowly corrupting me.

"We'll leave at dawn tomorrow. I just came to let you know."

But when I finally do give into temptation and turn, all I see are the remnants of his phantom traveling. His lingering shadows whispering a kiss goodbye on the air.

CHAPTER THIRTY-FIVE

We have to use orange ward stones for Scarlentta.

It's too far for Bayne to take all four of us, and the strain on his magic would be painful.

I'm not sure why it comes as a surprise to me, but as fate would have it, the region isn't all sand. I suppose I just assumed it would be, and while that was naïve, I blame it on the fact that I never got to travel with Perry like we talked about. Like we planned.

I wonder if Bayne would ever take me.

I frown at myself, disappointed in my thoughts. He's grieving, and I'm planning for...what? A future he's already promised me we don't have?

So when we're left standing on a cliffside similar to Marintha, I'm surprised to say the least.

Reading my thoughts, Bayne speaks in my head. *"East cliff of Archendia. Few miles from the closest village, where she grew up."* A long silence follows, as if even his thoughts are holding their breath. *"My mother, too,"* he adds.

I turn to him, nodding. Our hands are still intertwined from traveling, and I move to let go.

Only, he holds steady. And I let him.

Dawn is breaking over the cliffside, pinks and blues swirling into each other as they dance in the sky. Water crashes against the rock below, the only sound among us. The dry air is stark compared to the serenity surrounding us. As if nature knows it lost another soul.

Axl takes the crystalline container, tears strolling silently down his face. He's quiet, his hands shaking as he takes the lid off, giving it to Jesminda. She takes it, her tears mirroring his own. His soft whimper is all it takes for her to pull him to her, holding him tight as they both cry.

The sight of her rubbing his back as he sobs into her shatters my already splintering heart.

It isn't until I feel a gentle squeeze on my fingers that I realize I've started to cry again, too. None of it, and yet all of it, is too much for me all at once. I squeeze back, trying to give Bayne a fraction of the strength he's giving me.

When I meet his eyes, they're glassy, though he doesn't cry.

"Are you okay?" I ask.

He nods, turning slowly to watch Axl and Jes again, but I keep my eyes on him. He must be in such inner turmoil, suffering this immense grief and yet, he refuses to let it show. Is it an authority thing? Should the royalty of Second not *feel* as the rest of us? How can they be expected to live their lives as martyrs, knowing to let no one glean an actual emotion?

How incredibly lonely.

Without thinking, I step into him, wrapping my free hand around his arm. As I lay my head on his shoulder, he flinches, and though the reaction stings a little, he then melts into me ever so slightly, and it's enough.

To know that I've given him a semblance of comfort when he feels he cannot show it.

It's enough.

We remain like this, the four of us, until the sun crests in the sky, telling us it's time to go home. Axl and Jes take out an orange ward stone as they walk hand in hand. The transporting stone wastes no time in turning them into a citrus mist on the wind, taking them back home.

Lifting my head off Bayne's shoulder, I look at him. "Are you ready to go?" I ask, not wanting to rush him.

"Not yet." He unwinds himself from me to sit on the edge of the cliff. When I move to sit next to him, he stops me in my tracks, surprising me. "Just leave, Arden." He sounds broken, a shell of the prince who holds the weight of Marintha.

"Excuse me?"

His jaw clenches as he grits out, "I said, *go*. What do you not understand?" His dark eyes are unfeeling, chilling the once dry air.

"No."

He stands then, towering over me as he takes up my space, stealing my oxygen. "Get out of here," he shoves another stone into my hand, forcing my fingers to close around it. "I don't want you here. I want you to fucking leave me alone. Crawl back to whatever trash pile you came from."

A single tear falls down my cheek uncontrollably, as his words sting like papercuts on my heart. But he's not winning this time.

Stepping back, I hurl the stone into the ocean, waiting for the splash before I watch true horror flit over his face, only to immediately be replaced with visceral rage.

"Seven Hells, raven! Why would you do that?"

I shove a finger against his chest, making myself as tall as possible. "I get that you're grieving, I do. But you don't get to shove me away right now. You want to be alone? Fine. But I'm giving you ten minutes, and then I'm coming right back here, and you're going to phantom travel us back." I jab my nail again, harder this time. "I know you're mad at the Gods and not me, so I'll let this slide one time. Then I'm hauling your royal ass back to Marintha, whether or not you want to. You don't get to choose when to stop caring."

He stares at me wide-eyed, stunned silent by my outburst. More tears start to flow now as I clench my fists. Storming away down the hill, I leave him to his pity party of one.

I refuse to let another man manipulate me the way Perry had. He wants to lash out? Fine. Not tolerating it anymore.

I take deep, steadying breaths, trying to slow my pounding heart. Wiping the tears furiously off my face, I find the edge of sand where it meets the water, lapping up to kiss the rock and simultaneously pulling sand back under each time, only to replenish and repeat.

I drag my thoughts away from the complication that is Bayne, focusing instead on Jesminda and Axl. He never did need my advice, but despite the poor timing, I'm glad they've settled whatever it was. They deserve to be happy. Someone at least should be in a healthy—

"Raven—they're—run—"

"Bayne?" I call back, glancing up the hill as my heart sinks into my feet. No answer.

I'm sprinting up the hill now, my legs burning with each stride.

"Bayne!" Calling out again, I can't see anything at the top as smoke and shadow blend in a brewing storm. Panic tries to seize me with each ragged breath as I push myself harder. Desperation seeps into my bones like poison, and I can't breathe. I shove it all down as hard as I can.

I need to see him, I need to—

I stop dead in my tracks, pulled to my knees as terror slices me in two.

Bayne is gone.

The only thing remaining is his sword, shoved into the ground, surrounded by a puddle of familiar, cobalt blue blood.

A single piece of parchment lays in the puddle—an invitation.

If you want us, Nightkiller, come and find your prize.

He won't last long. See you soon.

CHAPTER THIRTY-SIX

He's gone.

Nightkiller? I—

I'm wasting time. Jumping to my feet, I rip his sword out of the ground, dragging it through his blood pooled beneath. I reach out with my mind only to find a solid wall of granite.

Except it's all wrong. It's suppressing something that's trying to break through.

The Shaded. It has to be.

They couldn't have gone far, especially with someone as big as Bayne. He would've put up a fight, he—

He *did* put up a fight. He still is.

Fuck, fuck, fuck—I have to find him.

I look both ways, frantically running my eyes over anything that could be a clue. The wind whips at my hair as I turn, trying to block my vision.

I don't know anything about this region. Hells, I thought it was entirely sand four hours ago.

I shake my hands as I pace back and forth, trying to calm my nerves as they spark out of control.

Placing a hand on my chest, I force myself to stop and breathe deeply, slowing my heart rate. *Calm yourself, Arden. You can find him, just focus.*

Stuffing the note in my pocket, I look over the edge as if the water will have the answer. Gods, smite me, I'm so fucked.

The crown prince is going to die because of me.

I shake my head. No.

I refuse to let it end that way, out of spiraling fear.

That's when I see something poking out where the water meets the rock. *Sand.*

There must be something there. Land, a cavern, I'm not sure, but I have to check. If it's dark and nearby, they can phantom travel just as well as Bayne. I saw it that day when he plucked me out of the alley.

Pain, excruciating and white hot, has me keeling over, grabbing my stomach on a sharp scream that rips from my throat. *I've been stabbed. I won't even make it off this cliff, won't*—pulling away my hand to see the damage, it comes back clean.

What the—

It's Bayne's pain. *He's been stabbed.*

Stumbling down the hill, almost tripping twice, I send a quick prayer to Midnight, promising that if I find him, I'll be a better devotee.

When I reach the beach once more, I keep close to the edge of rock, hoping to find...*something.*

But the sand stops. Not nearly close enough where I can see around the bend. Disappointment tries to slap at me, but I shake it off.

Focus.

Bayne's sword is heavy, weighing me down. I can't justify ditching it, not when I'll probably need it.

Setting it down to use my own dagger, I cut a piece of my shirt off to make a strap. I wrap the fabric around the sword once, then pull it flush to my back. Tying it over my chest, I fasten it into a knot that I hope stays put.

The waves don't seem that deep here, especially if there's sand close by, but I can't risk it. Taking one step into the water, I plunge into the deep end, shock muffling my scream. I sink quickly—even faster with the added weight of the sword.

Struggling against the current and my burning lungs, I swim for the surface with everything I have. Desperation propels me forward, even as I feel another slicing pain in my abdomen, reminding me of what will happen if I don't hurry.

Sputtering water as I break the surface, I wheeze as I attempt to tread, then swim through what must be liquid snow. The chill is already starting to seep into my bones, chattering my teeth as I shiver.

Keep going.

Rounding the bend of rock, I nearly sob at the strip of sand, providing a narrow island and—*thank you, Midnight*—a cave.

I swim even harder, pushing myself to my limit when I finally hit sand once more. Pulling my body up over the sandy edge proves more difficult with frozen fingers, but I manage to flop my soaking, shivering form to dry land. I only take a small moment to compose myself before I'm rolling over and clambering back to my feet.

Stumbling toward the entrance, I feel a sharp cut across my back, making it arch away, as if it can dull the ache.

Though he cannot hear me, I reach out anyway. *"I'm coming, princeling. Try not to die before I get there."*

The second I cross the threshold, a chill colder than the water skirts over my skin—death.

I can feel their suppressant magic from here, which is as dreadful as it is a relief. They're all dead when I find them.

Every last one will feel his pain tenfold, praying to Maveth for mercy I will not show.

Once I'm in the dimly lit cavern, I notice that it has several reverberant tunnels on both sides, all leading in different directions.

Great.

I hasten my steps, calling out for Bayne with my mind, our bond. Entering the first tunnel, it leads me around, depositing me right back to the entrance once more.

Frustration grows as I keep trying tunnel after tunnel, only to find dead ends and looping circles. I know he's here, despite the maze. I can feel that familiar prickle on my scalp—I would know it in every life after this one.

I pause, centering myself.

Where is the—*got it.*

Following the tug to his presence, I trek down one of the further tunnels slowly, pressing against the rock to stay hidden. I walk forward for what feels like ages, the tunnel getting darker with each step—telling me this is the right way.

When light spills in once more, that's when I see him. My hand flies over my mouth to stop my gasp, but it can't stop it from shaking with horror at the sight.

Bayne is shirtless, chained to the wall like some kind of wild animal. His head is bowed, his hair obscuring his face, but not the blue blood that drips off the tip of his nose. Splashing on the floor like liquid starlight.

There's a blade lodged in his lower abdomen, staunching the wound. Hardly. Long cuts decorate his chest, illuminating his blood even brighter against his tattoos.

My heart twists, only to be replaced the next beat by something more useful. Rage.

I hear their voices first.

"How much longer do we keep at it?"

A beat of silence. "Until she shows, I guess."

"We should kill him now, be done with it. It's been hours."

Hours?

"Risk the wrath? No, the plan stays."

I lean closer, peering in as best as I can. I catch sight of one...two—no, three of them, all men.

All wearing that ridiculous head to toe garb, concealing their faces. Like it matters. They're all going to bleed the same filth on this rock. I guarantee it.

For Bayne.

For me.

Untying his sword at my back, I flex my wrists, testing the swing, silently thanking Harrison for picking up swords that day.

When the group approaches his limp body, I move.

CHAPTER THIRTY-SEVEN

Swinging the sword at a brutal angle, I bring it down on the first man's neck, effectively decapitating him in one fell swoop.

The putrid smell hits me before the blood spray does, but I don't let it stop me as I leap over the falling body to ram my blade through the next. Wide, surprised eyes meet mine, and the sight is so lovely I can't hold back my grin.

"Sorry, am I interrupting?" I tilt my head as I kick the dead Shade off the blade, watching him crumple to the ground.

A low groan from Bayne draws my attention, and the lapse in focus is all it takes as I feel my skin melt.

Fucking Infernos.

Yelling in pain as I grasp my now-charred forearm, I drop the sword in reflex. The last Shade approaches slowly, flames flicking up his hands, ready to throw another ball of fire.

"*Bitch,*" he spits at me. "I can't for the death of me imagine why they need you, but he never said I had to bring you in one piece. Only breathing."

I take a step back, keeping myself between Bayne and the assailant.

"Who wants me?" I try my luck, stalling. "Why do they want me?"

He scoffs like he's conversing with a child. "Get out of the way, girl. Before I make your death as accidental as his."

Fear tries to flicker back to life in my chest, but I douse it quickly. There's no room for fear here. No time.

Silently, slowly, I reach my uninjured arm to the backside of my hip while I try to keep him talking.

"Please," I plead with fake begging. "Please don't kill him. I—I need him. If you tell me who wants me, I—I'll help you kill him, I swear it."

The demon-blooded scum prowls closer, forcing me to match his steps backward.

"If you think that impotent, puny human shit works on me, you're mistaken," he hisses. "I can just take you now." He pauses, considering. "He'll be taken by the poison soon enough."

Dread claws up into my throat, and I have to swallow my bile.

"He—he's got the Shade poison?" I stare wide-eyed, right as my hand clasps what I'm looking for. *Gotcha.*

The man-husk laughs, cold and empty. "That is not *Shade poison*, little girl. It belongs to Qin, our master."

I don't hesitate as he takes one more step, finally within range. Swinging my leg out, I kick him in the balls swiftly, bringing him to his knees. Flames erupt outwardly, singing my skin, but I funnel the pain out of my brain.

I drive my precious dagger through his throat, ripping it up his esophagus as I twist it, making him feel every slice of the blade.

"Tell Maveth I said hi when you meet her again."

Yanking it back out, black blood spills from the gaping hole in his neck. It pools across the floor toward my boots, and I'm entranced by how satisfying it feels to be the one to end them.

A wet cough bounces off the wall, snapping me out of it. "Bayne, oh my Gods." Panic seizes me once more as I hold his face in my hands, tilting it up to meet mine.

He smiles weakly, despite being still chained. "You were just *waiting* to tie me up, huh?"

Rolling my eyes on a scoff, I let his head loll back against his chest. His groans of pain echo, only making me work faster. Analyzing the chains closer, they emit a horrid energy that makes my head throb. As if even my blood knows something is *off* about them.

"They dampen. My power. The chains," he muffles.

Gods, how painful.

"Hold on," I say, picking up the sword once more. Bayne picks up his head, and for the first time, he looks worried.

"Listen, raven, we can talk about this—"

I swing with all my waning strength I have left, and I cut the rusted iron pinning the cuffs. As his knees hit the floor, he catches himself to stop his body from falling on the knife.

"Oops," I mock him.

He cuts me a glare, sitting up as he pries the restraints open. But true terror starts to slip in as I reach for him, remembering the poison.

"We need to go," I say hurriedly. I cut another strip of fabric, trying to staunch any of his wounds. The cut on his forehead isn't as bad as it first gleaned, but the knife still lodged in his stomach is not promising.

His eyes flutter, most likely from extreme blood loss. Tapping his face, I tell him, "Stay with me, stay awake."

"I'm...tired, raven...my little raven." His eyes close once more, making me scream in frustration.

"Bayne! Phantom us out, *now*. Then you can rest." Pulling his sweat and blood-slick body against mine, he wraps an arm over my shoulders.

Shadows envelope us as he opens his eyes just enough to meet mine. "You reek, raven. But you're still radiant regardless."

When the darkness fully holds us, he intakes a sharp breath, squeezing the life out of my shoulder. As they dissipate and light leaks back in, it reveals us in the middle of a forest.

The smell of smoke and pine hits my nose like a sore memory, dragging me back to every hunting lesson with Perry.

Archendia.

"Bayne, this is not where we—"

Turning to face him, I scream in horror.

Anxiety ricochets up my spine as I hopelessly watch blood spill over his fingers. Traveling by his shadows has ripped out the knife keeping him alive.

Where it once was is now a gaping hole. Blood drips steadily on the forest floor. His eyes meet mine, full of shock, pain, and most abhorrent of all—defeat.

They roll into the back of his head as he slumps in my arms, falling lifelessly to the ground.

CHAPTER THIRTY-EIGHT

His deadweight tackles both of us to the ground, landing sharply on twigs and what I can only hope is mud.

"Bayne, wake up right now!" I hiss at him, shaking his shoulder.

His blood trickles from the wound now, slowing down after losing so much.

"Bayne! Wake up!" Tears prickle my eyes, threatening to spill over.

No, no, no.

My heart is beating out of my chest as fear grips it, panic flooding my veins with every second he remains still.

"Listen here, bastard," I say, the tears flowing freely now, hot and unrelenting. "You cannot leave me here. You are not him, do you hear me?" A sob hiccups out of my chest as I frantically rip the bottom of my shirt off to try to staunch the blood.

"You are *not* Perry. You do not get to fucking leave me, do you understand?"

I apply as much pressure as I can, but Bayne still lies lifeless on the ground. Desperation wraps her cold fingers around my throat as I scream my throat raw, trying, begging him to wake up.

The wind is warm against my tear-streaked face as I sit back on my heels, defeat settling in for the kill.

"Please," I croak. "Please, anyone."

"You won't save him with a shirt, love."

That *voice.*

I freeze as all the breath dissipates from my lungs.

Looking up from my blood-covered hands, my suspicions are confirmed the moment I look into those violet eyes. Her purple cloak hides most of her figure, but I could never forget her.

The vendor from the Laine—the one who spoke.

"Wha-what are you doing here?" I whip my head around looking for others, but we're alone.

"Child, he won't survive. It's best to leave him, make your own way home."

Her comment is a slap to the face. Anger festers deep as I fight the urge to kill her, right here, where there are no witnesses.

"I have to *try,*" I spit out. "Can you help me? Or are you going to just watch him die?"

She steps closer, the scent of lilacs drifting to my nose.

"Why do you wish to save him? Is he yours?" Her face is impassive as she tilts her head, questioning me.

I look at Bayne, really look at him. His skin is lackluster now, missing its usual golden hue. His face, his lips—those same lips that kissed me reverently, even if he didn't mean to.

"Yes," I tell her confidently. "He's mine."

She nods, stepping closer to assess.

"If he were to survive the wound, he would still be poisoned."

I look away as my heart sinks with the weight of her words. She's right.

"What do I do...?" I whisper.

"Don't you usually pray in a time like this, Arden?"

Whipping my head back to hers, she's closer now. "How do you know my name?" My hackles rise exponentially.

"I know the names of all my followers, love. I also know you do love to take my name in vain, do you not?"

I study her, puzzled for a moment. Until it hits me.

Midnight.

"B-but..." I shake my head in disbelief. "You're a...a..."

"Goddess, yes," she finishes.

I see it then, like a veil has suddenly been taken off my eyes. Her subtle glowing presence, the finery of her clothes, her jewelry. Those eyes—why did I brush it all off?

My hands shake now as sweat falls, mixing with the blood, dirt, and tears. "Why are you following me? Why help me—"

"Are these the questions you want to waste, child? Or do you wish for my help another way?"

"Yes, please. Save him."

She nods, and another sob falls from my lips, only it's in relief this time. "For a small bargain, yes, I will save the one you claim."

Anything.

"What do you require?"

"I deal in secrets, love." She brushes a hand down my cheek affectionately, but Bayne's shadows have felt more tangible than her hands.

"I don't—there aren't any secrets I have of value," I rush out. "I do not remember anything past my life in Second. I swear it, I—"

"I can offer you something else." She speaks softly. I pause, unsure. "I can offer you another option."

Another option? The question must be written across my face, because she continues.

"You can save him," she points to Bayne, who is fading faster now. "Or I can restore your full memory."

I sputter, my world tilting on its axis.

"You can do that?" My tone is incredulous as I gape at her. She only nods once. "I can't," I breathe the words out, cleaving my heart in two over a fresh wave of tears. "I need him more."

Even if it takes everything from me.

"Shame. Perhaps the next secret you'll offer, hm?" She waits expectantly, but I have nothing to say. Midnight paces the forest floor, seemingly bored.

"What secret do you wish for?" I finally break the silence.

"It must be true to your heart. If it is not, you and I will both know. No lying, love."

I rack my brain, but I have nothing. Nothing of value to her.

"There are some secrets we have not even admitted to ourselves." She gestures to Bayne, then back at me.

I know what she means.

And I let my shoulders sag as the tears freefall, every drop in shame of what I've let myself do.

"I love him," I whisper, but it's Bayne I'm looking at. "That is my secret. I love him."

When our eyes meet again, she smiles, radiant and lovely. It feels like home, comfort.

"So you do," she says. Bending over him, she brushes hair off his forehead in a motion that feels too intimate for my comfort. "I was hoping you'd pick your memory. But perhaps another day, another life." She sighs, as though I've inconvenienced her.

"He'll be fully healed, yes? No poison. Not actively dying."

"Ah, too much time spent with the prince, I see." Her smile is feline, and I'm certain she enjoys this too much. "Yes, your specifics to our bargain will be taken care of. Be warned, my child, the bargain that ties your life to his will no longer remain. Is this still the choice you want to make?"

I nod, not caring for consequences. I'd stay even if the bargain killed me instead.

"Remove your hands, love, if you wish to keep them." Her voice is pure persuasion, forcing me to listen.

She taps his forehead, closing her eyes. Her other hand traces from the hallow of his throat, down his chest to the wound in his abdomen. To my utter fascination, her magic works just as we always prayed.

Each of his cuts from the Shades' knives slowly stitch themselves back together. Midnight concentrates as she heals, my tears of gratitude falling at the color coming back to his body.

When the last of his wounds finishes closing, she straightens, running her hands down her cloak. The motion is so human, I almost forget who she is when I ask, "How do we get home?"

"I can send you home, but it is not where this man lives."

I pause, understanding seeping into my bones.

"I know." I sigh. "But please send us back to Marintha. I cannot—he's too heavy to move."

Bayne's chest rises steadily, and the motion makes my heart swell. I run my hands over his heart, as if I can read how he feels by doing so. I take what feels like my first breath now that he's breathing again.

"Just this once, child." She holds her palm out, an orange ward stone in the center. "Do not toss this into the waves again. I'm not a fan of the water, you know."

"Thank you." I nod gratefully. "I'll always remember this."

"I know that already. I'm counting on it, in fact." She winks, smiling once more as she disappears in a cloud of purple smoke.

I hold tight to the ward stone in one hand, my other grasping Bayne's, holding his body close. The adrenaline has begun to fade, and I've never felt so tired.

I focus on my destination and hold onto Bayne as we're whisked away in a mist of orange. It's only a moment before we're back in the castle, my knees hitting the library floor with a thud. Bayne's head is on my lap as I hold it, tears and exhaustion taking their toll.

He's alive. He's going to be okay.

I press a kiss to his forehead, then put my brow on his. It isn't until Axl and Jes clamber into the room that my eyes grow heavy with sleep. Welcoming the darkness I've grown so familiar with, I greet it like an old friend, surrendering.

CHAPTER THIRTY-NINE

"So, this is all you guys do?"

Edene kicks the stones underneath her feet as she walks next to Perry and I. He holds my hand, my head on his shoulder. A perfect fit. Right where we belong.

I laugh at her question. "What do you mean? You don't like the Gardens? You wear flowers all the time."

I give her current dress of yellow with forget-me-nots dotting the hem a pointed look.

She smooths it down self-consciously. "It's not the same, and you know it." She upturns her nose, declaring the debate over.

"Arden, why don't you wear more dresses, doll? You'd look captivating in something like that," Perry says, and I know he means well. Truly. But it doesn't stop the thoughts of doubt. The sharp pang of hurt.

He doesn't like the way I dress.

I should look prettier for him...right?

"I'm sorry, Per." I look up at him, but his eyes are fixed on the road ahead. "I'll dress up for you later, if you want." I poke him in the side playfully, but he pulls away from me, releasing my hand.

"Arden, not in front of Edene. That's embarrassing."

My face is hot with shame. I can't believe I did that to him.

When I look over at Edene, she's watching us closely, and I can see her picking him apart again.

She's made her distaste for Perry evident, but she hides it well when we're all together. Edene loops her arm with mine, not missing a beat.

"Arden, why don't you help me pick out some flowers for my shop? I think it'll bring in more customers if I keep pretty arrangements in the windows."

I force a smile, even though I'm grateful to her for shattering the awkward moment.

"We'll be back," I tell Perry, leaning in to give him a kiss.

He closes the space between us, my eyes closing. But when his lips hit my cheek instead of my mouth, I can't help the instant sinking of my heart.

"I'll see you soon."

I nod. "I love you, you know."

"I love you, too, Arden."

I smile, less forced this time, but his declaration is still missing...something. I'm not sure what.

Perhaps I am being selfish.

Ungrateful.

Perry has shown me everything. He's taken me under his wing, ensured I survived. Took me into his home when I had nowhere to go.

I will do better.

I will be what he needs me to be. I would do anything for Perry.

Even die.

Edene sits at my bedside, fussing with the bedsheets.

I groan, turning over to lay face-down on my pillow.

Edene?

Flipping back over, I sit up, my entire body protesting the movement. "Edene? What are you—how are you here?"

She smiles, looking more alive than she has in weeks.

"What did I tell you? I *knew* you'd fall for him, Arden." She shakes her head. "I can't believe you fell in love!"

My stomach plummets with her words.

Oh my Gods. *How does she even know that?*

"What are you talking about?" I ask precariously.

She leans in, mischief glinting her eyes. "I can see the future."

My mouth drops open in disbelief. It's only then that she laughs, breaking the charade. "I'm just kidding. *Obviously.* You talk in your sleep. It's cute."

She leans back in the chair, a self-righteous smirk over her face. "So. Tell me. When did you fall for him?"

I narrow my eyes at her, flopping back on the bed. "I'm not—"

Wait.

Whipping my head toward her, my eyes widen. "Bayne." I need to see him, need to make sure he's okay. I rip the covers off, sitting up again.

"Arden, wait—"

I ignore her, putting my feet on the cold ground. I need to see him. I grab a silk robe, matching my lavender sleeping attire. I move to hastily tie it around my waist when Edene catches my hands.

"Arden, listen. He's still unconscious." Her words are like a slap to the face.

"What do you mean, *unconscious*? He's fine. He is supposed to be fine." My hands shake as I keep trying to tie the robe.

"He is, I checked on him. So did Franswon—nice man, by the way. If he weren't only into men, I'd definitely be seeing what healers can do." She smirks, but when my face remains stoic, it falls. "He's okay, Arden. Just relax. Fran says you both need a lot of rest, then we need to talk about what happened to you guys."

I don't waste a single moment. "We were ambushed by Shades. They almost killed him. Almost killed us both. Midnight saved us. Truly, if she hadn't shown herself, I—" Tears well unbidden in my eyes, spilling instantly.

All the fear of losing him crashes over me violently, all at once. Flashes of him chained to the wall in that cave. Almost drowning. Still flirting with me to the last second as the light flickered out behind his eyes. The Shade poisoning. My murder spree.

It's too much.

Edene wraps her arms around me without question, holding me as I sob. I scrunch her top in my hands, trying to ease the stabbing ache splitting my heart in half.

We made it. We're safe.

I cry on her shoulder for what seems like hours as she rubs my back in soothing circles. Like she used to. A comfort I'll always cherish with her.

It isn't until I feel like I'm ready to fall asleep that I peel my cheek off her shoulder. "Can you take me to him?"

She nods, wordlessly understanding the turmoil I know is written in my eyes. "I would say protect your heart, love. But we both know you gave it away to him long ago."

I nod back imperceptibly.

Relief, sadness, exhaustion, and grief all weigh me down as I follow Edene through the winding hallways. She does a double take at my favorite painting—the moon.

"It's pretty, right?"

She nods, mouth parted slightly. She lays a reverent hand on it, hypnotized. As if it bit her, she yanks her hand back sharply.

"Sorry. It was just beautiful, but I probably shouldn't touch it." She flashes me a sly smile. "Don't want to upset your *lover.*"

Giving her a small shove, I egg her on. "Let's get moving, Ede. It's already nightfall, and I need to be there when he wakes up."

She doesn't retort, and when we finally reach a strange door, it's only then that it dawns on me—I've never been to his bedroom.

I hesitate before grabbing the gilded handle, and push my way inside. Jes and Axl sit tangled together in an armchair next to his bed, and both heads turn to smile at me as I enter.

They cross the room to me, hand in hand, each of them giving me a hug.

"I'm glad you're both alive," Jes says. "It would've been really boring to be the only interesting one again."

Axl pouts at her, but it only makes her grin as she kisses it off his face. "We'll leave you be, Arden. We'll see you around."

She moves to leave, but Axl stops her, wrapping me in a second hug, tighter this time. When he pulls back, his blue eyes shine with tears. "Thank you. Truly. He's...all the family I have. Thank you."

I nod, my own eyes burning at his words. When they leave, I take the seat they occupied, staring, waiting.

"I don't know if you can hear me in there," I say in his head. *"But I need you to wake up. Today if you could, princeling. Knowing you, you'll take your time, but I need you. Wake up and fight with me. Wake up and fight for me. For us. I need you in my life. In Death."*

Sighing with resignation, I make myself comfortable as I watch his chest rise and fall. Each breath he takes fills my own lungs, as if the bond between us also links our oxygen.

As my eyes grow too heavy, I relax for the first time in a year, knowing that he's alive. Edene is alive.

Everything is going to be okay.

Once he wakes up.

Chapter Forty

I startle myself awake, a small gasp whispering off my lips. I hadn't realized I fell asleep in the chair next to his bed.

Moonlight streams in through the windows, refracting shards of it across the room. The pale glow allows me to see his chest moving up and down with each steady breath, smothering the anxiousness in my chest. Rain pours down outside, as if the sky also mourns for its prince to wake.

The stubble that adorns his face looks as tempting as it does out of place. He never lets it grow, but I suppose a few days of bedrest makes it difficult to shave. I love it.

There I go again. Using that word.

I'm sick of crying over it. My eyes are still puffy from the lack of sleep and tears. I feel all cried out, and then I start again.

I'm a fool.

He's already made it evident what this is. A mutual attraction at best. Can we even say we enjoy being around each other?

I know I do—hells, I love him. His laugh, his commandeering presence. His eyes. How he gets under my skin, but always knows what I need, anyway. The way he takes care of me, of Edene.

I'll never forget how he visited her every day. *How he spoke to her.*

Is it not enough that he has a grip on my mind? Do I have to offer my heart so willingly, too?

A slight movement catches my eye, and when I turn, I see Bayne awake, staring at me.

"Arden?" he whispers my name, but it feels like a plea as much as a question.

Without thinking, I reach for his hand, lacing our fingers.

"Hey," I whisper back, "I'm here."

"It's the middle of the night, raven, we should be sleeping."

I laugh softly. "Yes, probably. I couldn't sleep well. Not until I made sure you were okay."

He sits up, his face a breath away from mine now. "I'm okay." He smiles, and my chest tightens.

"You scared me..." My voice is small as I admit it. It's easier to be honest in the dark. "You almost died, and I don't think I could've handled it. I just—" I shake my head, unable to finish.

Bayne takes my face in his hands, brushing his thumbs over my cheeks as he shushes me. "Don't cry, Arden. I'm right here. I'm okay." Each swipe stops another tear that falls.

I nod as best I can, then he pulls my forehead to his own, making me close my eyes to take a deep, steadying breath. My hands find his wrists, keeping him in place.

I use the scent of him to ground me. *Home. He smells like home.*

"I'm glad you didn't bleed out. That would've been quite selfish of you after everything."

He chuckles softly. "And deny you the pleasure of my company?"

I smack his arm in a mock scold. "You're such a prick," I whisper. But my answering smile gives me away.

"Thank you," he whispers back, brushing his lips against mine. It's soft, sweet, and far more intimate than any we've shared before. My heart flips as I kiss him back, sighing contentedly as he pulls back.

"You should rest."

I pat his thigh, moving to stand, but he snatches my hand before I can.

"Stay."

"I should—"

He yanks me into his lap, trying and failing to hide his wince. I make a face at his disregard for Franswon's orders, yet I make no move to get off him.

"Stay, my little raven." He plants small kisses on my neck, utilizing every weakness of mine that he's learned against me.

My hands find the hair at the back of his neck, closing the space between our bodies. It's become impossible to ignore the pang in my heart hearing him say *my*.

"Fine," I breathe, tilting my head for better access. "But I'm not staying up all night just because—"

Before I can finish, he flips me next to him, and we land horribly wrong. His scrunched face tells me all I need to know before I scold him for being too rough.

"This is *exactly* what I was trying to say before you cut me off. You need to be careful, Bayne." I place a hand on his cheek, his features smoothing back at my touch.

His brown eyes blink back open at me, something unreadable flitting through them.

"Maybe I like to be rough, *Arden*," he whispers my name like a prayer, but I roll my eyes at his innuendo.

"Maybe I like you in *one piece*, and who knows what the goddess did when she saved you."

"You saved me. Not her."

"No, she took the poison—"

He silences me with a kiss, as equally punishing as it is endearing. "You. Midnight didn't come for me, didn't unchain me and drag me across the ground. That was all you, angel." He smiles.

"Hey! I didn't mean to, okay? You're heavy as deadweight."

He tosses his head back and laughs, sputtering out on a choked cough. The sound is beautiful all the same, and I could listen to it for the rest of eternity.

"You saved me, Arden." Worry gleams in his eyes as he ponders his next thought. "How *did* you get her to save me?"

Do I tell him? Will it make it too obvious?

He brushes a hand down my hair, and I lean into the touch. "I can see you fighting yourself in there. You don't need to tell me what you—"

"She offered to give me my memories back."

Bayne freezes, his whole body halting at my words.

"She did?" His eyes bounce between my own as I nod.

"She said I could choose to save you," I trace a finger down his chest, "or I could have my memories back from Living."

He shakes his head at me. "You should've. Everything would've been okay, Arden. You deserve to have that returned to you, and it's—"

I silence him with a kiss, wordlessly pulling him closer. He tugs me against him in response, wrapping his arms around me.

"I needed you more, Bayne," I murmur against his lips. "I've gone this long without them; I'll find another way. Or not. I truly can't say my life will be all the better with it."

He kisses me again, this time with more heat. His hands move lower to my ass, pulling me against his obvious arousal, making me moan. He uses it as an invitation to slide his tongue against mine.

Desire floods my system at how badly I want him—here and now, but he's healing.

I break the kiss, both of us breathing heavy.

"We shouldn't," I pant, one hand on his chest.

"And why not?" He smirks as he raises a brow in question.

"You're still hurt. It wouldn't be wise to risk—"

He cuts me off again as his lips dust over mine, then down my neck. "Then I guess you'll have to be gentle for once." I can feel his smile against my skin.

"You're the one who cut my clothes off last time, if I remember correctly."

He pauses his perusal of my body to latch his gaze on mine. "You're right. But this time, I plan on savoring every." *Kiss.* "Single." *Kiss.* "Second." He punctuates with a final kiss, making my heart speed up.

I love him.

I know it as surely as my own name, and yet, it's trapped behind my lips.

So I show him instead.

CHAPTER FORTY-ONE

Heat envelopes my entire body, almost overwhelmingly so.

I open my eyes slowly to find Bayne already awake.

"Were you watching me sleep, princeling?" A smile tilts my lips at the thought. I could get used to waking up with him.

He steals a kiss, only making my smile grow. "I'm drawn to admire beauty when it lays before me."

I mockingly roll my eyes at him. "So poetic."

"You love poetry."

"I like *reading*. I never said I liked poetry, Bayne. Perhaps you should listen better next time. Might get you laid." I wink poorly at him, making him laugh.

Laughing, I roll over to look out the window. A sharp gasp falls out of me, not having seen it in the dark last night. "You have a fucking balcony?! That's so unfair, I want a balcony in my room!" I turn on my side back toward Bayne, slapping his arm as he grins at me, chuckling at my expense. Suddenly, he grabs my hip, rolling me onto my back as he presses his weight on top of me in the most delicious way. My blood sings with the promise in his eyes as he holds weight on his elbows, caging in my head.

Yes.

He trails kisses up my neck and back down, causing my eyes to flutter closed. "If you want a balcony, Arden, say the word and I'll reconstruct this whole palace so you can have the view you desire." He continues his onslaught across my clavicle, and I arch my neck toward him in encouragement. "As long as I am sleeping beside you, so that I can have the best view in all of Second."

My heart stops in my chest, robbing my lungs of air. I open my eyes to find him staring at me with an adoration in his own that makes my heart soar. My whole body warms with an internal glow, and I mentally trap this memory in my head, as to never lose it. Gods, he is so beautiful, it's almost physically painful the way my heart squeezes when he looks at me.

Like I'm something precious. Something worth memorizing.

Bayne reaches up to brush a stray hair off my forehead absentmindedly, the touch so gentle I can't help but return the favor. I run my fingers up his bicep, to his hair to push it back when he seizes my hand, laying languid kisses across the back of my hand and up my arm. His eyes remain locked on mine, drunk in a haze of lust and longing. The sheer intimacy of it causes my breath to stutter, and I squeeze my thighs together to quell the building need of him back inside me.

Ridiculous, considering we barely slept at all last night because he was all over me.

"What are you thinking?" he whispers against my skin as he keeps up his pursuit.

"I'm thinking...that I'm happy." I smile at him, reflecting the one that splits his face. I can only hope he doesn't see the stars in my eyes that are dancing on the inside in response.

"Oh?"

I knit my brows together at his reply, but I quickly shake it off as soon as it comes. "Yeah," a wry grin spreads across my face, "is that okay with you, your highness?" I pinch his side with my free hand, grabbing nothing more than toned muscle. His eyes light up with a dare as he snatches my other hand and pins them both into the mattress. Bayne leans in close, brushing his nose against mine.

"Just, happy?" His smile is devilish, and it makes me swallow roughly. I can only nod in reply. "Well, Arden. It seems you have some sincere apologies to acquiesce for."

My confusion must muddle across my face, because his smile is so lascivious as he says, "Let me apologize for only making you feel happy. I hold my standard at nothing short of *euphoria*."

He kisses down my body, releasing my hands so his can follow his mouth's passionate assault. Starting at my neck, he bites the skin and soothes the pain with his tongue shortly after. I don't even feel the pain as it all morphs into pleasure, extracting a deep moan from me. Using his knees, he nudges mine further apart in a swift movement to settle his own between them. I can feel the evidence of his arousal, his cock hard again as he grinds his hips against mine.

Midnight smite me for thinking so, but nothing has ever felt as good as Bayne does. I've never needed anyone the way I need him, right now. Forever.

I moan mindlessly as he kneads his hands where his mouth was. Every touch, every sensation radiates through my body. I can feel my heartbeat between my legs, my arousal damn near embarrassing, the way I know it's running down my thighs.

Closing my eyes, I run both my hands through his hair, cradling his head as his mouth finds my breast, sealing his lips over it. He repeats his assault on my nipple and I gasp, arching into his bite, pulling his hair in return. His teeth pull on it, laughing darkly as he lets go. "So testy, little raven."

A bite to my stomach flashes my eyes back open with another gasp and I meet Bayne's dark eyes, almost wholly black with how blown his pupils are. "Eyes on me, Arden." He traces a finger lazily over my stomach, sending goosebumps over my skin. "I need you to stay still while I worship every inch of you, so I can burn it into my tongue forever. I'd hate to leave you...unsatisfied." His face is serious as his features burn with hunger.

I think I nod yes, but I can't be sure. He moves down past my navel to my hip bones, trailing his tongue out as he moves side to side. Groaning in frustration, I try to push him exactly where I need him most. He clicks his tongue in admonishment. "*Sooo* impatient," he coos.

"Bayne, please," I beg him. My eyes flick between both of his, trying to read how long this torture will ensue. His mouth pulls up at the corners.

"See? I told you when we met. I *knew* you'd be a good beggar when the time came."

Before I can retort, he covers his lips precisely where I need it, and mine part in a silent scream at the overwhelming sensation.

Gods, he is so fucking good at that.

I toss my head back in pure bliss, giving myself over to the pleasure. He suctions my clit as his tongue moves back and forth, sending stars to dance behind my eyelids. All of a sudden he stops, so I open my eyes again, not realizing they shut.

Shit.

Before I can move, his hand is wrapped under my jaw, pulling it back down to meet his gaze. Dark fury shines in his eyes, and it should scare me, but instead heat swirls hotter under my skin.

"I thought I told you to keep these pretty silver eyes on me." He pulls my face closer. "Unless my beautiful raven doesn't want to come, I suggest you listen for once." His mouth shines with me, and I can't help myself. Holding myself on one elbow, I reach out with my thumb and rub it across his bottom lip.

"I thought this was an apology to me."

He watches me mesmerized as I hold his gaze and put my thumb in my own mouth, cleaning it off. Bayne groans, his hips flexing into the mattress out of desperation. "Fuck, Arden." He smashes his mouth to mine, and I can taste myself on him. He licks the seam of my lips and I let him in, our tongues in sync as we fall back into the mattress. He breaks the kiss for a breath, closing his eyes for half a heartbeat. "You are the finest creature I've ever set my eyes on. I don't think I will ever get enough of you."

My reply is cut short as he slides back inside me, causing us both to moan. Bayne grabs my hips roughly, probably bruising them.

Good. I want to bruise with his mark.

His thrusts are relentless as we steal more kisses from each other. He kisses me with his whole body. I rake my nails down his back, nearly drawing blood. As I do, it spurs him on, snapping his hips faster until I'm on the precipice once again.

"Please," I whimper, my words weak. "Gods, I need you." His answering grin is damning, as he slides his hand from my hip to press his thumb against my clit.

"Come for me, baby. Scream my name so they all know who you actually pray to."

His words send me over the edge, my release ripping through me as he keeps moving, drawing out every ounce of pleasure. "Fuck, Arden. You've been such a good girl for me, haven't you?" I can only whimper in reply as I come down, squeezing tight around him.

I drag my hands down to his ass and pull him in deeper, my eyes rolling back. Bayne grabs my knee and pushes it up to my chest, holding the back of my thigh as he drives into me. It only takes a few more thrusts from this angle before he groans and snaps his hips once, twice—spilling his release deep inside me. His eyes droop as he pants, as out of breath as I am. Our breath mingles in our shared space, and I feel on top of the world.

He puffs a laugh at me as he smiles and pushes my wild hair off my face again. "How are you feeling now?"

I smile hazily at him, returning his laugh. "Euphoric."

The look on his face makes my heart soar, and I try to tamp it down, but I fear it might be too late for that.

CHAPTER FORTY-TWO

Every day since I gave in to loving Bayne is better than the last. I burn to tell him how I feel, but it never feels like the right moment. Every time I almost say it, something tells me not to. That I'll ruin this.

I know what I'm doing, though.

I'm letting Perry hold space in this—whatever this is between us. He has no room here. Regardless of my past, I am Bayne's. Even if he is not fully mine.

Oh, but how his words sing to my heart.

Sighing, I lean over the balcony railing, breathing in the salt air. It's different now, or maybe it's just because it's attached to his bedroom. The ocean is the same. Marintha hasn't changed—it's me who's changed.

When did I become the woman afraid to speak her opinions? It's silly. Bayne has made me stronger, feeling love like I've never known. I want to tell him—no. I *need* to.

Even if he doesn't say it back.

I don't need it back, not in this moment, anyway. But I can't live in a world where the people I love don't know how much I love them.

And he is so deserving of love.

Of me, my heart.

I didn't think I would ever fall again after losing Perry. And now that my soul belongs to Bayne, I can't hold it back anymore.

The next time I see him.

As if I summoned him, swirls of shadow reveal my favorite prince. Well, the only prince I know.

I smile, and he matches it, immediately taking me into his arms, kissing me hello.

"Hi," he whispers, burying his face in my hair.

"Hello, *darling*," I say.

He laughs, the sound sparking a light in my chest. "Are you mocking me?"

Even though he can't see it, a sly smile cracks over my face. "Maybe."

His hands find my waist, tickling me until I give in. My 'apology' is swallowed by my cacophony of laughter. When he finally lets me breathe, I pull back to see him watching me. His eyes look lighter today, despite the storm approaching on the horizon. Full of adoration and admiring me in a way I know I've never been looked at before.

He feigns a pout, making him look all the more adorable. I kiss him, an apology and everything I struggle to voice.

He holds me against him, and we stay like that for a while, swaying with the waves, just the two of us.

I want this forever.

Fear slithers down my spine, but I steel myself, finding the courage.

"Arden, there's something you should know," he says before I can say anything.

I look up at him, dread and anxiety pulsing through me. "What is it?"

Is this it? Will he say it first?

"Edene is a witch."

I cackle at his joke. "She's not *that* bad." I smile.

"Arden." He grabs my arms, putting a fraction of space between us. His face is serious now, halting my laughter.

My smile melts.

"Edene is not a witch. I would know! I lived with her, for crying out loud!"

He shakes his head. "No, you wouldn't."

I shrug off his touch. "Yes, *I would*. Edene is a healer—she doesn't even have magic!"

"She *does*, Arden."

"NO."

Tears burn, ready to fall. He's telling the truth, I know it in my head.

But my heart rejects it.

"She's been crafting the ward stones, angel." His voice is soft, imploring the tears to fall. "I suspected. So did Jes. Her siren ability, it's warped, but she could sense something was off."

I put my hands over my ears, squeezing my eyes shut as I shake my head.

Not Edene.

She wouldn't.

"It wasn't until she recovered from the poisoning, after she spoke in her state about the elixir." He pulls my hands off my head so gently I open my eyes again. "That's why I was in Voltus that day we met. I had heard about a potions master disguising herself as a healer. Imagine my surprise when I was in the shadows of that alley and found you instead—slaughtering a Shade on pure reflex."

I watch him, my mouth parting with surprise.

"You were in rough shape, and I thought I was going to have to step in. But then you got up. You had this." He taps my dagger where it rests in its sheath. "I had to know you, know how the smell didn't affect you. Because their blood alone, raven—it slows the rest of us down. It gives them an advantage, and you walked away like it was nothing."

At my frown, he corrects himself.

"Well, you didn't exactly *walk*, but you pushed on, regardless. I knew you would need a healer. I was just hoping it was the one I needed."

"So you were using me?"

"No, it's not like that. I needed the antipurzon—"

I shove him away, needing space to think.

"I need to talk to her. I want to believe you, I do. But I need to hear it from her."

"She's in her room."

Without another glance at him, he hangs his head as I storm out of his room. I use my fury to keep me bounding up the stairs to Edene. To my answers.

I throw open the door to find her already packing a bag.

"So it's true?"

She doesn't look up as she continues to place clothes and crystals—*ward stones*—in her pack.

"I knew he'd run his mouth the moment he saw you." She sighs.

"No."

She looks up then. Her gray eyes, once as familiar as my own, now look hardened behind her lies.

Her façade.

"So he didn't tell you?" Her brow raises, crossing her arms. She's unrecognizable.

"You don't get to tell me about Bayne. You get one chance to explain. *One.* Because I love you. Or whomever you were pretending to be."

Her eyes well with tears, but she sniffs them back down as she bends to keep packing.

"I am exactly who I said I—"

"Look me in my eyes as you say it."

She does, her tears spilling free now. "I have never lied about who I am, Arden. I am exactly as I look, except there are things that were not safe to tell you and—"

"*Bullshit,*" I hiss.

"It is the truth." She exhales shakily. "Whether it's what you can accept or not, then I can't help you. But the Arden I knew wouldn't have trapped herself here. She would be fighting to have freedom."

"I am free! He saved you!"

"No, love. My magic did. He simply found what he was already looking for. He just collected you along the way."

Her words slap me, leaving behind the intended sting.

"Get out."

Hot, angry tears burn my face as I spit the words. Edene reaches into her pack, pulling out a clear ward stone, one I've never seen.

"Even if you never want to see me again, even if you never trust me again," she places it into my hand, "hold onto this. Always. It'll keep you safe, even when I cannot."

"You're a witch." Disbelief rings in my head, in my voice.

"I am."

"And you didn't trust me enough to tell me."

She gives me a sad smile, closing her bag and throwing it over her shoulder. "Everything I've done has always been for you. Even though I couldn't bring back your memories, please understand that, Arden."

Before I can answer, she twirls her wrists, and when she claps, she disappears in a cloud of purple dust.

Taking the rest of the life I knew with her.

CHAPTER FORTY-THREE

I sigh, sinking back into my favorite chair in the library. The book in my lap is long forgotten, blurred through my tears.

Edene.

A witch.

I know witches are forbidden creatures—too much power for one human to hold. But why? Or was that a lie, too?

My headache splits my brain in half as I rub my temples to no avail.

Everything is so much more complicated than it already was.

Edene lied about who she was for over a year. My heart splinters even more as I think about every precious moment we shared.

Was any of it real?

Would she have even told me if it was?

She was irritated with me, with Bayne. As if she wasn't pushing us together just last week. I always knew there were two sides to Edene, but I never would've thought one of them was against me.

My lungs struggle not to collapse in on my heart, already in ribbons.

I close the book, tossing it onto the floor. Pulling my knees to my chest, I let myself sob. An ugly cry, with no one to bear witness, no one to coddle me and tell me it'll be okay. No one to rub circles on my back. It isn't until the tears have long dried that I sense he's joined me.

"Hi," I muffle against my knees.

"Hello, darling."

I peek an eye out to see Bayne crouched on the floor beside my chair, one hand on the armrest.

"You were right," I say, my voice impossibly small.

Pain—my own pain—reflects in his eyes. "I wish I wasn't." He moves his hand to cover mine. "Do you want to get up?"

I shrug, unsure of anything.

Of everything.

He stands, holding his hand out. I take his silent invitation, letting him pull me into him. His scent comforts me. My oasis.

"Do you want to dance?"

My eyes grow wide. "Right now?" I look down at my sleepwear, my slippered feet. It's in direct contrast to his finery. So much so that it could be laughable if I wasn't distracted.

"Yes." He laughs.

That's when I see it.

His crown.

It's silver, intricately woven with amethyst jewels. Each stone rests under a peak, the shine of it contrasting his inky black hair. And the beauty of it—of him—steals my breath away.

I reach up to touch it, until I think better of it.

"You're wearing your crown," I say.

"So you noticed."

I smile, but it's replaced by a gasp as he lets go of me to remove it, placing it on my own head.

"Now you're just as royal as me."

I mock a wave to a fake crowd, making him laugh. Locking eyes with him again, my heart swells with the love that pours out of it. For him. Only him.

"It's heavier than I thought it would be."

"Well, I'd better get used to it. I should probably wear it more often. But I plan on crafting one just like it." He pulls me into a slow sway, spinning me out, then back into no rhythm except our own.

"What do you mean? Why would you need two?"

"My queen will need one to match."

My stomach freefalls with dread.

"Right," I mumble, unable to hide my disappointment. I'm not royalty, and surely he will need to marry a royal one day. Right?

"Arden, I meant *you*." He rolls his eyes at me, pulling me closer.

"You...did?"

We stop, locked in time.

"Oh, my little raven." He brushes my hair behind my ear, cupping my cheek. "How can you not know? Do you not feel the way my heart beats only for you? Only because of you? I was a dead man."

I shake my head, unable to process what I'm hearing as my heartbeat roars in my ears.

"I love you, Arden. I don't much believe in the Gods myself anymore, but you've changed me. Because I've found myself on my knees, found myself worshipping you. You were all it took to get me bowing my head, *praying* for one more taste, one more kiss. So if this is Hell, allow me to serve Death herself. Allow me to be a believer only for you. You've given a dead man life. I love you beyond the comprehension of two souls so intertwined like ours. But you are the breath in my lungs, the sunrise on the ocean every morning. I thank every divinity I can think of that I found you that day."

A lone tear falls down my cheek before he swipes it away gently.

"I love you, too, Bayne. I think I have for a while, but—"

His mouth is on mine before I can finish. He grips my face in both of his hands, pulling me closer to him. It's not enough.

I need our love to be marked permanently on my skin.

Our kisses are messy and heated as he ushers me backward until my back bumps the bookshelf. Without hesitation, Bayne picks me up to set me on the edge that sticks out, never breaking our kiss.

His hands find my hair as mine find his belt, working desperate fingers to un-loop it. I use it to tug him even closer between my legs, the ache for him rising exponentially. He groans with the force I use, my tongue finding his. He sucks on mine, stoking the already blazing fire.

I get his belt undone and off, tossing it to the floor. Wrapping my legs around him, I pull his shirt up. He breaks the kiss to rip it over his head. He wastes no time in tearing my top down the center, baring my body to him.

The fabric tearing elicits a gasp from me as the cool air kisses my skin. But the heat of his mouth follows shortly after, kissing down my body, burning hotter with each press of his lips. I moan, arching into him with encouragement as my hands find his soft hair.

It isn't until he's on his knees again that I realize his intent. But I'm too desperate for him.

Shaking my head, I try to pull him back up, but he doesn't budge. "I need you inside me. Now." My chest heaves, ready to break as soon as he does.

His smile is lascivious as he pulls out his knife, swiftly cutting my shorts off. "I think," he blows cool air between my thighs as he spreads them wider, "you never listen to me."

He looks up at me as he throws one of my legs over his shoulder, and the sight alone almost makes me come. He trails his hand up and down my thigh; teasing, taunting.

"Wha—what do you mean?"

"I told you." He leans in to lay a light kiss to my inner thigh, making me squirm. He tightens his hold, not letting me move. "Eating is one of my favorite pastimes."

When his mouth lands on me, I can't help but pull him closer. Each lick and tease of his tongue works me higher, every moan encouraging him to work faster. Just as he sucks my clit into his mouth, he slides two fingers inside me, making me scream out his name as I grab the shelf behind me.

"*That's it, scream my name. Ride my face, baby. I want to watch you fall apart.*"

"Fuck. I can't—I—"

He suctions harder and I crash over the edge, falling over and over with each wave of pleasure. He doesn't let up until my legs are shaking and I've grown overly sensitive.

He sets my leg down, scooping me up as we travel to his room. His kiss is all-consuming as we fall to the bed. I can taste myself on his tongue and it reignites my desire tenfold.

In a blink, his pants are gone, and in the next second, he's back inside me as we both groan. I need to pull him closer, even though it's not possible. I wrap myself around him, dragging his lips to mine.

"I love you," I say against his mouth.

"I love you more."

His declaration is more than enough as I come for the second time, taking him over the edge with me. We collapse in a haze of love, holding each other close. I hope with each slowing breath that I never lose him—lose this.

I'm not certain I would survive it.

I wouldn't even want to.

CHAPTER FORTY-FOUR

Hands slide over my shoulders and arms wrap around my neck. I smile as soon as his lips hit my cheek.

"Good morning, angel."

Bayne sits down beside me at the dining table, grinning wickedly.

"Is that really necessary?" Axl groans. Jesminda leans over to pinch him.

"You didn't care when Jes kissed you hello," I chastise. Turning fully toward Bayne, I place my hand on his knee to kiss him properly, making Jesminda giggle.

When I pull back, I can't fight my satisfied grin. Axl gags, making the two of us laugh. Bayne intertwines his hand with mine, and I can feel the warmth of his love dousing my entire soul.

To love and be loved—that's what it's all for, right?

It used to be for Edene.

Her lies still sting as cutting as they were yesterday before Bayne tried to kiss them all away. I look over to catch him staring. Again. *"Can I help you, my love?"*

His eyes glitter with warmth and a promise that makes me squirm. *"I think I like that better than 'princeling'."*

"You don't get to pick your nickname." I poke his side playfully. *"That ruins the fun."*

His brow quirks up. *"Can we have my kind of fun?"*

"You had your *fun six times last—"*

"So," Jesminda cuts in unknowingly, "I suppose we should clear the air on what happened with the witch."

"Edene," I correct. Bayne gives my hand a gentle, steadying squeeze.

"Witches are outlawed. There's a reason your friend hid her power behind the guise of an apothecary." She taps her red nails on the table. "The only way she would've been allowed to keep her magic is if she was a selection of the crown before the war. She didn't live here, obviously." Golden eyes watch me curiously, cautiously. "Did Edene have any connections to the Ziineth royal family?"

I shake my head. "No. I would've known. Edene didn't even mention the royal families."

"Edene lied to you," Axl says softly. "It's normal to not want to accept that, but she did."

My knuckles turn white against Bayne's fingers, trying to extract every bit of his quiet strength. "I understand that. Believe me, I do. But she lived in Voltus the whole time. During the war, and before it. The people there, they know her. She had a business, a life. If she had connections to the royal family, she would've boasted about it loud and clear."

Silence rings throughout the dining room with the shifting mood. I'm not even sure why Axl and Jes needed to talk to us so desperately if they were only going to rip apart my friend. Or—my ex-friend.

I would've been perfectly content to roll around my prince's sheets all day, blocking out the real world from our love bubble.

Speaking my thoughts aloud, Bayne says, "If that's all you wanted us to meet you for, this could've waited." He traces small circles over the back of my hand, grounding me.

It's Axl who leans forward, though, his face stony for once. "It has to do with Genevieve."

Bayne freezes beside me, going impossibly still. *"My aunt."* His clarification echoes in my mind.

"What about her?"

"Her death, it—" Axl takes a shaky breath as he fights the tears threatening to spill. "The ward is down, Bayne."

"Down? What do you mean it's down?"

"Marintha is no longer hidden." Dread crawls up my spine, stiffening it with each word.

"How is that possible? I wove those spells myself. They are tied to *me*. Not Gen."

Axl shakes his head solemnly. "You know we're weaker every time another Vail dies. I feel it, you feel it. Hells, I bet even Arden can feel it."

I try not to feel offended at his remark.

"So, what's the problem? If people know that Marintha is still standing, then maybe they'll fight for it. Stand up to the Shaded, maybe even put the patrol guard to use."

"No, Arden, we can't," Axl says. "The patrol guard is another piece of Second. They belonged to Ziineth—to Midnight. You can't *use* them for anything. They were demons programmed to uphold the law who have since lost purpose."

Hope starts to deflate in my chest, but I refuse to let it win. "Well, let us be a beacon of hope for the people then. If Marintha opened its doors, especially to the families of those who are disappearing—"

"Disappearing?" It's Jes who cuts in this time. I nod.

"Yeah," I tell her. "People kept going missing. Unaccounted for. At the time, I thought it was just...my *friend*, but it was a few people."

"How many people did you know of?" Bayne squeezes my hand in question.

"I think three total. Well, perhaps two?" Shame internally slaps me for even bringing it up.

Two people are missing, Arden? You've killed more than that.

"Well, maybe if it was closer to twenty or so, it'd be worth looking into. But we can't justify allowing the public back in so soon," Axl states.

"It's not like you can hide a whole castle! People *will* notice."

"Not if Bayne can re-raise the wards over us."

"Why should we live in safety for everyone else to suffer? Have you ever starved for anything? Barely scraped by? No. People don't need to live here, but we can offer assistance. It's better than waiting for them to be poisoned and corrupted or die. But what do I know? I'm just powerless and useless."

I stand, pushing back on the table. Bayne stands with me, muttering something to them I can't hear.

Stupid magic.

"Arden, wait," Bayne calls after me. I don't stop as I march down the hall. In an instant, he's beside me, shadows dancing over my skin in invitation.

I roll my eyes at their blatant disregard at reading a mood.

"My love, please wait."

I halt where I am, halfway up the stairs. Without turning toward him, I speak. "That's not fair. You can't call me *love* to win an argument."

Hands grip my shoulders, forcing me to turn. "I would never call you that for something as juvenile as winning an argument." He brushes my hair off my face gently, tilting my chin up to meet his gaze. "It's because I love you, and I want the world to know."

Failing to stay angry with him, I give in, pulling him into a hug. His firm chest is my comfort, his scent bringing me to the home in my heart. I breathe him in for several heartbeats, brushing away my conversation with Jes and Axl to the back of my mind.

"Why do you call me all the other names then? Since you only seem to call me *Arden* when you're inside me." My voice is muffled into his shirt.

He laughs, the vibration soothing. Pulling back a step, he lightly tugs me up the stairs with him. "While I love being inside you," he says, like he's going to try the minute we reach his room, "you already know why I call you raven." He flicks a piece of my hair where it sways off my shoulder. "But I also like *darling*, just to get under your skin."

"What about *angel*?"

"Because you're an angel, a divinity. Because you are my salvation as much as you are my damnation. And I want to pray for forgiveness just to keep you by my side, forever."

Without thinking, I pull his mouth to mine. He matches it without missing a beat. What was supposed to be soft, quickly heats. I pull back, breaking the kiss, one hand resting over his heart.

Thump, thump, thump.

"I'd like that," I whisper. "Being by your side...forever."

He grins with childlike wonder, making my heart soar. "You'd make a fine queen, Arden." He kisses me again, reluctantly stopping it. "An even finer wife. I'm sorry Midnight made you choose between knowing yourself and saving me."

"I'm not."

He takes a sharp inhale, admonishing me. "You don't mean that. You don't know what you're saying."

I nod. "Yes, I do. Because I knew it then, and I'll tell you every day if I have to. I love you. And despite what you may think this is or was, I'm not letting you go. Because losing you," my voice wavers, "was worse than Death. I'd have rather met Maveth at your side than live this life without you in it."

He's silent for a beat, absorbing my words.

"Marry me, then."

The words clang through my skull, reverberating like a staccato. *He doesn't mean that, does he?*

"Bayne, I—"

"There's no reason we shouldn't." His eyes search mine frantically, desperately. "I mean, unless you don't want to, then I'll wait. But the courts don't exist anymore, so even though you're not from a noble family, there's no one to get approval from."

"I'm not saying—"

"But if you're just not wanting to marry me, it's alright." He takes my hand, and the softness of it makes my eyes water. "Don't cry, my love." He brushes a fallen tear off my cheek.

"If you'd listen, I'd have given you an answer already." I smile through my tears.

He's silent, waiting impatiently.

"Of course I'll marry you, you fool. Why would you ever think—"

But I don't finish.

Because in the next breath, his hands are on my face, pulling my lips to his. He takes my air like he needs me to breathe, devouring everything I have to give. I throw my arms around him, as if it's possible to get any closer. Tears of happiness continue to flow freely. He breaks the kiss suddenly, leaving us still intertwined but breathing heavily.

"Why are you crying?"

I smile, unable to put the euphoric bliss I feel coursing through my veins into words. But I try, anyway. "I'm happy."

He smiles then, wide and unrestrained. Bayne hugs me close, spinning me around. Letting me go to reach into his pocket, he pulls out the amethyst ring he placed on my finger months ago for our ruse.

His mother's ring.

"Bayne, are you sure you want to use that ring?" I look at it as though it might bite me.

"Do you not like it?"

"What? No! I love it." I hold out my left hand for him, waiting for the familiar slide of the cool metal. "I just didn't want to take it from you. You don't really mention her...and you don't have to explain anything to me about it. Trust me, grief is an old friend of mine. But I only want you to be sure."

He's silent for a few heartbeats, and I try but fail to stop my own from sinking at the idea that he's reconsidering.

A soft smile tugs at his lips, melting me. "There is nothing to second guess," he whispers, sliding the ring on. I can't help but think about the first time he did, and how different this is—how far we've truly come. "My mother would've wanted you to have it. She would've loved you as I do."

A thought niggles at me, unbidden. "But Axl—"

"It was *my mother's* ring. Not Genevieve's." He says it with such finality, there's no room for doubt.

When it's firmly back on my finger, I kiss him briefly once more. "Well, thank you. It's beautiful." I twist it, admiring it.

"You know…there's more satisfying ways to thank me." His grin is nothing short of devious and evil as his eyes sharpen with desire.

I roll mine, stepping back from him. "Later. We need to focus. You can't be distracting me with…well, *you* when we need to figure out why the Shaded want me."

The happiness drains out of me instantly, unwarranted as I see it.

Godsdamned kleptomaniac.

The moon painting.

It's gone.

CHAPTER FORTY-FIVE

The next month flies by in a blink.

Axl and Jes were ecstatic to hear of our engagement, though Axl did comment on Bayne's *quickness*, resulting in a fistfight. Jesminda, of course, demanded to be my maid of honor. I told her I didn't care, but in truth, I was only trying to shove down the Edene-sized hole of hurt in my life. It's been hard for me to even think about a wedding.

I'm not sure where she went, why she stole the painting, or if I'll ever see her again. I'm not sure if I even want to.

I can't help but kick myself for not looking deeper than the surface. She was always there, picking up my pieces. Maybe it's on me for being naïve, but she still lied.

Everything I've done has always been for you. Her words ring in my head, giving me a headache.

I press my hand to my forehead, trying to relieve the ache as I sit down on the sofa next to Bayne, but it's no use.

"Are you alright?" he whispers in my head. I only give him a nod, and what I hope is a reassuring smile.

Today is my birthday.

I think that's why I don't feel well. As if even my body knows today it ages—even though I know I won't look older. Ever. And the last one, I spent in the arms of a very different man.

Or maybe, it's the worry of marrying a Vail, knowing that he might not know me in the next life the way I do.

Or maybe I forget everything all over again.

I could never forget Bayne.

Right?

"—and that's why we think they're in those caves." Axl's voice rips me out of my inward spiraling.

Three sets of eyes turn to me waiting for my response, but I haven't been listening. Not even slightly.

"I—um, yes?"

Bayne chuckles as Axl sighs, exasperated. Bayne brushes a piece of hair off my face, tucking it behind my ear, like he has so many times before.

"Darling, we were discussing that Axl thinks we've pinpointed the base location for the Shaded." His words are soft, but his dark eyes glimmer with worry.

"Oh. Right," I force a smile, "so, when do we leave?"

Jesminda smiles deviously. "Well, you two lovebirds are going to scope it out. When you give us a confirmation, we'll all form a plan of attack, and ambush them. Hoping their leader is among them."

"Where are we supposed to 'scope out'?" A chill runs its hand down my spine at the thought of returning to those horrible caves in Scarlentta.

Bayne breathes deeply, hesitating before he speaks. "Voltus, unfortunately."

My heart squeezes painfully in my chest, knowing what and *who* waits there.

"Saffron," I grumble.

"Saffron," Bayne confirms.

After we solidify our plans to leave the next morning, we retreat to the dining room for breakfast. I hold Bayne's hand the whole way, like he might disappear if I let go.

I should tell him it's my birthday. He's going to be my husband, after all. I don't even know when his birthday is.

Do I know him at all?

I cut the thought of doubt out of my heart. I *do* know him. I just don't know myself.

Before we reach the dining room, he stops, making me halt with him. Turning to me, he studies my face.

"Are you sure you're okay, my love?" Genuine concern twists his face, and I feel my heart tear at the sight, knowing I put it there.

"Yes," I say, giving him a chaste kiss. "I'm just in my head today. That's all."

"Is this about today being your twenty-fourth birthday?" A sly smirk spreads across his lips, making me smile, surprised.

"How do you even know that?"

His eyes glaze slightly before admitting that *Edene* may or may not have slipped and told him before she left.

I shake off the dejected feeling, not wanting to let her ruin the mood when she's not even here.

"Well, yes. That's part of it," I confess. "But I just think it's silly to celebrate the day I was born, and yet, I can't even remember when I died. I don't know much about myself."

"I wish I could give you all the answers you're looking for, Arden. But know this—I love you, and I know you." He presses a kiss to the back of my hand, reminding me of when we met. "You're stubborn as hell, vicious, and have a smart mouth."

"Hey!" I protest, pouting, but he kisses me swiftly, melting it away.

"But I love all of those things about you. I love how you have such a big heart, even though people who did not deserve it, held it recklessly. But I love even more that you've entrusted it to me. And I vow to prove to you every day for the rest of our eternity that I am worthy of it. Of you. The most radiant soul to ever grace my life."

I smile through my burning eyes as he kisses me once more. "Are you really trying to make me cry on my birthday? Who knew the Prince of Marintha was such a softie?"

I turn to enter the doors, but he stops me, pulling my back flush to his front as he traps me in his arms. His breath coaxes the shell of my ear, sending excited chills over my skin.

"I promise you, my little raven," he drags his nose down my neck, pulling a soft whimper from me, "there's nothing *soft* about me."

That's when I press my hips back, feeling the evidence of his threat pressed against me, jolting need through my veins.

When he releases me, I immediately mourn the heat of him.

"Time for your breakfast." He grins, throwing open doors to a feast fit for a queen.

I raise my brow at him, crossing my arms. "*My* breakfast? What are you going to eat if not this?"

His hand finds my ass, smacking hard enough to make me squeal, but not hard enough to hurt. "You, *later*." His eyes darken with the promise, doing nothing to douse the rising flame of desire. "But for now, we'll eat this. Then I have a present for you."

I want to be excited, and some small part of me is—but shaking the memory of my last birthday is hard. Even when I want for nothing.

Perry truly warped my sense of self.

But Bayne is slowly bringing me back. And I love him even more for it.

After breakfast, he still makes me train with him, but he lets me win for once. It isn't until after we bathe and get back into his room—our room—that the promise of his gift comes back in full swing.

"Close your eyes, stay right here." He presses a kiss to my forehead, and then I feel him vanish.

Peeking my eye open, I see a lingering shadow twirling around my ankle. It makes me smile, and as soon as it starts to grow, I close my eyes again to Bayne reappearing.

"Okay..." he trails off, "open."

When I do, I gasp. Air is trapped in my lungs, making it impossible to breathe. Between his fingers dangles the most beautiful necklace. A long, slim, silver chain and at the very end is a small raven charm.

"I love it," I whisper, reaching out a hand to touch it.

"It was my mother's, too," he says sheepishly, "but I had it made into a necklace and polished." He moves to put it around my neck, and I help him by moving my hair to the side. When it's clasped securely, my hand fiddles with the charm, testing the weight of it. "My father gave it to her. And about a year before the war, she gave it to me."

"She did?"

He nods, continuing. "My parents saw an oracle, trying to seek help for the war effort. They didn't get what they were looking for, but my mother told me the oracle said I would need it. To guide me to the light." He smiles, drifting to the memory. "At the time, I thought it was silly. After they died, I almost got rid of it. Wearing a crown, I felt like a fraud. I wasn't a ruler, I was hiding. But then I met you, and I knew it was for you. The light bringing me out of the darkness."

Tears stream down my face as my heart simultaneously breaks but heals all at once.

"I love you," I tell him, wrapping my arms around him.

My home. My love.

He presses a kiss to the top of my hair as I close my eyes.

"I love you more."

CHAPTER FORTY-SIX

Standing in Violet Gardens should make me feel better, but even as I release my hold on Bayne's tunic and open my eyes to the bright colors welcoming me back, this place fills me with nothing but dread.

A place I used to call home.

The idea that Perry could pop up anywhere with *Chandler* makes me want to peel my skin off my bones. If I see her again, I *will kill her.*

Especially now that I know just how to draw it out. Every painful cut will demand to be felt.

"You've got your evil smile on." Bayne watches me, amused.

"I don't have an *evil smile.* Why does everyone keep telling me that?"

He laughs as we start walking toward town, and I sweep my eyes over the field as if one of the poppies might bite.

"Maybe you should stop grinning like that, and maybe you'll stop hearing it."

I ignore him, stomping forward.

When we reach the edge of the field, both of us pull our cloak hoods up, concealing ourselves as much as possible. Slipping through the alleys, a thought occurs to me.

"Why don't we just phantom inside Saffron? It'd be a lot quicker," I tell him, climbing over a fence.

He follows me, keeping close behind. "*Because that isn't safe.*" He gives me a pointed look as he lands gracefully. "*If they have it warded—which if that truly is where they meet—then every precaution needs to be taken.*"

I roll my eyes where he can't see them, continuing along the wall.

"*I can feel your annoyance, angel. It radiates off you like—do you hear that?*"

Stopping to listen, I strain my ears. but don't hear anything. Turning back to him, I shake my head. He points to the wall, but it's also the general direction of the market square.

That's when I hear voices, vaguely in the distance.

Fucking service day.

"Godsdamnit!"

Bayne lunges forward, slapping his hand over my mouth. I kick myself internally for letting my emotions get the best of me.

His eyes look wild, and when the voices get louder, he pulls me into him and against the wall. We watch the opening with each heaving breath, my heartbeat roaring in my ears.

It isn't until a group of villagers walks by, unnoticing, that we relax. Bayne releases me, and I try to slow my heart from beating out of my chest.

"Thank Gods—"

It's the last thing I hear before the whole world tilts sideways, and I'm left with a ringing in my head.

I stand over the broken stone, littering the once beautiful courtyard.

He killed them. Every last one is gone.

Qin.

Now he'll pay. And I'll be the one to do it.

He stands on the far side of the yard, leaning against a tree, thoughtless arrogance. The Shaded leader, come to kill the last remaining royal. I can't even mourn my family—not yet. I pray that Aiden slipped away, unscathed.

Right now, I have to give him all the time I have. Even if Second breaks with me.

"What a precious little doll," he drawls, stepping toward me. "A princess, in way over her head."

"Oh, look. A false prophet, in over his head, leading a poisoned cult under the guise of a better afterlife. How cute."

He smiles, venom and evil dripping from the corners of his lips. "So you think I'm cute?"

I scoff, disgusted. I refuse to encourage him anymore than I already have. I draw out my mother's dagger, the sapphire hilt glimmering in the sunshine.

The sun feels like Burnus is mocking me, shining when such destruction has broken our shores today.

Qin starts to close the distance between us, but he draws no weapon. Not yet.

I start for him, but the moment I swing my arm up, an arrow goes through it. My dagger falls into the grass as I howl in pain like I've never known.

He shakes his head at me, like I'm a disappointment.

"Did you know, doll, that the Shaded need fresh blood?" His words send chills down my spine as I back away from him, but he's too close. His hands wrap around my arm, right where my blood drips blue from the arrow piercing bone. I scream, wriggling in protest.

He takes a deep breath, soaking in my power, my magic that he draws from my blood. "Vail blood always tastes better, you know?" I try to kick him, try to scratch him, but he isn't their leader for nothing.

As if on cue, his face contorts from the handsome man to the demon I've seen all too often in my dreams—my nightmares. My scream isn't loud enough to convey the unfiltered terror his demon face elicits from me.

His blood magic is too strong, too overwhelming. I don't have enough time. I've barely lived, barely seen any providence outside my own.

And now Qin is here to collect on his promise.

My death.

I swing, scratch, and kick, but it's no use. He's sapping my strength, taking all that I am.

I sag, open-mouthed to my knees as I feel the last of my Persuasion drain from me, useless battlefield magic that it is.

But it was the power I was born with, the magic my parents gifted me. It was mine to carry. And he stole it.

I glare at the demon as mud and dirt soak cold into my bones.

Midnight, I pray for you to take my soul with theirs—my parents, my brother. Let us know Peace as only you can gift and let—

"Are you seriously praying right now?" Qin snarls at me, as though the prayers in my head personally affect him.

I ignore him, continuing my prayer. He bends to pick up my dagger where it fell, morphing slowly back into the handsome-faced man he dons.

Wrapping his hand around my throat, he cuts off my air supply, digging his nails into my skin. Darkness clouds my vision, and I internally beg for it to be quick.

"You...you might be useful, you know. I think I'll keep you."

My eyes bulge as he picks me up, my feet kicking for a purchase that isn't there.

No.

"You won't need these pesky memories, though. Once you wake back up, you'll be mine." He hisses the words, making my stomach twist as bile burns my throat.

No.

I can't speak as he taps two fingers against my temple, and the last thing I see is a set of emerald green eyes, glimmering with what can only be described as hunger.

CHAPTER FORTY-SEVEN

My head is torn in half.

I can't open my eyes, and my wrists feel raw. I can't move. Only feel.

Was that a memory? Or a nightmare?

I think I'm going to vomit. I groan, trying to let the wave of nausea pass me by.

That's when I get slapped in the face. *Hard.*

"Time to wake uppp!" A screeching, sing-songy voice cuts through my haze. I can't lift my head or react. My veins are filled with sludge, keeping me prisoner in my own head.

Another smack lands on my cheek, even harder. My eyes crack open to find blurred vision.

Another hit makes my numb face feel like it's burning. "I said, *wake up* you stupid bitch!"

I know that voice.

I blink as much as I can, and when the feet beneath me start to clear, I see another set standing in front of my own.

"Maybe you should stop hitting her. It's not like you can slap the drug out of her system."

I know that voice, too—deep and resounding. Once comforting.

Surely not—it can't be.

"But it's way more fun if I beat the shit out of her before he comes."

Before who comes?

My heart beats faster, but my body is stuck in molasses, unable to show the fear that grips me in a vise. A sharp nail pinpricks my chin as it's forced up, and I meet a set of cutting, blue eyes.

Chandler.

I must be hallucinating.

She smiles cruelly at me, like prey in a trap. "Finally." She turns to the figure behind her, but it's too dark to make out. "I told you that would work." Her face snaps back to mine, and I see an emptiness behind her eyes that wasn't there before.

Genuine concern tries to bubble up, but I shove that bitch down and lock it up tight.

"Hello, Fallon," she purrs.

I don't speak, unsure if I even can.

"Don't you look so pretty strung up like this?" She pulls hard on my arm, making me wince against the pain. "It's so *cute* that you thought you could hide your bloodline from us, Nightkiller. After all this time, too!" she sneers, shaking her head, making her blonde hair swish with the motion.

"I'm...not hiding...anything." My voice cracking from not being used. I'm just grateful it still works.

"Liar!" she cries, slamming her fist against the stone.

I flinch, not out of fear, but reflex. She doesn't care though, because her grin returns in full.

"Always so scared, pretending to be brave." She drags a nail down my cheek, slicing my skin like a razor blade. "I saw the fear, the anger in your eyes that day. When you knew he was *mine* to play with now. And he'll be mine for the rest of eternity, as I serve by his side as queen."

I bark a laugh, but it feels like I swallowed gravel.

Chandler slaps me again, and the other body steps forward.

"Alright, that's enough." The deep voice echoes off the walls, and I squint to try to see who it is.

When his face comes into view, my heart stops altogether. Those brown eyes that were always so kind. His cropped, brown hair, his tanned skin.

Kaisen.

No.

I don't want to believe it, but I can't deny the facts in front of me. Kaisen is working with Chandler? I try to look around, but my head feels heavier than lead.

That's when I see Bayne, strung up beside me in identical chains, his head hung low as he remains unconscious. My heart shatters at the sight as guilt grips me. This is all my fault—if I hadn't opened my mouth, we wouldn't be here at their mercy.

The last thing I remember is we were hiding, and the next, total darkness. So why? Why Kaisen? Why Chandler?

My eyes water against my will as I look at Bayne, crushed by the dread that this is it—this is where we die.

It's all my fault.

"Arden, it'll be okay if you just cooperate," Kaisen says.

Chandler snorts. "Don't lie to her, pretty boy." Her eyes narrow on me once more. "She'll be left to rot here. And that's if I'm feeling merciful." She tosses her hair off her shoulder as she speaks.

"What do you want with us?" I grit out.

"We just need you to help us," Kaisen almost pleads, as if there's a scenario where I make it out alive.

"What help? Why did you take me?" I glance between the two of them, trying to decipher this.

Kaisen's face becomes serious once more, unrecognizable from the kind soul I thought I knew. "He needed to finish it."

"Who!" I scream at him. My entire world has flipped, and I can't even trust my own mind right now.

"*Wake up, Bayne!*" I urge him silently.

Kaisen shakes his head as he brushes my hair off my forehead. I recoil at his touch. He has the gall to look offended.

"It'll make sense soon," he promises me. Turning to Chandler, he asks, "How much longer are we supposed to wait? I don't think we were supposed to wake them up."

She shrugs as she makes her way over to Bayne. As she lifts her nail—a *talon*—I scream at her to stop.

"Ooh, touchy, are we? Don't worry, I don't want your little plaything. Not when I have the one I really wanted." She preens.

Perry?

"Please. You can have him. You always were after my sloppy seconds—"

Her palm whips my face hard enough to jerk my head. Harder than what should be possible for her...unless . . .

I taste blood in my mouth, spitting onto the floor as I look back at her. "You're one of *them,* aren't you?"

Shade scum. She grins, confirming through her silence.

"You're disgusting." It all makes too much sense. Saffron. The lies about *people disappearing.* They both played me. For what? Power? Magic?

"You always thought you were so smart. Chasing a ghost that didn't want to be found. You know, he told me your cunt was so loose—"

But I don't hear the rest of what Chandler says.

Her head is twisted at an unnatural angle, a sickening crunch filling my ears. Two hands release her as she falls lifeless to the ground, and it's all I can do to just gape at her as she crumples.

Until I hear a voice, slick like oil. It slithers over me, thick and heavy. Even as I see who it belongs to—who I know it belongs to—I'm in denial.

"I never did care for her screeching."

A set of emerald eyes. Ones I used to love, that haunted my last nightmare as he morphed into Qin, emerge from the shadows like an omen.

"Hello, doll."

Chapter Forty-Eight

Perry.

In all his horrid glory, smiling at me with no warmth. He's as much of a stranger to me in this moment as he ever has been.

I never really knew him. Every memory, every time he said he loved me, it was all false. Calculated.

How is this possible? How did I not see through it?

I thrash against my restraints, trying to escape. I look to Kaisen, even though I know he won't help me.

"Why? Why Kaisen?" Tears fall, but it's anger that fuels me, not sadness.

"He promised me you," he says softly, but it tramples me like ten horses.

Glancing between the two of them, I can't quite put it together. My brain is whirring a mile a minute, and each breath escalates the beating of my heart.

"I don't—I just—"

"Shh," Perry coos. He reaches a hand out, making me flinch, but his touch never lands. When I open my eyes, there's a knife protruding out of Kaisen's throat, black blood oozing down his neck.

His eyes are wide with shock as his hands helplessly scratch at the wound to no avail. He sinks to his knees, and his last breath of life is gone before his head hits the ground.

"Why? Just *let us go*," I beg him. When I hear Bayne groan next to me, I suck in a small breath of relief. Knowing that once he's awake, he'll figure out a way for us to escape.

Perry takes notice of him waking slowly and punches him square on the jaw. I gasp as Bayne absorbs the hit, flexing his jaw to ease the pain.

Pain I feel.

But I shouldn't...right? Our bargain was broken, so the only way we would be connected...

I didn't even question his bond to my mind. It's still there, like a tether between our souls.

"A soulbond," I whisper aloud to myself.

Except both men jerk their heads to me. Bayne's dark eyes look fearful as they come to the same conclusion I'm drawing. Perry barks a laugh, nearly doubling over as he gestures between us.

"Oh, *Gods*, you really did it, didn't you?" Perry looks to Bayne, sharing a look that I know nothing about.

"We can't have one," I press. "I'd have to be a Vail."

Perry gestures to my bloodied wrists, as if I have to accept it as truth. But it has to be a lie.

Otherwise...*everything else I know is a lie.*

Perry rolls his eyes. "Gods, you always were so *daft*, weren't you?" He stalks toward me, flicking out a knife. Fear grips my chest heavy like a stone fist. Next to me, Bayne pulls against his own chains.

"Don't touch her!"

Perry doesn't even glance his way as he lifts the blade and brings it down on my forearm, slicing the skin effortlessly.

I hiss, scrunching my eyes to the pain. Chains rattling echoes off the walls of the room, but the ringing in my ears isn't from them. Bayne's shouts of promised violence can't even pierce through what truth is dripping down my skin.

Blue.

But it's not cobalt like Bayne's like I first thought—no, it's darker than that. A deep, navy blue.

That's not—it's not—

Perry's grin is cold as he puts space between us.

"Yes, doll." His face morphs into a mask of fake empathy. "You're a Vail. How unfortunate we didn't work out. Truly." He turns to a shocked but seething Bayne. "She is quite a good fuck though, isn't she?" He laughs darkly at Bayne jolts against his restraints.

"I don't understand," I say softly, shaking my head. "It's not...you found me. I *died*. I wasn't born here, I—"

"Don't remember," Perry interjects, finishing my sentence.

"No," I whisper, but it's a futile defense against the truth. Because I don't. And he knows it.

"I may have manipulated the color of your veins, but we couldn't exactly have you running around Voltus bleeding a different color, could we? It would've raised too many questions." He taps the side of my temple, the way he always used to. Except now, I recoil in disgust.

"How."

It's not a question, but a demand. I have to know.

"I'm sure you've been dreaming about me, Arden." And that's when I see it. *Qin.*

The swirls of black take over his irises, but they're gone as soon as they appeared.

"You're him. You're Qin."

He shrugs, twirling the blade. Before I can blink, he flicks the knife at Bayne, sinking deep into his side. Bayne can't hide the look of pain and shock off his face that reflects my own. I scream for him, tears pouring down my face.

This is my worst nightmare come to life—everything I feared as the man I love is tortured by the one I thought I did.

Bayne groans as Perry rips out the knife, spilling his blood down the tip of it. He holds it up to me, as if in offering. I can barely see through my tears now, unwilling to watch Bayne die again.

Perry approaches, and as he scrapes my own dripping blood off to mix with Bayne's, I watch in horrific fashion as they mold together, swirling and bending.

"Ooh, what a *pesky* little thing soulbonds are," he ponders out loud, clicking his tongue. Pointing the blade between us, he continues. "Is that what that whole ring thing was in Voltus? You sly, sly creatures. Vails. Always trying to outsmart the rest of us, always thinking you're better than us."

But we're not soulbonded.

He...said we weren't. He promised me we *weren't*.

"Bayne?" I whisper.

Perry sees the devastation written on my face, making his emerald eyes sparkle with elation.

"This is too good, truly." He places a hand over his heart. He pulls Bayne's head up from where he was keeping it bowed, unable to look at me. "You didn't even tell her that you tethered her to you forever? Bold move, my friend."

Bayne's face twists with rage as he spits in Perry's face. He wipes it off, chuckling. As if our impending demise is enough for him to forego all other priorities.

My head pounds, and my heart is twisting as if that's where the blade cut and not my arm.

Tears continue to fall, but I steel myself. I will not let Perry take anything else from me.

"Raven, I—"

"Stop," I hiss. I can't look at him right now. I love him so much that it's physically painful. That even though he lied—I could never let him go. And that's killing me more than any revelation Perry could show me.

"Aw, trouble in paradise?"

I know that voice—I *love* that voice.

Axl.

He stalks in, covered in black blood, reeking to the Seven Hells and back. Beside him is Jesminda, her auburn hair braided back and matted with the same blood.

They're here. *They came for us.*

Perry whips around wasting no time, throwing the knife but missing as Jes dodges with a swiftness I've never seen her use. In the same breath, Axl sprints to us, removing the rough restraints, helping me down first. I nearly sob with relief as I throw my arms around him.

He catches me, giving me a tight hug.

I keep an eye on Jes and Perry, as each strike of their swords reverberates in my ears. Moving to Bayne, I assist Axl in helping him down, his arms finding my own, pulling me close on instinct.

He claps his hand around Axl's neck, touching their foreheads. "Thank you." They pull apart, and Bayne turns to me, the apology I know he wants to give on his lips. But that's when I hear it.

The scream.

It splits the air, silencing the world around us.

Everything freezes in time.

If I don't look, it's not real.

This is not real.

Turning around, bile rises into my throat as my heart plummets to Maveth.

Perry's sword is shoved through Jesminda's ribs, her golden eyes wide as her mouth is parted in shock.

It's Axl's scream I hear first before reality shatters.

CHAPTER FORTY-NINE

Jesminda.

Sweet, golden-eyed Siren.

Perry rips his sword out of her body, her red blood spraying her hands as they try to keep the wound closed. Perry takes one look at us and bolts. *Coward.*

"No!" Axl screams, running to catch her before she hits the ground. She smiles at him weakly, and he bows his head crying as he cradles her dying body to his chest.

I'm stunned into place, unable to do anything except process this hellscape before me.

"It's okay," she whispers, "Peace has found me."

As Axl shakes his head, it's all I need to take off after Perry. I run through the dark tunnels, realizing the prisons we've been taken to are a system of caves, much like the ones I saved Bayne in.

The caves. Axl was right. That must've been how they found us.

"Where are you?" I scream, anger boiling me from the inside out.

He'll die. For everything.

I run mindlessly around corners, not knowing where I'm going, and it isn't until I've turned myself around that I hear Bayne calling out for me. The minute our eyes meet, hands wrap around me, yanking me back *hard*.

I land on the ground with a grunt as I'm thrown down. My scream must've echoed because in a moment, Bayne is beside me, helping me up.

Bayne slips a protective arm around my waist, and we're greeted by Perry's eyes ignited with hatred. "I see it was easy for you to get over me. So quick to spread your legs for someone else." He spits at my feet, his face crinkling with disgust. "Whore."

Embarrassment floods me as my face flushes red. How can he still make me feel guilty? He left *me.*

Bayne lunges for him, grabbing him by the throat and slamming him against the cave wall. Perry's laugh is manic as his face reddens, then purples slightly from the lack of oxygen. His laugh becomes garbled, but he looks me in the eye as he chokes out, "Did you ever tell her?"

I freeze, the blood in my body turning to ice. I watch as the muscles in Bayne's back tense, and my stomach drops in tandem. He's hiding something. After all this time, *he's still hiding things from me.*

"Bayne," I say slowly. "What is he talking about?"

He doesn't speak.

"What. Is. He. Talking. About," I grit out. My hands are fisted by my sides as he slowly turns, releasing Perry. He keeps his hands up in defense, like I've reverted to that skittish animal he could scare away. Perry slumps to the floor, hunched over and hacking up a lung to regain his breath.

"Now, little raven, it's not what you—"

"No." I cut him off, as though it can stop the pain before it starts. "That is NOT my name. My name is Arden!" I scream.

My identity is cut into pieces. He is all I have left.

I can't take the shattering of my heart; the splintering feeling of it ripping apart the seams he so carefully stitched together. I'm no oracle, but I know what he has to say is going to break me apart.

"Arden," he says. I feel the walls inside me shooting up, trying to harden what's left of my heart so I can make it out of this alive. "It's not what you think. I've never lied to you." His gaze shoots to Perry, still trying to pull himself together. "But him and I, we've met before."

I'm taken aback by his words.

"Before Voltus?" My voice is surprisingly steady.

Bayne nods. *He's met Perry before? How is that even possible? How did I not know? Why did he never tell me?*

"I hadn't met you yet, I swear it," he continues. I feel physically sick, bile rising in my throat. "We made a deal. I didn't know who he was. He offered me his magic in exchange for a ward stone. It wasn't uncommon, people who were melancholy enough often ventured to Meadows to try to find me. Most never can, as you well know."

I remember. The magic veil surrounding the castle that no longer stands. I nod slightly, giving him permission to continue.

"He offered me a power I hadn't seen before. It wasn't so much the deal itself, but what his power meant for my people. *Our* people, Arden." My eyes burn at the implication. "The power to manipulate what people remember could keep all of us safe. I did what I needed to then and I don't regret taking it in exchange for one guy to be able to transport. I see now, the mistake in not killing him the minute he entered."

I'm confused where this is going, and why Bayne kept this a secret all this time. Why keep me in the dark? He was there to pick up the pieces when Perry broke my heart again. *Why* is all I can ask. I keep my face as impassive as possible, just like he taught me.

Perry wanted a ward stone? That's why I couldn't find him. He must've absorbed the magic from it somehow. The pieces coming together hit me in the gut so hard, the tears that had been threatening to fall make silent trails down my face.

"If I could go back and change it I would. I never would have kept it from you. And I didn't lie to you, I swear—"

"Omitting the truth is the. Same. Thing," I choke out. My tears fall hot and heavy with every blink. I can't snuff out the fire now brewing in my chest at his blatant deceit.

"I never wanted to hurt you, Arden. I made a mistake, but I lov—"

"Do not finish that fucking sentence!" I hiss at him. I could kill him right now, just for thinking *this* is the time and place to say those words to me.

Bayne looks like I've stabbed him in the heart as his shoulders slump, icing over the cold already creeping into my heart.

"Finish the story." A command, no room for argument. He wants me to act like a queen, so I'll give him one with no mercy. "How does he still have magic if he gave it to you?"

"The Vail who died," Perry chokes out from the ground. "She was the only person standing between me and the Shaded from taking back magic."

Bayne kicks him swiftly, flipping him into the wall. He turns to me, desperate to keep his hold on the conversation.

"That day we made the bargain and you came to Meadows—to Marintha, I knew you had gotten under my skin. I knew as much as I wanted to fulfill whatever deal I made, I wanted you that much more. I threw away their safety for you. For us. And I don't regret that."

The ward falling, Perry getting his magic back. It's all my fault. Bayne selfishly gave it up for me. It gnaws at the walls around my heart, but it can't chew through stone.

"That was incredibly stupid, princeling."

His face looks crestfallen as he says, "I know, but I mean every word of it. And I'll spend the rest of my eternity proving it to you. If you'll let me."

A cackle comes from the floor as Perry stumbles to his feet, smiling to himself. That once dazzling face holds nothing but contempt. His once warm eyes are cold emeralds, like he wishes to cut me open with a look. How had I never noticed such evil? How could I be so blinded by his charms?

"What the fuck are you laughing at?" Bayne snaps, cutting Perry a scathing look.

Looking around, I realize I do recognize this place—from the book of folklore. Maveth had these as her temple once.

I rack my brain for the passage, trying to remember.

Once entered, Her temple cannot be abandoned without sufficient sacrifice.

"We're stuck here," I say.

"What do you mean?" Bayne asks, coming to my side. I shrug off his touch, too overwhelmed by everything.

"This is Maveth's temple." I glare at Perry. "A sacrifice must be made if you want to leave."

A chill wraps its hands over my skin, echoing the dread filling my veins. I pull out my dagger—*or my mother's dagger*—palming the usual weight of it.

"If you want your memories back, I'd think long and hard about what your sacrifice should be. After all, I'm not like you." Perry's eyes morph into black voids, and as his body shifts, my choice becomes clear.

What I need to do to save Bayne.

I look at him, hot tears streaming down my face as I raise the blade.

"I love you," I tell him. He nods at me as I take a step, pointing the dagger at Qin.

But he doesn't know what choice I've made.

As soon as the demon lunges for us, I turn the blade.

The last thing I hear is Bayne screaming my name in horror as I drive the blade into my own heart.

EPILOGUE

I thought stabbing myself would hurt a lot less. Which is dumb, considering I've been stabbed before. It just wasn't ever the heart.

So if I killed myself, is this it?

Is this Peace?

Do the Gods even offer sanctuary to those of us like me? Everything is so dark here, I can't even see. Or I'm blinded in this life as punishment.

Wait. I remember it all...the temple, Perry, Bayne, Axl, *Jesminda*.

Her name chokes me as tears well in my eyes. Perry killed her. Like it was nothing. I can't stop the sob that escapes me.

"Are you seriously crying in your sleep?"

My eyes fly open, unaware they were even closed. When I find who the voice belongs to, I would've been better off succeeding.

Edene sits before the bed I lay in, hands folded in her lap over her crossed knees. She's dressed like I've never seen her before. Her curls are longer than before, with streaks of violet in them and pinned off her face. Her outfit is skin-tight and black, tucked into matching boots. But it's her jewelry and cloak that throw me off. Ward stones adorn each ring and necklace.

The one around her neck, clasping the cloak together, is shimmering onyx. *A hex stone.*

She catches me staring and self-consciously grazes it with her fingers. Her gray eyes study me as if I might bolt at any moment.

I probably would, too, if it weren't for the debilitating pain coursing through every vein.

She says nothing, just watching as though she can't believe I'm real. When I peel my eyes off her, I take in the room.

It's massive, with floor to ceiling windows behind Edene, an unlit fireplace, and sapphire canopies strung about the bed frame. Simple, elegant.

The moon painting from Marintha stares back at me. Cold and unassuming. "Where am I?" I croak out. *Am I dead? Is Bayne okay?*

I try my best to swallow the panic that threatens to rise, but if I've moved onto Death, I need to know that he's alive. *My love.*

Edene plants her feet on the ground and leans forward. "This is Ziineth, Arden."

I search her eyes for any jesting, but there's none. I'm not dead. I'm still in Second. Some of the pressure sitting on my chest lets up, but not all of it.

"Ziineth," I roll it thickly over my tongue. "Where *specifically*? How did I get here?"

I'm tired of these guessing games everyone plays with me. Over and over. There's no one I have left that hasn't lied to me.

She leans back, releasing a sigh. "Your family's hidden estate. You got here because of me."

I shake my head, disbelieving every word that comes out of her mouth. Nevertheless, she continues.

"It doesn't matter if you don't trust me. But your memories will start coming back here soon, and it's going to be a lot, but—"

"What do you mean, *coming back*?"

"If you stop fucking interrupting me, you'll get your answer."

My head jerks back like she slapped me. Edene has never spoken this way to me. My already shattered heart splinters even further. I don't know her. I never have.

I stay quiet, letting her continue.

"I want to reintroduce myself to you. No lies, no pretenses, though when you remember yourself, you'll be able to see through that anyway." She straightens her spine. "I am Edene Elledge of the Vakharia Clan, the chosen witch for the Ziineth Crown, selected service to His Majesty, King Devon III. In my quest to secure my future, I became his trusted spy." Shadows fall over her face at whatever memory the name brings to her. "I searched for you for a long time, Arden. After the war, I traveled all over Second, and when I heard rumors about Voltus, I fell into a new role as an apothecary."

I blink back the tears that burn my eyes. "So Burtons? It was all a setup, a scam?"

She shakes her head. "No! Gods, I wish. It'd been ages since I'd made potions, but I had to have a cover. It wasn't until Perry brought you in that day that I realized you were different."

"That's why it felt like I knew you," I whisper as tears fall. "When we met—I swore you felt familiar. I guess you were." I laugh humorlessly. "Were you ever going to tell me?"

Her smile is full of pity. "I needed you to remember on your own. I wasn't expecting you to have no memories when I found you."

I hold up the healing gash on my arm where I bled dark blue. "So this has to do with my missing memory?"

Edene grins at the injury. "Yes. Your blood is important. Do you know why it was showing up red?" She leans forward, waiting.

"Perry...he's Qin."

Her face falls for a moment before she masks it, reaching for my hand. "I'm sorry. That must've been devastating for you."

I jerk my hand away. I don't want comfort from a stranger. She sighs in resignation.

"There's more to tell you, but we haven't the time today, and you'll hopefully start remembering on your own. All you need to know right now is that you're here, *alive*, because of me."

"Why? How?"

"I gave you that ward stone, but it protected you from Death. I didn't spend all that time looking for you, only to lose you again. Whoever tried to kill you, they wouldn't realize you weren't really dead before you turned into stardust."

My mind is reeling with everything she's dumping on me. "So wait, why do you need me? You said this is my family's? Where are they?"

I have no desire to spend any time with Edene.

She gestures to the room, exasperated. "Because you are the heir to the crown. Your eyes, that silver? It's a marking here." The breath leaves my body at the conclusion I'd been trying not to draw. *The dream was real.* "And we need to find Aiden."

My brows shoot up, remembering that name from the dream. "Who's that?"

Edene grimaces, mumbling something to herself.

"He's your brother."

"I'm sorry—*my brother?*" Where is he? Does he remember me?

She nods. "You'll remember it all soon, I promise."

"How can you be so sure? I can't trust you!"

"Trust in the magic then." She pulls out a ward stone, similar to the one that allegedly saved me. "I spelled it specifically to protect you. But you still *died*—just for a moment. That would've ended any lasting hold Qin had on you. Memories will come back from before, but just brace yourself to feel them. It'll be...uncomfortable."

This whole time...I've had a family. I just didn't remember them. This is their—*our*—house.

"Fine. I'll help you. But I want out after we find Aiden."

Edene rolls her eyes, but then they find my hand. She grips the left one like she had that day at Meadows, except there's not much to say this time. The ring feels tighter on my finger with each passing second. I don't know how to forgive him, but part of me already has.

"You're not seriously—"

"Yes," I interrupt, ignoring her exasperated sigh. "You don't get to judge me. After this is done, I'm going straight back to Marintha."

She stands, then bows at the waist, looking more like a soldier than my old friend.

"As you wish, your highness."

Looking out the window once more, I see rolling green hills with pops of color. I urge myself to feel the familiarity, but all I want is to be back in the same bed as Bayne.

"When do we need to leave?"

Edene grins.

ACKNOWLEDGEMENTS

Personally, I used to ignore this section of the book.

Story over, book closed, onto the next. But once I started writing my own, I really stopped to look at who the author would thank at the end.

The absolute village that it takes to bring a book to life is uncanny, and I doubt fifteen-year-old me would believe where we are a decade later. It only makes me that much more excited to see the next decade, and I hope all of you are there with me.

First, I want to thank Allie White. Sunshine, this book is dedicated to you, and I know you'll cry when you find out, just like you sobbed when you read the ending for the first time. (But I love you more for it.) This story, this series, would've died (pun intended) without you. I never had anyone encourage me to keep writing in the way you did. The way this story meant as much to you as it did me was anything and everything I could've ever asked for. I hope I get to hear your crazy theories for life.

To Catherine, for taking me on when I was very naïve and didn't even have my first book completely written! You were so kind, and you remain a confidant and a friend. I was so nervous to have you be the first person to read entirely through *Staying Dead*, but I will cherish your kind words forever.

To Kelly, who's convinced I'll be a NYT Bestseller, and for always having higher dreams for me than I have for myself. I love you like a limb.

To my Rhy's pieces, you girls are my rock. Thank you for keeping me sane and always being down to beat a dead horse or two. I love you guys so much.

To my beta readers, Cassie, Alana & Brittany, thank you for your invaluable feedback, and for loving this story at its barest bones.

To my friends and family, I will never be able to express what your support and commendations mean to me. I love you with my whole heart and maybe even a little bit more than that.

A special shout-out to Amanda, my favorite sister-in-law. Thank you for your undying support, always hyping me up and for being there for me for this whole journey. I love you bunches and having you in my family is one of my favorite blessings.

Last but not least, thank *you*, dear reader. Without you and your support, indie authors would not be able to do what we love and human art in all forms is precious. I can't thank you enough for taking a chance and reading Arden and Bayne's story, and stay tuned! There's many more secrets to uncover in your next life...